Indonesia

A Hedonist Production

Editorial

Editorial

Larry Blair, Jeremy Goring.

Art

Nick Baron.

Photography

Hilton Dawe, Tim McKenna, John Hepler, Bernie Baker, Jeremy Goring, Sean Davey, Paul Rubies.

Contributing writers and thank yous

King Kong, Peter Cox, Harry, Clayton Barr, Ronal Ketut Mcdonal, Mamtas, Stu Horstman, Tom Plummer, Dr Andrew Griffiths, Nev Hines, Rocky Made Senaya, David Wyllie, Anssi Kauppila, Brett Court, Julian Groom, Henry Yamada.

Surfing is a dangerous sport.

Web-site; www.wave-finder.com email; info@wave-finder.com

How to use Wave-finder

How does Wave-Finder Work?

Wave-Finder uses **Surfer's Eye Maps** and **icons** to help you quickly identify the key features and best conditions for each break. The icons also indicate wave type and direction; see next page.

What do I look at first?

You can find your desired break by looking at the area map for each section. Find out what area you are in by looking at the contents pages overleaf. There's also a break index at the back.

How do I find the best spot for the conditions?

Each spot has its own **Surfer's Eye Map** showing the main streets and landmarks nearest the break. Look for the **icon box** located in the corners. This contains info on wave direction, bottom type, best swell direction, best tide, and best wind direction. **Wave locators** in each map show position and direction of waves.

About Data-maps

Scales marked on maps relate to the 2cm **scale bar** in the bottom corner.

In this case the bar is 0.75 kilometers so the whole map is about 1.5km long. All maps face **north** but scales **vary** in order to fit important features in.

How do I get there?

Concise directions, usually from the nearest hub, are in the text. To get to these hubs, check the back of the book under "How to get to".

Additional Info

Surf **data-charts** for each ocean zone show seasonal conditions & hazards etc. There are surf travel tips and forecasting tools at the back, or try **www.wave-finder.com**.

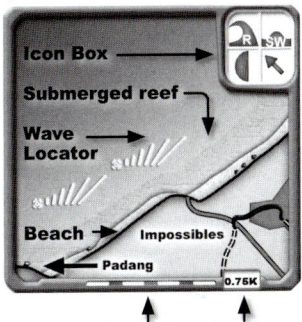

Icon Box

Submerged reef

Wave Locator

Beach

Impossibles

Padang

0.75K

Scale Bar **Scale**

3

Surfer's Eye Maps: Icons

Wave Locator

Left	Right	A-Frame	R Point	L Point

Wave Type - Wave icon shows **direction**, letter in center shows **bottom type**.

	Right, R = Reef bottom		Right Left Beach break
	Right, S = Sandbar/River		Left, P = Pointbreak

Swell Direction - Shows **best** swell direction. **Other swell directions may also work for this wave.**

	North swell is best		NW-SW is best
	NW -W is best		SW is best

Best Tide - Shows **Optimal** tide heights. **Can change subject to sand movement and swell direction. Other tides may work.**

	Low is best		High is best
	Mid is best		Low - Mid is best

Best Wind - Shows wind direction for a **perfect** off-shore. Long curved beaches will show a range of directions.

	Westerly (from West)		North to Westerly
	Southwesterly		Easterly

Special Icons - You will find these at the top of certain spots. They indicate other features about the break.

	Handles huge swells		Protected from winds
	Swell Magnet		World Class Wave
	Best in Wet Season		Best in Dry Season

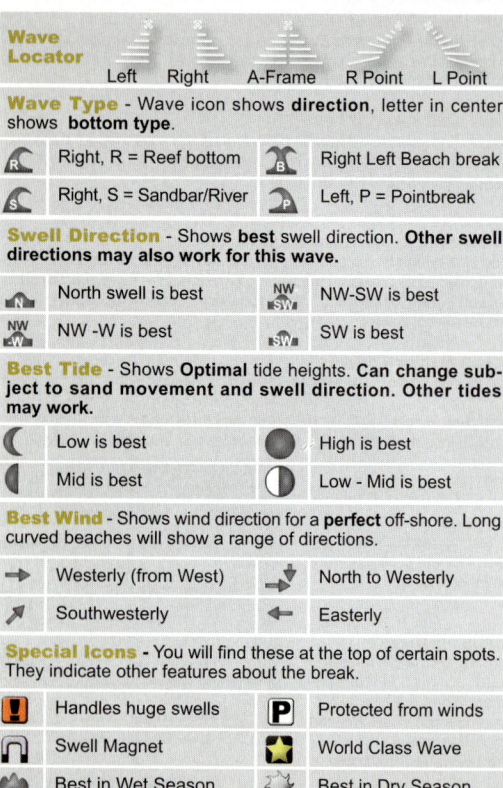

Surfer's Eye Maps: Legend

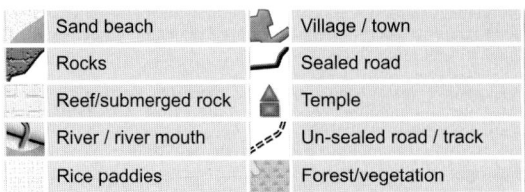

	Sand beach		Village / town
	Rocks		Sealed road
	Reef/submerged rock		Temple
	River / river mouth		Un-sealed road / track
	Rice paddies		Forest/vegetation

Scales

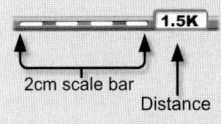

2cm scale bar

Distance

Surfers Eye Maps attempt to fit in all important features of a beach, and so work to different scales. The figure in the scale box relates to the distance covered by the black and white scale bar, which is 2cm long.

Area maps: Legend

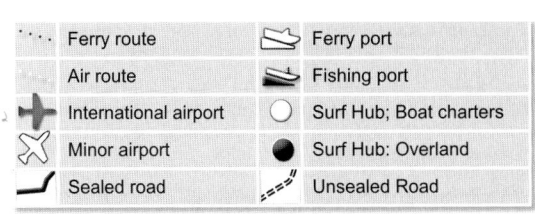

	Ferry route		Ferry port
	Air route		Fishing port
	International airport		Surf Hub; Boat charters
	Minor airport		Surf Hub: Overland
	Sealed road		Unsealed Road

Surfer's Eye Maps are just that; they are an overview of the surf setup, and as such are designed to be intuitive rather than exhaustive.

Foreword

When I first surfed Uluwatu in 1974, hardly any of the waves in this book had ever been ridden, and more than half of them would remain that way until the late 'eighties.

Back then, I was staying in a *losmen* owned by Ketut "King Kong" Kasih, who became our tour guide. I think he was quite happy to have a surfing buddy because in those days not many Balinese would go near the water. A belief in the evil spirit of (among others) Nyai Loro Kidul meant that the ocean was far from the comfort zone of most Indonesians. They would fish in it, look for oil under it, harvest seaweed from it, but swim in it? You must be "Gila"! Ketut however, had learned to surf before he could swim, thanks to an American who'd donated a board on the beach in Kuta. He spent his early surfing career unable to ride waves in water that went higher than his neck. As he says, he knew he loved the ocean, he just didn't have a method of getting close to it back then; surfing gave him and many Balinese that gift. He took me to all the hot spots: Kuta reef with nobody out, Padang-Padang, and "Chang-Goo", the location of which I was sworn to secrecy about. King Kong and his mate Wayan Swenda were so adamant about this that I still won't tell anyone where Canggu is today, thirty years later, even though it's the most well known spot on the west coast!

Because I had behaved well all that first week, they took me to Uluwatu, where this gorky 15 year old grom had his first brush with celebrity. The only other surfer out on that lumpy high tide day was Gerry Lopez and it was he who showed me how to line up at the peak, and get back in unscathed through the cave.

King Kong's final tour de force was hooking us up with Thornton Falander and a friend who had a yacht. We left Benoa harbour at dusk, passing the jagged wreck, and motoring through the night. At dawn we were anchored off "Gru-ga-gan". An enormous fish swam under the yacht, which guaranteed that Ketut would be a no-show in the line-up. As a result, I surfed most of that first day alone and terrified. Up until Bali, I had not surfed anywhere outside of Maroubra and Bondi, and these were the longest, biggest, noisiest roundest barrels I had ever seen. It remains the most frightening experience of my surfing career.

Since then I've surfed places that get bigger and maybe a bit more powerful, such as the North Shore in winter. There are also places where it's easier to surf, like most of Australia. Nowhere else however, has the abundance of perfectly shaped reefs lying at perfect depth, at the end of an optimal fetch and presenting precisely opposing angles to the prevailing winds. As a result of these four factors, the shape and length of the waves in Indonesia are better than anywhere else on earth.

With Wave-finder, we've attempted to give you detailed information about a large number of surf spots from every corner of this nation. It's a surf guide, for surfers by surfers, and for this reason we don't talk about travel or culture in any great depth; I strongly recommend that you consult our bibliography at the back, and do some reading if you want to get the best out of your travels through this epic, beautiful, evocative group of islands.

We provide you with the information you need to go and get awesome waves in any corner of Indonesia. Certain surf spots however, do not make it into Wave-finder because they may be as yet totally unknown outside a small group of surfers. These surfers may have spent years of hardship finding them. We spend hours deliberating over the inclusion (or not) of these so-called "secret spots" and as a result, our offices are littered with maps and sketches that have been kept back from publication. Please forgive us that.

If I had to summarize what makes the surf so special in Indonesia, I'd just give you a Top 10. Dangerous, almost unmakeable waves at Panaitan Island, the pure natural-foot perfection of Lagundri Bay, ocean-going adventure off the Mentawais, the dense jungle lifestyle of Grajagan, volcanic black power at Canggu, madness and fun at Halfway Kuta, impossibly long lines at Impossibles, shallow green reef barrels at Padang, mellow high tide at Geger, the "waiting game" at Desert Point, & Sumbawa's 20ft pythons and it's crowded Lakey Peak. OK, that was 11.

Larry Blair, November 2004

Indonesia

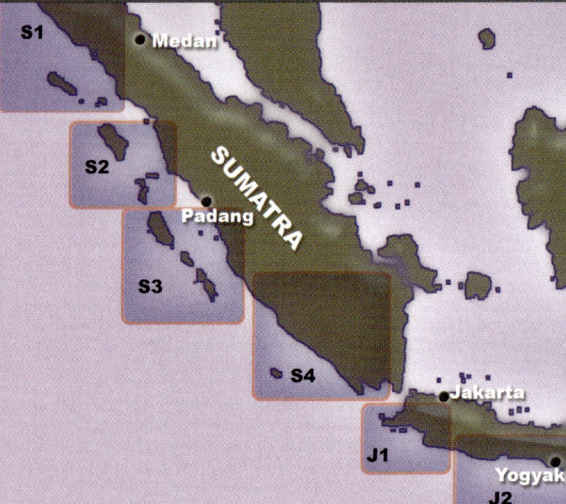

S1
● Medan

SUMATRA

S2

● Padang

S3

S4

● Jakarta

J1

Yogyak
J2

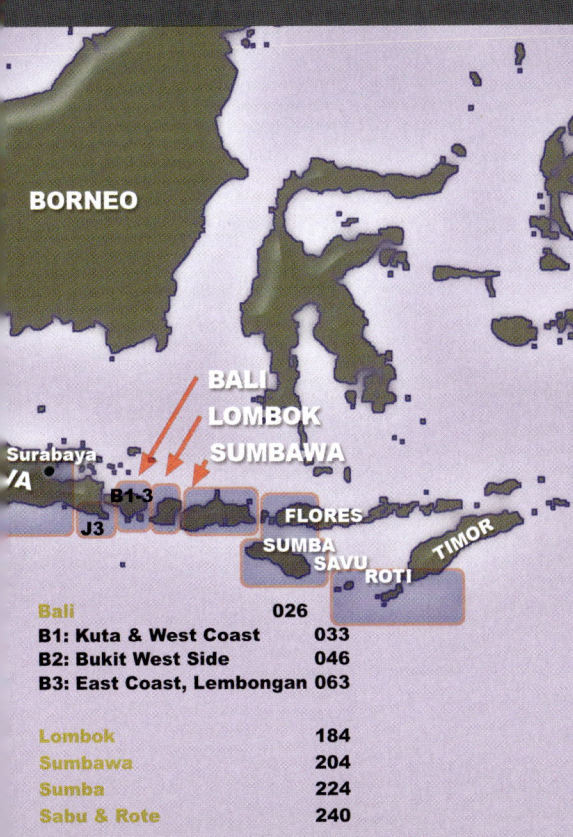

BORNEO

BALI
LOMBOK
SUMBAWA

Surabaya
/A

B1-3

J3

FLORES

SUMBA
SAVU
ROTI

TIMOR

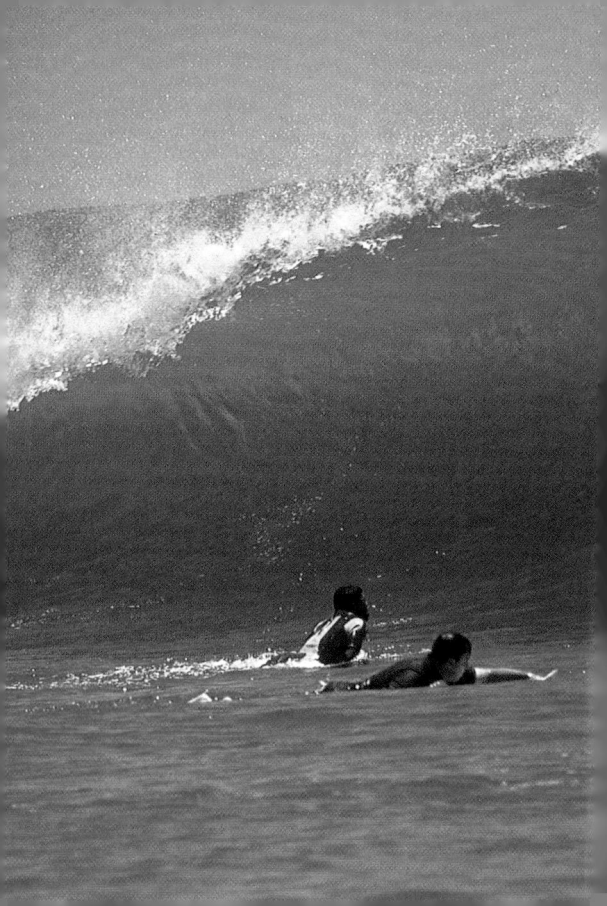

Kuta Reef, where it all started / Hepler

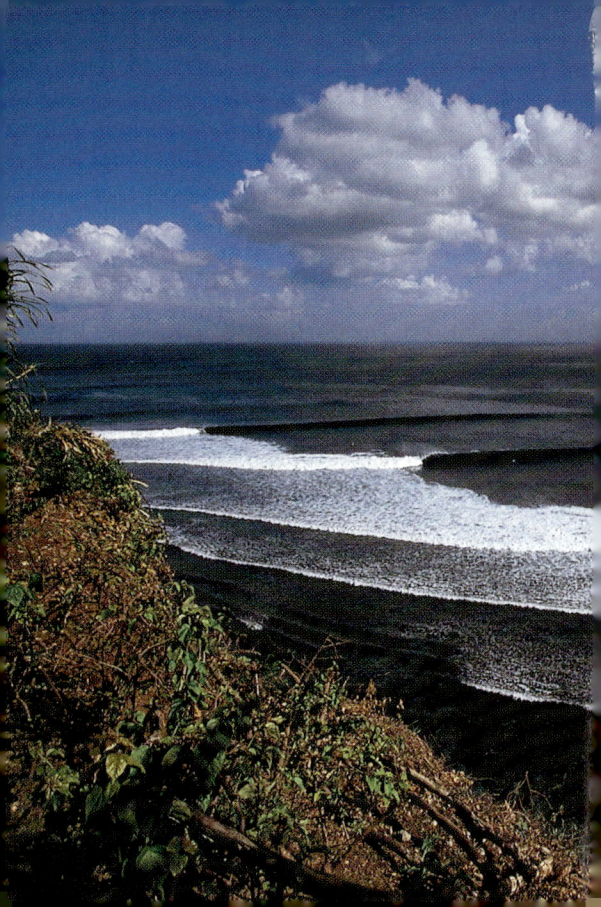

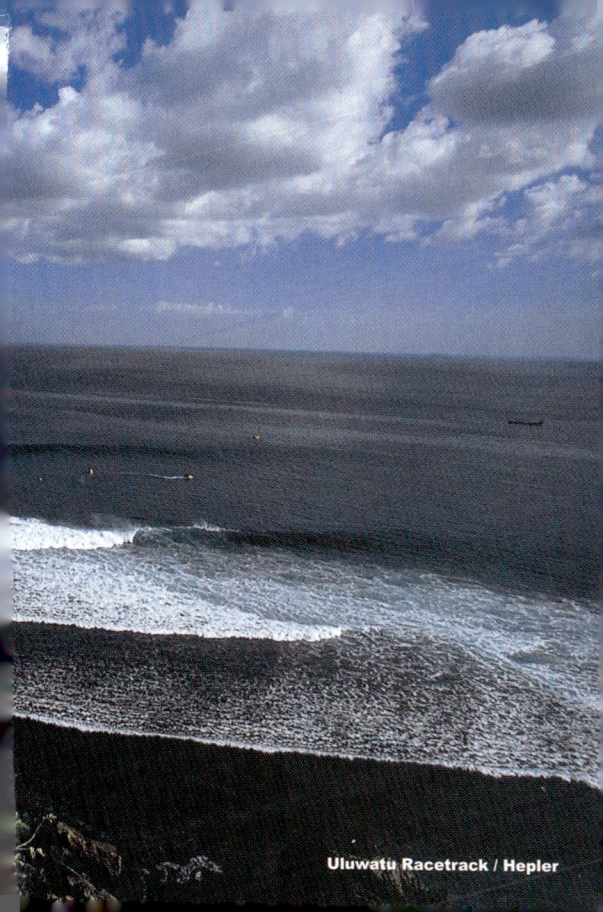

Uluwatu Racetrack / Hepler

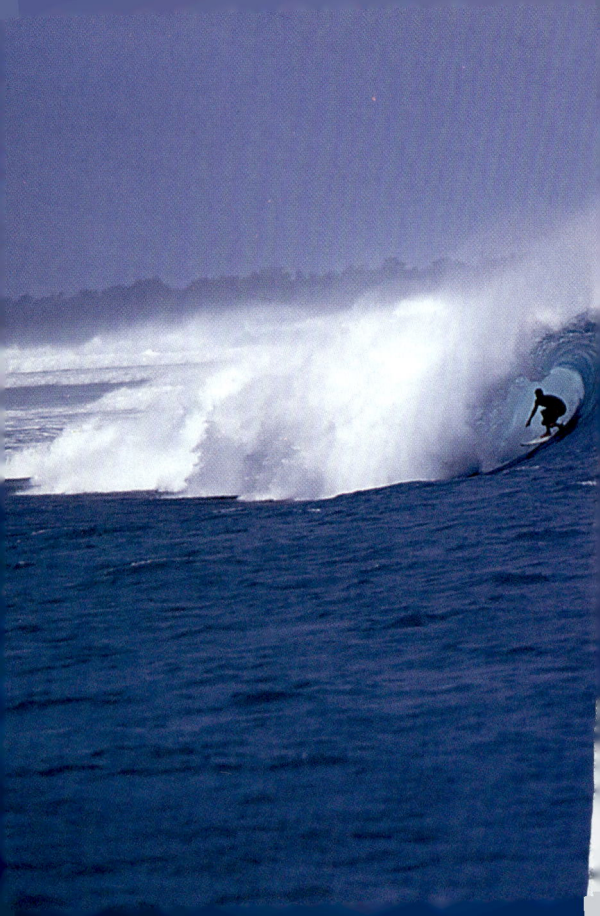

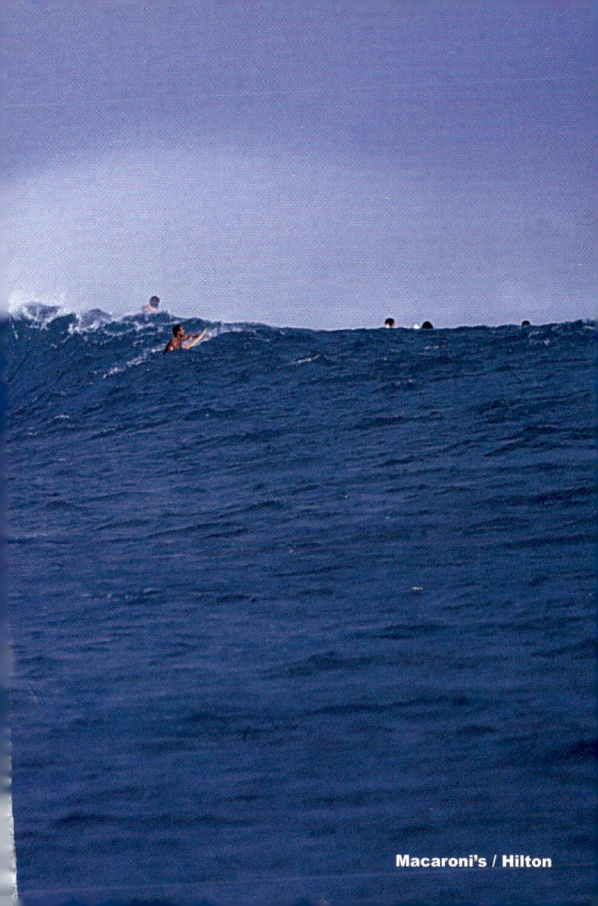

Macaroni's / Hilton

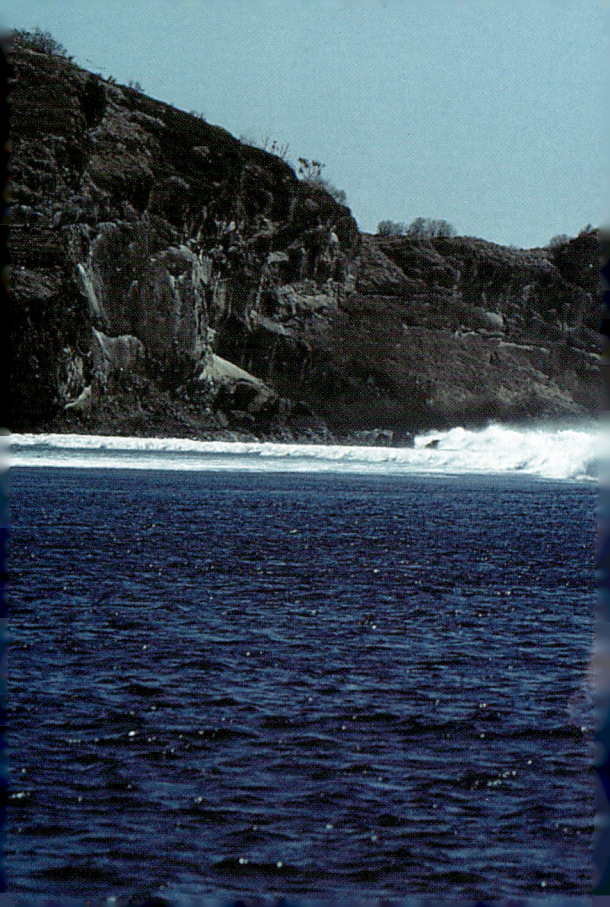

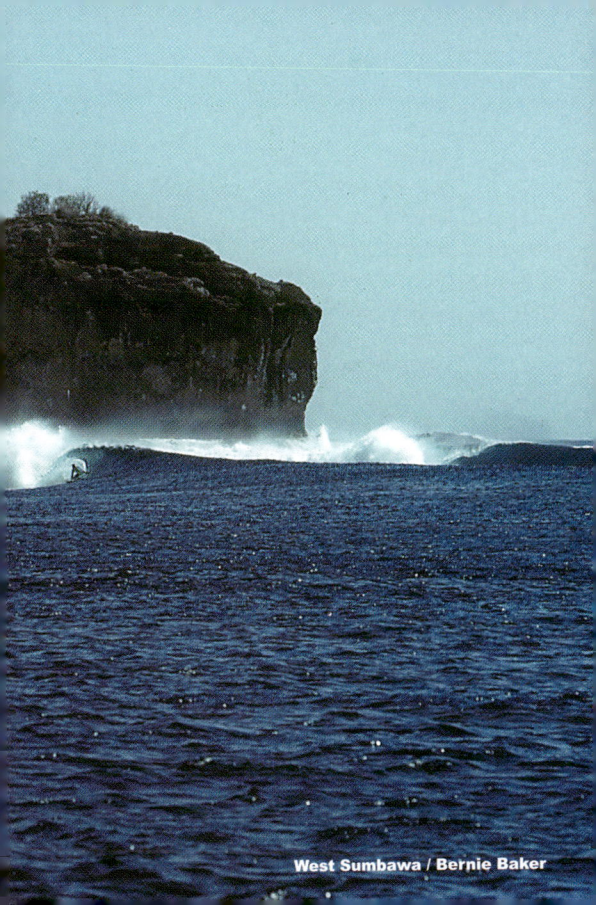

West Sumbawa / Bernie Baker

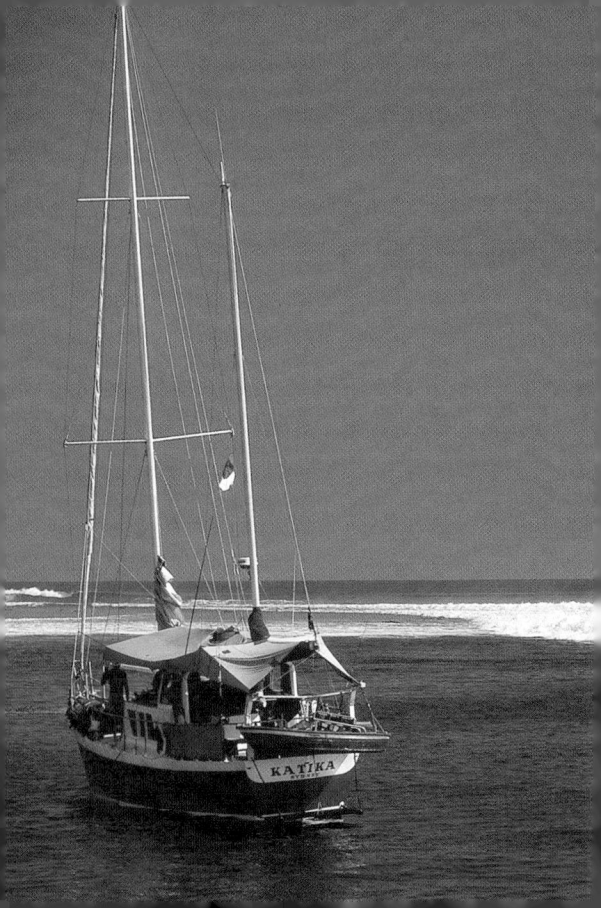

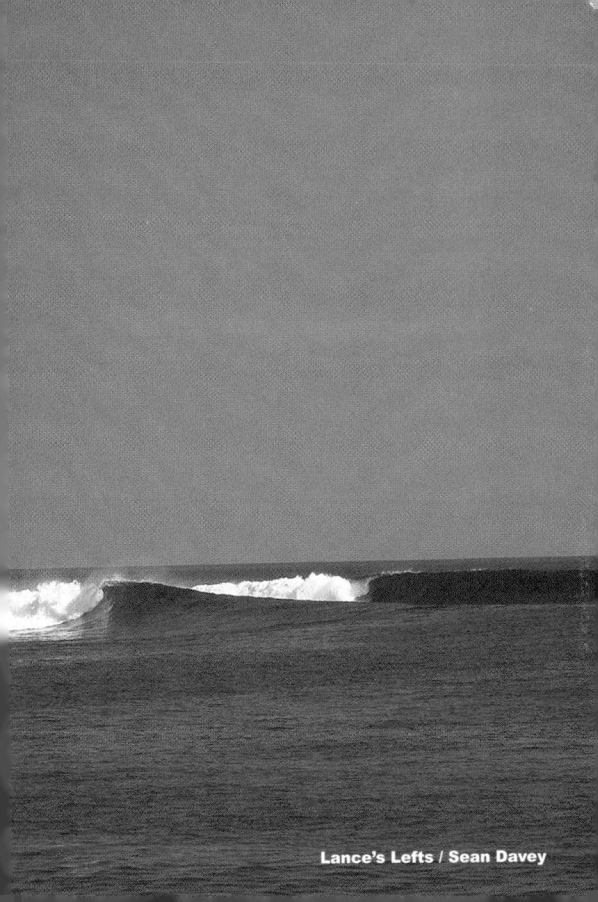

Lance's Lefts / Sean Davey

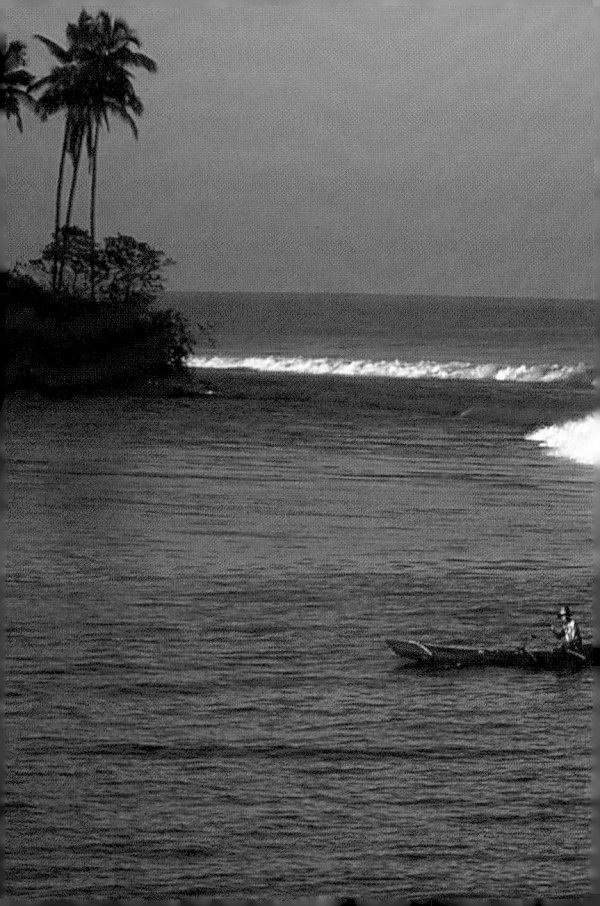

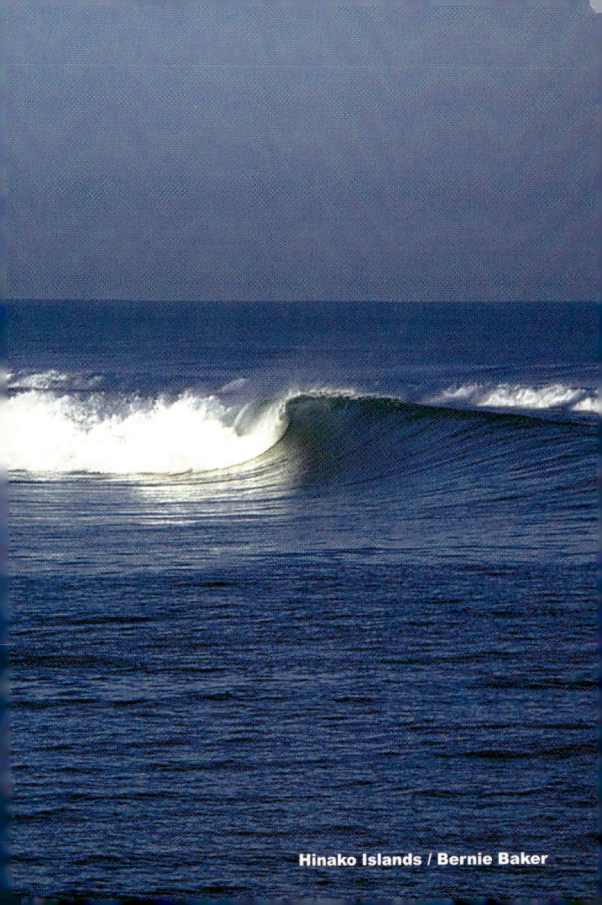

Hinako Islands / Bernie Baker

Contents

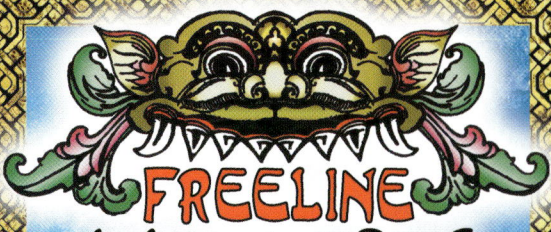

Contents

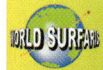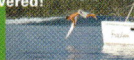

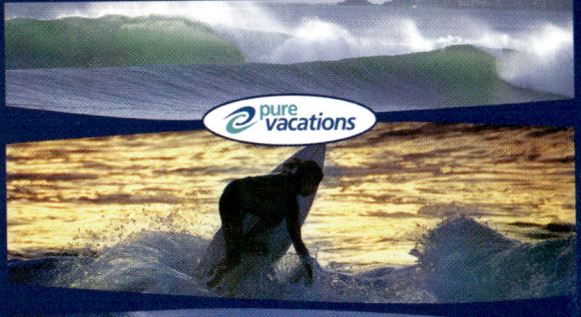
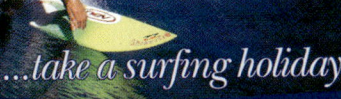
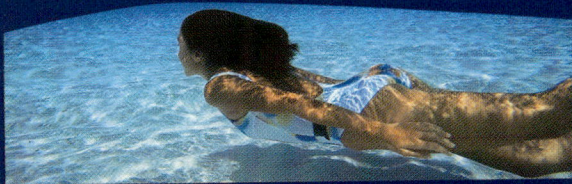

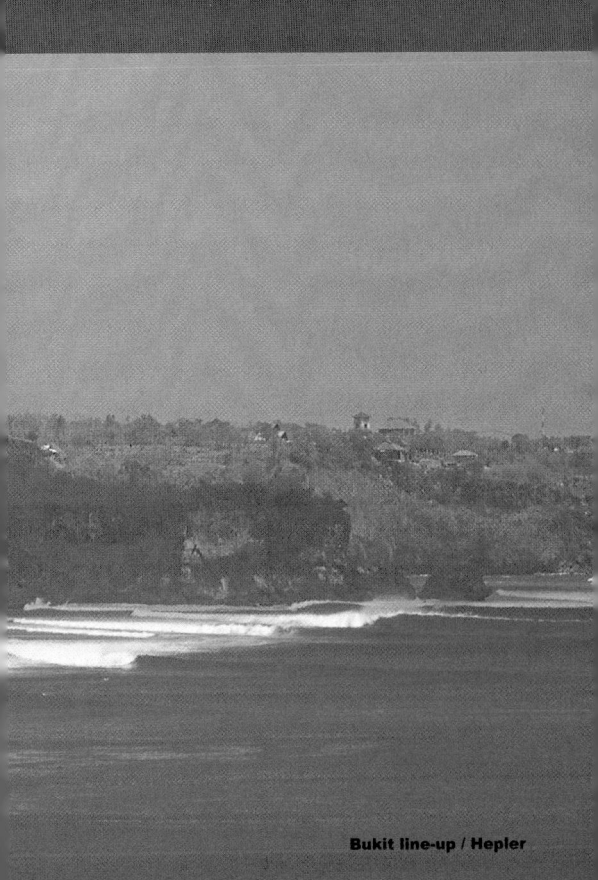

Bukit line-up / Hepler

Bali: Surf data

Where

Right in the middle of the southern trade-wind belt, Bali lies between latitude 8 and 9 degrees south. It is the most tourist-ready place in Indonesia, with an international airport accepting direct flights from Europe and Australia, as well as good connections for the USA.

Background

Bali is a densely populated island of over 3 million inhabitants. Hindu religion and culture permeate all areas of life, noticeable in the many ceremonies and colourful processions. Tourism, the mainstay of the economy, has had a massive impact, yet the strength of the Balinese culture has somehow survived, as has the warmth of the people.

The Setup

There are varied topographical and bathymetric circumstances on Bali. The Bukit in the south is a dramatically steep limestone peninsula fringed by shallow tables of coral that drop away reasonably severely. Fast reef breaks predominate as a result. The neck of the island is hard-packed sand with a mix of volcanic and calcareous grains, so dumping beach-breaks are no surprise. The body of the island is dominated by enormous volcanoes that have created black-sand and lava reef breaks, punctuated by the occasional river mouth.

The Waves

Whilst it is often used as a jump-off for other Indonesian surf adventures, Bali is where the whole thing started in the early 70's. It's still the centre of Indian Ocean surfing, and has at least 6 of the worlds top 100 waves. There is a smattering of beach-breaks and some very high quality rivermouth and even cobblestone point-style waves. What attracts the world surfing community however, are the long, perfectly formed reef-breaks of the Bukit peninsula down south. Uluwatu, Padang-Padang and Bingin are 3 unbelievable and unique lefts, while Nusa Dua, Hyatt Reef and Sanur offer 3 complementary rights of equally immense quality.

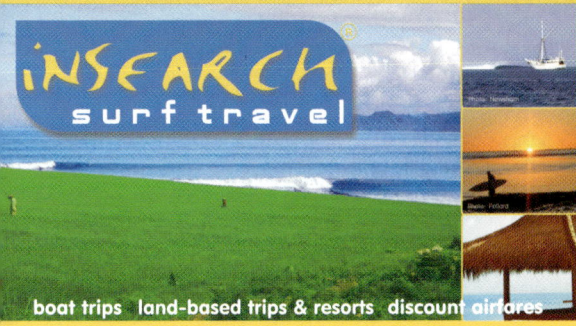
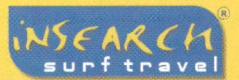

Bali: Surf data

Tides

As in many parts of Indonesia, the character of waves in Bali changes dramatically according to the depth of water over the bottom. What may have been a grinding barrel at low tide, can become a group of playful peaks on high, although every spot is different. You can either get a tide table from a local surf shop, or just turn up and enjoy the different moods of the spot. If you miss the "optimal" tide, bear in mind that you will probably still have a fun surf, and you may also have missed the crowds who like to descend on the place at just the right time.

Winds

Many surf spots really come into their own when trade-winds kick in and comb the faces into perfect lines. Unlike, say, Southern California, glassy conditions are not always best, and can give a spot a kind of shapeless lethargy, or "morning sickness". Uluwatu is a good example. With winds kicking in around 10 a.m. onwards in dry season, you may therefore find that some spots are less crowded in the early mornings, and, whilst not necessarily at their almighty best, can offer you more waves per hour.

Season

Bali surfing is generally divided into 2 coasts and 2 seasons. In essence, the west coast is off-shore throughout the **dry season**, from around April to September (and later if you are lucky). Winds are predominantly east - southeast. This is also the major swell window for the Indian Ocean's big south pulses. It is southern hemisphere winter, and therefore peak season due to Bali's proximity to Australia. For these reasons, the west coast waves, which are predominantly lefts, are the most well known and busiest. You can still surf these spots on lucky days off-season, and early mornings, so goofy-footers do not despair.

Wet season, from mid October to mid April, brings northwest trade-winds and quite a bit of rain. Some lucky travellers will only get wet at night , others will arrive in time for a full week or torrential rain; it's a lottery. The up-side is less crowds, and a selection of awesome right-handers up the east coast from Nusa Dua to Sanur. Whilst there is less swell during this season, the more consistent spots like Nusa Dua itself will still be firing, and there are super-hollow, extremely long waves like Hyatt Reef to look forward to. Another factor is less Australians. That isn't Xenophobia, it's just that Aussies surf pretty well so it's harder to get waves when they are there en masse. Wet season falls across the northern hemisphere winter so the flavour can be more European.

M	Swell Range		Wind Pattern		Air		Sea	Crowd
	Feet	Dir'	Am	Pm	Low	Hi	°C	
J	2-6	SE-SW	NW LO	NW MOD	22	27	26	HI
F	2-6	SE-SW	NW LO	NW MOD	22	27	26	LO
M	2-6	SE-SW	NW LO	NW MOD	22	28	26	MED
A	2-8	S-SW	SE LO	SE MOD	22	30	26	MED
M	2-10	S-SW	SE LO	SE MOD	22	30	26	HI
J	3-10	S-SW	SE LO	SE MOD	22	30	26	HI
J	3-12	S-SW	SE LO	SE MOD	22	30	26	HI+
A	3-10	S-SW	SE LO	SE MOD	22	30	26	HI+
S	2-8	S-SW	SE LO	SE MOD	22	29	26	HI
O	2-8	SE-SW	NW LO	NW MOD	22	28	26	LO
N	2-6	SE-SW	NW LO	NW MOD	18	27	26	LO
D	2-6	SE-SW	NW LO	NW MOD	19	27	26	HI+

Transport

Hiring a *Bemo* (minibus or big car with driver) is by far the best way to maximize your surf time and avoid getting lost and frustrated. Even if you can find your way around alone, chances are you will get stopped and fined by the police for not having a proper international licence (there's a notorious police station on the way to Uluwatu). You can arrange drivers through any hotel, or at Bemo Corner (or any street) in Kuta. They aren't as expensive as you might think, especially when shared between mates, and the drivers are always interesting, friendly guys who will look after you, point you in the right direction, and enrich your stay more than you enrich their pockets. See the **Surftrip Planner** at the back. Many surf spots require a boat to get to, and all of these are well serviced

Bali: Surf data

by Jukung (wooden canoe with outrigger and motor) owners who line the beaches at Kuta, Nusadua and other spots. Pay your small 2-way fare nicely, and enjoy the ride; it's all in a good cause and paddling 800 yards to land, alone in the dark is not worth the saving.

Crowds

You will not escape people in Bali, whenever you are here. Lucky it's a party island so you can get up early and avoid them.

Boards

As in most of Indo, your usual board plus 6 inches length, and 1/4 inch thickness, will cover most situations. Waves are hollow and straight, so the rhino chaser approach doesn't always pay off, tending to limit your position changes in the barrel, or even catch. If your short board is a 6'3" then the ideal plan might be to take it along plus a 6'8 and a 7'2".

Hazards

Shallow reef means cuts are common. Sneaker sets on bigger days. Crime is not a big issue but be careful late at night anyway.

Bali Bomb post-script

Almost every Balinese person you meet, is deeply saddened, and strangely embarrassed by the events of October 2002. The devastating attacks left wounds that will take a generation to heal. It's extremely likely you will meet somebody whose lost a family member. On a materialistic level, the economy of the Island has been dealt a knockout blow and there are many families living close to the bread-line. Bear this in mind when negotiating the price of your ride or T-shirt, and think of it as a tribute to the Balinese people that they remain the most warmly welcoming bunch of guys you are ever likely to meet. Whilst it is natural to fear going to a place that has been the target of a major act of bastardry, it's impossible to ignore the fact that Bali is still today, a safer place to be than most western cities.

Bali: Kuta and west coast

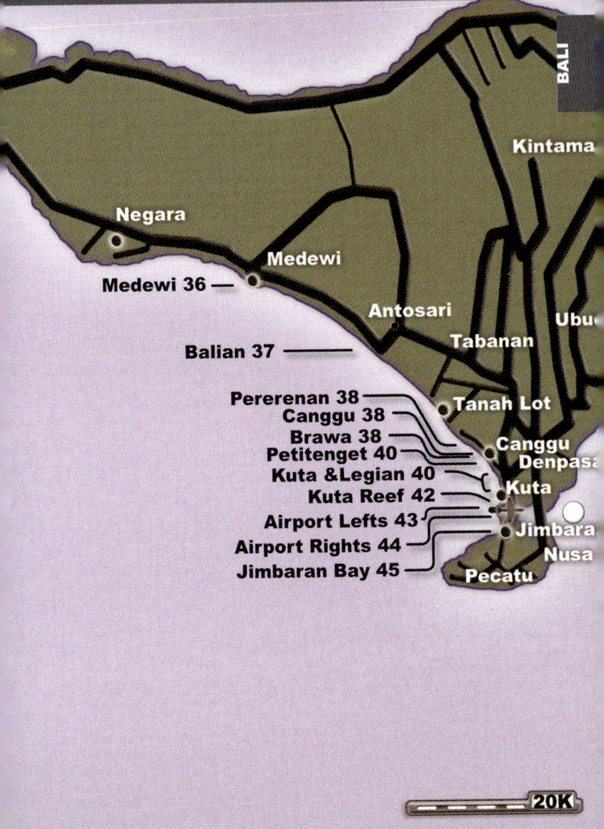

BALI

Kintama

Negara

Medewi

Medewi 36 —

Antosari

Balian 37 —————

Tabanan

Ubu

Pererenan 38 ——— ● Tanah Lot
Canggu 38 ———
Brawa 38 ———— Canggu
Petitenget 40 ———● Denpasa
Kuta &Legian 40 ——
Kuta Reef 42 ——— ● Kuta
Airport Lefts 43 —
Airport Rights 44 — ● Jimbara
Jimbaran Bay 45 — Nusa
Pecatu

20K

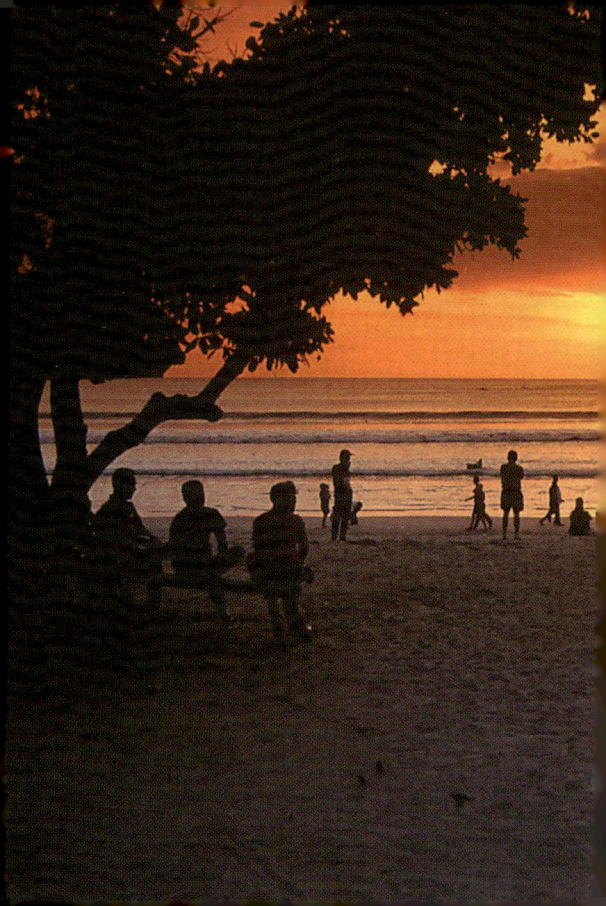

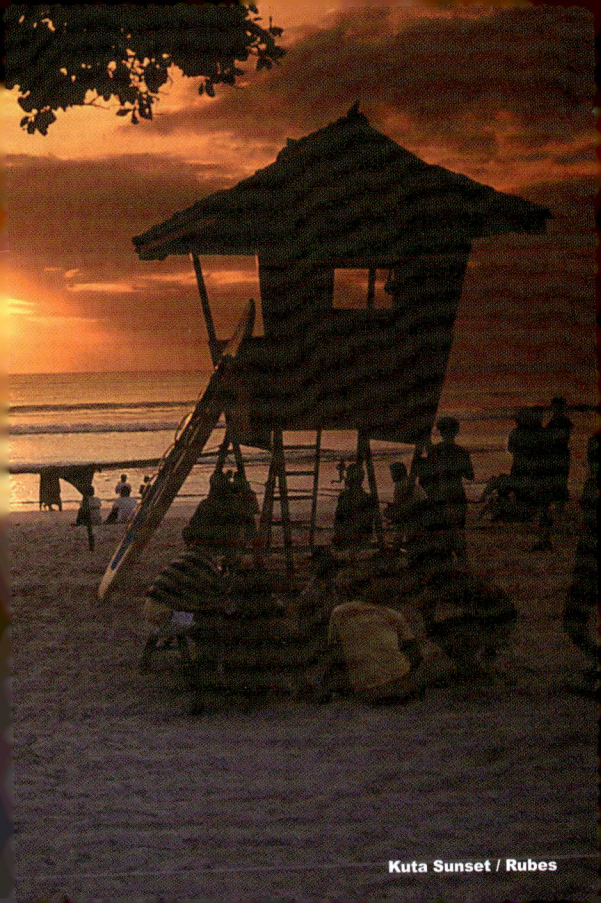

Kuta Sunset / Rubes

Medewi

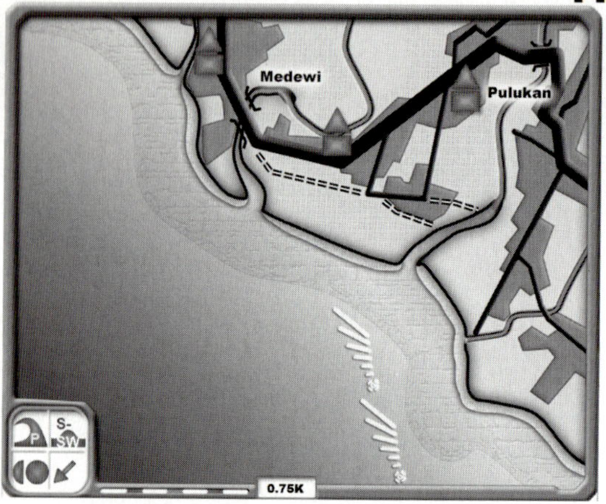

Head north out of Kuta through Tabanan, to the T-junction at Antosari. Take a left down to Soka Beach and you'll rejoin the coast road which bends right to the north-west. On, on, on past Balian about 10km to Pekutatan. There's a signed left down to the beach which is about 1.5km off the main road.

Very long, fun left-hand cobblestone and black sand point that delivers its best experiences in the early mornings. Dry season trades are cross-on-shore. When on, expect long lined up walls that are smash-able and fast. There's a quality inside peak called Pulukan. It's one of the furthest surf-spots from Kuta but still popular as there's plenty of accommodation at the break. Ideal warm-up spot, and rarely very hollow or steep. All levels. Fairly consistent. 3 good river mouths in the area.

If you really have time to spare and feel like wandering, you'll find some nice right beach peaks 1 bay up, and more lined up lefts in the Negara district around Pangambengan and even further towards Candikusema.

Balian

It's about half way between Canggu and Medewi. Head north out of Kuta through Tabanan, to the T-junction at Antosari. Take a left down to Soka Beach and you'll rejoin the coast road which bends right to the north-west. After about 9km you are there; you'll see it down on the left from the bridge.

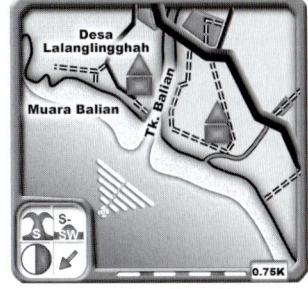

Consistent, well shaped rivermouth / beach break (with a few cobblestones thrown in). Generally gutless although can get hollow, but is more likely to be breaking than most spots on this stretch. Lefts can really line up. If beaches at Kuta are 2ft, it might be 5 up here, but the trade-winds ruin it so get up early. Any tide can work. Crowds variable but rarely bad. All levels unless big. Water gets dirty. Soka Beach itself may be worth a look on the way although it's quality isn't as recognized as Balian. It's a pleasant spot for a re-fuelling at any of the *warungs* while you check the surf.

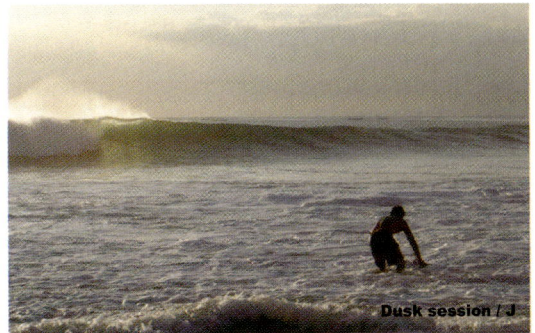

Dusk session / J

Canggu & Pererenan

Canggu: North from Kuta, through Seminyak and beyond. Just past Kerobokan and through many a rice field, via Padang Linjong Village, you'll see signs to "Canggu Surfing" & Echo Beach". There are 3 access points.

Black lava sand beach with 2 areas to surf, over sand and lava rock. If you ever catch it with nobody out it can be eerie, but that is not likely. Canggu ("Changoo") is the main escape route from Kuta beach-breaks. Best surfed early morning before the trade winds, up to about 6-8ft. Waves tend to peak up out of nowhere here in the black water, and low tide can get sketchy on the inside. Low lying cliffs and steep beach at high are a hazard. Advanced. On moderate swells if Canggu is crowded, you can check the black sand beach-breaks at **Brawa** (Berawa) a kilometre south.

Pererenan: Right next door to Canggu and often considered part of the same spot. Road ends at Pondok Wisata Losmen right at the break. Quick way is via Kerobokan towards Tanah Lot, but at Pererenan Village go left at "Pantai Pererenan" sign.

Left and right peaks over sand and lava best on higher tides unless small. Both peaks shoulder out into a well defined channel although you can take the "wrong way" on each depending on tides and size. There's sometimes a bit of a crew here but crowds are well absorbed by the shifting peaks. Afternoon breezes are side-onshore. All levels if small. Advanced when big. Consistent spot pulling more swell than Kuta beach-breaks.

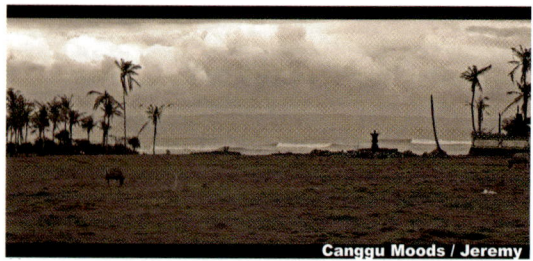

Canggu Moods / Jeremy

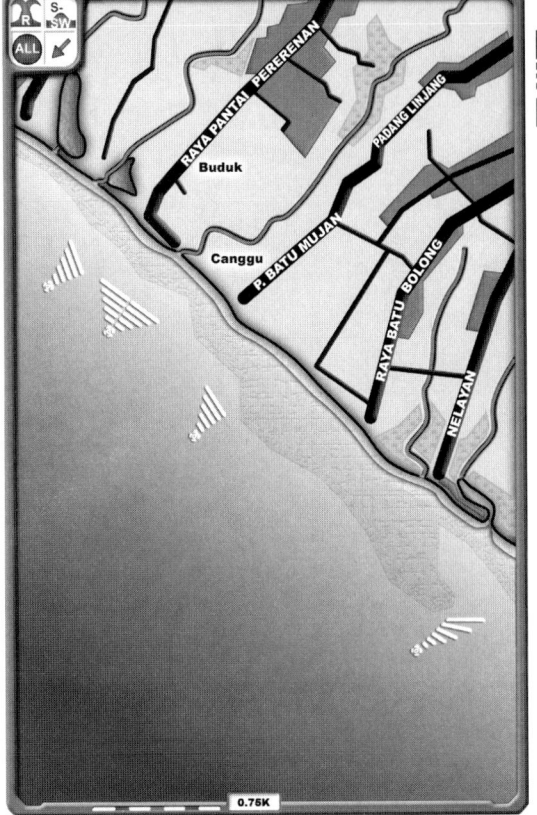

BALI

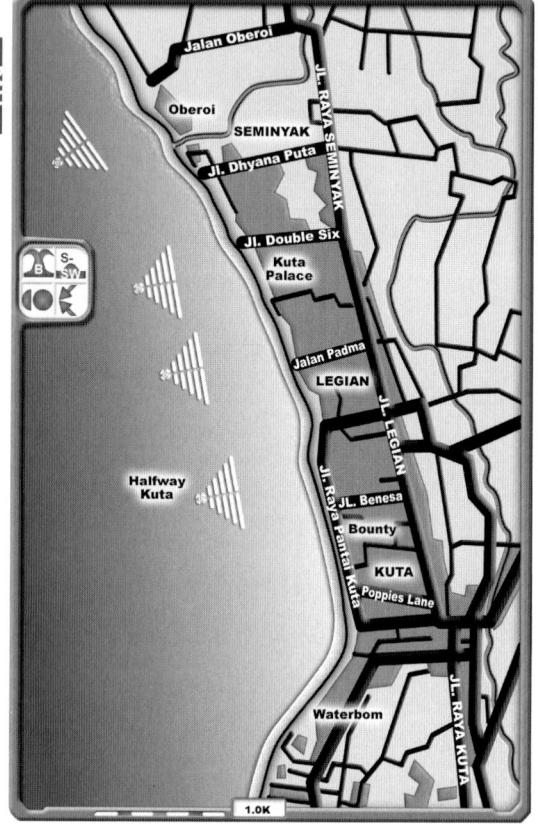

Jalan Oberoi

JL. RAYA SEMINYAK

Oberoi

SEMINYAK

Jl. Dhyana Puta

Jl. Double Six

Kuta
Palace

Jalan Padma

LEGIAN

JL. LEGIAN

Jl. Raya Pantai Kuta

JL. Benesa

Bounty

KUTA

Poppies Lane

Halfway
Kuta

JL. RAYA KUTA

Waterbom

1.0K

Kuta and Legian beach-breaks

For many, the brown-water beach-breaks stretching from Kuta Beach up to Seminyak are the first waves they surf in Indonesia. Not an inspiring introduction to Indian Ocean power, but these fairly consistent black sand beach-breaks are a great warm-up and jet-lag reviver, close to the action.

Kuta Beach itself, the large strip centred around Jalan Pantai Kuta, can be the worlds worst close-out, especially at low-tide. At best, you can get fast cover-ups, and the up-side is the waves are usually super-hollow, and offshore in the southeast trades. At the west end of that street, you can jog up and check for the best peak. **Halfway**, located level with Poppies Lane 2, often has the best peaks. You'll spot it from almost anywhere because there's always a solid group out there. It gets a bit more wind than spots down the beach but holds better shape thought the tides and is pretty consistent, and usually hollow. If its over 4 feet you will get thumped! **Padma**, at the end of the street of the same name, is one of a number of well-frequented sections of beach running north from Kuta to Legian. If you're in a *bemo*, you might want to check the spots up and down Jalan Raya Kuta and find the best on the day. Body-boarders and a regular crew surf outside the **Blue Ocean** Hotel at the end of Jalan Putra, and there are plenty of peaks running across this area. The whole strip is often very murky, with plastic items floating in the water and washing up on the beach. Best avoided after rains.

Further up towards **Seminyak** are more low tide peaks, getting more consistent but messy as you head north. Best on morning glass or opportunist NE winds. Of note is the beach-break called **Petitenget**, near the Legian hotel.

Breaks from 1-6ft (more if lucky although often the bigger swells are a suicide mission involving heavy close-outs). Higher tides generally best. Ideal for beginners on most days. Can be used as an indicator for Ulu's and Bukit breaks; if its a genuine 4-6 feet here pack your gun and head south: Uluwatu could be 10 feet, Padang may well be breaking, and Green Ball will be too big by far.

Kuta Reef

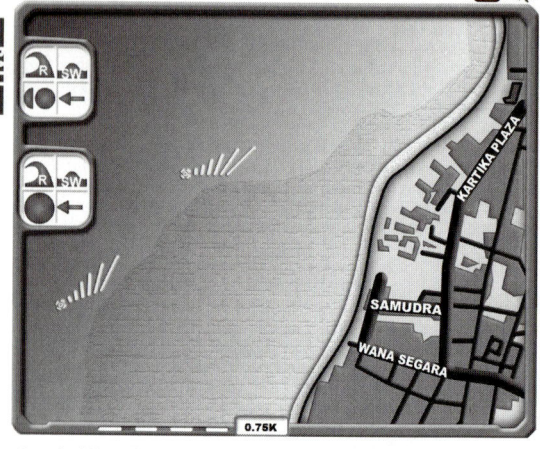

S end of Kuta Beach at end of Wana Segara Street. Get a *Jukung* and politely pay your fare, about 20'000RP each way.

This classy reef left-hander reels for long enough to fit in multiple bottom turns, and can feature very makeable barrels. Needs solid swell to get going (Ulus will usually be several feet bigger), but is the best wave near Kuta. Extremely crowded unless you go very early, and these days that means a dawn raid. Afternoons get wind-blown (cross-off-shore) as it's far from the lee of the land. A few hundred metres south towards the airstrip, but further out to sea, is **Middles**. Generally less crowded, bigger, but not as barrel-rich, Middles is a straight-forward take-off into a long wall with a few turns possible before the close-out section. Sometimes it lines up further, but riding beyond and inside the reef-line leaves you fully exposed to multiple hold-downs. Below mid is a close-out. For both spots book a ride both ways as it's a 20 minute paddle home. 2-10ft. Intermediates plus.

Airport Lefts

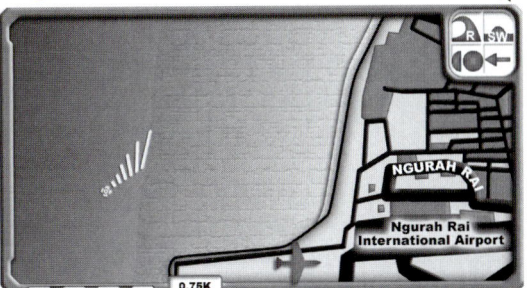

NGURAH RAI

Ngurah Rai
International Airport

0.75K

Off the end of the runway. Catch a *Jukung* from South Kuta unless you are training for an Ironman contest. Superb left-hand reef on the same coral base that was used to anchor the runway. Sections are more fun and bash-able than most Indo breaks. Usually less crowded and bigger than Kuta reef next door, but its still worth going early to get an easier session in before the crowds. A second peak absorbs the numbers. Suffers from strong cross-offshore winds on dry season afternoons.

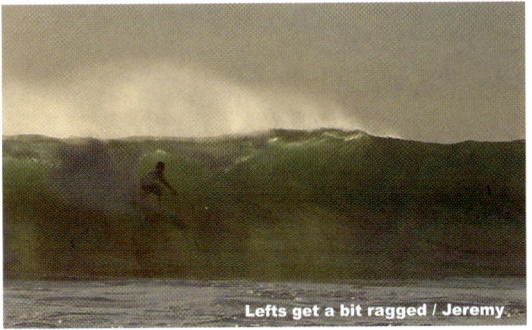

Lefts get a bit ragged / Jeremy.

Airport Rights

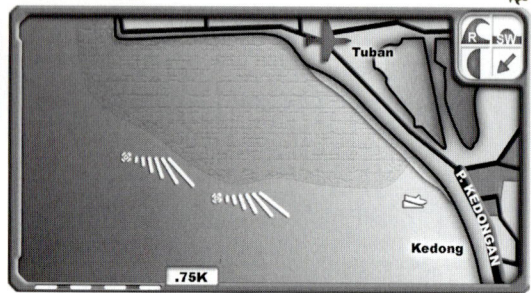

On the southern side of the airstrip, Jukungs can be hired from the top end of Jimbaran bay, where there is a large fishing fleet.

Right hand reef break over a double curve of coral reef, that can barrel from start to finish and will be, at the very least, extremely sucky. Of all the Kuta area reefs, this one is the shallowest, and the most likely to cut you if you fall. When it's around 3 feet on middle tides, it is a racy open tube all the way across. When it gets bigger, it just breaks on another section of the reef, just as shallow and round, for the most gaping stand-up tubes a man can want. On a 5-6ft day of low-ish mid tides and gentle easterly wind, it can dish out the best barrels of your life, although the exits are not always guaranteed.

Airport rights requires more swell than Lefts or even Kuta Reef if it is to fire; Kuta beach-breaks have to be at least 6 genuine feet. If you catch it on day one of a swell it'll be relatively uncrowded, but once word gets out every natural footer in town will show up looking for a break from surfing back-side. Although a dry season break, it is best early in the day before the winds get onto it; strong southeast trades create heavy cross-chop in the afternoons; it'll still barrel but the bumps can be harsh. 3-12ft plus. Advanced.

Jimbaran Bay

Nestled in between the airport and the beginning of the Bukit Peninsula.

If there's a very big southwest swell out there it can offer beginners waves across the strip at low tide, breaking on sand and getting bigger the further N you go. There is a very rare right reef off the Four seasons at the S end, and 2 left points in coves further round. Both need low tide and huge swell to show, with SE winds off-shore. A bombora right left combo works way off-shore in similar, and might make a good tow-in spot.

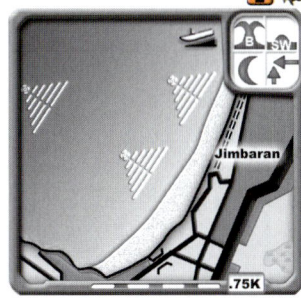

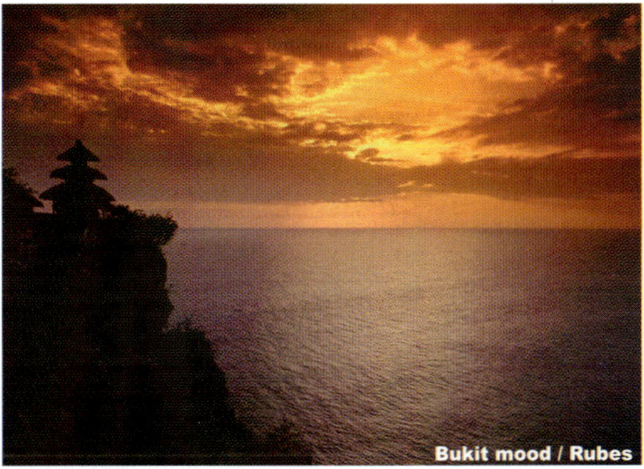

Jimbaran

.75K

BALI

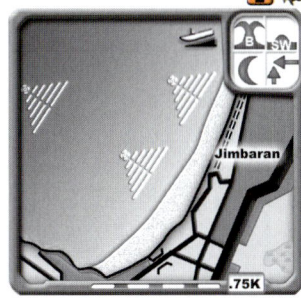

Bukit mood / Rubes

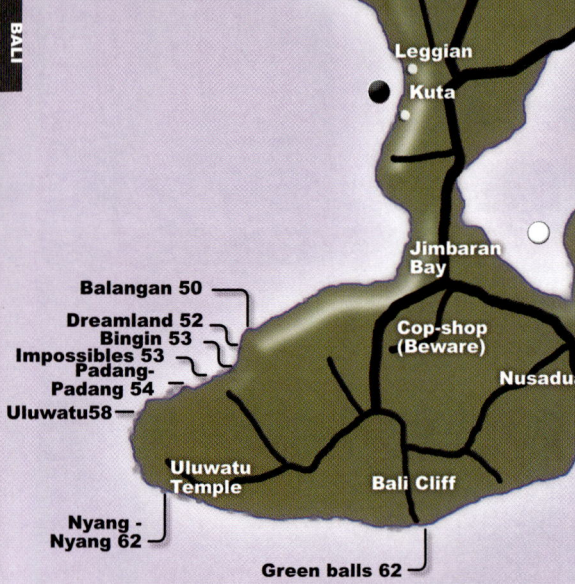

Leggian

Kuta

Jimbaran Bay

Balangan 50

Dreamland 52
Bingin 53
Impossibles 53
Padang-
Padang 54

Uluwatu58

Cop-shop
(Beware)

Nusadua

Uluwatu
Temple

Bali Cliff

Nyang -
Nyang 62

Green balls 62

5K

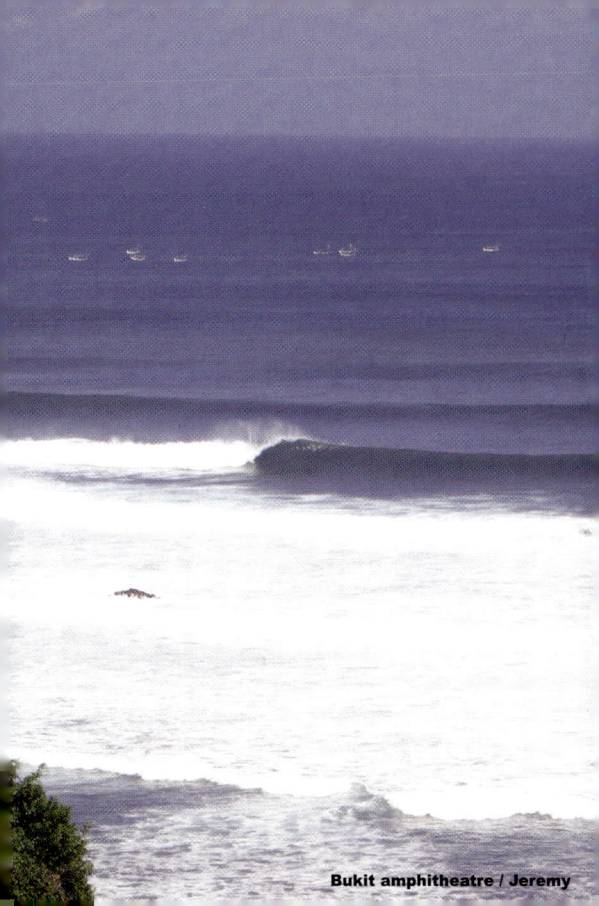

Bukit amphitheatre / Jeremy

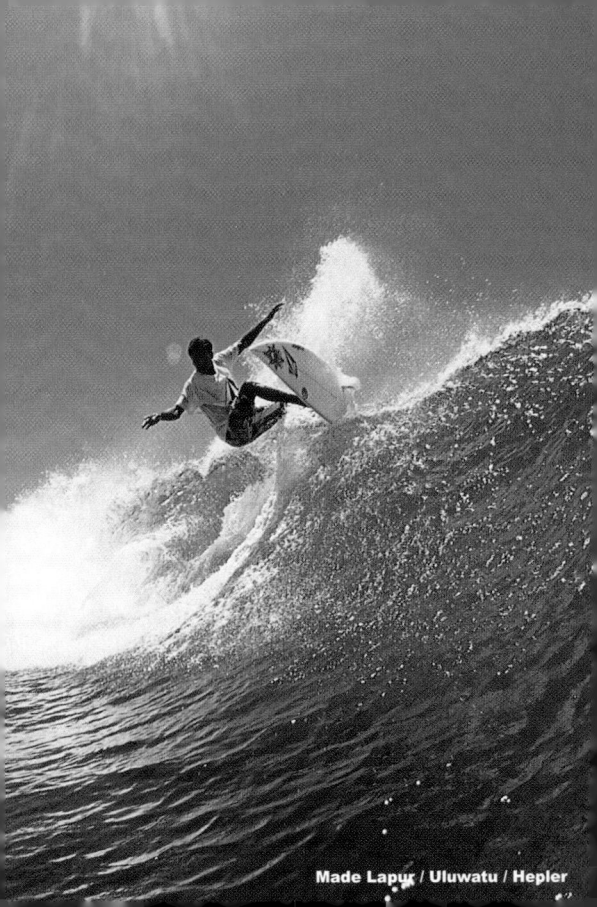

Made Lapur / Uluwatu / Hepler

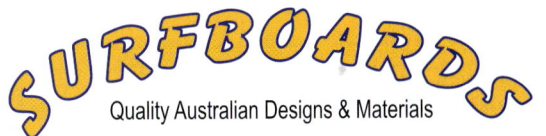

SURFBOARDS

Quality Australian Designs & Materials

CUSTOM MADE IN BALI

Indo Guns, Short Boards, Mals etc.
Covers & Accesories available
Pick up in Bali or Jakarta

ORDER IN ADVANCE

NAGA SURFBOARDS
AUSTRALIA INDONESIA

FREELINE SURF DESIGN

OnLine

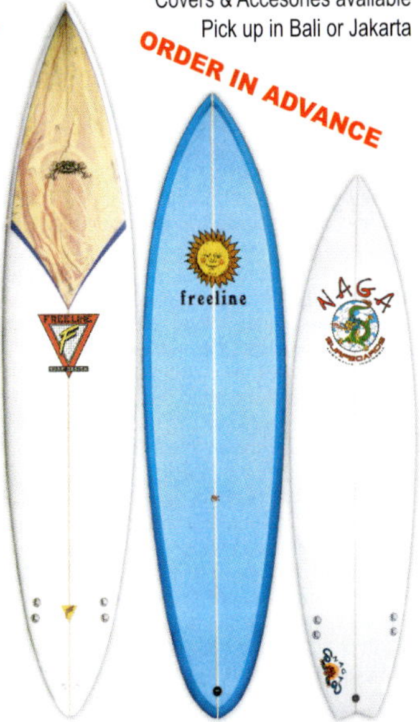

freeline

NAGA SURFBOARDS

Contact Nev Hines Email: nev@freelinesurf.com.au
www.freelinesurf.com.au/surfboards.htm

Balangan

From Kuta, take the main road south through Jimbaran towards Uluwatu. Once through Jimbaran, the road splits 3 ways; take the middle road "Uluwatu". After about 4km there's a crossroads with Balangan signed as right; ignore it & go straight. After another few hundred metres (after the police stn) go through the gateway on R marked "Griya Alam Pecatu". All the way down palm-lined rd, past the

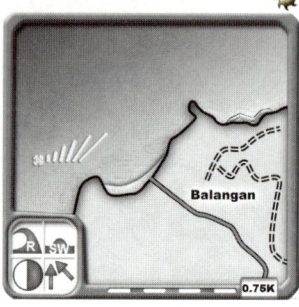

Dreamland sign, then next left. On a low tide you can walk round the point to the left and hop off. On high, it is possible to walk left along the cliff and lower yourself down a rope inside the cove.

A truly beautiful beach hosts this very long left-hand reef/point that often looks more makeable than it actually is. The endless lines seen from the top can be deceptive. On an average day, there are 2 main take-offs; The Point, and the middle of the beach. Good days are on low tide and 4-8ft of swell, when point waves will start with a benevolent take-off then barrel all the way to the 2nd peak, where it is a toss up between a close-out or a gloriously accelerating 2nd barrel section all the way through. Taking off on this 2nd peak is always an option, and is often more critical, leading straight into the faster part of the wave. As the tide rises, it is more of a fun peak, with 2-5ft being playful, even limp, with split peaks. The real Balangan however, shows itself on a very large swell and full moon super-high tide, when the inside reef fringe is fully submerged allowing it to line up all the way through. Level of expertise required generally correlates to size and tide at this spot. Small urchins pepper the reef; boots a must at low tide. When trade-winds are more south oriented, this spot will be cleaner than Uluwatu or Bingin/Dreamland, but is generally the smaller of the Bukit surf grounds.

Great *warung*s on the beach; spend the day. This entire area is slated for resort development so it's quirky charm will be short lived.

50

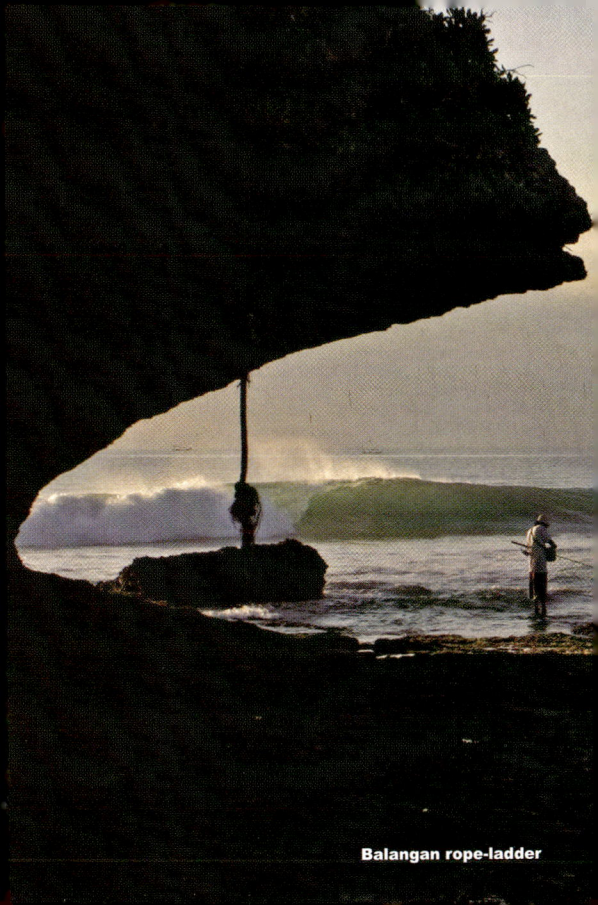

Balangan rope-ladder

Dreamland

Take Balangan directions, but turn off left at that Dreamland sign and follow the short coral stone track to the car park.

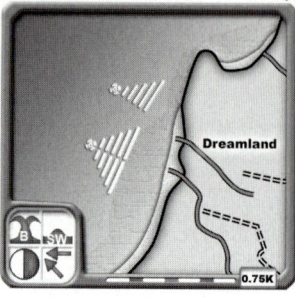

Not the most classic long wave in Bali, but probably it's most beautiful beach. Primarily a left and right A-frame reef with a big drop and barrel, tapering into the channel. Lefts are longer and usually more shack-rich, rights are often just the drop and the shoulder, although they can be quality. Inside reforms close out near beach. Further up the beach are some more lefts towards Balangan. Close outs are common, and the wave is fickle in all respects, requiring a major swell to show it's real character. On an average small day it can resemble a typical home-town beach-break. It is a place to head when Uluwatu is solid but these days you'll have to share it with many. 2-8ft. All levels.

Land here has been "redistributed", first by Tommy Soeharto, then by the administrators of his assets following his incarceration. The result is locals losing their land to a proposed resort development. It means bad aura, imminent loss of character, (this beach has the best *warungs* and *losmen* on the Bukit), and the probable ruination of another surf spot.

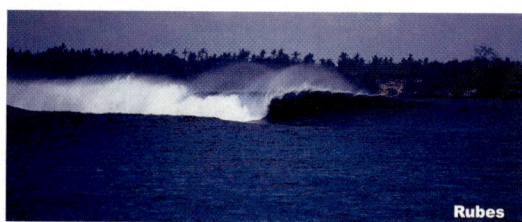

Rubes

Bingin

As for Padang, but take a R 2km before marked "Surfing beach Bingin - Impossibles". You can stay in the *losmen* at the bottom of the cliff, eat cheap, and even get your board carried back up the steep path.

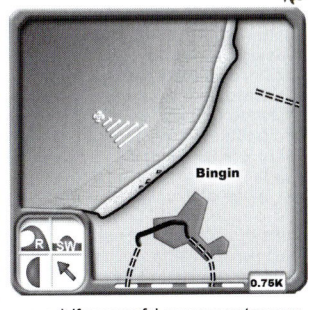

Super-hollow, classic left shared with a tightly packed group. Everything is focussed on the tiny take-off point, and if you actually get a wave to yourself it's likely you'll have to dodge helmet-cams bobbing around. If successful, you can get square, perfect barrels even on a 2-3ft day. Advanced, but easier on high tide. Sharp coral. Beautiful spot for late p.m. Bintang and noodle soup.

Impossibles

Visible looking south from Bingin, with easy access from Padang Padang; the first peak is out the front to the right of the beach, where there's a good channel.

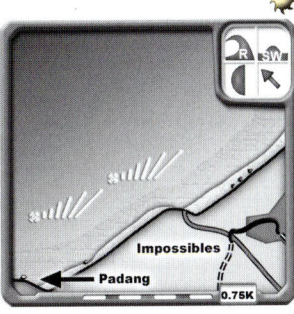

This is a mad, very long, fast left-hand coral point that barrels hard over a sharp shallow sea bottom, offering only a slender chance of making an exit. It needs a very large swell to get going (Ulus needs to be over 6ft), and isn't always the fairground ride it may appear from the top. The most usual scenario is take-off into barrel, get out-raced, start again. Lower tides best. Currents. Long paddle. Advanced.

Padang - Padang

Head S from Kuta through Jimbaran. At the end of Jimbaran is a 3-way split. Take middle road marked "Uluwatu". After 4km go straight across crossroads, and another 4km approx. Take R at shop down Jl Labuansait all the way to the bridge above Labuansait Beach. Park. Down steps through rock tunnel. The main take-off is around the point to the left. You can walk around on low, or use the deep channel.

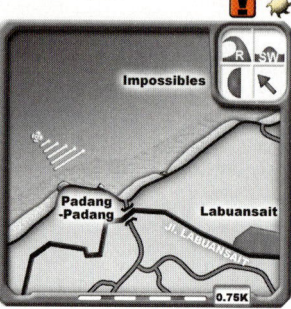

Classic, extremely hollow, very shallow left-hand reef break for experts. Padang is Bali's most consequential wave, but it needs a major ground-swell to show; think minimum 6ft plus at Uluwatu. Being clearly visible from the road, easily accessible, and unchallenging in the paddle-out, this spot gets very crowded indeed. The small take-off zone exacerbates the situation, so you need to be skilled and tactful to get your share of waves here. Even on a small day, take-off is usually straight into a yawning, turquoise, oval barrel, just like Pipeline. Then it's a matter of maximum speed, sight your exit, and stand solid all the way to the deep channel. A fall here is punishing, with pointy, lava-based shallow coral forming holes and spikes.

Padang works through the tides although low is extremely serious and should be avoided by newcomers. Mid tides still toss up perfect barrels and there's a good channel from mid to high. It's worth wearing reef boots at all times so that you can put your feet down when wiping out. Some even wear spring-suits; ostensibly for nipple-rash, but usually to give a little protection from the pock-marked reef. Experts only. Fickle. 3-10ft. Heading on up the hill towards Uluwatu there's a right to "Thomas Homestay". The beach under this is also known as Padang-Padang, and can have waves away from the crowds. Buy a cold drink and enjoy the view.

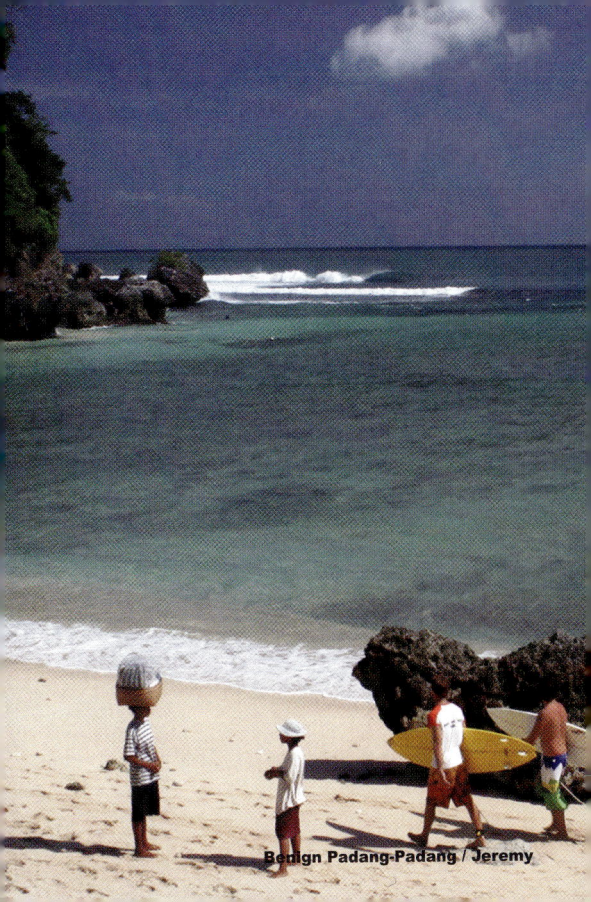

Benign Padang-Padang / Jeremy

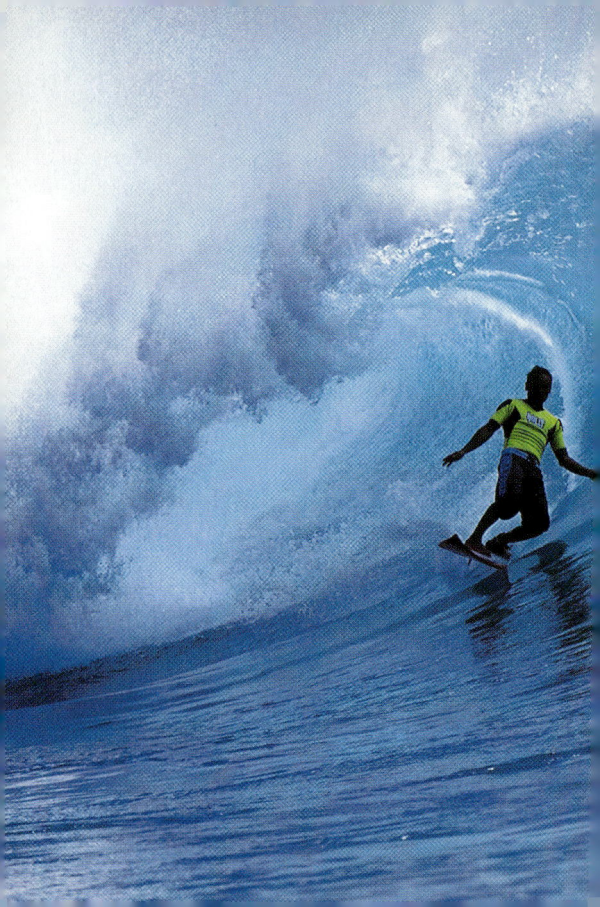

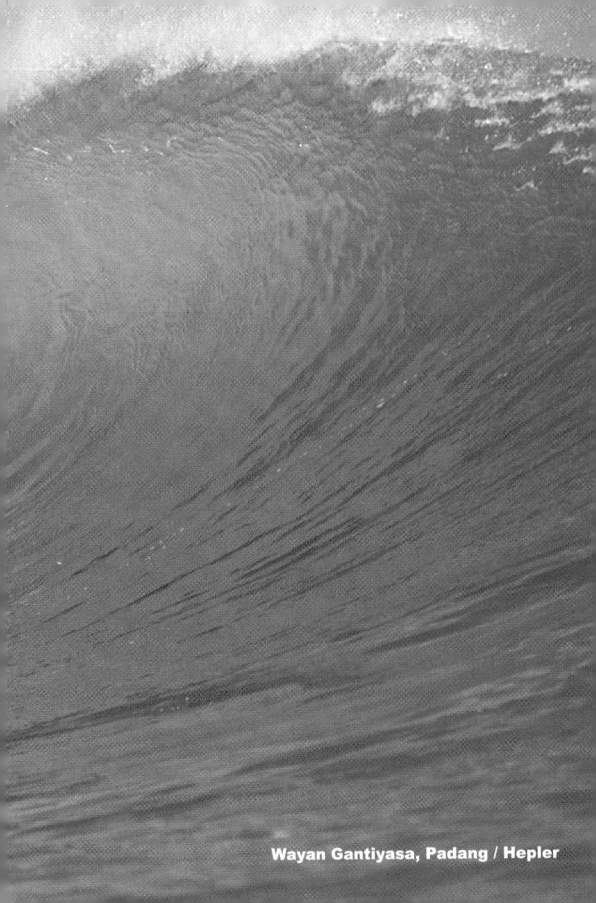
Wayan Gantiyasa, Padang / Hepler

Racetrack

Outside Corner

Peak

Temples

Suluban

Songbintang

Uluwatu

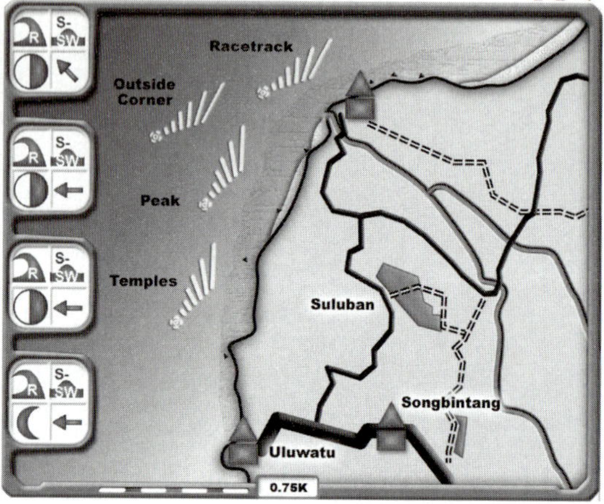

0.75K

As for Padang Padang, then continue south for about 2k. First turnoff is now cut off by new resort, although you can park just inside the first gate and walk about a km. 2nd turnoff is best, and takes you straight to the cave via some concrete steps and the Rip Curl toilet.

The romance of Indonesia's first surf mecca was being strangled for years, and has now finally been killed off. The major development on the northern cliff, with the original *warungs* clinging desperately to the slopes underneath, is an omen for the whole peninsula. Access is still through the famous cave, but even this now has concrete steps to replace the old bamboo ladder. This is all quickly forgotten once out in the line-up however, which still comprises some of the most consistently good lefts in Indonesia.

At high tide you enter the cave, paddle fast and accept the current, which takes you over to the right but eases off on the outside. On low

Uluwatu

tide you have to hop off the edge of the exposed reef between sets. Essentially a series of left-handers breaking on quite sharp coral (reef boots a must) with many different personalities and take-off points depending on the tides and swell size. Ulus is essentially a dry season wave although it is one of the most consistent waves in Bali, and can be surfed on windless mornings all year round.

Moderate east to south-east trade-winds comb it into perfect shape, but conversely it can suffer from a lack of shape or "morning sickness" on early mornings with no breeze. On smaller days and higher tides in those conditions, it can be a fun, even flaccid spot, and crowds are often much smaller because most arrive from Kuta later in the day.

Temples, out the back over on the far left-hand side, is your best chance of a peaceful surf. The longer paddle thins out the numbers although there is another, dangerous, access point. Fun on high tide (unless it is big), it is a nice left-hander away from the main area. Not usually as lined up as The Peak or Racetrack, but can get good and hollow on it's day. 3-12ft. Advanced. Needs bigger swells and low tide.

The Peak, in front of the cave and slightly to the left, is the most ridden peak, and best at mid tide. It features a punchy take-off and good opportunities for barrels. You will often need to kick out early or face a nasty shut down; the inside section is very shallow. When the reef outside the cave is fully covered the sweep can be wicked. This means that to get back in you need to take a wave, straighten out and ride the foam as far back right as you can to avoid missing the entrance and having to start again. Lost boards at these times mean a swim to Padang, or clambering back up and across some evil, pointy rocks. 2-10ft. Advanced. On average swells and higher tides, intermediate peaks open up between here and Temples and the set-up is unpredictable. On big days, a small high tide can be good and lined up.

Race-track, just right of the cave, is the last section of the wave. It works best on low tide to 2 hours either side. This is a super fast, bending, hollow speed ride, and once barreled you either blast out

Uluwatu Continued

gloriously or get crushed as the sections increase in size. It gets super shallow as it wraps around the point towards Padang. Experts only. 2-8ft.

Outside Corner: On bigger days and lower tides, out the back to the right side of the set-up is this big-wave arena for experts. Outside corner, when working, is a heavy, sucking left-hand barrel that can hold very solid swell. On dry season afternoons with 8-10ft+ swell, it'll assume Hawaiian proportions with harsh wind-driven spray pushing you off the back or forcing you to take off extremely late. 6-15ft. Big boards required. Experts.

Overall hazards include craggy reef at low tide, when reef boots are a must. Currents on higher tides although the reef is nice and deep at this time. Major crowds after 10a.m.

Buy a tee shirt or 3 from the lovely ladies at the cave car-park or in the *warungs*. Make a small contribution to have your gear looked after too and, finally, enjoy the afterglow over a Bintang and some healthy cheap food overlooking the peak.

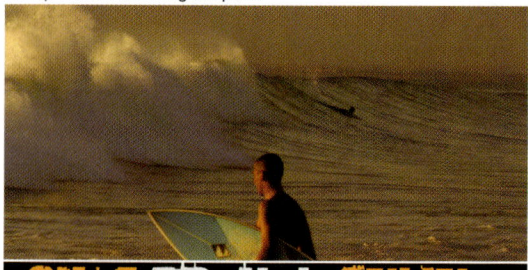

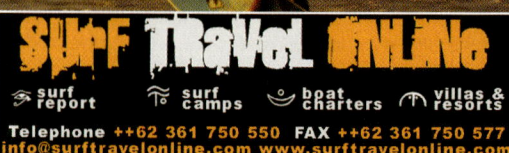

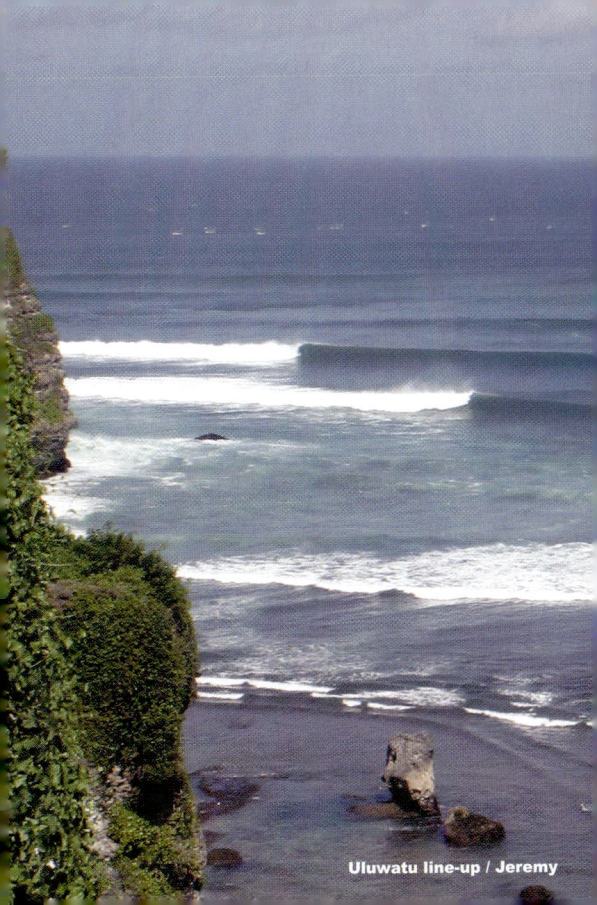

Uluwatu line-up / Jeremy

Nyang - Nyang

From Uluwatu Temple, take the main Pecatu road. After a few km go R by school down rough 4WD track. Fork left at V.

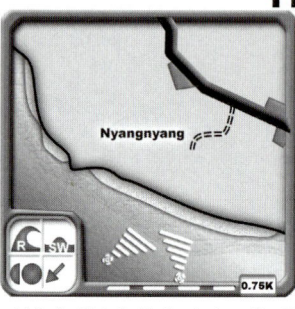

Only head here if you've checked Uluwatu and it is too small for you. Nyang - Nyang draws any available swell to its mainly right reef pass setup, breaking into a good channel on mid to high tide. It doesn't handle much size, with 4ft and over being heavy. The reef here is riddled with intimidating holes. Surf it early morning. Consistent. Bad currents. Sharks sighted. Advanced. The view from the top is as staggering as the walk down.

Green balls

Head past Ulu turnoff and go to the southern tip of the Bukit, following signs to the Bali Cliff Hotel. Its at the bottom of the huge cliffs here.

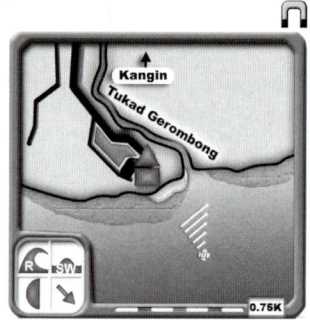

The most consistent wave in Bali. If Green balls is flat, so is everywhere, and in fact it is often to big and messed up to ride. Essentially a short right breaking over coral into a channel. There is an occasional left that may tempt on the other side of this channel but it rarely has any shape. Best surfed on small days, early morning. Both the wet and dry season trade winds badly damage it. Currents. 2-8ft. Other peaks east to be discovered, via the seaweed farms.

62

Bali: East Coast & Lembongan

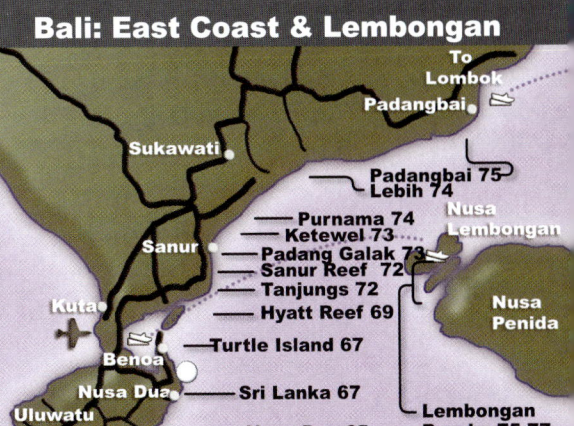

To Lombok

Padangbai

Sukawati

Padangbai 75
Lebih 74

Purnama 74
Ketewel 73

Nusa Lembongan

Sanur

Padang Galak 73
Sanur Reef 72
Tanjungs 72
Hyatt Reef 69

Nusa Penida

Kuta

Benoa

Turtle Island 67

Nusa Dua

Sri Lanka 67

Uluwatu

Nusa Dua 65

Lembongan Breaks 75-77

15K

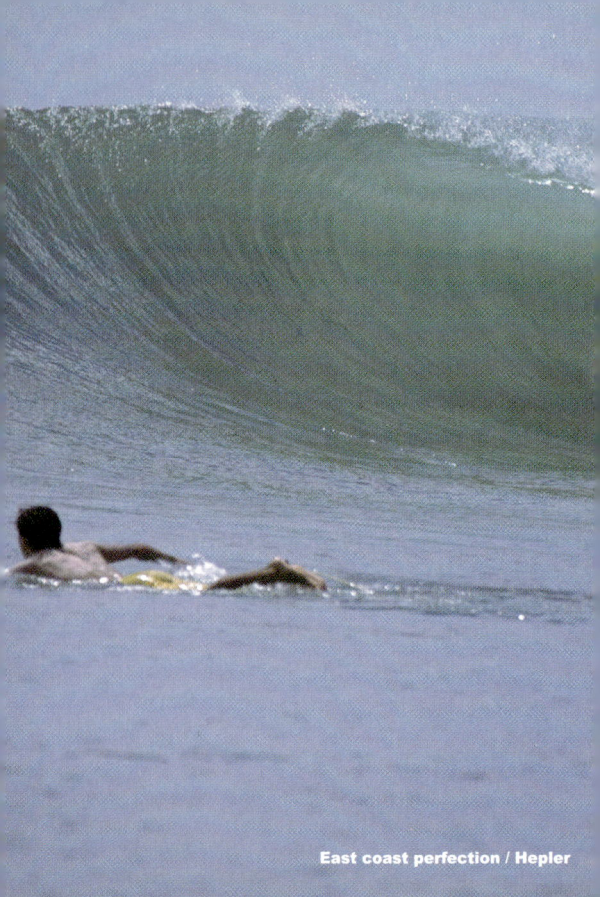

East coast perfection / Hepler

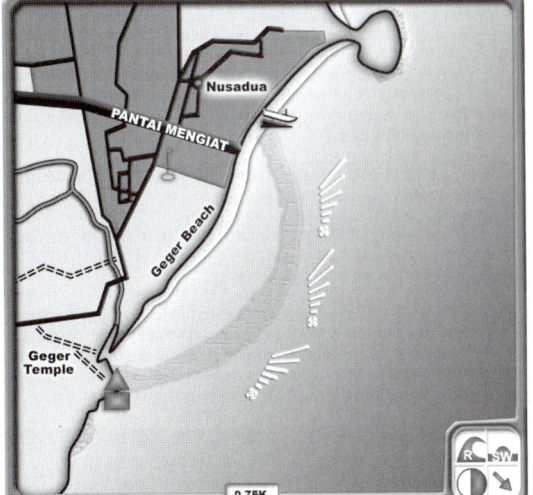

In Nusa Dua, take Jalan (street) Nusa Dua Selatan and Pantai Mengiat through the golf course and follow sign left to "Geger Surfing". It branches off right to Geger Beach (Pronounced Gerrgerr).

Open ocean right-hand reef break of immense quality and size. At 3-5ft on mid to high tide this is a bash-worthy, fun, fast, long beauty with at least 3 main peaks. On these days it merits a 4 hour session. On big days it is a heavy cloud-break experience; still the long walls, but barrels and huge drops too. The power of this place is phenomenal, but the even delivery of speed across it's length allows you to hone your skills. There is also an inner peak, north of the big outside wave, that delivers long, hollow lefts winding across the coral

Nusa Dua cont'd..

after a steep jacking take-off. On bigger days there are waves way out the back, and it can hold a genuine 12ft plus or more. On some days it is hard to really see where "out the back" really is as peaks stretch into the distance. The rights south of the Nikko and Geger Temple break on a similar but more exposed arc of reef and can be high quality and consistent. Wet-season wave, but if the south-east trades are strong it is pretty windy out there and some sections are cross-offshore.

Missing your boat back to land here is common in the excitement of a great session, but costly on the arms; it really is a long way to paddle and usually a long walk to wherever you left your ride. Those who have paddled out when boat captains are at a ceremony will tell you it is a gruelling, demoralizing experience struggling towards peaks that seem to just get further away.

Between the 2 islands are some fast (often too fast) hollow barreling rights. They merit inspection if there's enough swell, and if winds are south. Another fat left breaks off the south side of the island, and this can be hollow and fast. Hazards include long paddles, urchins (wear boots at low tide), sneaker sets and north-going currents.

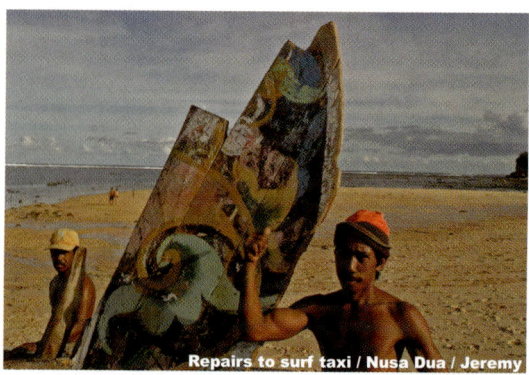

Repairs to surf taxi / Nusa Dua / Jeremy

Sri Lanka

One of a number of little gems in the area north of the Nusadua islands. Drive up towards Benoa and its on the right next to Club Med.

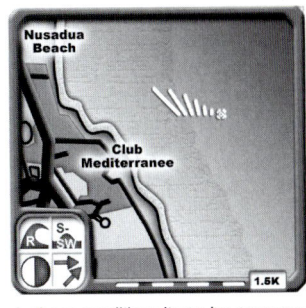

Right-hand reef that gets very hollow and can be fast and challenging. Check it on big days in the wet season; an awful lot of swell is needed for it to break properly (Nusadua 8ft+) although very straight south swells get in. Low tide is the barrel time, up to mid. On a big day in these conditions it can be a reverse Padang. It can be surfed on higher water but it needs to be big. All levels but shallow. Crowded. Check it when Nusadua is huge.

Turtle Island

You can drive here now. AKA Serangan. From Kuta, head towards Sanur on the By Pass, and follow the Turtle Island sign to the right before you get there. Once on the "island" you can take a right and look left for the breaks.

Previously only surfed by a few lucky locals, now this spot has a daily surf report to itself and is becoming the preferred off-season spot for long-timers and tourists alike. It's a trio of reef based lefts and rights with patchy sand, best on high tide as water submerges the main reef. There is a left, a right, and a Left-right combo, and the setup holds some major size. Consistent by east-coast standards. Sometimes pretty busy with more and more *warungs* to service the surfers. All levels. It can get very big indeed. Some local surfers know it as "Tartarellan", or "Tirtaarum". Can be invaded.

See map over

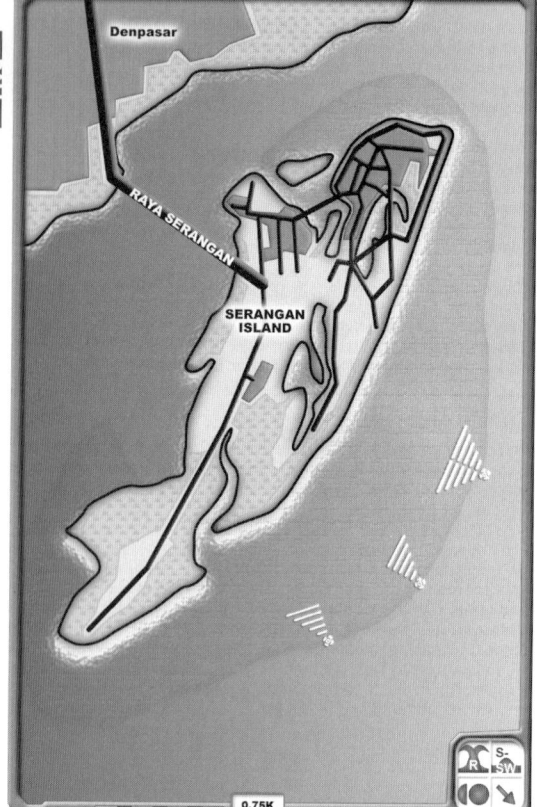

BALI

Denpasar

RAYA SERANGAN

SERANGAN ISLAND

0.75K

Hyatt Reef

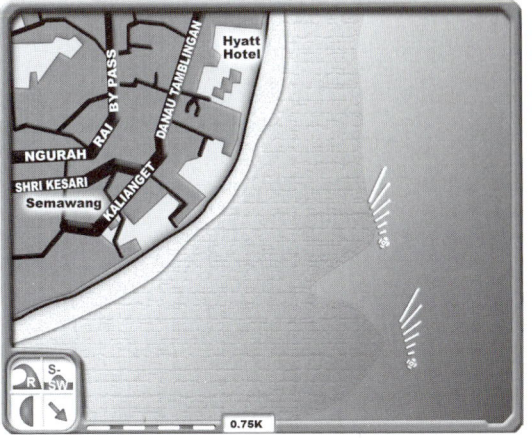

Head to the end of Kesari St in the Semawang district south of Sanur and it is out the front. Hire a *Jukung* to get out to the spot. Some locals know it as Semawang.

Curious to find a spot like this right out the front of a strip of resorts populated by elderly Internationals. A shifty, fast, long, cavernous right-hander breaks way off-shore. Sometimes closes out, sometimes lines up, always powers. It can deliver the best barrel of your life if you hang on in, although this sometimes results in a vainglorious stack on the inside slab. There's an inner peak that can be more precise on smaller days, but at low tide it is very shallow. This inner peak is usually the favoured spot for the keen local crew, who have it's take-off perfectly wired; give way to the experts and wait your turn. Inconsistent. All in all an advanced spot due to sneaker sets, horrific current, windy faces and the long distance. If it's on, it will be crowded unless you catch it early.

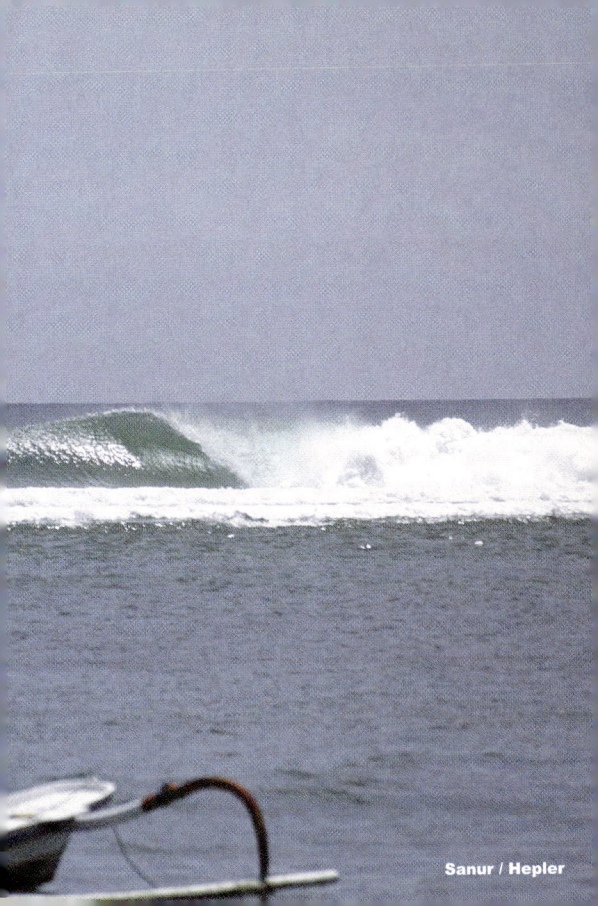

Sanur / Hepler

Sanur Reef and Tanjungs

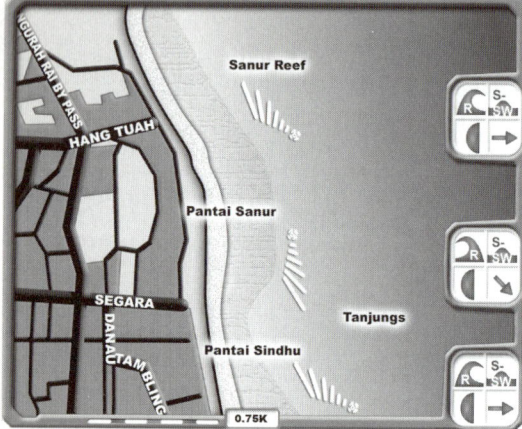

Tanjungs: Off Jalan Tegeh Agung by the beach markets in the Sindhu district. A left and a right reef pass, both requiring major swell and west trade winds to form up correctly. The rights (**Tanjung Sari** from the hotel of the same name) can be long and very hollow on lower tides, although hard to predict sometimes. All tides are OK with high more fun and sectioned. The **lefts** across the channel by the markets can be wedgy and steep, although often leave nothing to savour after the initial drop. The set-up can spread the crowd a bit so worth a look. Some days are awesome. All levels.

Sanur Reef: In the heart of Sanur, in front of the Grand Bali Beach Hotel. A rare, incredible right-hand reef breaks with precision over a straight-edged coral table. This is a wave that can barrel and wall for an extremely long distance, starting with a very steep take-off and requiring straight-line speed all the way to it's bitter, close-out end. Unfortunately it is one of the least consistent, most crowded waves on the east side unless you are on it on the first day of a very, very big swell. 3-12ft plus. Advanced.

Padang Galak

Head north out of Sanur towards Padang Bai on the Bypass for about 1.5km. Take R by Paramitha Hotel through the rice fields.

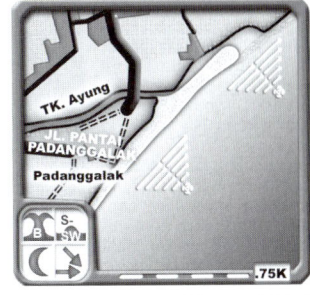

Semi consistent low tide beach-breaks over black, hard volcanic sand. This spot really needs a north-west wind to hold up well; wet season southeast winds are onshore and morning glass can leave it disorganized. Best in the 2-5ft range, which is when Nusadua may be 8 feet and firing! All levels. High tide is for kamikazes when over 3ft, but low is also closed out often.

Ketewel

North from Sanur, after about 4 km, is a small turnoff through the rice paddies.

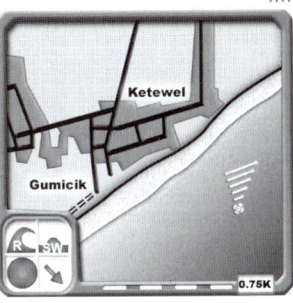

Shallow lava base right-hander off the black sand beach, and lefts too. This is a small-wave spot that gets super-hollow on its day, and always has power. Low tides are virtually unsurfable, and high is best. Any strong trade-winds from either side will affect it badly, and early morning glass is the best option here. Advanced and unforgiving, especially on lower tides. Plenty of other options around this area if you are willing to explore.

Purnama Beach / Sagara

Head north from Sanur on Ngurah rai bypass then r onto Kusamba bypass. After about 4km is the Ketewel gas station. After another 4 go right to Purnama Beach.

More black sand beach-break for early morning sessions or quiet wet season surfs away from the crowds. This strip of coast is laden with opportunities to get a tune-up on this type of break.

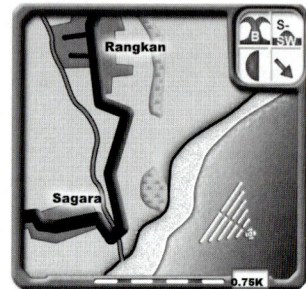

Lebih

Head north from Sanur. A few kms after the halfway mark towards Padang Bai. Lebih is sign posted through the rice fields.

Lava base rights needing straight south swell and preferably a rare north wind. Early mornings are best, when mountain airs drop down and can blow off-shore for short periods of time during the wet season. 2-5ft. All levels. Similar to Keramas. You're in the real Bali at last, the food is good and cheap and the locals are mellow. Many acres of beach and lava reef heading south.

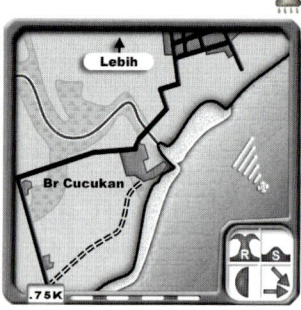

Padang Bai

If you are getting the Lombok ferry from Padang Bai, then this spot might be worth a look if there is a major south swell. It's iatthe harbour.

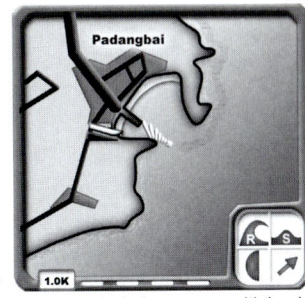

Essentially a right-hand point beaking into the harbour in sometimes black water, Padang Bai can offer some long rides and less crowding. There are great places to eat fish nearby, so all is not lost if you fail to score. Needs off-season west winds or none, with loads of swell, and is horrific in the dry season. Extremely rare. All levels. Pollution.

Nusa Lembongan

There are many boats from Benoa Harbour near Nusadua, that will take you across to Lembongan for the day. It's a great fun intro to boat trip surfing, if a little expensive in proportion to the hours surfed. You can also get the ferry from Padang Bai or a *Jukung* from Kusamba, which go via Nusa Penida. There's accommodation right on the beach.

2 quality, well-surfed classics draw in the swell which funnels up the Lombok Strait out of very deep water, to unload with un-filtered power on sharp, shallow coral.

Shipwrecks

The first wave of note is a fast, fairly short, jacking right-hand barrel machine. Mid to high is best, with high handling the bigger swells up to 6ft or more. Arriving by boat it might look small and easy from the back, but outside sets can come from nowhere and terrify. There's a fairly menacing rock-pen and ship remains on the inside should you

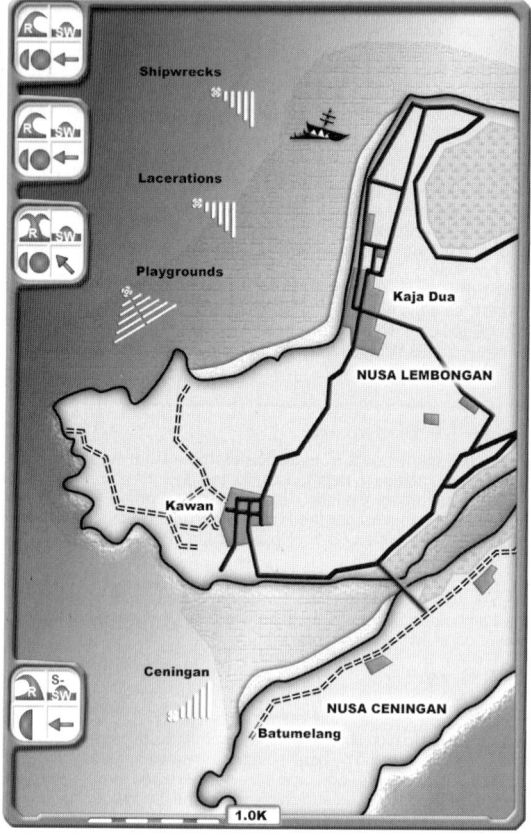

Shipwrecks

Lacerations

Playgrounds

Kaja Dua

NUSA LEMBONGAN

Kawan

Ceningan

NUSA CENINGAN

Batumelang

1.0K

BALI

Nusa Lembongan cont'd..

come un-stuck. Medical assistance is not available anywhere near. Advanced. Currents are hell during spring tides. Next door, **Razors** provides super-hollow pits that are hard to exit. Boots essential; you'll need to be able to put your feet down on the reef.

Lacerations

Over to the right as you look from the back of the wave at Shipwrecks, is a very fast, shallow right with wide barrels in anything from 2-5ft of swell. Low tide is very critical and shallow so newcomers surf mid tide or higher. Lefts break off the same peak, and they are sometimes makeable. Experts even if small. Lassos' alter-ego, **Noman's**, can offer some extremely hollow pits with barely any escape channel.

Playgrounds

On the southern end of the bay, this spot seems to be a more approachable, less critical left and right reef break to be checked if the above 2 spots are too big for your tastes. It is however, just as hollow and fast, with just as much potential for getting skinned. It works on all tides, with mid to high being good. On small days of heavy southeast trades, it will be cleaner and more fun here.

Ceningan Island

Lying to the south of Lembongan is a less surfed little patch of fun. There is a very consistent left-hander which, while it will not handle bigger swells very happily, is easier to surf than most Bali spots and can line up very well. Sticks poke out of the water courtesy of seaweed farming. Tiger sharks spotted. Doesn't react kindly to trade winds. A good bet when tide too low for Lasso's etc, on small days.

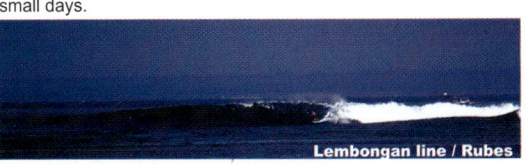

Lembongan line / Rubes

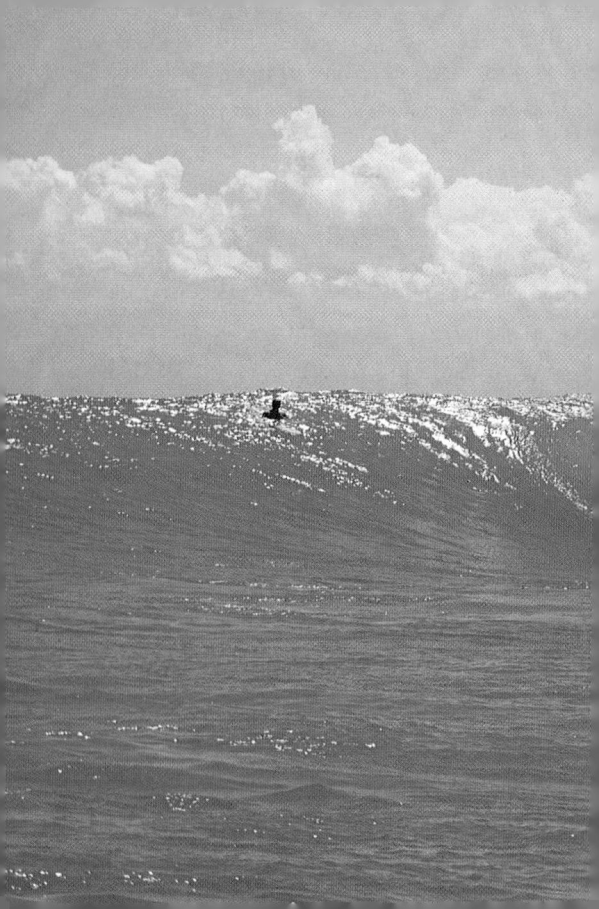

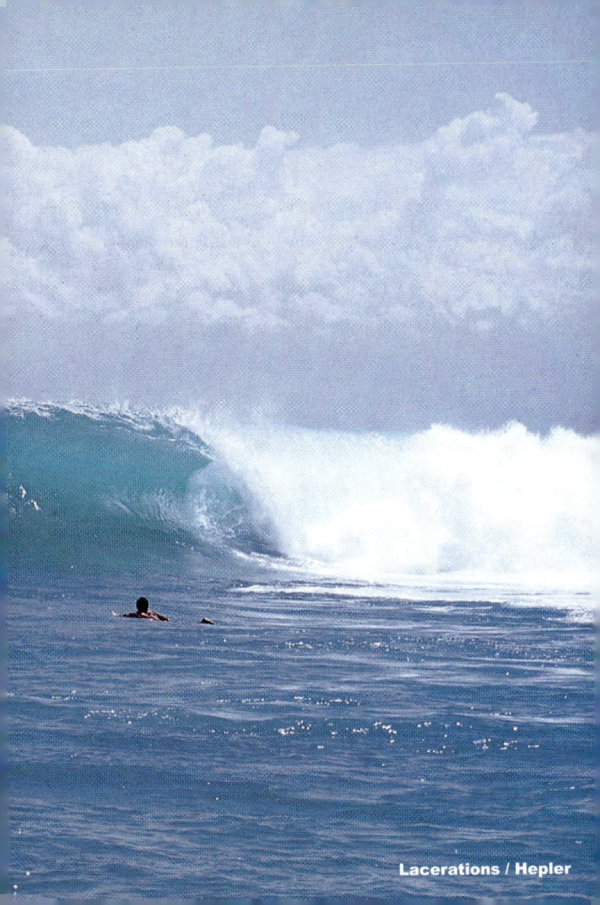

Lacerations / Hepler

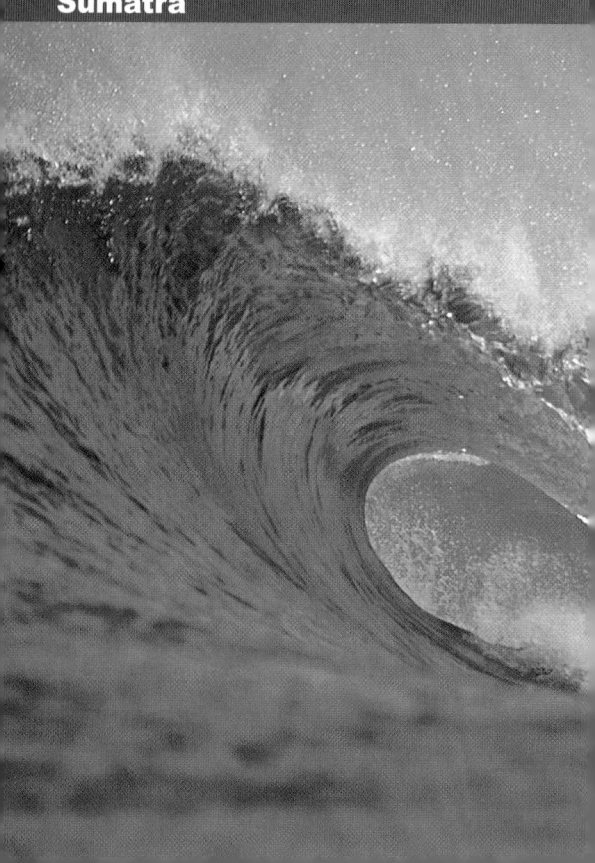

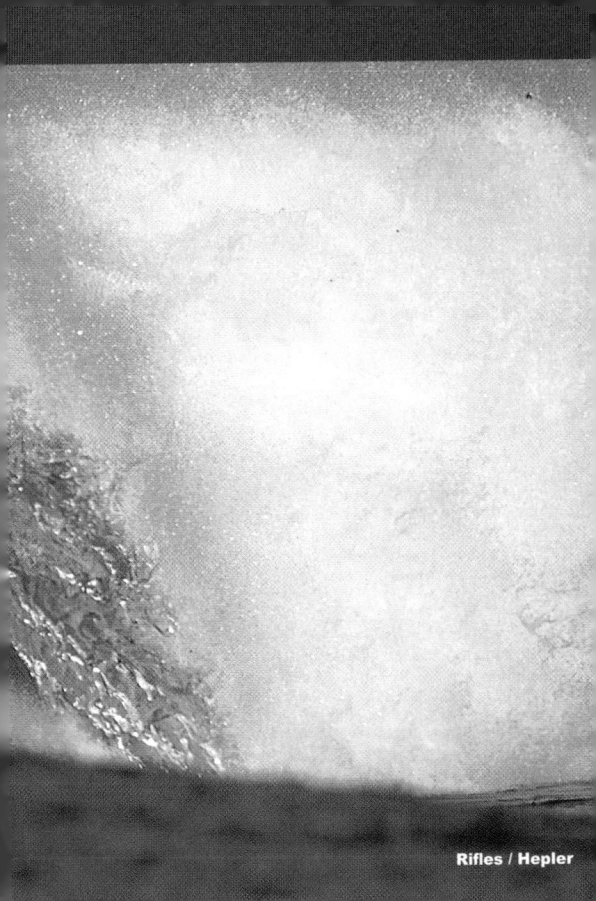

Rifles / Hepler

Sumatra Surf Data

Where

Indonesia's westernmost and largest island straddles the equator from latitude 6 degrees north to 6 degrees south.

SUMATRA

Background

Sumatra is over four times the size of neighboring Java, with less than a third of the population. There's a diverse ethno-cultural mix of Acehnese, the formerly cannibalistic Batak, the isolated Mentawaians and Niassans, Minangkabau and others. Whilst swathes of land have been cleared by loggers or for palm plantation, the network of national parks and hinterland have wildlife diversity and natural beauty to rival anywhere on earth. There are over a dozen active volcanoes.

The Setups and Waves

The most consistent surf in the Indian Ocean, with the longest fetch and exposure to the prevailing south-southwest swell, is found along the west coast and islands of Sumatra. Much of the body of the mainland is shielded from regular swell by islands, but overall there is no continental shelf, and 6000 metre depths of water persist close to land allowing undiluted wave power to unload. The volcanic origin of the landmass contributes to steep drop-offs around the reefs, further assisting formation of powerful waves.

The northernmost province of **Aceh** has an untold wealth of surf, although access is limited due to a long running civil insurgency. One day it will open up to the world and we'll start to see it in magazines. Of all mainland Sumatra, Aceh is the most open to swell, having less islands shielding it, and protruding too far west for any other land mass to block it. With plenty of it's coastline facing due west, it is well set up to refract south swells into long lines, and very much off-shore in southeast trade winds. The corresponding island of **Simeulue** is also hard to access, although boat captains quietly acknowledge its potential with a certain reverence.

The **Banyaks** and The **Batu Islands** (Including **Telo**) are also only just being really charted. **Nias** and it's incredible right-hand point at Lagundri Bay is perhaps the most well-trodden surf ground, with an array of surfer accommodation and all the trappings that go with it. Just off-shore, the **Hinako's** have 2 of the best waves in the area, one of these being as thick and heavy as any Hawaiian break.

The **Mentawais**, comprising a group of 4 major islands and countless islets, probably encompasses over a dozen of the worlds top 100 waves, and at least a few contenders for world's best. It has a name for hollow fast shallow reef-breaks, but there is plenty of variation, ranging from the heavy, intimidating **Thunders**, to performance-orientated **Macca's**, the aptly named **Burgerworld**, and everything in between. There is very little accommodation in the Mentawais although commercialism is creeping in with resorts planned at several name surf-spots. This means boat charter is the most realistic way to get to waves (see back). There are over 40 recognized boats plying this area so choosing the right one is crucial if you want to avoid crowds.

The southern provinces of **Lampung** and **Bengkulu** also have some great waves for overlanders. A deep ocean trench deviates close to shore contributing to consistent and powerful surf. There are many world class reef-breaks here, that can be surfed without large numbers, many with *losmen* (accommodation) right on the break. This southern area has wind patterns similar to west Java, so check the swell charts in that chapter.

Seasons

Unlike the southernmost islands of Indonesia, most of Sumatra lies in what sailors call "the doldrums", a latitude between the tropics that is not subject to regular trade winds. Roughly speaking, the area from the southern Mentawais north falls into this zone. What this means is a lot of glassy days, and negligible seasonal wind predictability year round. One day might be glassy from dawn till dusk, and the next might see a fast moving storm system with cyclonic winds

Sumatra Surf Data

that change direction all day. You cannot plan for a wet/dry season surf like you can in Bali, but with so many different angles, if one side of an island isn't firing, the other may well be.

When to go

Despite the above climatic situation there are some rules of thumb affecting the larger part of the Sumatran surf zone. 1. Swell increases dramatically from April onwards, with June to August being peak wave period. 2. July and August is the busiest time of year. 3. May and June are often drier than the rest of the year...often but not always! 4. Boat charters operate between April and October/November each year. 5. It is always hot. Temperatures reach 30 degrees almost every day of the year, and the humidity can be extremely high.

Crowds

The Mentawai Islands are flavour of the moment, and easy access is limited to the "dry" season. At the peak of this season it can therefore be very crowded at all the name breaks. Nias has always been known for its semi permanent population of wave hungry surfers, although staying there as a base for exploration to the Hinako's or Telo can yield uncrowded sessions. Southern Sumatra (Bengkulu and Lampung) has managed to stay out of the limelight although aficionados are fully aware of the quality on offer. Being an overland destination, with the risk and lack of comfort that can imply, keeps the crowds at bay.

Boards

The same principles apply as for Bali: boards that give you extra paddling speed without losing manoeuvrability are ideal. Big wave guns in the 8 foot plus range can make heavy going of the hollow faces that are common, although there are some Hawaiian style bombs that merit them. Take as much equipment as you can carry, especially spare leashes as you wont find many surf shops!

Hazards

See medical section at end. You will most likely be very far from help, meaning first aid supplies will be crucial. Full medical evacuation insurance is a must. Malaria, common throughout Indonesia, thrives in the wet equatorial climate, with Nias and other islands famous for some very nasty cerebral varieties.

All the usual reef cut provisos also apply. Overland surf trips in Sumatra can be heavy affairs; many locals don't speak Indonesian let alone English, and thorough planning is required unless making use of any of the hosted overland options on offer in the travel section at the back of the book. Generally it is advisable to reserve a spot in one of the surf camps, (again see back) and base surf discovery trips from there.

Boat charters insulate you from many of the irritants of individual land travel, but also from some of the interaction with locals, and other happenings that often define a memorable surf adventure.

M	Swell Range		Wind Pattern		Air		Sea	Crowd
	Feet	Dir'	Am	Pm	Low	Hi	°C	
J	2-6	WSW	LO	VARI	22	28	26	LO
F	2-6	SW	LO	VARI	22	28	26	LO
M	2-6	SW	LO	VARI	22	28	26	MED
A	2-8	SSW	LO	VARI	22	28	26	MED
M	3-10	SSW	LO	VARI	22	28	26	HI
J	3-12	SSW	LO	VARI	22	28	26	HI
J	3-12	SSW	LO	SE MOD	22	26	26	HI
A	3-12	SSW	LO	SE MOD	22	26	26	HI
S	2-10	SSW	LO	VARI	22	26	26	HI
O	2-8	SW	LO	VARI	22	26	26	MED
N	2-6	SW	LO	VARI	21	26	26	LO
D	2-6	SW	LO	VARI	21	28	26	LO

Sumatra: Aceh & Northern Islands

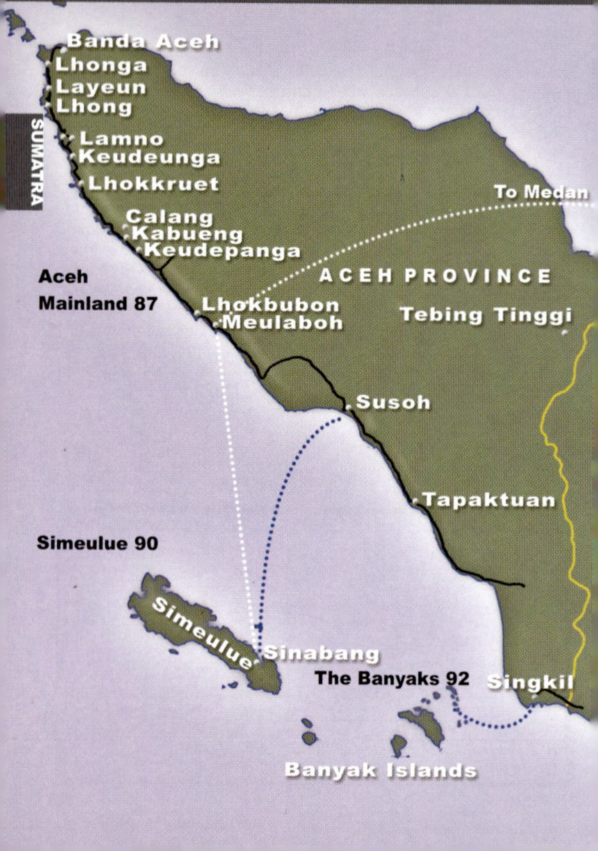

SUMATRA

Banda Aceh
Lhonga
Layeun
Lhong
Lamno
Keudeunga
Lhokkruet
Calang
Kabueng
Keudepanga

To Medan

Aceh
Mainland 87

Lhokbubon
Meulaboh

A C E H   P R O V I N C E

Tebing Tinggi

Susoh

Tapaktuan

Simeulue 90

Simeulue

Sinabang

The Banyaks 92

Singkil

Banyak Islands

Aceh Province - The Mainland

A separatist movement, recently lifted martial law, a press blackout, and a total ban on access by foreigners; not a recipe for casual surf travel. Indonesia's northernmost province has been under wraps for several years although it seems that access will soon be granted again. Aceh's west coast has a makeable road that flirts with the coastline all the way from Banda Aceh to and beyond the port town of Meulaboh (250km). Travellers along this road will see awesome forest and mountains, and get glimpses of pristine beaches, some backed up by grade A surf. Beyond Meulaboh towards the ferry town of Susoh (for Simeulue), and Singkil (For the Banyaks), lies possibly the most uncharted surf territory in Indonesia.

The surf around the capital of Banda Aceh on the northern tip has been documented by stoked adventurers since the 1980's. Surfers have even made their mark on **Pulau Breueh** and **Pulau Weh**, both accessible by ferry from Banda Aceh. Weh has some of the most beautiful palm fringed beaches and lagoons in Sumatra, with basic accommodation available. It is more famed for it's diving (whale sharks and turtles) than it's waves.

Easier access is at hand for **Lhok Nga**, a scenic spot about 15km south of Banda. In this area you can sniff out a beautiful little surfy village with a consistent, perfect "A" frame reef break at it's epicentre. A little further down, the very, very fickle hollow long rights of **Pantai Camara** can be worth the wait. Tides here are never a problem, but winds need to be right. Mami Diana's Losmen is a good base from which to find your own favourite spot. A ride further south still near **Lamno**, you might be lucky enough to glimpse good wet season rights at the river mouth, and a quality right point.

There are reef breaks all the way down the coast at and around **Keudeunga**, **Babah Nipah**, and all the way to **Meulaboh**, which has both long lefts and rights either side of a major headland. Serious travellers only. Medical help is far.

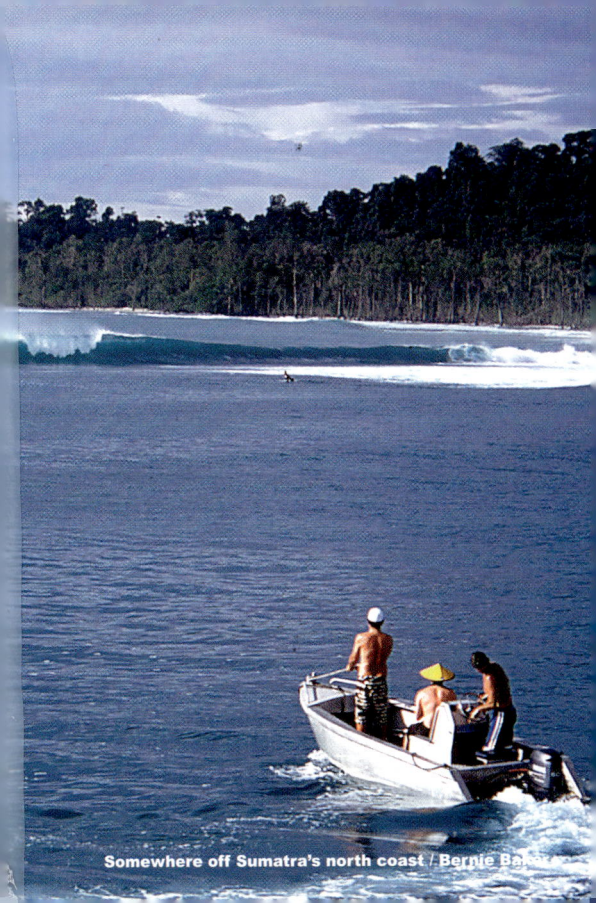

Somewhere off Sumatra's north coast / Bernie Baker

Simeulue

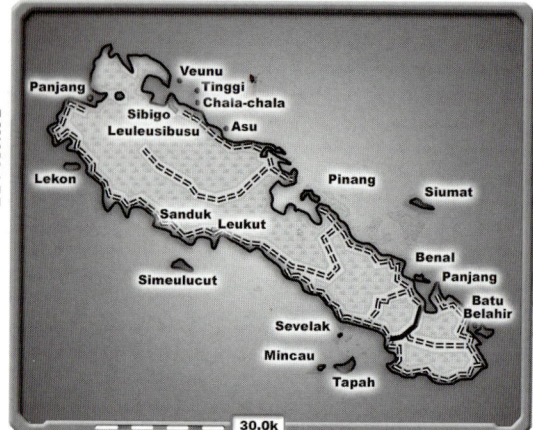

Panjang · Veunu
Tinggi
Chaia-chala
Sibigo · Asu
Leuleusibusu
Lekon · Pinang
Siumat
Sanduk · Leukut
Benal
Simeulucut · Panjang
Batu
Belahir
Sevelak
Mincau
Tapah

30.0k

90NM west of Tapaktuan on Sumatra.

Part of Aceh Province, Simeulue and its satellite islets are as deep into frontier land as you can get. Essentially a volcanic island that is densely forested and surrounded by coral at varying depths, there isn't much "civilization", and accommodation is minimal (a new surf camp, Baneng Island, opens down on the southwest corner as we go to press).

Palm lined beaches and beautiful bays with great diving. Sketchy air access is available from Medan when politics allow, although once there, access to surf is harder than hard core. In addition, malaria is a serious problem here. If you want to go surf there, the only truly safe options are via established yacht charters (see back) or by pre-arrangement with the new surf camp, which has charter flights out of Medan, and which will no doubt be the first of several.

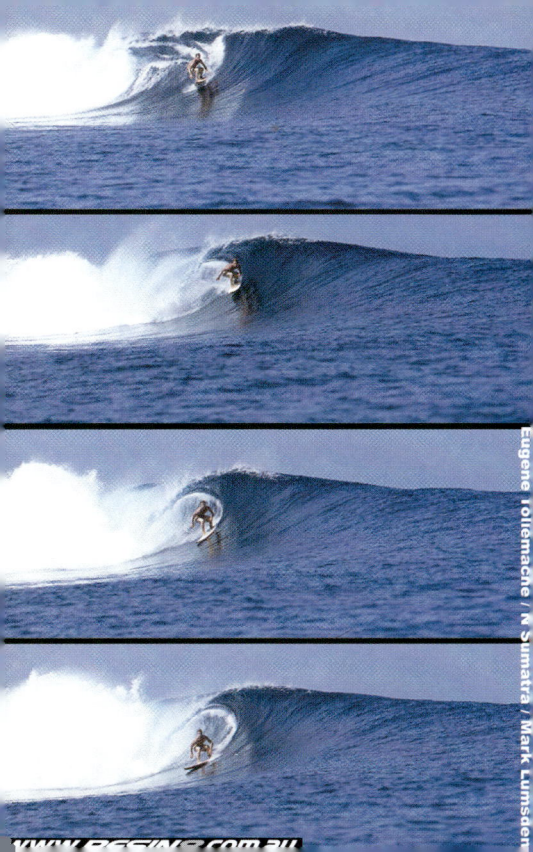

The Banyaks

Declared off-limits to boat charters by the Indonesian government, the Banyaks lie 20 NM offshore from Singkil on mainland Sumatra. Overland and ferry access from there will only get you to the leeward island of Balai, useless to surfers, although onward journeys on small boats can be negotiated from here if you are immensely patient. The only meaningful way to surf the islands is by yacht charter as and when the ban is lifted (see back). What accommodation there is, is centred on Pulau Palambak Besar, consisting of leaf houses and home-stays. Prepare yourself for a low "surf to hassle ratio".

The 99 islands harbour a cache of surf spots that will one day be "discovered" by the world at large. Treasure Island / Machine Gun Rights is perhaps the most talked about wave here. A superb lengthy right coral point that has been seen to form precise lines and almond barrels over hundreds of yards.

Hazards; very little accommodation. Malaria.

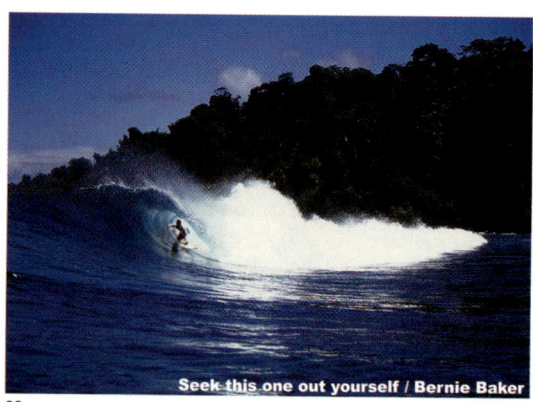

Seek this one out yourself / Bernie Baker

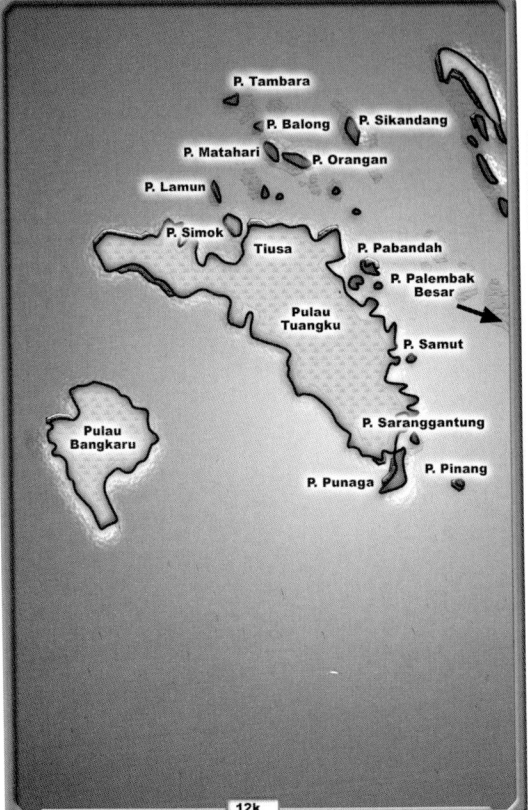

P. Tambara

P. Balong   P. Sikandang

P. Matahari   P. Orangan

P. Lamun

P. Simok   Tiusa   P. Pabandah

P. Palembak
Besar

Pulau
Tuangku   P. Samut

Pulau
Bangkaru

P. Saranggantung

P. Punaga   P. Pinang

12k

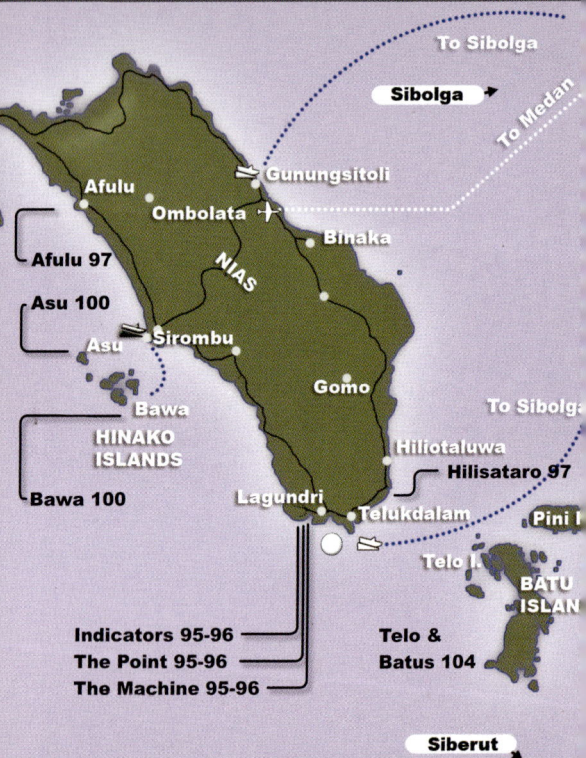

Sumatra: Nias, Hinakos & Telos

To Sibolga

Sibolga

To Medan

Afulu

Gunungsitoli

Ombolata

Binaka

Afulu 97

NIAS

Asu 100

Asu   Sirombu

Gomo

Bawa

To Sibolga

HINAKO ISLANDS

Hiliotaluwa

Hilisataro 97

Bawa 100

Lagundri

Telukdalam

Pini I

Telo I.

BATU ISLAN

Indicators 95-96

The Point 95-96

The Machine 95-96

Telo & Batus 104

Siberut

30K

Lagundri Bay

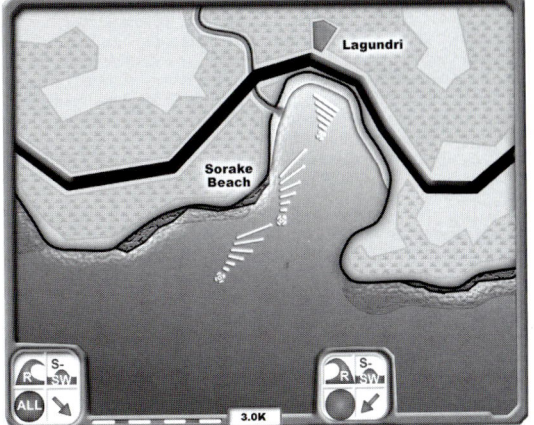

An arduous journey is required. From Telukdalam on Nias, (See "How to get to" section), get a truck ride or *opelet* (minibus). It's 13km west and well known. The main wave is at Pantai Sorake, which is littered with *losmen* accommodation (see back).

One of the worlds's very best right-handers peels into Lagundri Bay. Once the ultimate surfari destination, Nias has lost it's forefront position in the collective surfers' conscious, but it's still a veritable surf hub, teeming with surfers from across the globe. There are still uncrowded days to be had outside of major European or Australian holiday periods. There is plenty of accommodation, with over 20 *losmen*, and a heap of watering holes and *warungs*. Despite all this modernisation, Nias is in a malaria zone, with resistant strains appearing in recent years. Major flooding is possible in wet season, with severely destructive deluges over the last few years. Rip-offs have been on the increase in and around the surf village at Sorake Beach, which attracts a few shady characters.

Lagundri Bay

The Point: Opposite the tower on Sorake Beach, lies the perfect right-hander that we have salivated over in surf magazines since the late '70's. South to South-west swells wrap around the outer headland and unload onto the table reef, bulging and jacking up at the take-off zone. The wave is often an extended barrel from thereon to the finish, and works from 3 to about 12 ft plus. There's a good deep paddle-out channel to the right of the take-off zone. On the inside, smaller forgiving peaks are good for warming up and getting your bearings; this fun wave with few consequences is sometimes referred to as Kiddieland.

The Machine: Right inside the bay is a perfect left-hand barrel machine requiring very large swell from the south. It's the spot to check when The Point is too big. Most tides OK although full moon high is the most likely to yield quality.

Indicators: Way out the back to the right of The Point is a heavy, current affected, hollow right-hand reef break that's often more exposed to winds. On lower tides this is a dangerous spot, but whatever the conditions, it's for the experienced only. On high tide it is more makeable but still for hell-men.

Hazards; Reef cuts, urchins, malaria, rip-offs. Roads go quite a long way up both coasts, enabling some excellent exploration expeditions. To the west, spots such as **Sobatu** (for pros only), **Northern Secrets**, or **Lantana Lefts**, can be sniffed out with the help of local guides. Teluk-dalam itself has a couple of valid waves in it's vicinity, including a good right-hander. The locations of these waves is best left vague, in order to sweeten the thrill of finding them.

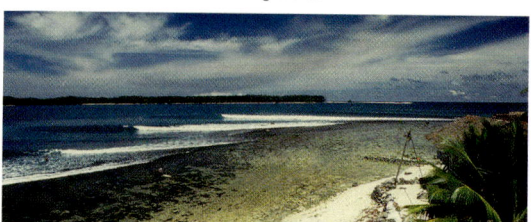

Hilisataro Village

You can check this area out from Lagundri, hiring a local guide or renting a bike and heading east past Telukdalam.

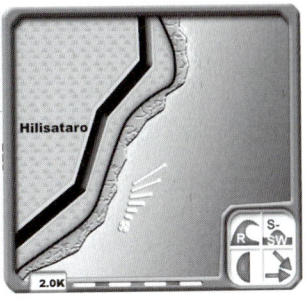

If there's a solid south swell, a couple of good waves can be found here, notably a right-hand reef/point that get good when winds are either zero or northwesterly. Middle tides best. Not the most consistently big spot, but will often have a wave of sorts.

SUMATRA

Afulu Beach

In the northwest sector of Nias. An hour's boat ride from Asu, which is your best approach; you can arrange it from Hinako's Hideaway or Patrick's on that island.

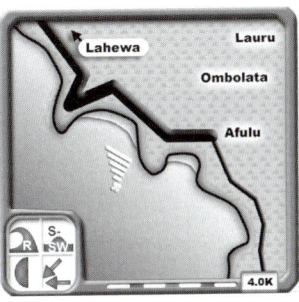

This is a perfect reef break left to check when Asu or Bawa are too big. Clearly it needs a solid swell, but when on, Afulu is an incredibly well sculpted wave. Whilst it is generally smaller and less heavy than its neighbours, the take-off is critical and the face is beyond steep. A solid board is still useful to get into the wave. Intermediates plus. Semi-consistent.

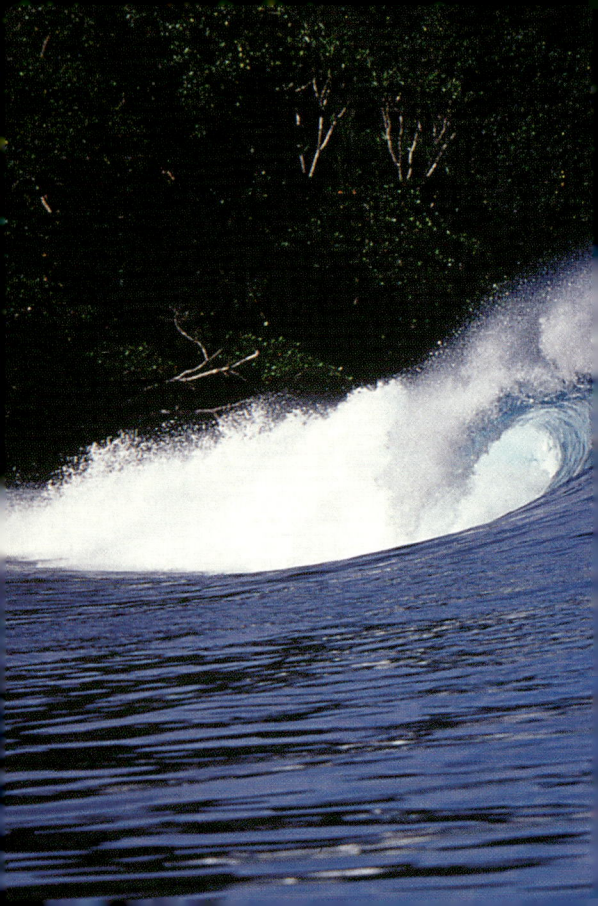

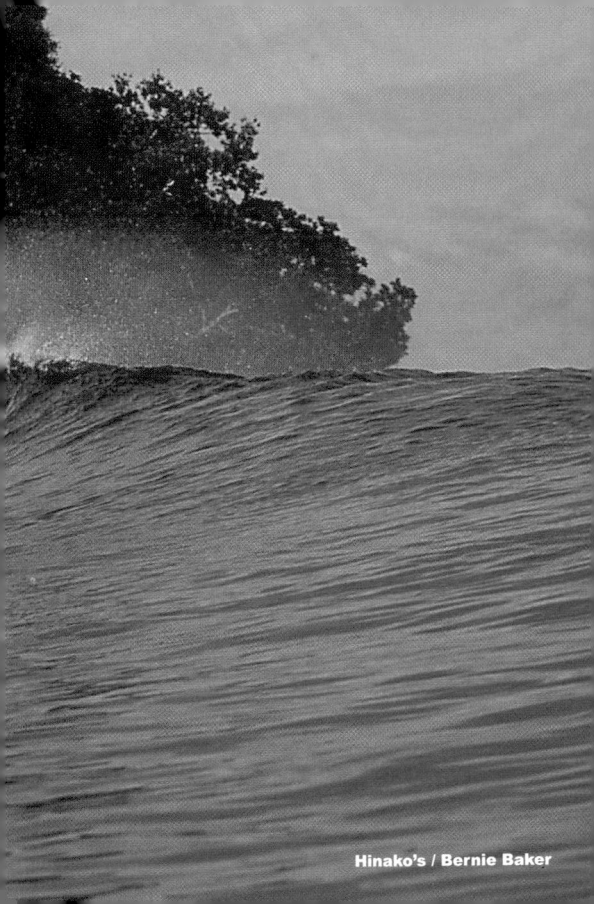

Hinako's / Bernie Baker

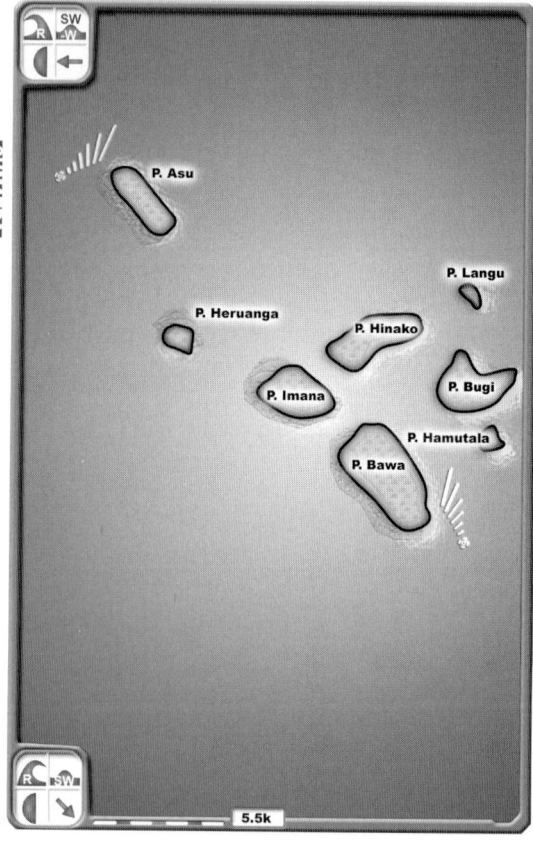

P. Asu

P. Langu

P. Heruanga

P. Hinako

P. Bugi

P. Imana

P. Hamutala

P. Bawa

5.5k

The Hinako Islands

Located off the west of Nias, this little archipelago is as exposed to swell as you can get. The Hinakos are home to 2 well known legendary waves, and a host of quality reef lefts and rights that you'll have to scope out for yourself. The keyword here is HEAVY; these spots hold size, are thick, and are suited to expert surfers only. They have become more accessible than in the past although still require major journeying. Accommodation has improved on Asu, where there is a very good surf camp (see back) as well as a couple of less salubrious options. An hour by boat from Sirombu on Nias' west coast, or charter a 5 hour ride from Telukdalam / Lagundri. World Surfaris or Pure Vacations (see back) can hook you up. As in all parts of Nias, malaria precautions are strongly advised.

SUMATRA

Asu

With it's evocative palm forest as a backdrop, the wave is located off the top of Asu Island, the Northernmost in the **Hinako's** Archipelago.

Long, almond-barrelled left consistently drawing swell onto its uniformly shallow reef point. Asu is a classic wrapper with a sometimes daunting wall that can appear unmakeable. It can get big; in the 15 ft range on it's day. Experts only.

Bawa

Bawa is the southernmost island in the **Hinako's**, with this eponymous wave off it's southern tip. You can boat it from Hinako's Hideaway on Asu.

Right-hand reef peak that rears up way out the back in anything from 4-14ft. Sometimes the photos make it look too fun; the peak shifts at times, and the inside section accelerates and gets sucky and grinding. An advanced, heavy wave, especially given the distance to get help. Works nicely when Asu is blown out. Very consistent, bring your big board. Bawa has a malarial swamp, which makes the prospect of staying on the island fairly unattractive.

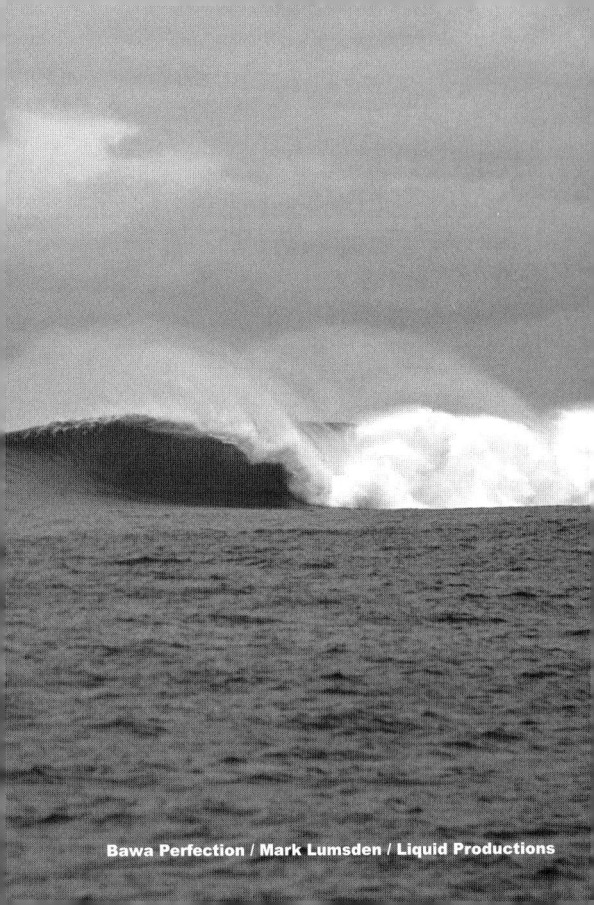

Bawa Perfection / Mark Lumsden / Liquid Productions

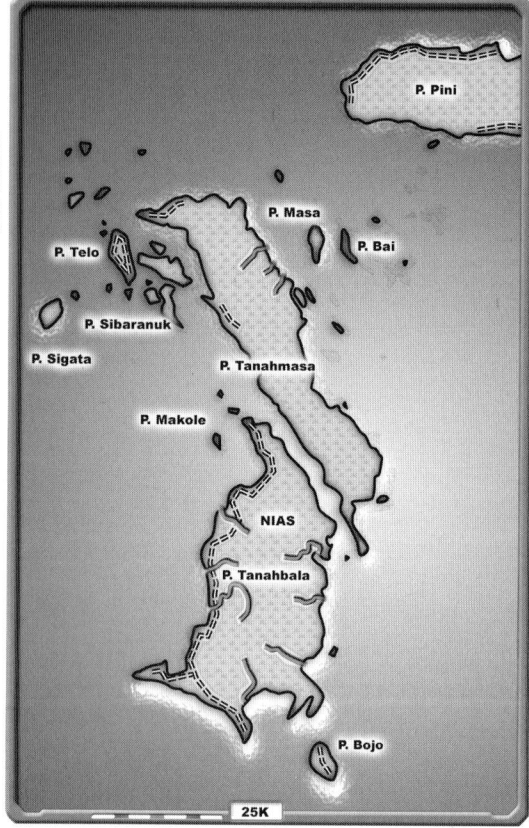

P. Pini

P. Masa

P. Bai

P. Telo

P. Sibaranuk

P. Sigata

P. Tanahmasa

P. Makole

NIAS

P. Tanahbala

P. Bojo

25K

Pulau Telo & the Batu Islands

The Batu Archipelago is known by surfers as the Telo's after the main administrative island of the same name. This eclectic group of 51 islands starts 40 NM southeast of the main Island of Nias and stretches 45 NM to the south. Wily surfers have negotiated their ride from Lagundri, having firstly extracted whatever information they can from locals. It's an extremely long and tough journey to make for some pretty fickle surf. To get the best of it, organized charters are the best method, with independent travel presenting tough obstacles that all add up to less time in the surf.

One of the more talked about highlights is a relatively consistent, sucky left-hand reef break that wraps off a tiny island in sight of a church. This wave is known for it's changeable nature: one day a whackable wall, hollow fast barrels the next, but never too punishing on the reef. A right breaks off the same island on opposite winds, and an outer bommie right renowned for tiger shark sightings is found off the island to the west. Another revered spot is a pretty, tiny island in the north where a rock with a lone tree overlooks a quality right-hander. Way down south you can stumble across other breaks, with one of the stand-outs being a series of lefts forming around an arc of reef that fringes a very remote island.

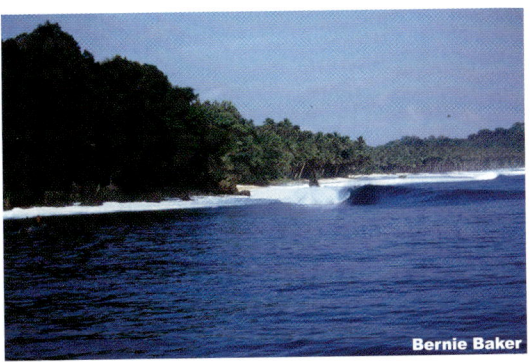

Bernie Baker

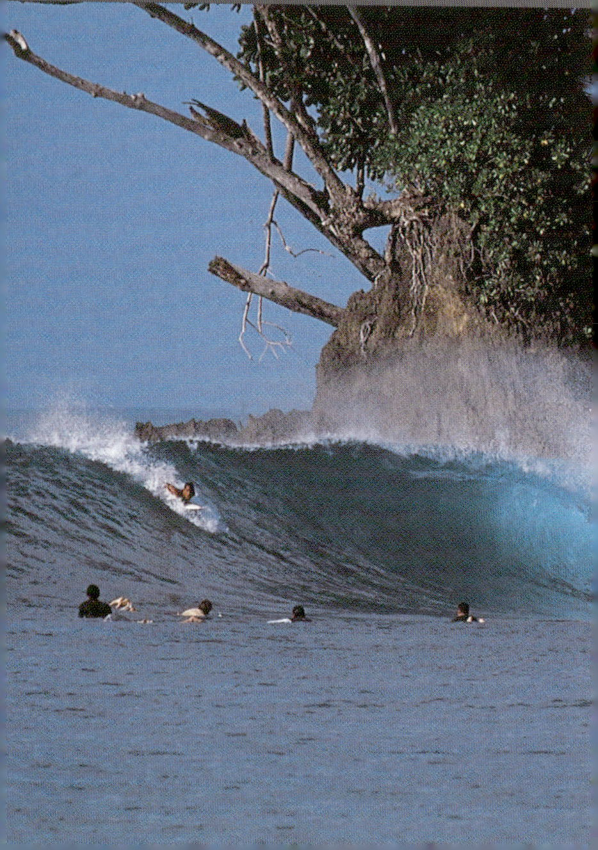

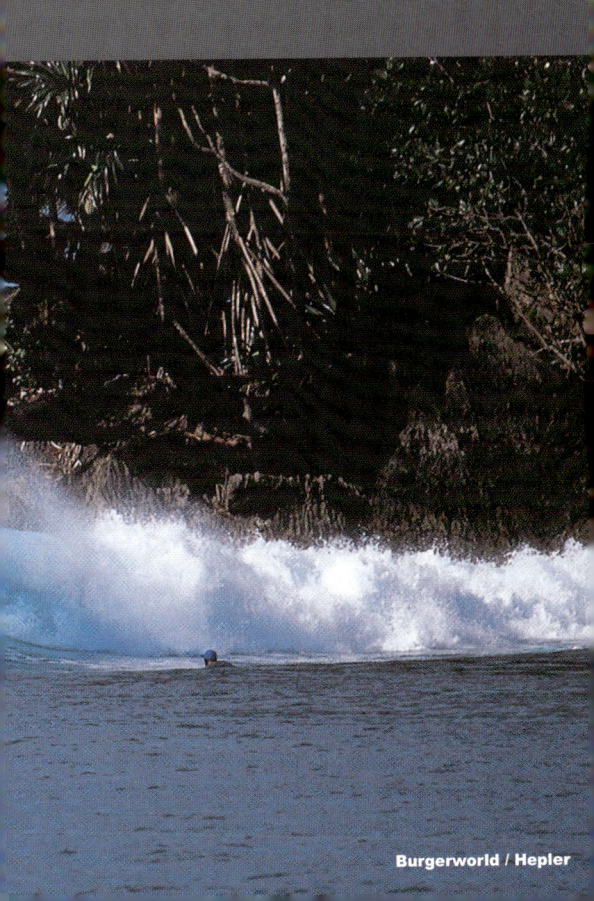

Burgerworld / Hepler

Sumatra: The Mentawais

Where

The Mentawai Islands, stretching from latitudes 2 to 3 degrees south, off the west coast of Sumatra, could easily merit a book to themselves. They are without a doubt the destination most aspired to by surfers worldwide, being home to a large number of the best waves on earth.

The Setup

4 main islands and dozens of islets are fringed by palm cultivations, 28 degree water and coral reef, and backed by dense jungle miles away from any western style "civilization". Like much of Indonesia, volcanic eruptions shaped the topography and sea bottom of these islands, making for extremely deep trenches in the ocean floor, and fast rising land mass close to the shoreline. The result is minimal dilution of swell energy, and funneling and refraction of waves to the enormous benefit of surf spots. In conjunction with the above, the Mentawais present almost the widest swell window and fetch in the Indian Ocean.

The Waves

The convoluted shorelines, deeply recessed bays and many islets also add variety of angle to swell and wind, so whatever the breeze or swell direction, somewhere will be offshore and lined up. It's a slam-dunk for surfers. Waves here tend to have considerable power without necessarily being heavy in the Hawaiian sense. Generally speaking, peaks are relatively predictable, enabling you to tackle larger waves than you might be able to at home. Intermediate surfers can get good waves although some of the celebrated waves are more challenging than they look in still photos. Prepare for anything from 2 to 10ft, but rarely more.

The Reef

The quality waves are over lava based coral reef lying at varying depths. Some are flat tables with a safe covering of water, others

Surf Data

are pocketed, pointy, shallow and hard to avoid in the event of a fall. Very few surfers come back from a trip here without some kind of a cut, so the medical section at the back is particularly relevant.

Crowds

There are well over 30 full time charter boat operators, with an average capacity of 8 -10 surfers each. If 5 of them decide that a certain spot is on today, instant over-crowding is the result. Have a good long chat with your tour operator or boat captain about how to avoid this situation. Not all charter companies will take you beyond the main areas closer to Padang, and some are only willing to surf the big name, easy access spots.

Season

Swell is in best supply from April to October, with July and August often representing the peak of consistency and size. This middle of season is also the driest and most crowded. Boat operations run from April to October/November for these reasons, and because after November, the weather can get pretty unsettled. Trade-winds do not operate this close to the equator, and winds are shifting and unpredictable. Many days are wind-free, or with the breeze veering 360 degrees in 24 hours. Thanks to this, goofy footers and natural can both get their fix on the same day, with rights and lefts often next door to each other.

Getting There

It is extremely hard to get waves when tackling these Islands overland. There is very little accommodation (see back) for land surfers, and outside the semi-sanitized environment of the surf camp, food can be a challenge, as can shelter from malaria carrying mosquitoes. Alarmist as it may seem, Malaria is a genuine problem throughout Sumatra and its outer islands. Boat charter is the most realistic way to get to the best waves, which is why we've dedicated a few pages to some of the main players in the back of the book. Most charters depart Padang on Sumatra's central west coast. You can get there from Singapore, or from Jakarta. Generally, a charter will be from 6 - 12 guests, so you will form part of a larger group.

Equipment

Take the full extent of medical and surf supplies listed at back. Boat trips provide some insulation from malaria carrying mosquitoes, but no guarantees. Spare board and leashes are essential. In addition, Stugeron or other sea-sickness pills are a must. Many charter boats are diesel powered and heavy, meaning they can have a particularly bad rolling action if big seas are running. Even the most hardened sailor can fall to sea-sickness in those conditions, and you will not be able to just get off the boat!

Boards

Generally, rhino chasers are not appropriate for these hollow waves; they make turns hard, are clumsy when trying to slot into the barrel, and can't be pumped or positioned easily. On an average 4-6ft day, an ideal board might be about 4 - 6" longer and 1/4 inch wider than your everyday short board. Taking both should therefore cover you for the good days and the small. Add another 6" again for your "big day" board and you'll have the ideal quiver! Bear in mind that snapping your only board on day one will leave you little else to do while everybody else is having fun.

Boredom

Most boat trips take 10 days minimum. When you are surfed out there will be little else to do. A few tips: Check if your boat has good fishing equipment - there's great tasty fish all around you here. Ditto snorkeling. Take those books you always wanted to read. Check that the boat will have a CD player, and, of course, that staple of modern living, the DVD player. Finally, ensure somebody in the group has a good camera. Some operators run cultural tours of the villages when waves are absent; check in advance. It's a shame to travel half way across the world and not meet a single local except your boat crew, and many surfers that come back rate these visits as the most memorable part of their trip.

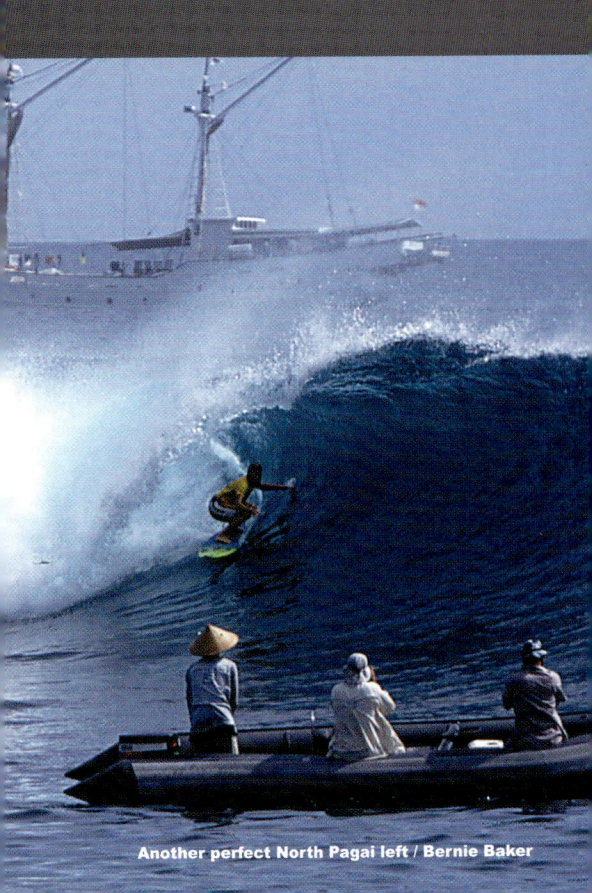

Another perfect North Pagai left / Bernie Baker

Sumatra: The Mentawais

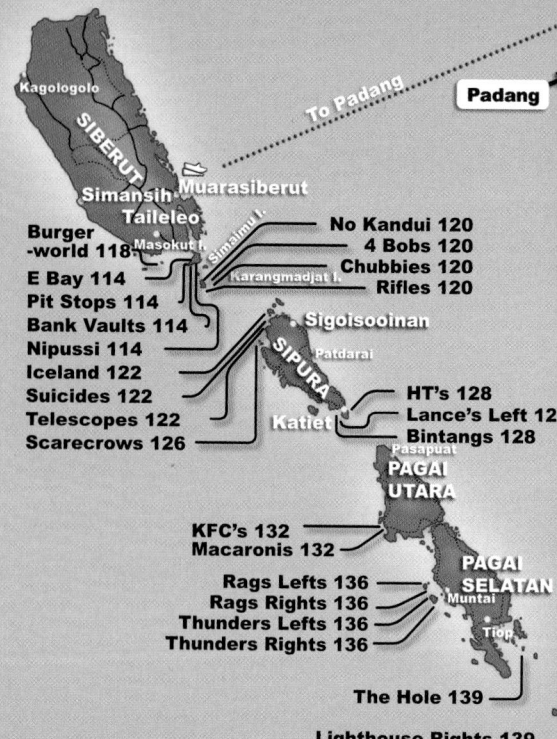

Kagologolo

SIBERUT

To Padang

Padang

Simansih
Taileleo
Burger-world 118
Masokut I.
E Bay 114
Pit Stops 114
Bank Vaults 114
Nipussi 114
Iceland 122
Suicides 122
Telescopes 122
Scarecrows 126

Muarasiberut

Simaimu I.

No Kandui 120
4 Bobs 120
Chubbies 120
Rifles 120

Karangmadjat I.

Sigoisooinan

SIPURA

Patdarai

Katiet

HT's 128
Lance's Left 12
Bintangs 128

Pasapuat
PAGAI
UTARA

KFC's 132
Macaronis 132

PAGAI
SELATAN

Rags Lefts 136
Rags Rights 136
Thunders Lefts 136
Thunders Rights 136

Muntai

Tiop

The Hole 139

Lighthouse Rights 139

35K

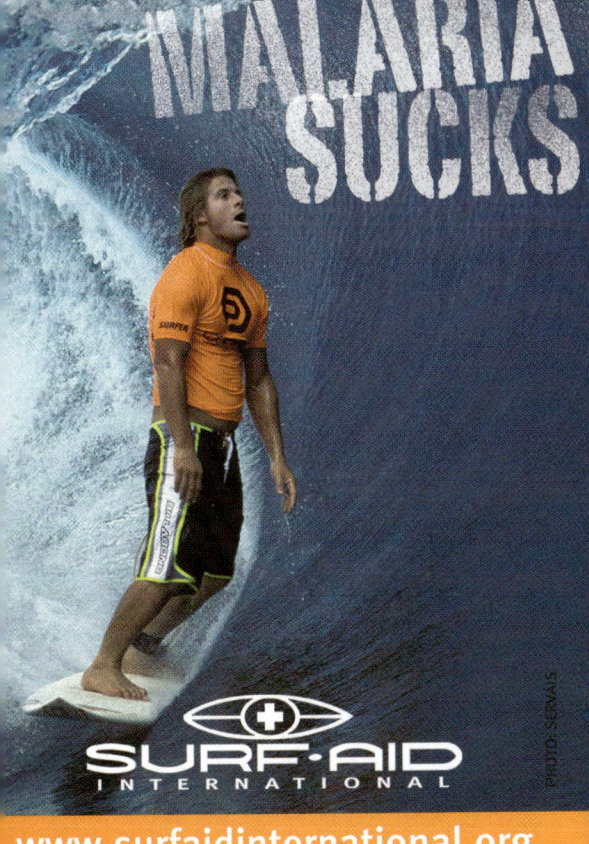

MALARIA SUCKS

SURF·AID
INTERNATIONAL

www.surfaidinternational.org

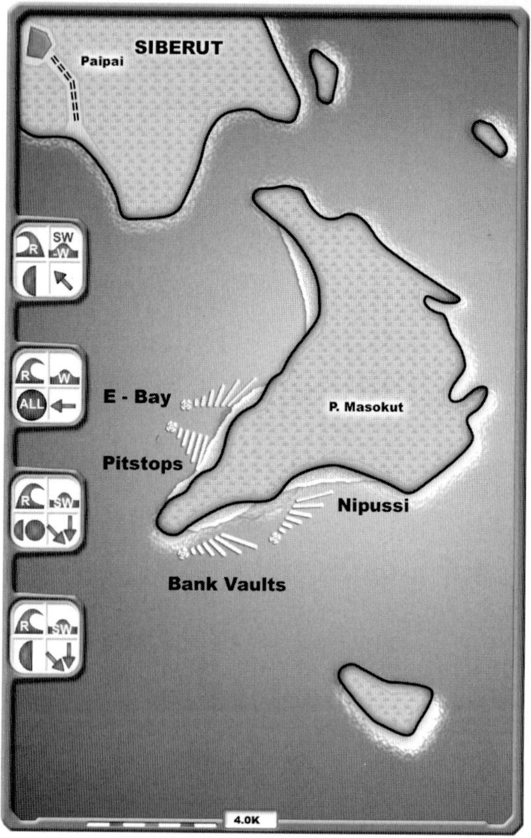

SUMATRA

SIBERUT

Paipai

E - Bay

P. Masokut

Pitstops

Nipussi

Bank Vaults

4.0K

E Bay

This wave wraps around a nobble of land on the west side of Masolut Island, lying off the south tip of Siberut. It's often one of the first stops on a Mentawai trip.

A fast hollow left pushes up onto a curved reef to create some perfect barrels over 50 to 100yds. Likes solid southwest swells and handles the more westerly swell directions even better. Southeast dry season trades preferred, of the light variety if possible. Can handle solid 10ft, and some of the best reported days have been in the 5-8ft range. It is hard-breaking with predictable lines and a good exit into the channel, but sharp shallow reef to castigate any low tide error. Surf it mid plus. Advanced. Semi consistent. Awesome jungle setting is site of proposed resort. When crowded here Keyhole may be worth a check for some quality lefts if swell is ample.

Pit Stops

Just around from E Bay to the southwest.

Benign right-hander over reef and sand. Recommended for first-timers and as jet-lag relief before tackling it's neighbours. Most tides are OK here too. 2-6ft. All levels.

Bank Vaults

On the south side of the west tip of the island.

If you like Sunset, you'll be right at home here. Powerful, weighty right-hander that works to almost any size, with sets coming in from anywhere when you least expect. The drop is often akin to a base-jump, with a lip that pitches thick and heavy. Not the longest right in Sumatra, but unforgettable. Another boat trip wave. 3-14ft with 6-8 best. Advanced. Consistent but not always perfect as doesn't like any south winds.

Nipussi / Bells

Breaking off a second protruberance of reef into a recess east of

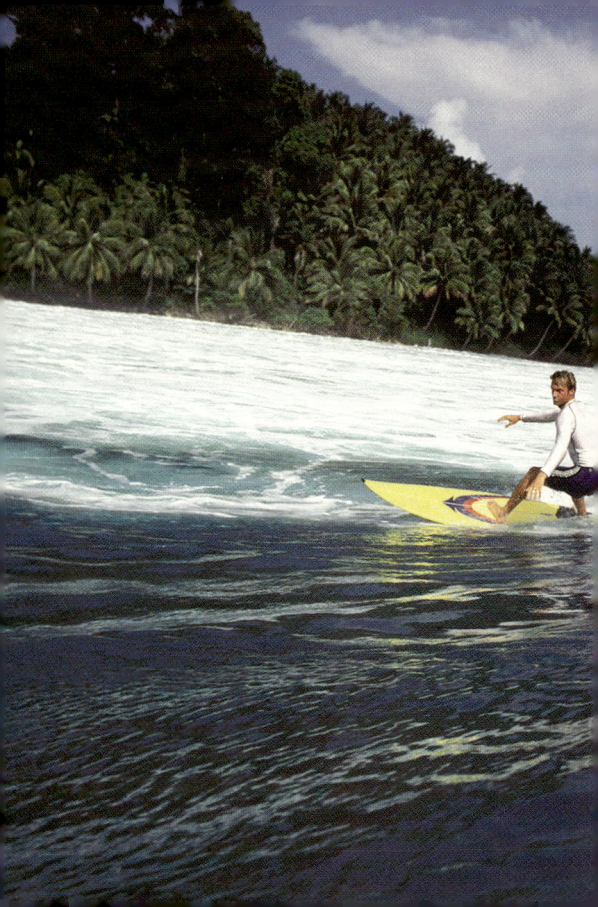

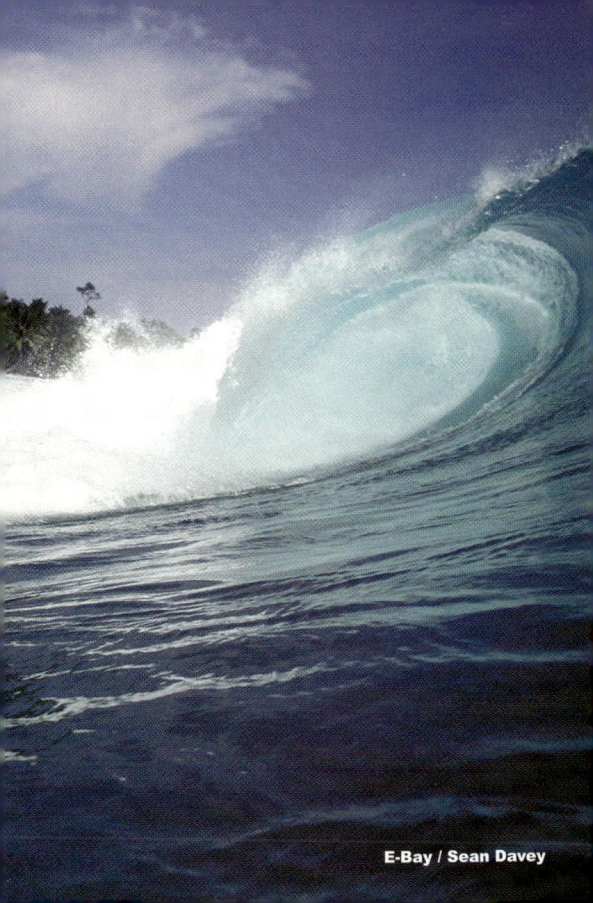

E-Bay / Sean Davey

Nipussi / Bells

Bank Vaults.

Consistent and approachable (by Mentawai standards) right-hand point / reef set-up, perfect for mid-size days when winds are light or northerly, and swell isn't igniting other spots. Likes south-south-west swell, with wests bringing wide sets. This wave can be fun, but do not exclude the possibility of getting barrelled, or held down. It's really only a boat access spot. If there is a crowd, it handles it well with multiple peaks in the bay. Intermediates plus. Holds 8ft, with 4-5ft perfect.

Burgerworld

Out there on its own on Dodiki Island, a few miles cruising west of E-Bay.

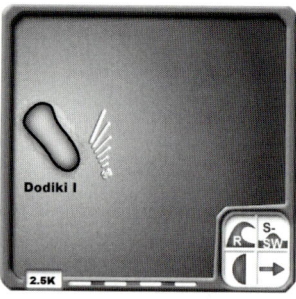

Dodiki I

2.5K

As the name suggests, this is not always a tube machine, rather a saving grace when the swell is too small for anywhere else to be working. A reef right winding off a coral-fringed rock outcrop, it delivers short sweet whackable waves on any tide, up to about 4ft. Consistent. All levels. Another, faster right-hander breaks just across the water if this is just too slow for you.

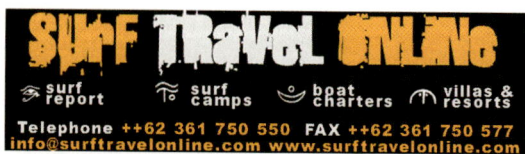

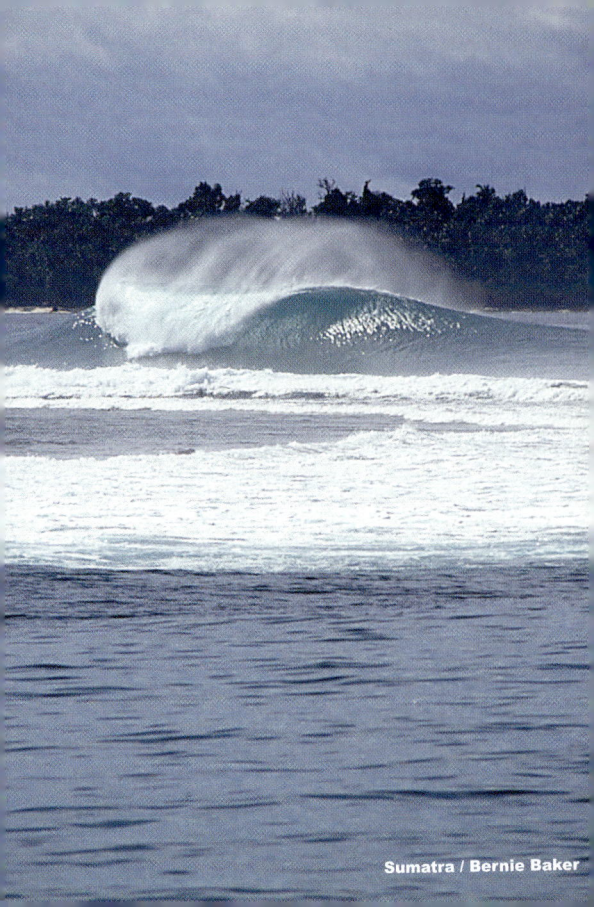
Sumatra / Bernie Baker

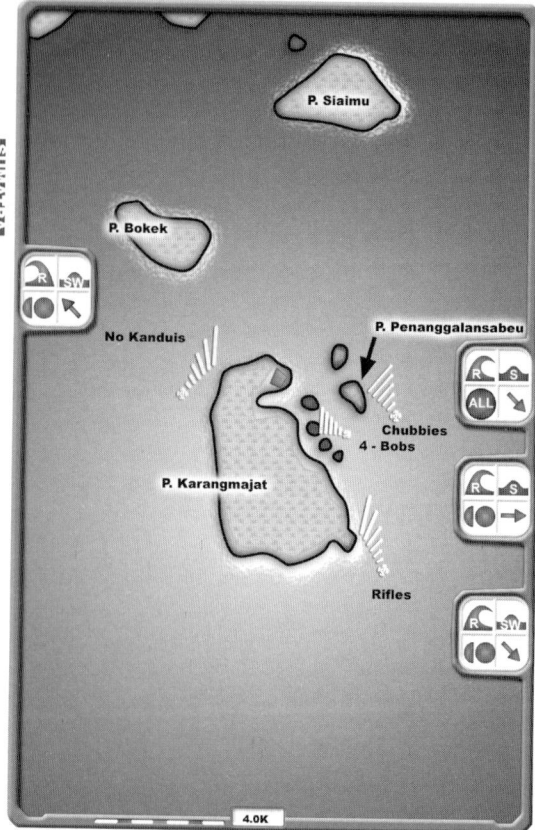

SUMATRA

P. Siaimu

P. Bokek

No Kanduis

P. Penanggalansabeu

Chubbies

4 - Bobs

P. Karangmajat

Rifles

4.0K

Rifles (Kandui)

Off the east edge of Karangmajet Island, 9nm off Siberut's southern tip & just across the water from Bank Vaults. Extremely long, hollow, fast right-hand reef break for pros and hell-men. This is a wave that bends and throws out surprise tubes or shut-downs, as well as everything in-between. Your best defence is a stout body, maximum speed and total commitment. Low tide isn't fun here, not that the reef is ever too far under-fin. Consistent although not always perfect. When it's on it is awesome.

No Kanduis

A wave of many moods, but when on this is a dream left-hander with awe-inspiring barrels from start to finish. To make this incredibly long wave without getting shut down you need lashings of down-the-line speed and the guts to pull in; there's no other route. Inviting at 3 feet, fast and challenging at 4, and jaw-droppingly hollow and powerful at 6 plus. Extended barrels are frequent, but lower tides and solid swell height bring consequences. Try mid tide on south-southwest swells and light southeast breeze. Advanced, although small high tides days can be fun.

Chubbies

In the lee of Karangmajat Island, you'll find a lagoon, and the peanut sized Penanggalan Island. Chubbies wraps around this. For Chubby, read FAT. Being hidden round a corner and protected from the full Indian Ocean energy, it throws up smiling right-hand walls ideal for cruising on. 2-6ft. Any tide. All levels.

4-Bobs

Just across from Chubbies. An easy right-hand reef-break tapering into a deep channel that is generally fat, fun and short. Errors are not heavily punished here, and the fact that it is sectioned and a little "ordinary" by local standards means mellow uncrowded tune-up sessions. Beautiful setting. Something different. Semi consistent although doesn't handle enormous swells too well. Mid tide upwards. All levels including Mals.

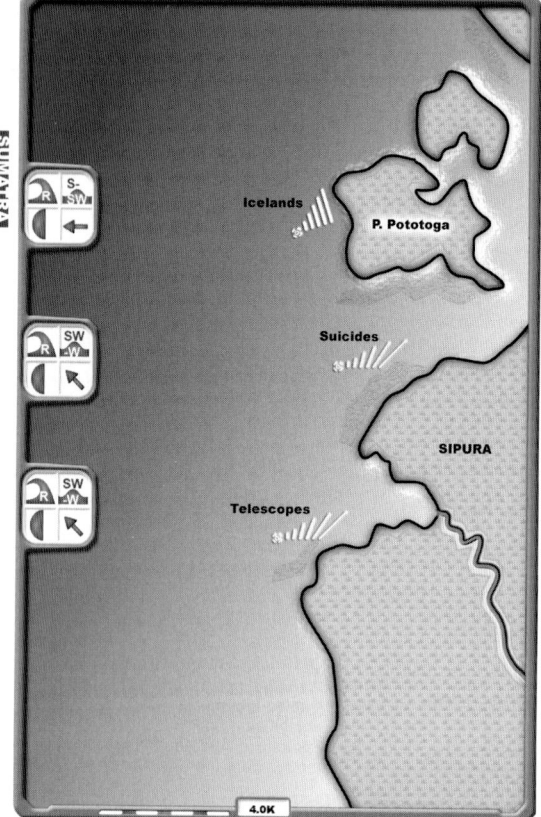

SUMATRA

Icelands
P. Pototoga

Suicides

SIPURA

Telescopes

4.0K

Icelands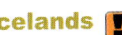

Pototoga Island lies just off the north tip of Sipura, with this classic wrapping into it's western bay.

Heavy, inconsistent left that is a test of machismo at any size. Deep water surrounds a steeply sloped reef, causing waves to pitch in a sudden, unpredictable manner and unload with awesome power and unexpected barrel sections from 4-15ft. Best surfed early mornings as most winds wreck it. Rights can work if conditions right. South swell best, wedged and terrifying on a west. Experts only.

Suicides

This wave wraps around a fringe reef off the northern end of Sipura.

Well-named shallow left-hander over (only just) live coral heads. It can be a fickle wave that doesn't show it's true nature very often, but throws up incredible barrels when on. A successful ride involves steep take-off on the shifting peak, followed by direct entry into the barrel and a short fast drive to the deep channel. Best conditions are south to southeast winds or none, and preferably a southwest swell. South swells need to be big to get in. Advanced.

Telescopes

A couple of miles south of Suicides, off Cape Kinilok on Sipura.

Like a fine piece of hand-blown glass, telescopes is a perfectly crafted receptacle for goofy-footed barrel seekers. Wrapping left along a curved table of coral, it's one of the most picture perfect waves in the world. On a good day, 200 yds of perfect tube maintains shape from start to finish. On a big day the set-up peaks way outside before re-focussing onto the main take-off zone with shape and power. It works from 3-8ft plus, but 5-6ft of southwest swell is just about perfect. Any tide cna be fine, but mid perhaps optimal. Classic. Consistent. Advanced unless small.

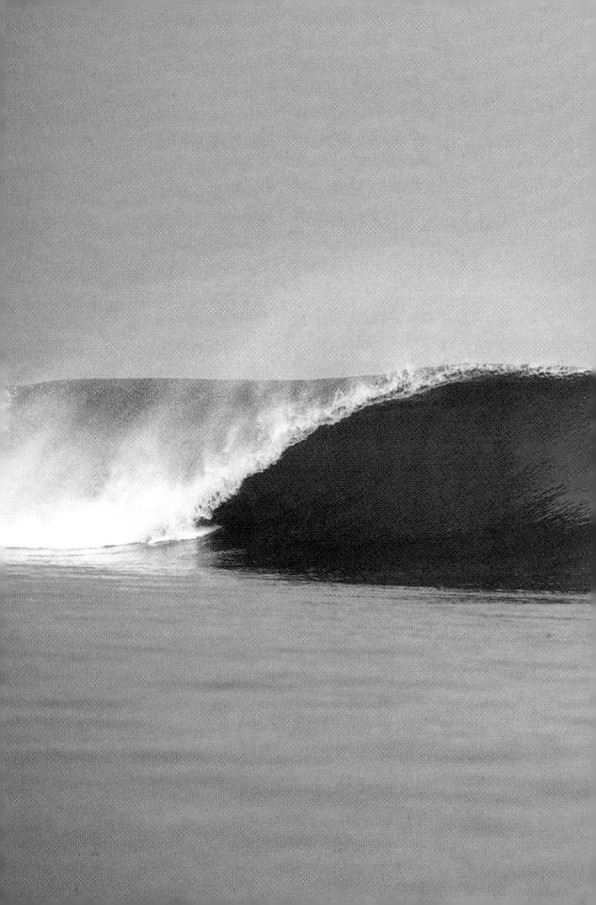

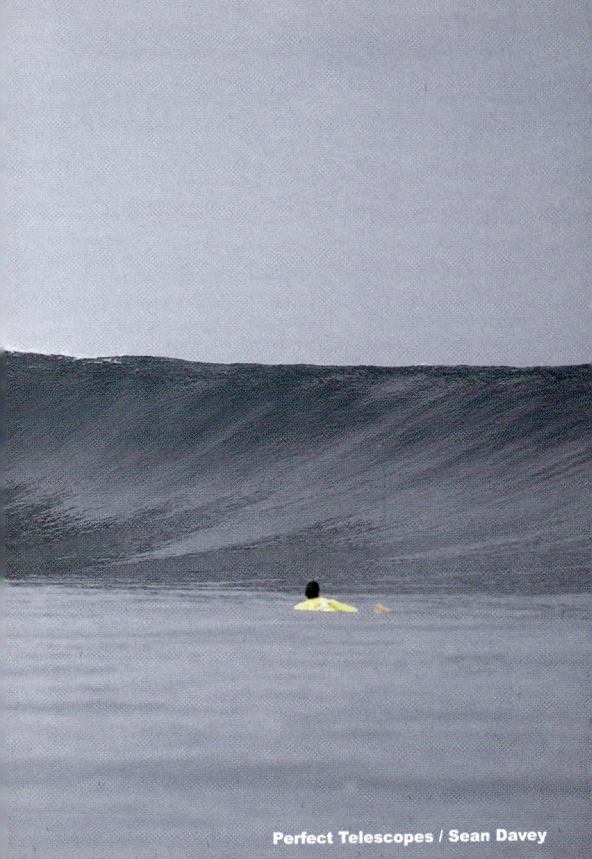

Perfect Telescopes / Sean Davey

Scarecrows

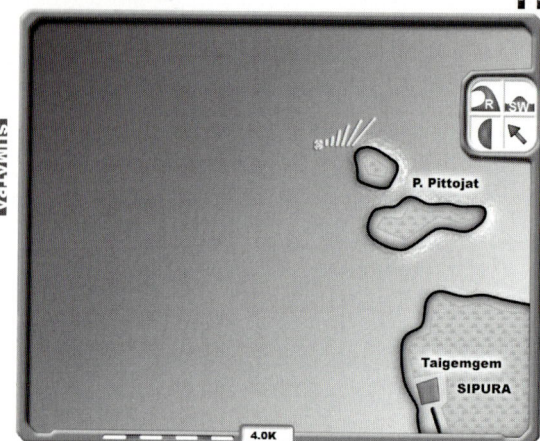

Sitting out in Siberimanua Bay, off west Sipura, is Pittojat Island. This wave breaks of the neighbouring football field sized islet.

Not the most perfect, ruler-edged wave in the islands, but this is a high quality, beautiful left with ample chances to get barrelled. Take-off is often a lottery, with shifting peaks and some considerable suck, depending on the tide. The wave can then speed up and section, requiring quick reactions and a readiness to pull in at a moment's notice. One consistent factor is the power and thickness of the lip; getting caught by it will result in being swatted like a fly. All levels can surf it unless over 4ft. It's right out there exposed to any swell going, thus a good option on smaller days with light southerly winds. Usually less busy than many nearby spots.

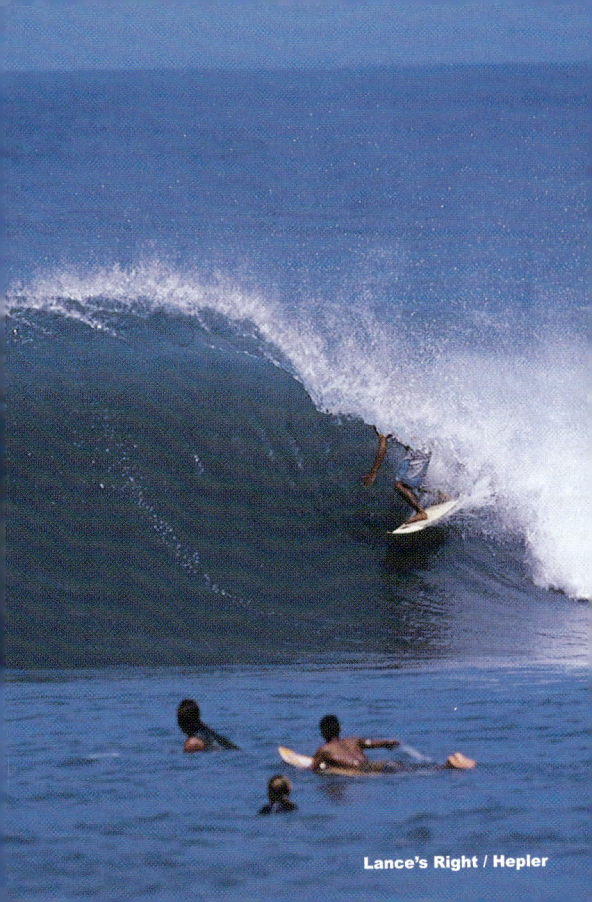

Lance's Right / Hepler

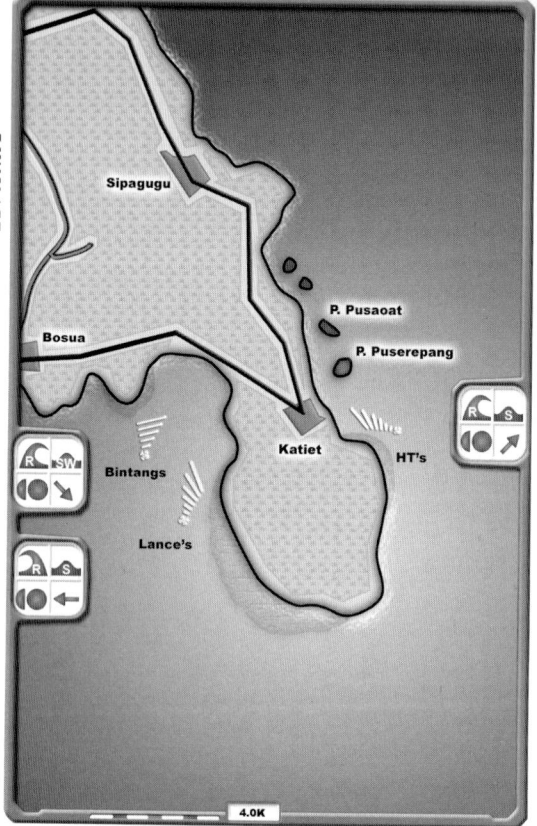

SUMATRA

Sipagugu

P. Pusaoat

P. Puserepang

Bosua

Katiet

HT's

Bintangs

Lance's

4.0K

Lance's Right

Located off Katiet, the main village on Sipura's southern peninsula. Named Lance's after it's discoverer, but some call it HT's after the hollow dead trees once found in the water.

Not always the longest, but definitely one of the best and hollowest barrels in the world. Endless videos of pro's taking off and pulling in here belie the evil nature of the spot; a sucky face and extremely shallow sharp coral make this a wave of consequence. Falls at the end section rarely go un-punished and low tide is risky. South to southwest swells have to have real power to make it around Cape Kinapat, so when it's on here, you know it's serious. The bigger days can see the whole lot line up into a much longer point-break. Smaller days split the wave into sections, with the legendary "office" take-off spot yielding the truck-size tubes. Breaks often but perfection is not guaranteed, needing morning glass or a west wind. 3-8ft. A wave to behold, but not to be surfed unless you are an expert, and even then, avoid low tide.

Lance's Left

At the edge of Katiet's western bay, at the southern end of Sipura Island.

Consistent left-hander and frequently surfed crowd-pleaser. Lance's has it's moods, but in east winds when HT's is onshore, and with a moderate southwest swell at mid tide, you can expect a 2 or 3 barrel wave and some workable but fast sections in between. Bear in mind that this wave is powerful and can be hard-breaking even on a 3 foot day, with craggy reef never too far away. Intermediates plus, but it holds a solid 10ft, when the experts take over. A brilliant wave, and open to any swell. 3-8ft, mid to high tides best, with low tide unpredictable and too shallow.

Bintangs

The left-hander across the bay from Lances left. If winds are north and Lances is onshore, have a look here. Rights break over an off-shore reef delivering short fast barrels. 2-6ft. Advanced. Breaks often, but doesn't like bigger swells. Consistent.

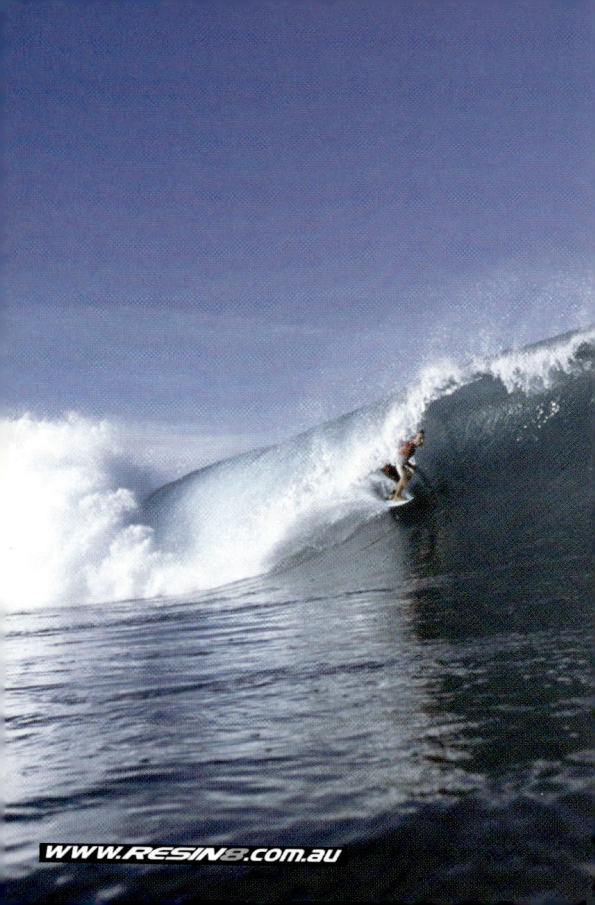

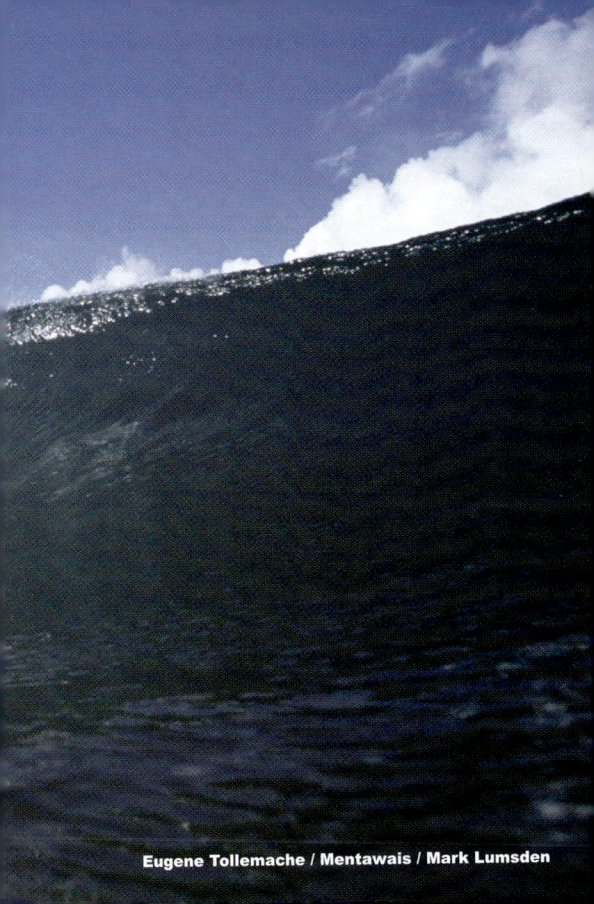

Eugene Tollemache / Mentawais / Mark Lumsden

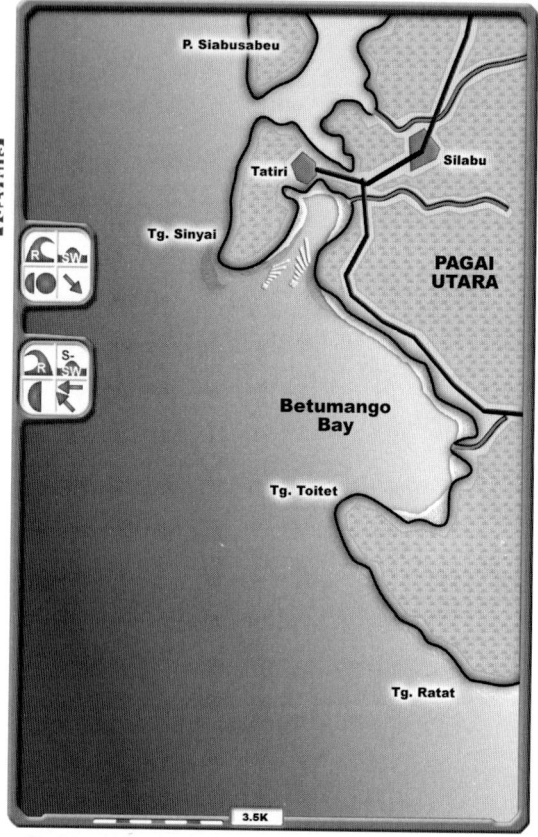

SUMATRA

P. Siabusabeu

Tatiri

Silabu

Tg. Sinyai

PAGAI
UTARA

Betumango
Bay

Tg. Toitet

Tg. Ratat

3.5K

Macaroni's

At the northern edge of Betumango bay on Pagai Utara.

If photos of this place don't cause saliva to drip from your lips, you need to see a shrink. Macca's, the most famous wave in the Mentawais, is the perfect left in the perfect setting. A typical take-off will be straight into a fine-lipped, feathering barrel that tempts you to stall and make the moment linger. The idea is to then come out of the tube onto an endless clean wall, with room to turn and throw spray. Sort of like 2 experiences for the price of one. It gets horrendously busy for the above reasons, but worth it. 3-8ft plus. 4-5ft is often best, with middle tides; low tide is pretty shallow. Sits in a protected bay thus requires solid swell to fire, preferably of the south-southwest variety. Experienced surfers, but intermediates will get waves on most days. An hour's cruise south can yield less crowded options.

KFC's (Macca's rights)

Off Sinai Cape, which lies to the southwest of Tatiri Village on west Pagai Utara. Opposite Macca's in this quite spectacular bay.

The rights at Macaroni's are relatively approachable and will often be working when Macca's is not. The wave wraps into a curved section of reef on the west side of this heavily recessed bay. On low tide it's unappetizing sections are barely recognizable, but when the water pushes in, some long lines will start to appear. The best time to catch it is when the winds have completely switched off, or on slightly rare north-westerlies. Consistent if tides right. All levels. 3-8ft. The whole setup is as picturesque as can be.

A few miles north on the other side of the peninsula, **Silabu** hosts a fairly consistent left-hander that is worth inspection if the crowds are up, or if neither Macca's nor KFC's are delivering your wave as ordered.

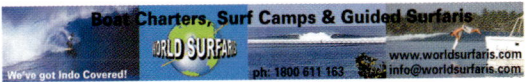

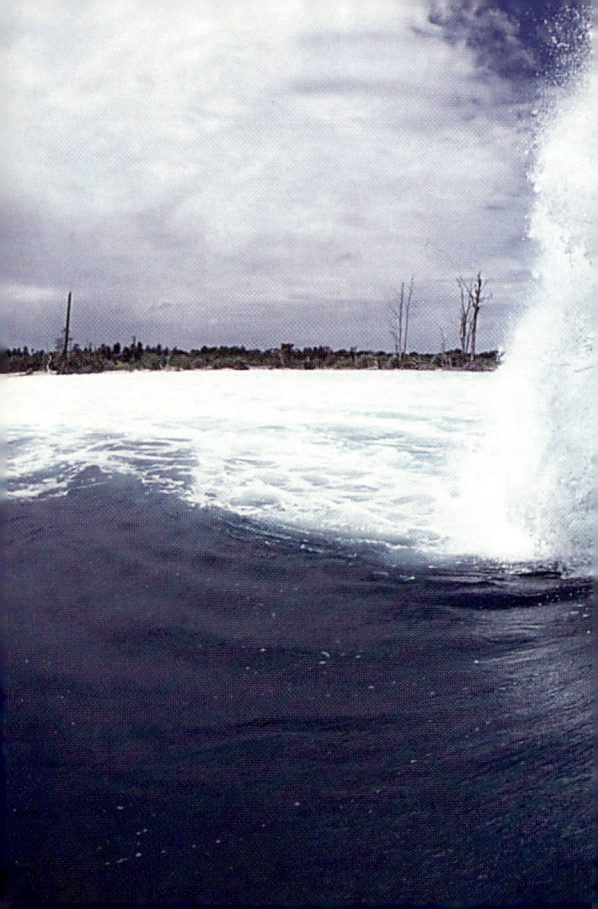

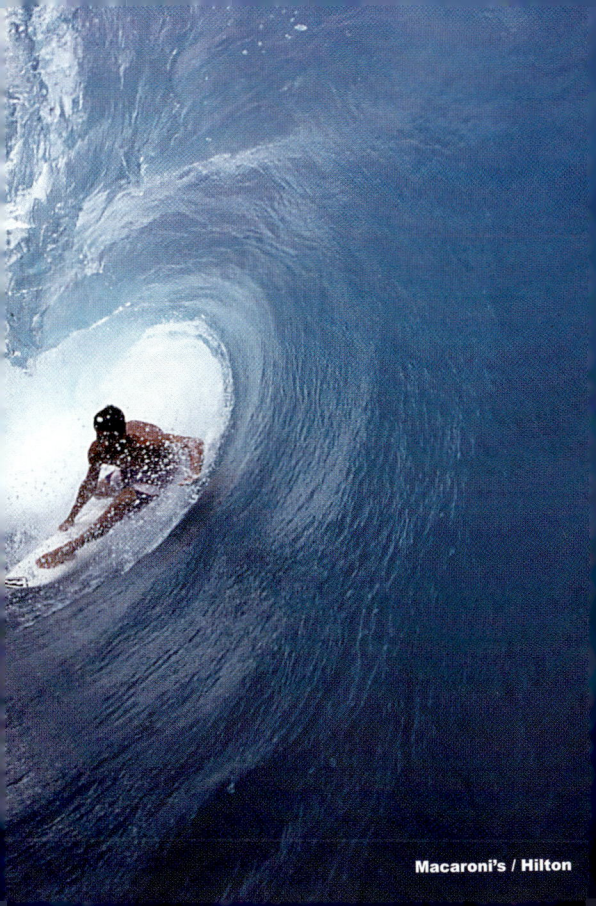

Macaroni's / Hilton

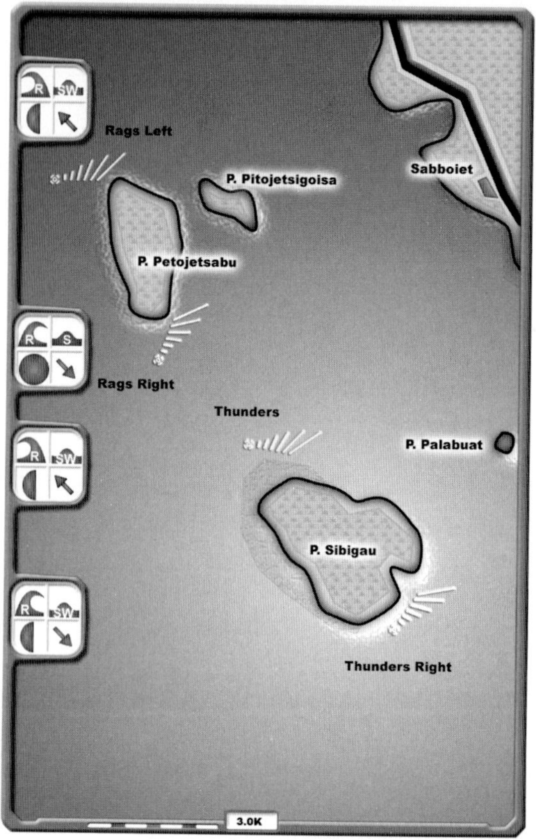

SUMATRA

Rags Left

P. Pitojetsigoisa

Sabboiet

P. Petojetsabu

Rags Right

Thunders

P. Palabuat

P. Sibigau

Thunders Right

3.0K

Rags Lefts

Petojet Sabu is a windward isle sitting opposite Sabojet ; an end-of-the-line village in the middle of South Pagai's west coast.

Endless left-hand barrels wrapping around the reef that bulges off the north side of the island, causing it to bend, clean up, and hollows out to perfection. 3-8ft. Mid tide and south wind/glass best. Good level required.

Rags Rights

Off the southeast edge of Petojet Sabu Island. Hard-core right-hand barrel over very shallow reef. Rights will not show every day, but on solid southwest swell and glassy or norwest winds, some of the most gaping barrels are to be had - but only by the pros. This is a dangerous wave with heavy water coming at you from depth, and the most threadbare covering over the reef. Low tide is for the slightly mad, and high is best although still for experts. Consistent if not always perfect.

Thunders Lefts

Sibigau Island sits off the west coast of South Pagai opposite the village of Bake. It's low lying malarial swamp gives way to a narrow beach and protruberant fringe reef.

This is a powerful, heavy left-hander rearing up in open water. Thunders is the hell-man wave in Indonesia, and it's many shifting peaks would suit tow-in surfing. It can handle almost any size, with big days often being better. Pros only. Barrels possible, but some days it's just the sheer size that excites.

Thunders Rights

Thunders' lesser twin rarely shows top-drawer quality, but in norwesters and west swells it can offer a solid option away from the crowds. High tide is lumpy and low can be a mess; time it right.

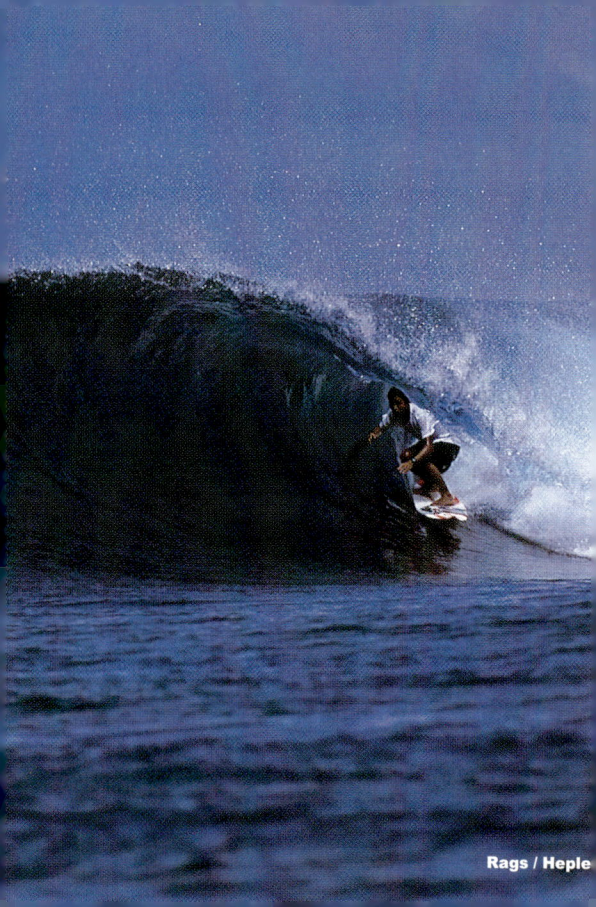

The Hole

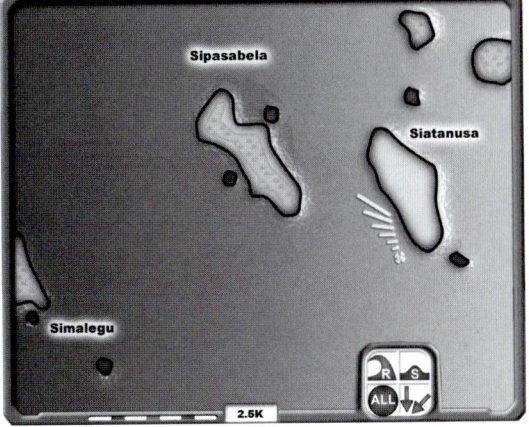

Off the western edge of Siatanusa Island, which lies east of the southern peninsula of South Pagai Island.

Hard breaking left-hand barrels over a shallow reef. Whilst the costs are dear for those who fall, the glory is eternal. Deep water jack-up on take-off, then accelerating wave bending around the arc of reef, making final exits difficult. Different take-off depending on tides, with high breaking on a very shallow slab. Advanced only. Fickle wave, and heavy. Other great lefts in the area, but the many islands here are in the lee of Cape Bio, thus requiring a very big swell with plenty of south in it.

Lighthouse Rights

Even further away, this shifty but lined up right-hand point works on anything from 2-8ft. Some power walls and barrels. All levels unless big. Low tide best, with any west wind...or no wind..

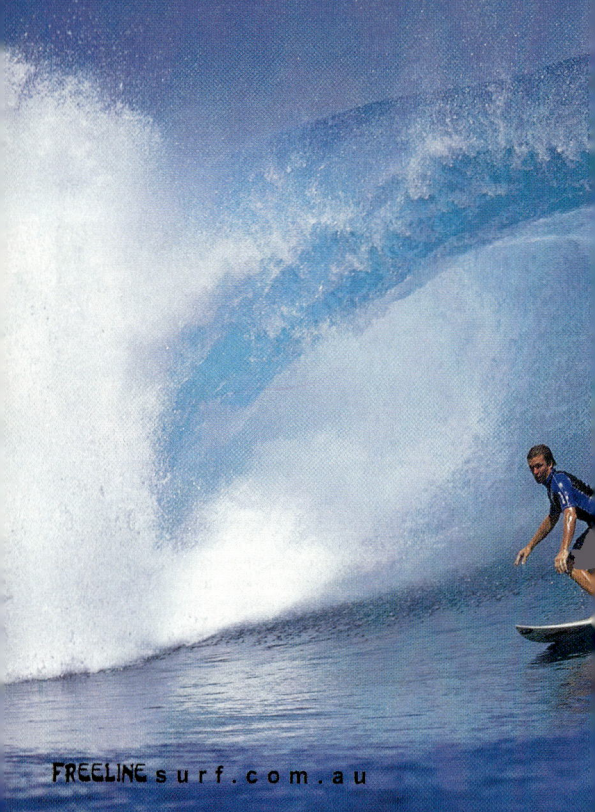

FREELINE surf.com.au

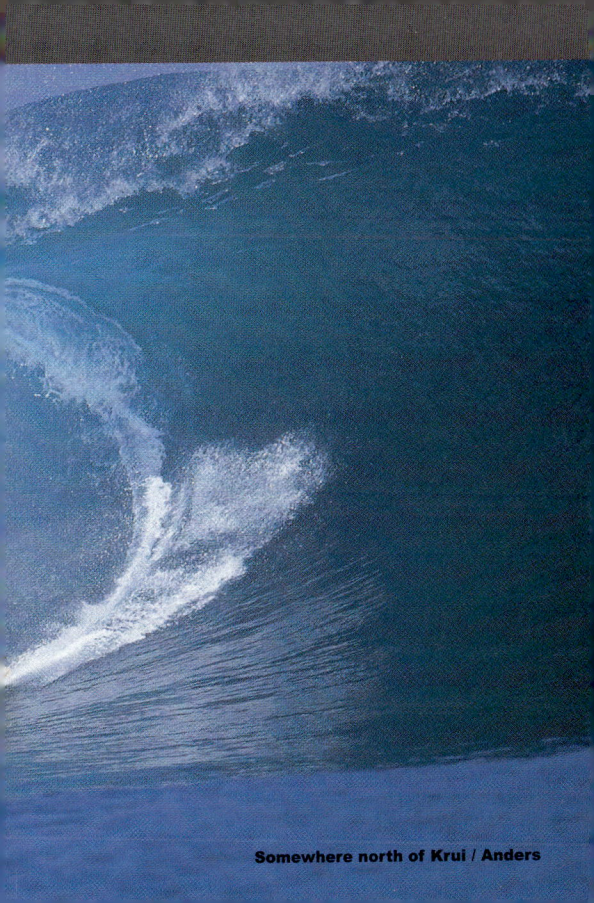

Somewhere north of Krui / Anders

Southern Sumatra

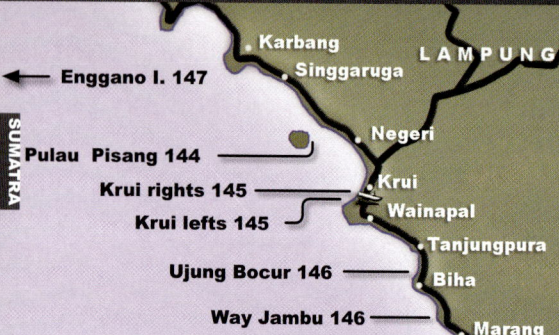

Karbang
Singgaruga

L A M P U N G

← Enggano I. 147

SUMATRA

Negeri

Pulau Pisang 144

Krui rights 145
Krui

Krui lefts 145
Wainapal

Tanjungpura

Ujung Bocur 146
Biha

Way Jambu 146
Marang

Banj
nege

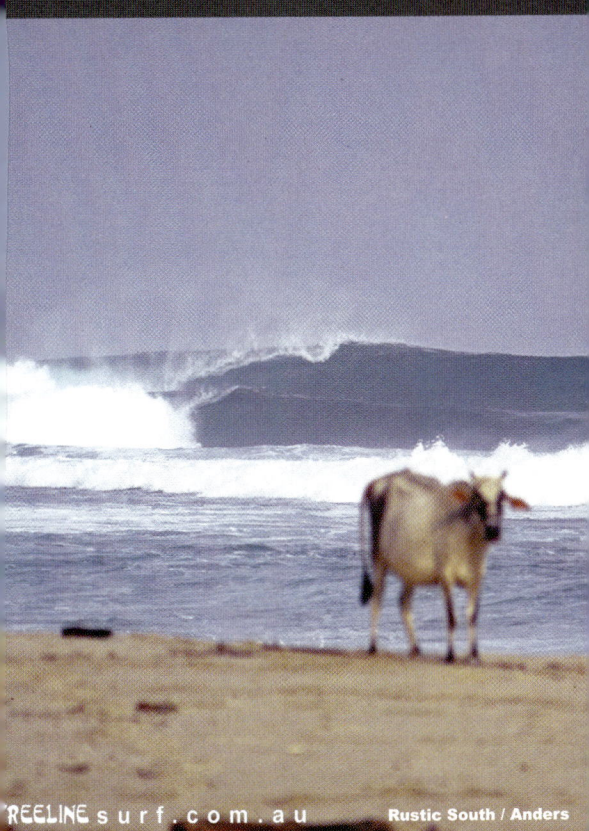

Rustic South / Anders

Pulau Pisang (The Island)

You can get a boat here, either charter or public, from Krui Harbour. The wave breaks off the eastern tip.

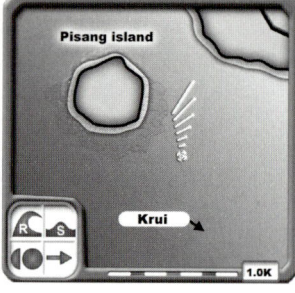

A heavy, jacking right rears up from deep water and wraps around an arc of shallow coral with undiluted energy. Not the longest wave, but the power per square inch is high, with challenging, spit-filled barrels common. The drop is usually a big one but makeable, and the paddle is easy. Mid - High tide best. 4 - 6ft plus. Advanced.

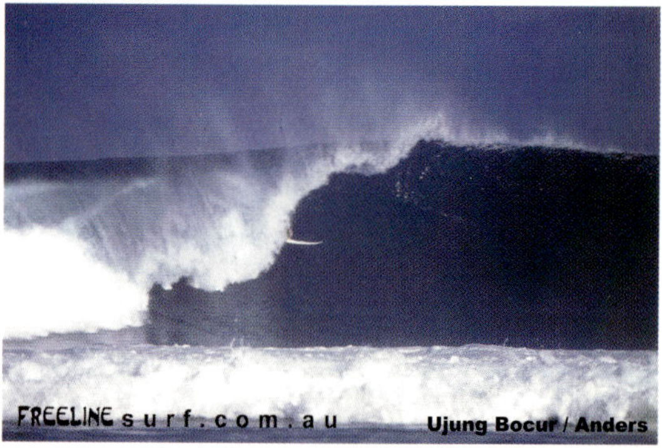

FREELINE surf.com.au   Ujung Bocur / Anders

Krui

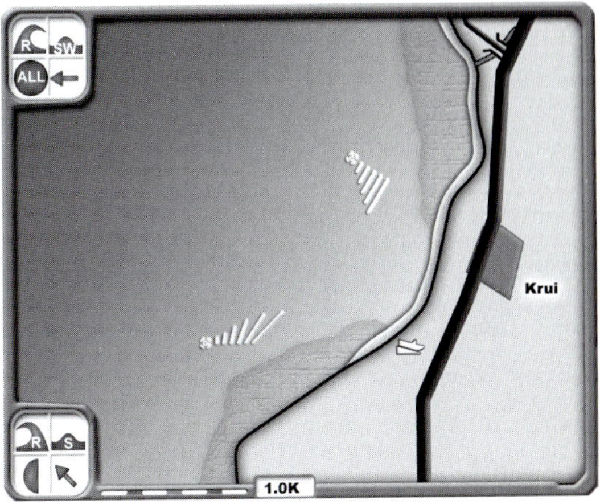

Krui

1.0K

2 great waves break either side of the beach at Krui.

Krui Lefts: A high quality wave, this left is approachable yet laden with barrel potential. Any tide will work although the low tides expose some reef spikes. It is an intermediate wave, but hold-downs can still be severe. Offshore in southeast winds. Needs solid southwest swell to work.

Krui rights: Off the reef fringed northern point of Krui's long curved beach. Hollow reef point almost guaranteeing a barrel from take-off. A short wave, but not a moment is wasted from start to finish as it barrels right across. All tides are OK, and even low offers a generous covering of water over the reef. Intermediate plus. East to southeast winds best. Requires large southwest swell.

Ujung Bocur

AKA SLL (Sumatra's longest left), it's right out the front of Ombak Indah Losmen at Biha.

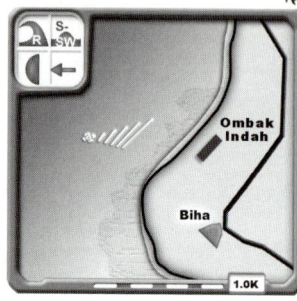

Quality long point reef in an idyllic setting. Orderly lines focus onto a predictable take-off, and then develop quickly into a barrel. Once you've pulled in, the wall usually tapers evenly and morphs into a fast but workable ride of up to 300 metres. South swell best, with E-SE winds. Low tide is fast and hard-breaking, mid perfect, high fun to fat. All levels depending on conditions.

Way Jambu

One of the widest barrels you are likely to surf. A pitching take-off over shallow reef is the intro to a barrel of up to 200 metres before final release into a channel. This wave may section and throw up surprises, but it rarely shuts down totally, meaning those who hang on and sight the exit are likely to prevail. Low tide is extremely difficult and risky, although awesome to see,

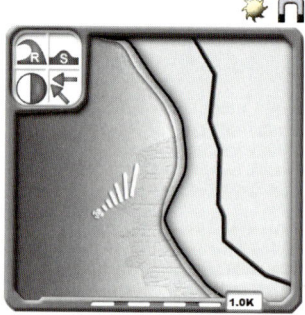

mid tide is perfect. High tide is full but still very high quality on a bigger day...and it is usually bigger than it looks courtesy of a very long paddle-out. 3 - 12ft, 4-8ft best. Advanced. Dirty beach.

Enggano Island

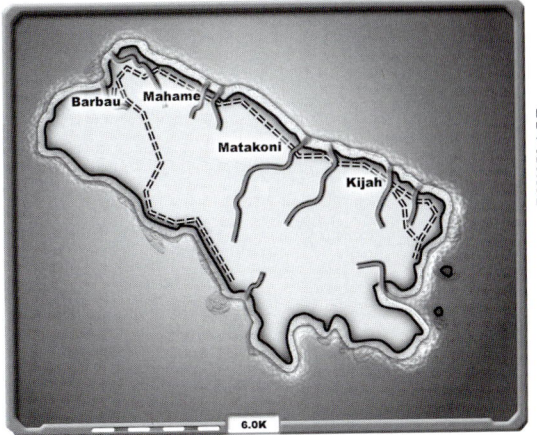

Barbau Mahame

Matakoni

Kijah

6.0K

Enggano Island is a fairly serious sail 90 nautical miles west from the port of Krui.

This remote island is hard to get to (Some boats go from Bengkulu to its only port of Malakoni), without much except medieval agriculture, wild pigs and buffalo. There is little accommodation in the 5 villages, and the locals just about speak Bahasa Indonesian but certainly no English. It is surrounded by beautiful white sand beaches, coral reef arcs, and a trio of stunning coral atolls although the interior is pretty flat and malarial. Only a very basic track circumnavigates the 30 by 50km island, but this doesn't fully service the south and east shoreline. It certainly isn't well charted territory. Getting waves here requires real commitment, and the ability to tolerate the hardships endured.

Risks include malaria, and the total absence of medical help.

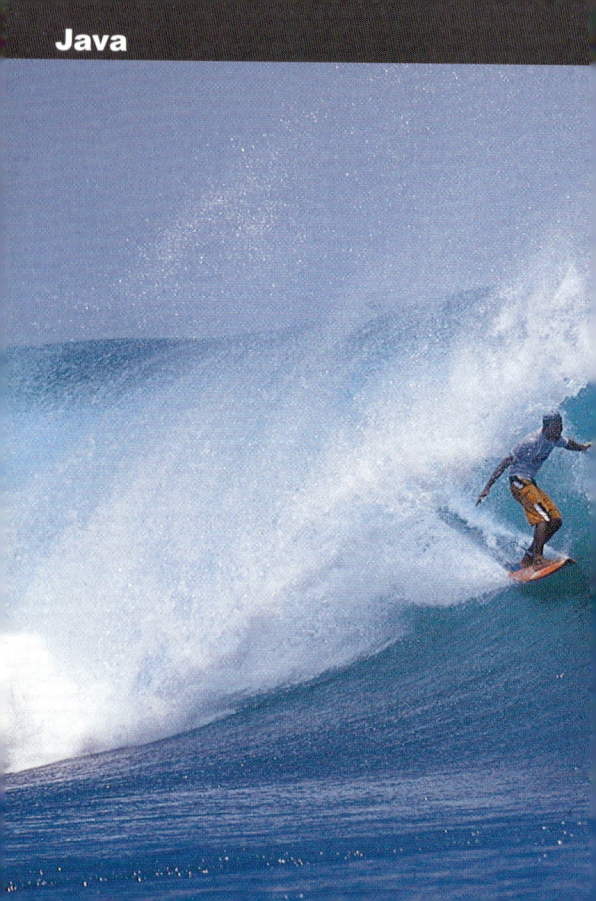

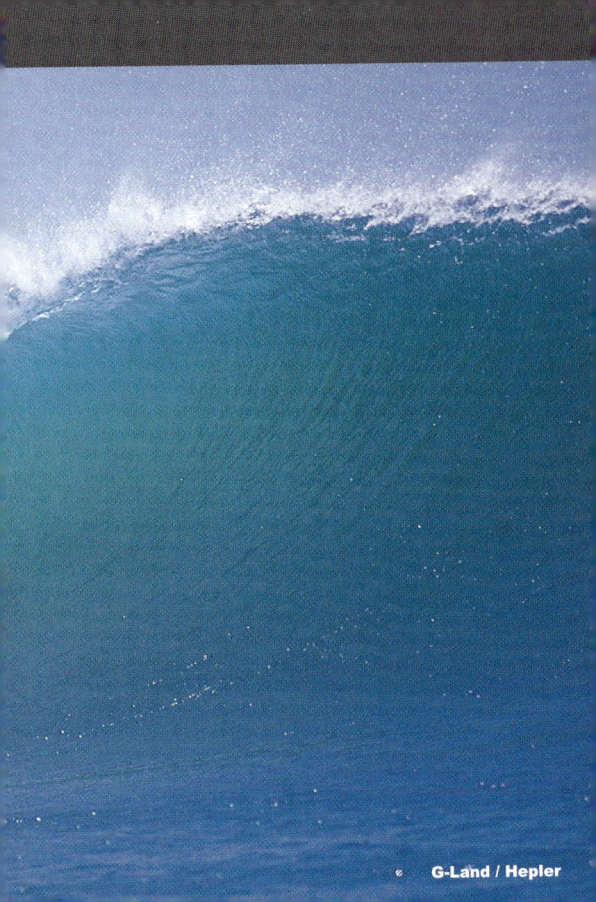

G-Land / Hepler

Java Surf Data

Where

1'000 kilometres long, Java has a surfable coastline facing south into the Indian Ocean, lying between the latitudes of 7 and 9 degrees 30" south.

Background

Indonesia's most populous island (compare it's 100M inhabitants with the 36M next door on Sumatra), Java is a predominantly Muslim island although it's culture is heavily influenced by Hindu and other beliefs from it's pre-Islamic past. It is the centre of industrial and government activity.

Java presents perhaps the ultimate overland surfing experience, with extreme opposites like the lunacy of Jakarta traffic situated just 6 hours from the primal beauty of Ujung Genteng and Ujung Kulon National parks. Some of Indonesia's most important temples, such as Borobudur, are found in Java, and a chain of volcanoes in various states of awakening stretches from east to west. Some incredible national parks such as Ujung Kulon in the west (of which Panaitan Island is an extension), and Alas Purwo in the east (where you'll find G-Land clinging to the edge of the jungle) straddle the mayhem of Java's sprawling towns. There can be no mistake, surf travel in Java is an adventure.

The Setup

The major part of Java's coastline faces into the southeast trade-winds, and perpendicular to the predominant swell direction, resulting in unruly, big, wind affected surf. Happily the contortions of the coast have created areas where the set ups are perfect. This has meant that a two key areas have become "established"; Pelabuhanratu in West Java, and Grajagan in the east. There is little in the way of a beaten path in between, which means unridden waves for intrepid explorers with time on their hands. As a guideline, find yourself a west (or east, in wet season) facing bit of coast and you'll probably score waves.

The Waves

Celebrity waves include the shallow fast reefs of **Panaitan Island**, waves for all levels at **Cimaja**, the mountainous **Ombak Tujuh**, Pangandaran's fun, dilapidated beach resort with waves to match, and the majestic **G-Land**; the epitome of Indo perfection with dry season lefts in a jungle setting.

Seasons

Surf is subject to the Indian Ocean wet/dry season cycle. Southeast trade-winds dominate from late April to October, accompanied by drier weather and increased swell peaking from June to August. November through early April is wet season, with northwest trades and decreasing swell. A typical January might have 400mm of rain, vs 50mm in August. West Java breaks work all year round; Panaitan has waves that are off shore in both predominant winds, as does the Cimaja area. G-Land is strictly a dry season wave, with on-shores frequent from October to April.

M	Swell Range		Wind Pattern		Air		Sea	Crowd
	Feet	Dir'	Am	Pm	Low	Hi	°C	
J	2-6	SE-SW	NW LO	NW MOD	22	26	27	LO
F	2-6	SE-SW	NW LO	NW MOD	22	26	27	LO
M	2-6	SE-SW	NW LO	NW MOD	22	26	27	MED
A	2-8	S-SW	SE LO	SE MOD	22	27	27	MED
M	3-10	S-SW	SE LO	SE MOD	22	27	27	HI
J	3-12	S-SW	SE LO	SE MOD	22	28	27	HI
J	3-12	S-SW	SE LO	SE MOD	22	28	26	HI
A	3-12	S-SW	SE LO	SE MOD	22	28	26	HI
S	2-10	S-SW	SE LO	SE MOD	22	29	26	HI
O	2-8	SE-SW	NW LO	NW MOD	22	30	26	MED
N	2-6	SE-SW	NW LO	NW MOD	21	28	26	LO
D	2-6	SE-SW	NW LO	NW MOD	21	27	26	MED

Java Surf Data

Crowds

Terrorism, and the Sumatran feeding frenzy have helped reduce crowds across Java in recent years. G-Land will always be G - Land, but if you are able to venture away from the obvious, you can find great waves with little aggravation in the water. 1500 km of coastline is a lot of waves.

Boards

Indo semi-guns are a useful piece of artillery right across Java, although some Cimaja area breaks are more fun / performance oriented, and the Batukaras area is ideal for longboarders. There are waves for everyone. Take plenty of your own supplies because surf shops are non existent, and board repairs are really only readily available in the Cimaja area and G-Land.

Hazards

All the usual Indo hazards apply, although road and accommodation infrastructure is relatively well developed. Of the places you're most likely to surf overland, spots west of Cimaja are pretty remote, and G-Land has it's own unique jungle backdrop although the accommodation is now westernized to the max.

It is a country where poverty is sometimes confronting, so there are theft hazards associated with that. Medical facilities outside of Jakarta are fairly basic; take first aid supplies.

All the usual Indonesian sea creatures abound, with urchins the main offender. Sea snakes are common, as are shark sightings though attacks are statistically extremely unlikely.

With much surf travel in Java being of the overland type, sickness and disease, including malaria and diarrhoea, is an issue to take seriously. Check the back of the book, and consult your doc about preventive medicine / shots.

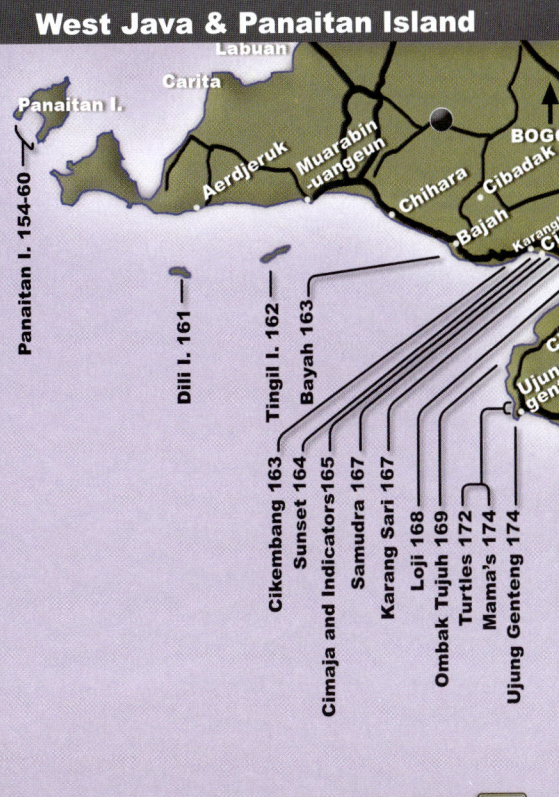

West Java & Panaitan Island

Labuan

Carita

Panaitan I.

Panaitan I. 154-60

Aerdjeruk

Muarabin
-uangeun

BOGO

Chihara · Cibadak

· Bajah

Karangha

Cir

Cir

Ujung
gent

Dili I. 161

Tingil I. 162

Bayah 163

Cikembang 163

Sunset 164

Cimaja and Indicators 165

Samudra 167

Karang Sari 167

Loji 168

Ombak Tujuh 169

Turtles 172

Mama's 174

Ujung Genteng 174

50K

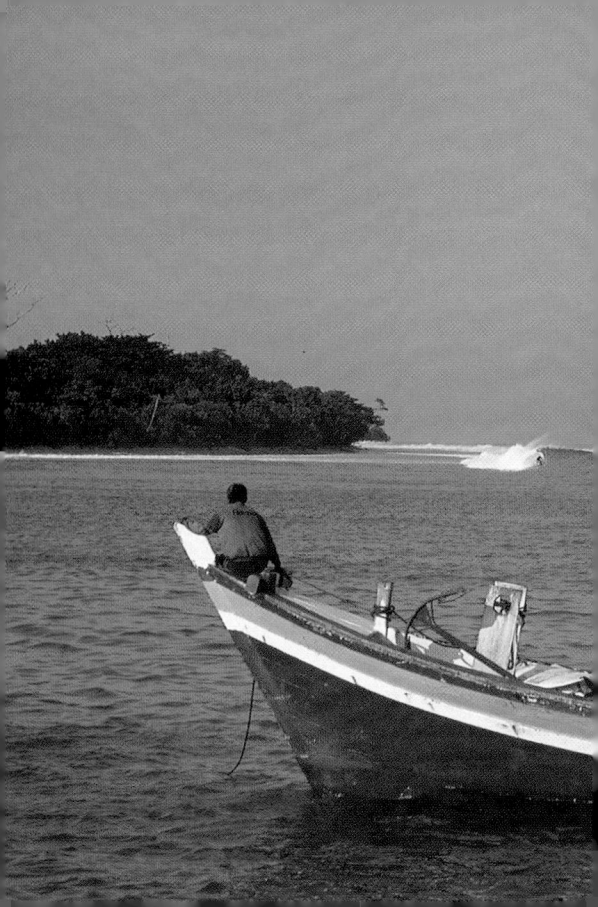

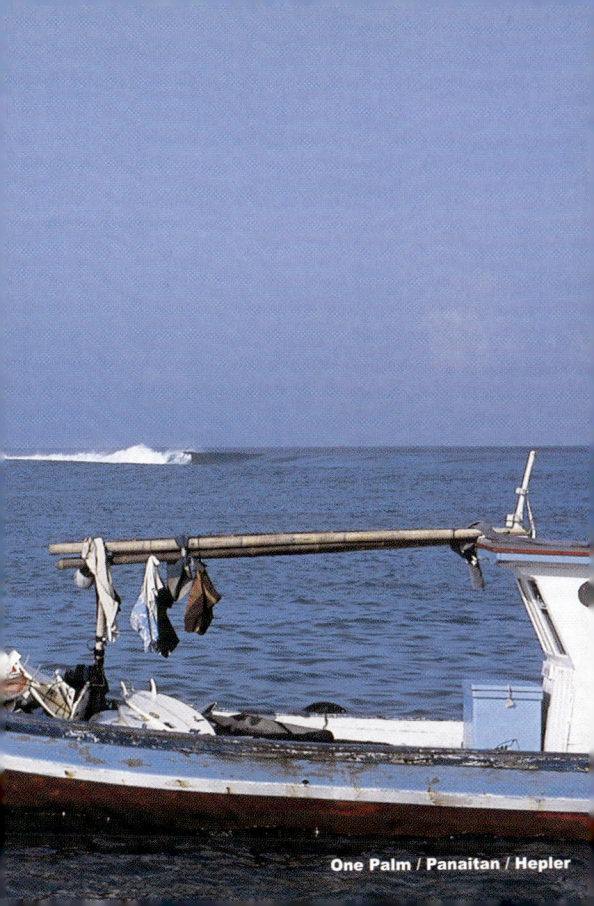

One Palm / Panaitan / Hepler

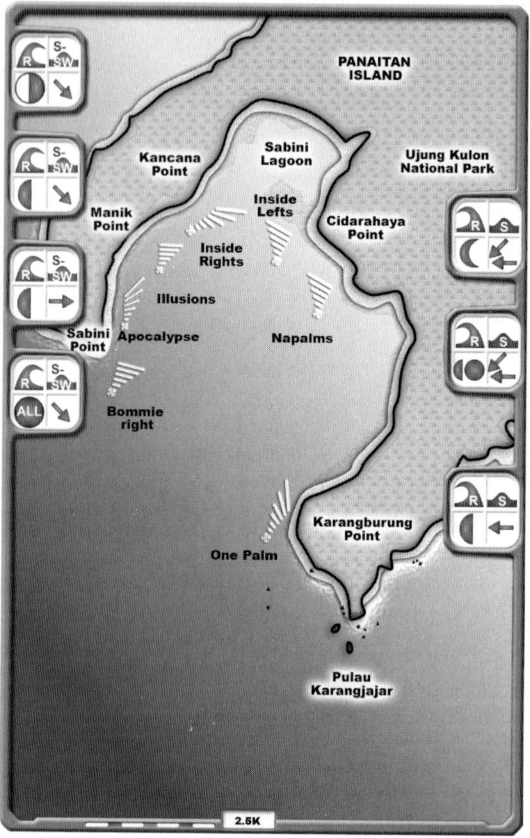

JAVA

PANAITAN ISLAND

Ujung Kulon National Park

Kancana Point

Sabini Lagoon

Manik Point

Inside Lefts

Cidarahaya Point

Inside Rights

Illusions

Apocalypse

Napalms

Sabini Point

Bommie right

Karangburung Point

One Palm

Pulau Karangjajar

2.5K

Panaitan Island

An island extension of the Ujung Kulon national Park off the western tip of Java, Panaitan is a large chunk of untouched primal wilderness fringed by dense palm thickets and a wide flat table reef. You can get here by surf yacht charter or by fishing boat from Labuan or Carita. "Proper" surf charters are a good option because there is no accommodation or food on the island. You can get picked up in Jakarta itself and do a 4 day trip, making this one of the easiest locations at which to access hard-core waves. It's also among the most cost effective boat trips you can do, for the aforementioned reason and because Jakarta is well serviced by major airlines. See back for transport details.

Waves at Panaitan are generally for experts only. Many amazing photos have come out of this place, with their freeze-frame view giving the impression that the waves are makeable when they are sometimes far from it. Quite a number of the more famous shots were taken immediately prior to the rider coming to grief on the barely covered reef.

One Palm Point

The wave that put Panaitan on the map. One of the world's longest (up to 800yds), most perfect, most dangerous shallow left-hand barrels reels across a reef point. You need a sturdy board to get into the wave as early as possible, then set a rail and go for maximum speed. Low tide is as hairy as any surfing experience imaginable, with mid tides best, and anything from 3ft of south to southwest swell. This wave is often unmakeably fast and hollow, and the consequences are real. Experts only unless small. Probably Panaitan's most punishing wave.

Napalms

Probably the most frequently surfed wave at Panaitan, and with good reason. The left-hand reef here delivers barrels with mechanical perfection, and they are more makeable than One Palm thanks to a defined channel. Take-offs are straight forward, then a lined up wall

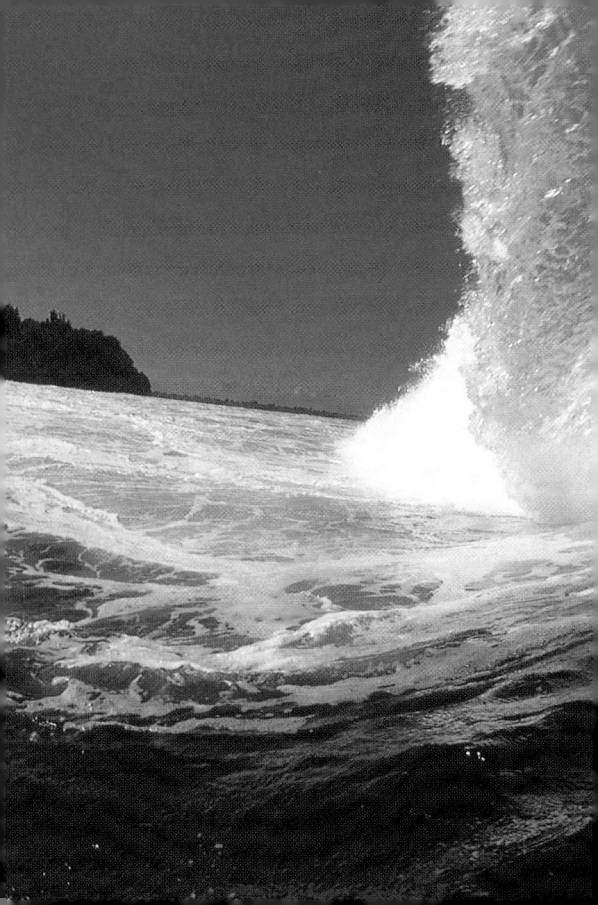

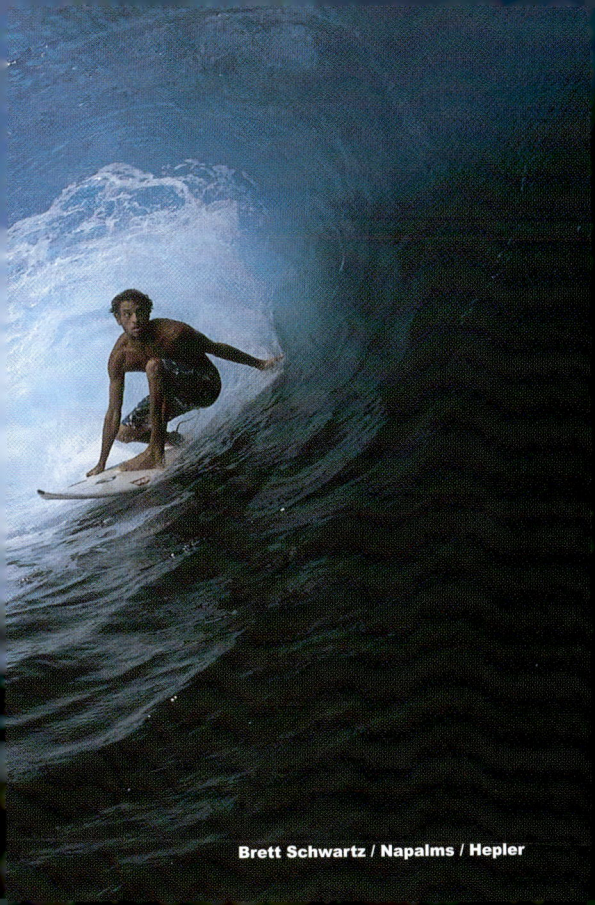

Brett Schwartz / Napalms / Hepler

Panaitan Island cont'd..

leads to a full-on barrel before tapering off into deep water. Higher tides are best if you want to avoid the shallow second section.

Inside Lefts / Pussy's

At the head of the inner bay are some very well lined up, fun long lefts. Generally a good warm-up spot for Panaitan proper, the lefts need a good south swell but work at any tide, although low is often best. All levels.

Inside Rights

Opposite the lefts, on the west side of the bay is a right-hand reef break that works on wet season west breezes and any swell direction. A solid south swell at low tide will get this alternative spot firing. Low to mid tides generally OK although depends on swell size. All levels depending on the day.

Illusions

Right-hand reef break with approachable take-off and variable barrel and wall sections. Advanced. It's a wave you may never see working properly.

Apocalypse

Extremely square right-hand barrel; pull in or don't go. Low tides are super-gnarly. Experts only.

Outside bombora waves

On the cruise to Panaitan you will see a number of outside reefs, all with potential. The rights off the western point are the most frequently ridden, but they need glassy conditions or northerly winds if they are to be worthy.

Dili Island

A 2 hour boat ride from Muara Binuange fishing port which is a good 2 hours west of Cimaja. Careful negotiation at the port can get you on a boat for a hefty price.

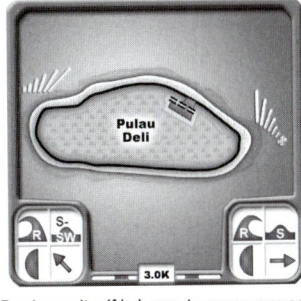

This reef fringed island forest is a sanctuary for the breeding of laboratory monkeys. Making landfall is an absolute no-no. Depending on wind direction, check either end for reef lefts and rights. Muara Buniange itself is home to some waves worth exploring.

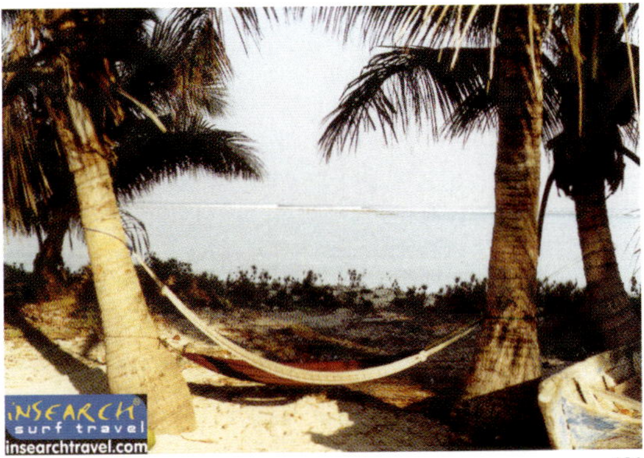

Tingil Island

As above, a 2 hour boat ride from Muara Binu-ange fishing port which is a good 2 hours west of Cimaja. This island is also restricted for the same reasons as Dili.

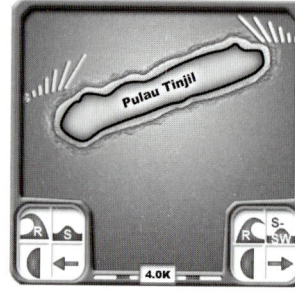

The western reef can throw up some solid left-handers, but it is open to swell and gets destroyed on bigger days. Strong trade-winds are also a menace. Both of these islands are worth investigating as part of a longer boat trip from Pelabuhanratu; making a dedicated visit is costly, and the results may not justify the hassle.

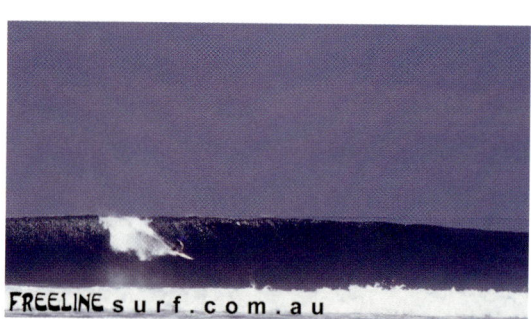

Never-ending race with the face at Ujung Bocur / Nev

Cikembang

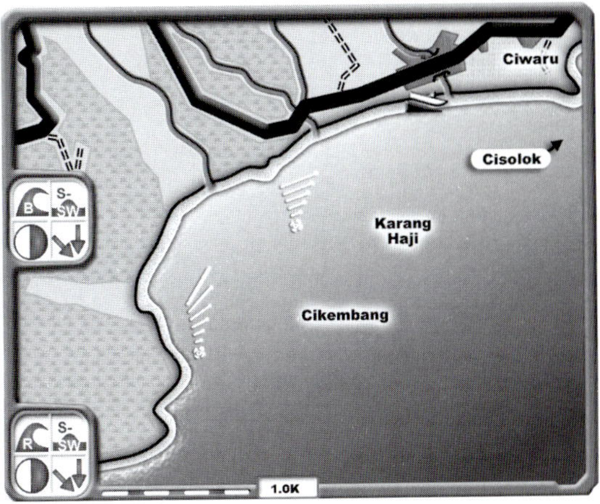

Ciwaru

Cisolok

Karang Haji

Cikembang

1.0K

From Cimaja, take a major drive west through Cisolok and Cibangan. After Cibangan, the road leaves the coast. Follow it up into the hills and back down to Pasirandu village. There's a left turn into a very poor track. Quite a trek. Best bet is boat ride from Cimaja.

Right point can offer quality rights over rock base. It's protected from any west winds, but it needs a very big southwest or solid south swell if it is to work. On the way, about 4km west of Cisolok, some check out **Karang Haji** just left of the Ocean queen resort. Mediocre quality lefts and rights on sand and rock ledge, requiring sizeable swell. Intermediates.
Beyond Cikembang, **Batu Marob** is a mystical reef break to stumble across. A more extended trip may lead to **Bayah** village, where an enormous strip of beach and reef break is visible in all its glory from the hilltop roads. The beach rarely has any shape and is usually blown out in trade winds, although the eastern point by the village can offer a bit of protection for it's rarely surfed lefts.

Sawarna

About 20k (2 hours on the weathered roads) west of Cimaja, this is a hard spot to get to. We recommend boat or guided trip from Cimaja.

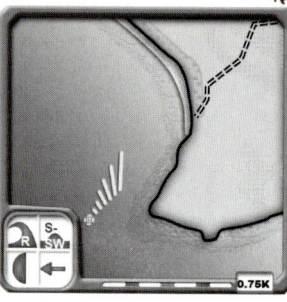

L point of consequence. Sawarna holds as much swell as the ocean can provide; the bigger the better. Fast, lengthy lefts fold in from the outer point and wind across a table reef all the way to the inside beach section. The angle of the reef makes it magnetic to prevailing SW swells, with more west directions providing dredging powerful waves best left to experts. Uncrowded. Not to be surfed alone.

Sunset Beach (Karang Hawu)

Head 2km west from Cimaja and stop at the beach,

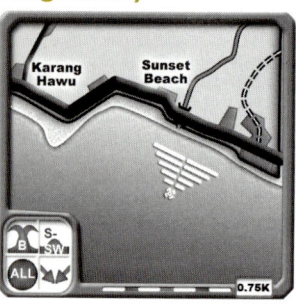

Fun beach-breaks when Cimaja isn't quite lined up properly. It's also a crowd avoidance strategy in season. Early morning off-shores or glass can result in some punchy beach-break rights and lefts on most states of the tide, with some shore-dump and rips to contend with. All levels. Consistent if not always perfect. On small days, some more fun low tide rivermouth peaks can sometimes be found by veering off the main road just before neighboring **Cisolok**.

Cimaja and Indicators

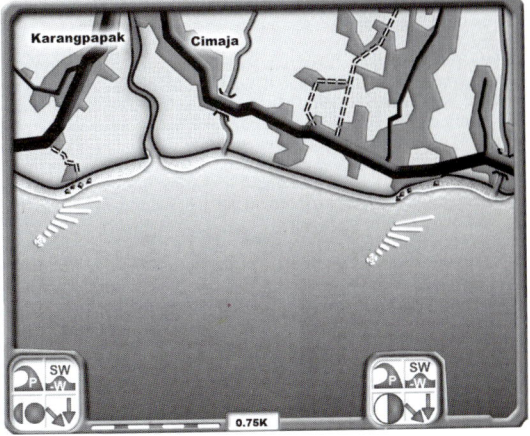

JAVA

Cimaja village and its surrounds are easily reached from Jakarta, taking the highway south to Bogor, then towards Sukabumi and Pelabuhan Ratu. Once in Cimaja fishing village, it's a hike through the rice paddies, and a cautious hop across the cobblestone beach.

Cimaja: Long lined up right-hand point break on a rock and boulder bottom. Cimaja is generally a fun wave (think Lower Trestles), but there are hollow sections and a shallow uneven bottom to contend with. On a good southwest swell at 3-6ft it will line up and offer barrels all the way to the inside. South swells can hit it too square and create sections; but it'll still be fun if unpredictable in these conditions. Lower tides tend to be better, creating more barrels although on larger swells it is not crucial. Southeast trades are onshore; surf early morning. 2-8ft depending swell direction. All levels, but beware boulders, shallow close-outs and currents. It's the favourite of Ja-

Cimaja and Indicators cont'd..

karta ex pats, a few locals and travelling all-sorts that base themselves here; therefore can get busy.

Out the back and to the west, the swell-pulling **Indicators** breaks right, over an outer reef point. It'll usually be bigger than Cimaja point, but on lower tides can be a close-out on the reef. Indicators holds almost any size, and is better when there is solid swell (think 6ft plus at Cimaja). On these bigger days it is for chargers and those with the will and ability to take it's very steep drops. Best surfed on high tide (when it is more makeable and you can avoid the exposed boulders) and morning glass or a north-west wind. It's an advanced break.

Heading west for a few hundred yards, across the river, you can check out the lefts at **Karang Papak**, which can be working when Cimaja is a mess. Generally the temptation doesn't pay off however.

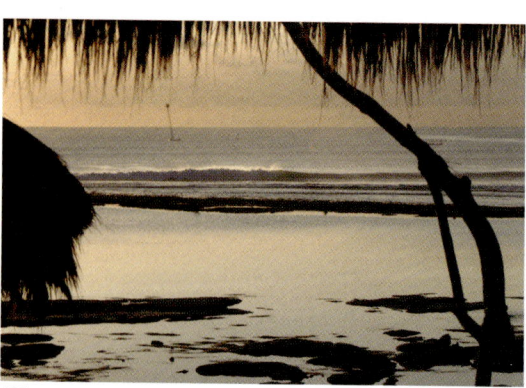

Samudra Beach

About 6km west from the port at Pelabuhanratu, you'll find the main strip of *losmen* accommodation starting at the 3 little bridges that offer a good view of the beach. Out the front of the Samudra Hotel.

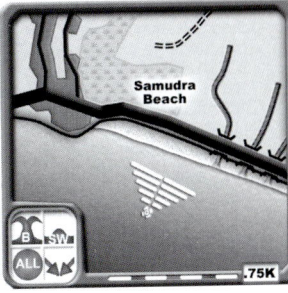

Average beach-break peaks on small swells, best surfed early morning. Normally Samudra is for the lazy, or beginners looking for a bit of space.

On northwest winds, the right corner can get reasonable, and the creeks can form good banks. 2-5ft. All levels. Consistent if not consistently good.

Karang Sari

In the north corner of the main beach at Pelabuhanratu, about 800yds north of the main harbour.

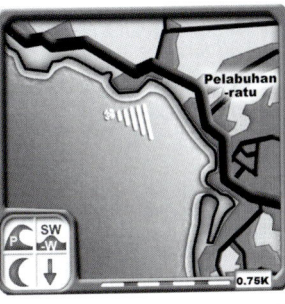

Short right-hand point style wave on sand bottom. Karang Sari is an easy spot close to town, and a good bet on big days when Cimaja might be ragged. It's protected from unruly south-west swells, which it can filter into shapely waves. Straight south swells are a mess here, as are dry season SE trade-winds. Northwest winds or early morning glass is best, and only works on low tides. All levels. Inconsistent.

Loji

Head due south from Pelabuhanratu. After a few km, cross the large bridge at Bagbagan. After another 3 km cross another bridge. After another 1km take a R at Cilangkap and follow the road for 2.5km through the paddies as it narrows into a track.

Long, well shaped left point-break over boulders, peeling in for 300 yards towards the beach. Pantai Loji is acknowledged as a saviour when Cimaja is too big, or is blown off by the southeast trade-winds that are perfectly off-shore here. It likes a solid southwest swell or big south, preferably in the 6-8ft range. In these conditions, Loji is a reeling left with fun sections all the way across. When swell is really pumping, tide is less of an issue.

If however, it isn't quite big enough for here, and winds are east to south-east, there are qual-ity lefts breaking into the rivermouth about 2km up the beach. Intermediates plus. Water can be dirty; avoid af-ter rains.

Cilagkap →

Warung

Cibuata

0.75K

Ombak Tujuh

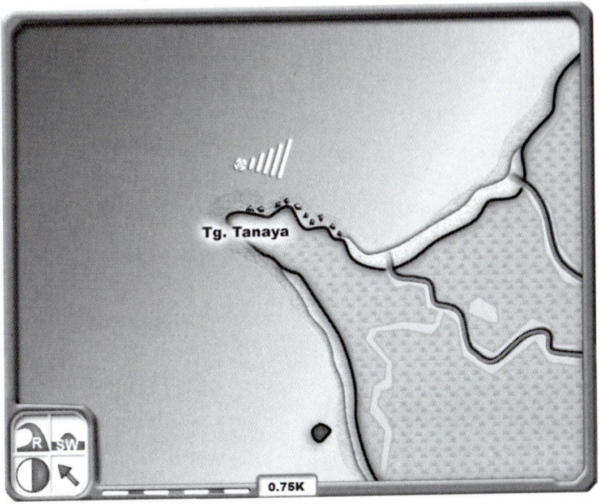

Tg. Tanaya

0.75K

10 nautical miles north of Ujung Genteng, or a major mission if going overland. 1 hour bike ride north from Turtles.

Deepwater left-hand reef break holding almost any size swell, this is the big-wave spot in West Java. If not always perfect, Ombak Tujuh (seven waves) offers some outrageous drops requiring serious commitment, and rearing walls all the way across. Makeable barrels are not as regular as some spots, but this is a hard-core adrenaline wave not unlike a reverse mid-tide day at outside Nusa Dua. Lower tides are best unless it's big, when higher tides work fine. Advanced only. Not to be surfed alone.

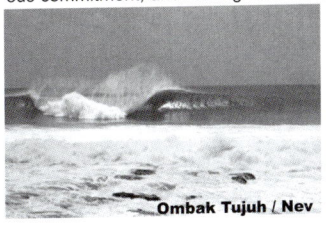

Ombak Tujuh / Nev

169

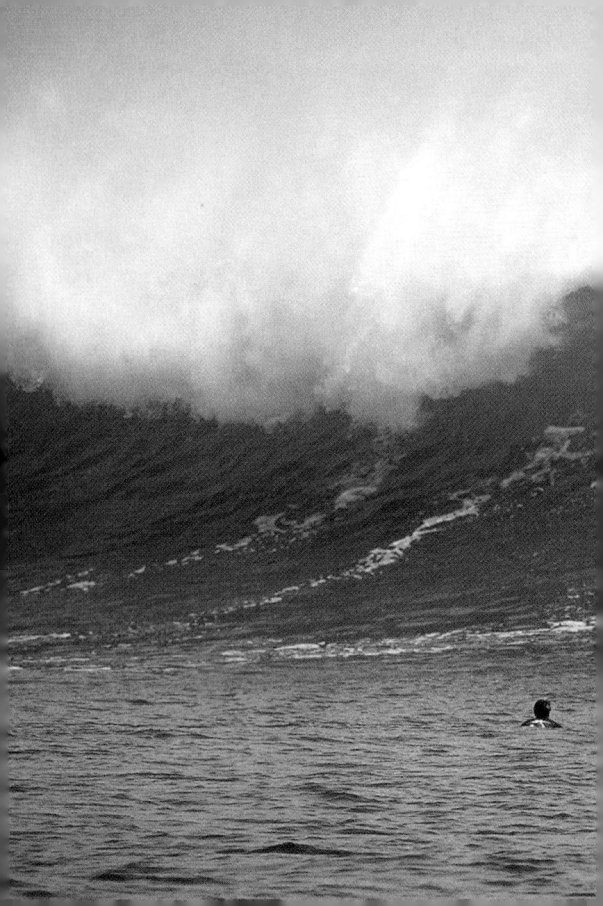

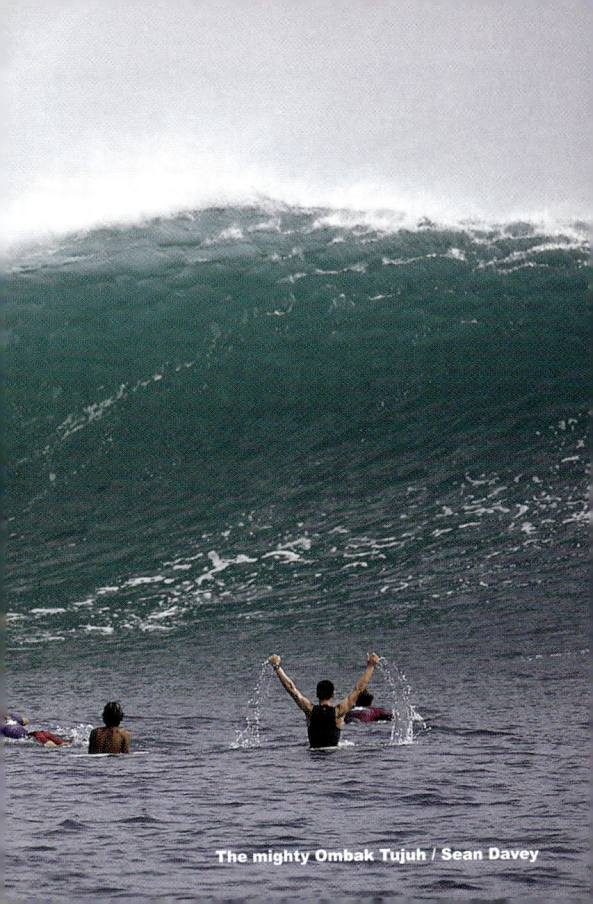

The mighty Ombak Tujuh / Sean Davey

Turtles

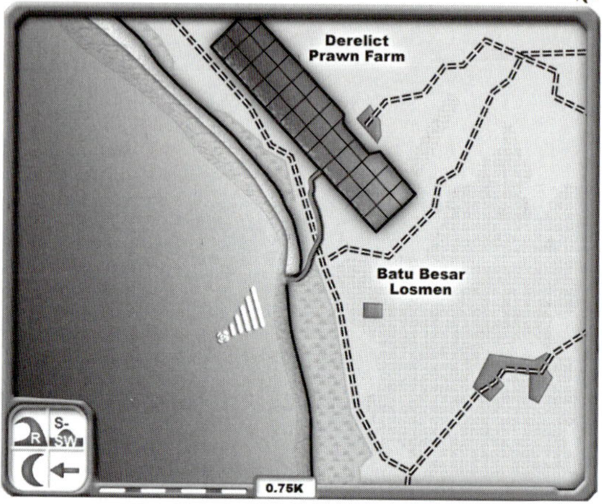

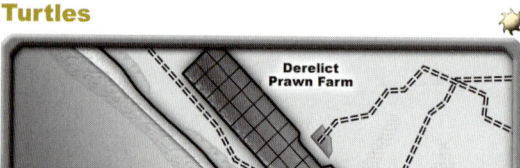

Derelict
Prawn Farm

Batu Besar
Losmen

0.75K

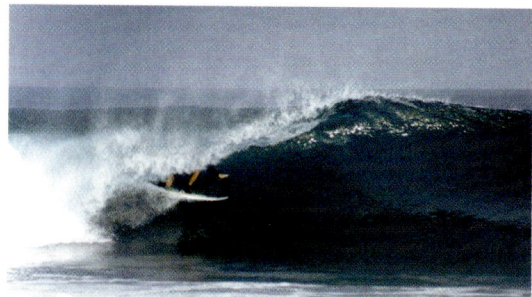

FREELINE surf.com.au

Turtles

Turtles

300m down the beach track from Batu Besar Losmen, 4 km north of Ujung Genteng.

Quality Left-hand reef with a high power to size ratio. The slightly shifting peak is extremely steep, and the barrels are square if unpredictable. The shallow reef isn't totally ruler-edge, meaning close-outs are a possibility, but often it will just keep on going. Lower tides produce the best, most lined up conditions, especially if combined with a south swell and east winds. Small days can be fun too, on higher tides, with the wave getting harder to predict the bigger it gets.

Advanced. 2-6ft plus. Consistent: In dry season it's a spot that rarely fails to deliver. There's a crew of surfers at the nearby *losmen*, and this is a perfect surfer's hangout from which you can explore Ujunggenteng waves as well as the mighty Ombak Tujuh.

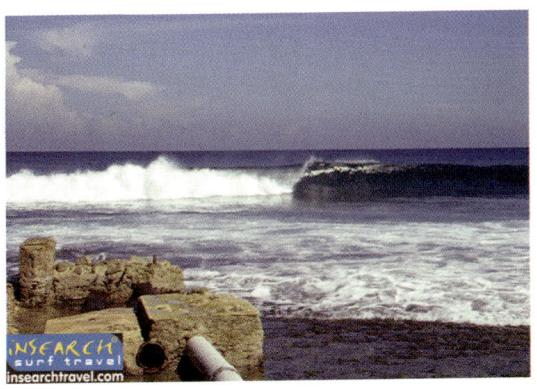

Mama's & Ujung Genteng

Take the road south from Pelabuhanratu, to the harbour of Ujung Genteng. This sleepy fishing village has a mellow if not pristine beach where you can drink coconut juice and explore.

At **Ujung Genteng** Harbour itself, you'll often see huge lines wrapping in from the outer point, way out the back. Inside this, and more protected from southeast trade-winds, is another left-hander that is ridden on occasion. Southwest swells are too perpendicular for the reef here to deal with, but straight south directions can wrap and create a fast hollow left-hander. This is a powerful spot for advanced surfers only. Higher tides make the entry and exit easier, as the exposed reef is hazardous at low.

About a kilometre and a half north of the harbour via a dodgy track, is Mama's Losmen. **Mama's** is out the front! A left-hand reef-break of many moods; from fat, to hollow to closed out. On some days it will produce quality; usually on southeast trade-winds, higher tides and a south swell. 2-6ft. Advanced. Sharp reef. Close-outs.

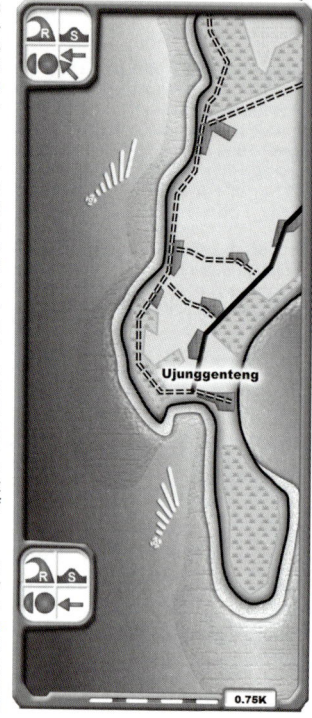

Ujunggenteng

0.75K

174

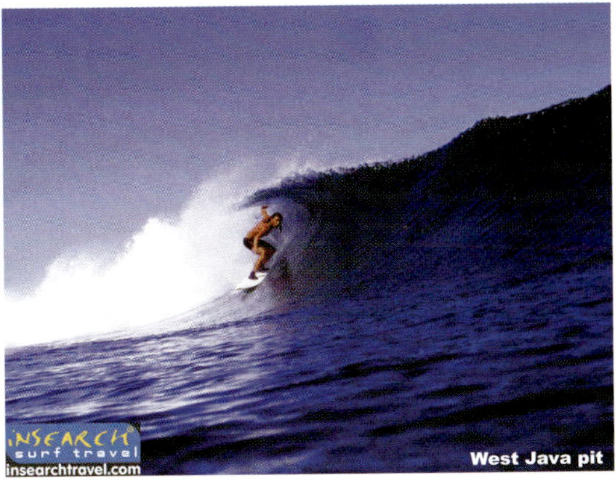

JAVA

West Java pit

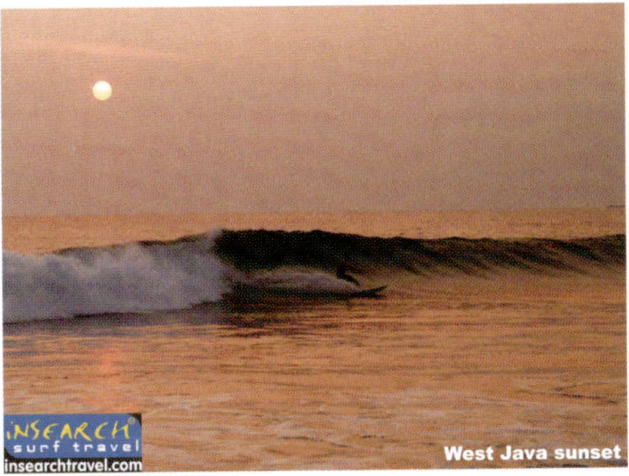

iNSEARCH
surf travel
insearchtravel.com

iNSEARCH
surf travel
insearchtravel.com

West Java sunset

Central Java

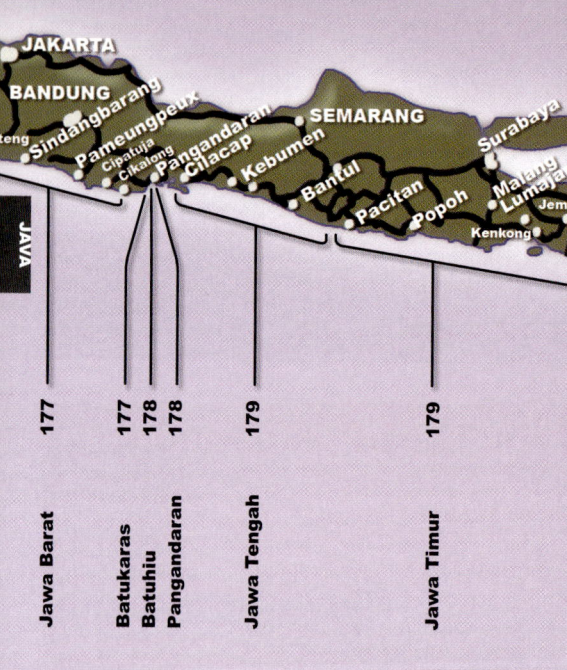

JAVA

JAKARTA
BANDUNG
Sindangbarang
Pameungpeux
Cipatuja
Cikalong
Batukaras
Batuhiu
Pangandaran
Cilacap
Kebumen
SEMARANG
Surabaya
Malang
Lumajang
Jember
Bantul
Pacitan
Popoh
Kenkong

Jawa Barat   177

Batukaras   177
Batuhiu   178
Pangandaran   178

Jawa Tengah   179

Jawa Timur   179

70K

With over a thousand kilometres of coastline in Indonesia's most populous, industrialized region, it is a surprise that so little has been photographed of or said about Java's central south coast. There is a smattering of quality set-ups along this coastline, but imposing cliffs and long distances in between the good spots have discouraged surf travellers. There's a mixture of volcanic black sand beach, and calcareous coral fringed varieties, many of which face straight on into wind and swell, creating huge expanses of closed out carnage.

Jawa Barat - the rest

JAVA

Outside of the Cimaja / Turtles area, the western **Jawa Barat** province is a secretive place. Dry season lefts of quality are rumoured at **Ciponkong** south of Bandung, as well as in the area of **Sadatau**, 40km east. Beyond Bayah, the very western tip of the province has been surfed by charter groups on their way to Panaitan, giving names to some of the waves.

Batukaras

Batu Karas is well signed west from Pangandaran, and the jungle point is easy to find.

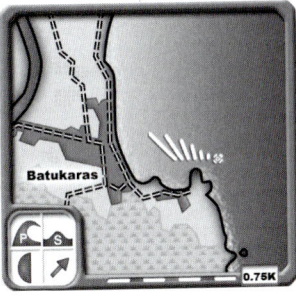

A fun, easy right-hand point-break that makes a change from the norm. The wave here ambles in over a mostly sand bottom for 100-200m, and is great for beginners and long-boarding. Ideal wind would be a rare south-westerly, so it is often cross or on-shore here unless you get up early. A mellow laid-back town with good cheap accommodation and great food...something different. Limp beach-breaks either side too.

Pangandaran

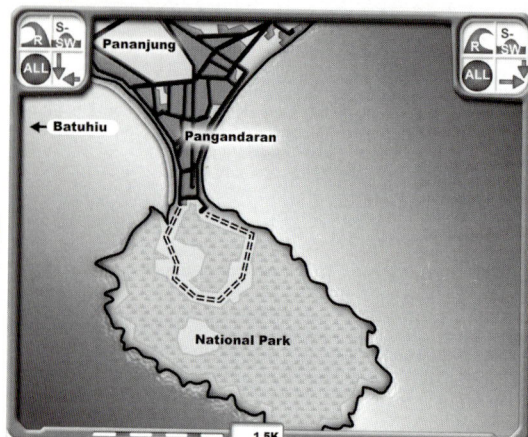

Pangandaran is a fun if tired resort town half way between Bandung and Yogyakarta. It is not worth the trip if it is surf and only surf you need. Roads are easy and there are also buses and trains from both cities.

There are low quality beach-breaks on both sides of the isthmus. To the east, very rare peaks can pop up near the park, and wind affected river mouth banks work towards **Karangsari**. On the west side, **Batuhiu** has a mellow beach with some lefts in the corner. Heading towards Batukaras, **Cijulang** has a rivermouth where a spit of sand faces east offering early morning or wet season potential. The peninsula itself is a forested national park with a series of small narrow beaches backed by cliffs and bluffs, facing all directions. A permit is required to go beyond the tourist area at it's entrance, and tracks do not cover the whole area. One of it's best offerings is a left-hand reef break about a km hike west of the parking area, at the west point of the peninsula; worth investigating on middle tides and east trade winds.

Jawa Tengah

Jawa Tengah is Java's central province, centred on Purwokerto. **Cilacap**, south from Purwokerto, is an industrialized town and harbour with some polluted waves about. East of here at **Ajah** (reached via Gua Petruk), the black sand beach of **Pantai Indah Ayah** can get good. Around the huge headland at **Karangbolong**, the prized swallow-spit nests are harvested high on the cliffs for use in birds nest soup and other Chinese delicacies. Rights are not unknown on this side of the point. Running east from here, the coastline faces straight into the wind and is punctuated by river mouths of varying water quality, that are generally only really surfable on small swells and no-wind days. Around Yogyakarta, the beach town of **Krakal** has been surfed for years. It's white sand beach is hidden behind one of the only protective outcrops on this stretch of coast, and some good lefts can pop up. iNSEARCH Travel out of Western Australia have good experience here and run guided tours through this territory, see back.

Jawa Timur

Away from G - Land, the eastern province has probably the most uncharted surf in Java but, if you don't find waves there are unbelievable vistas of towering cliffs, volcanoes, and some of the most pristine forest. Surf trips through this province should be looked at as a cultural adventure rather than a military style assault targeting maximum surf time. The rewards are there in the form of unsurfed reefs and beaches, but there are absolutely no guarantees, and access to beaches is difficult.

Near the town of **Pacitan** is the secluded, pretty beach of **Ria Teleng**, at the head of a huge bay. It has been surfed. Craggy cliff lined bays stretch east from here, many of them very hard to access, but brimming with potential. The area south of Malang has a string of beautiful beaches around **Tambakrejo**, with basic accommodation and some potential. The intrepid can take the main highway east from Jember, and turn off after the Meru Betiri reserve towards **Sarungan**, where a series of bays offer good angles. Hard core only because it is beautiful, but very remote here.

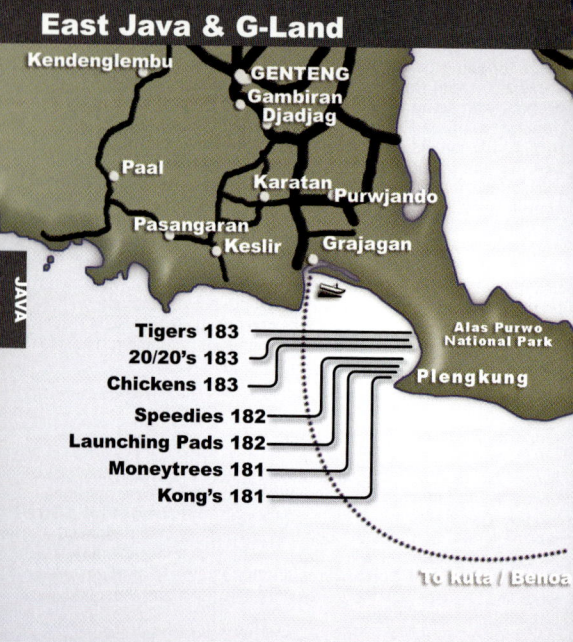

East Java & G-Land

Kendenglembu

GENTENG
Gambiran
Djadjag

Paal

Karatan
Purwjando

Pasangaran
Keslir
Grajagan

JAVA

Alas Purwo
National Park

Tigers 183
20/20's 183
Chickens 183

Plengkung

Speedies 182
Launching Pads 182
Moneytrees 181
Kong's 181

To kuta / Benoa

20K

G-Land

Located at Plengkung in the Alas Purwo Nature Reserve on the eastern tip of Java. **From Bali**: You can get a boat from Benoa Harbour or Kuta, and take the 3-or-more day return trip. The advantage of this is that you can check the swell and make a decision at short notice...if the camps have space. You can also get a seaplane from Benoa or fast boat from Kuta if you have the cash. The slowest, cheapest way from Bali is by ferry via Banyuwangi to Grajagan village, then a boat ride across the bay from there. Tour guides all over Kuta can arrange any of these for you, with easy options being via Bali based surftravelonline.com, or Australia based World Surfaris, who both have it wired. **Java Overland:** a *bemo* or major Javanese adventure drive to Grajagan followed by a boat ride. There are 2 main camps; Bobbys and G-Land Jungle. See our surf camp locator at the back for more details and phone numbers. You must book in advance.

Superlatives have been used about Grajagan since it was first discovered in the early '70's, and it has consistently justified it's reputation ever since. G-Land offers the most reliably perfect and power-packed left-hand barrels found. Like Uluwatu, it has a perfect position facing due west out of the trade winds, but it has more exposure to different swell directions, and is located adjacent to a 10km deep ocean trench so it has more power, and deeper, straighter, longer barrels.

Essentially 3 to 4 take-off zones, starting way outside on the outer point at **Kong's**, where some big, often unruly walls form up. Kong's can be quite whackable and approachable on it's day but is generally best surfed on low tide, light winds and a smaller swell. A 4 foot day with WSW swell in these conditions can see it barrel, but often it will be windy and uninviting. It's a fairly long walk and paddle or reef-hop, depending on tides. **Moneytrees**, the main take-off point, is across a useful channel from Kong's. A fast, extended, spit-filled barrel in anything from 2 to 10ft, it gets hairy on low tide with the coral table very close. Kicking out at the right time is essential as it is difficult, and the result of failure can be a good skinning. Mid tide

G-Land

sessions can deliver the best tubes of your life.

The next section, called **Launching Pads**, is an outside peak that can split the crowd. It can break a long way out the back and is generally firing if Money's is closing out. It is also the outer take-off for G-Land's most spectacular barrel provider; **Speedies. Speed Reef** is an appropriately named, shallow, heavy barrel for 150m or more at the end of the G-land reef set-up. On a big south pulse (preferably over 6ft), it wedges on take-off and bends into an ever-accelerating race for the exit. The barrel is often perfect for over 100yds, and has enormous energy and roundness. Lower tides are hazardous with the reef never far under fin.

All the sections change with the tide, and big days mean current and a permanent paddle. The reef is sharp, and there are coral snakes, urchins, even the odd shark (no recorded attacks).

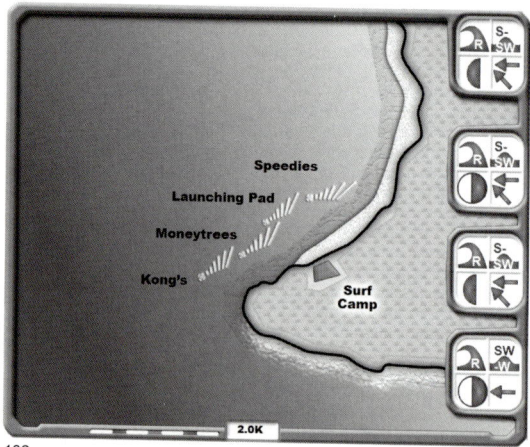

G-Land's other waves

On large days, **Chickens**, down the beach, can be a good warm-up wave; it will be smaller and more fun with some low tide barrels possible. Further along still, **20/20's** is a pretty good, quiet left-hand reef pass with a wedgy right next door. Again not a classic. **Tiger Tracks**, way further down, is a short fun right off the rocks.

On a macking south swell, early morning, **Tanjung Kucur** has a set of quality, very rare long rights. Ask your camp host how to get there because this is a major trek through the national park, and will more often than not be unrewarded.

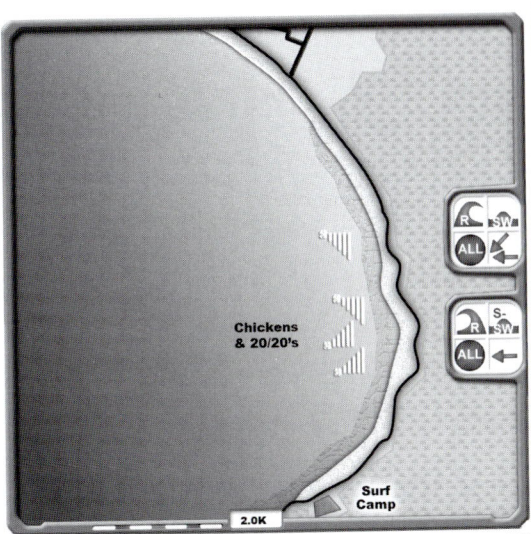

Lombok

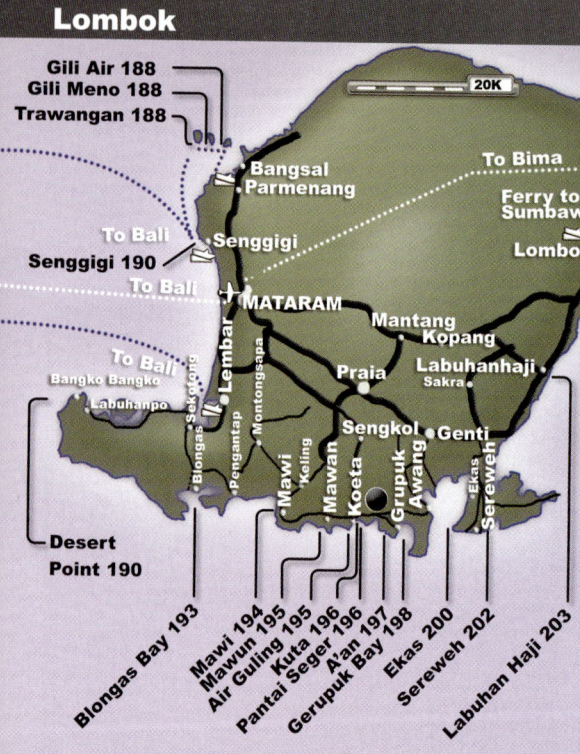

20K

Gili Air 188
Gili Meno 188
Trawangan 188

Bangsal
Parmenang

To Bima

Ferry to
Sumbaw

To Bali
Senggigi 190
To Bali

Senggigi

Lombo

MATARAM

Mantang
Kopang

To Bali
Bangko Bangko
Labuhanpo

Praia

Labuhanhaji
Sakra

Pengantap

Blongas Sekotong

Lembar

Montongsapa

Sengkol

Genti

Mawi

Koling

Mawan

Koeta

Grupuk
Awang

Ekas

Sereweh

Desert
Point 190

Blongas Bay 193
Mawi 194
Mawun 195
Air Guling 195
Kuta 196
Pantai Seger 196
A'an 197
Gerupuk Bay 198
Ekas 200
Sereweh 202
Labuhan Haji 203

Lombok Surf Data

Where

A stone's throw from Bali, Lombok rises majestically and suddenly out of the Indian Ocean. It sits between 8 and 9 degrees south, in the centre of the southern tropical trade-wind belt. This western most island of Nusa Tenggara is the beginning of the dry side of Indonesia; you'll notice that the forested landscapes give way to arid scrub. The whole deal is 80 by 80 km. Ferries and planes go from Bali, and the main airport, Mataram on the west coast, is well connected to most big Indonesian towns. It's in an ideal position for quick boat trips from Bali.

Background

Lombok is in some ways a flash-back to Bali in the 70's. It is considerably less developed for tourism, and has nothing like the volume of food and accommodation options. Apart from these obvious parallels, the comparisons falter. The population on Lombok is 90% Sasak, an ethno-cultural group sharing characteristics and beliefs with Javanese and Sumbawanese. People are very friendly, often surprising visitors with their generous hospitality, although you will not always find the universal openness to Westerners that sets Bali apart. The scenery is breathtaking; Mount Rinjani dominates the entire island, and the laid-back Gilis off the west coast have incredible diving and pristine beaches. The semi arid bays of the south coast, such as Selong Belanak, are an unforgettable backdrop to a surf session.

The Setup

Lombok's surf-rich south coast is a craggy stretch that offers enough angles to cater for both dry and wet-season wind directions. Whilst swell supply to some name breaks is not in ready supply, it's unlikely you'll go more than a few days without some form of rideable wave. Most breaks are coral reef based, and very much influenced by tide. Many of the best waves are in deeply recessed bays, requiring considerable refraction. A craggy bathymetry along the south coast results in waves funneling into unlikely places. The Lombok Strait,

Lombok Surf Data

running up the west coast, is an extremely deep bottle-neck of water, which is why currents here can be extremely strong between tides. Full moon surfing at mid tide Desert Point for example, can be an Iron Man's challenge. Beaches are mostly white calcarious sand, and among the most beautiful in Indonesia.

The Waves

Indian Ocean power reaches Lombok's south coast with similar intensity to Bali's southwest coast, yet there are waves here for all levels. Experiences vary from the hollow, critical and challenging Desert Point, to fat, fun Grupuk Bay rights. There are great waves on the east and west coasts too, but these are among the most fickle in the Indian Ocean. There is no predominance of lefts vs rights although the most famous wave here is the ultimate goofy foot experience.

Season

Typical trade-wind patterns prevail; east to southeast airflows in the dry season (May to September), and west to northwest in the wet (November to April). The south coast is most consistent in the dry season, but gets waves all year round. When wet season winds blow westerly, you'll find an array of reefs and right-hand points that will be perfect. The huge volcano and mountains of Lombok also assist between seasons, by giving some morning off-shores as the cool night air drops down and fans out. Lombok is a true year-round surf zone.

Crowds

Good waves are always crowded, but Lombok has been out of fashion in recent years. The south coast area around Kuta is a fairly quiet corner at the moment; if you spend a week or more there you will get some lonely sessions in. High season, from June to August, will witness crowds, and certain spots will get a sudden influx of boats at a given moment; it pays to be mobile, and to get up early.

Lombok Surf Data

Boards

Generally, your usual board plus 6 inches length, and 1/4 inch thickness, will cover most Lombok situations. Waves are hollow and straight, so the rhino chaser approach doesn't always pay off, tending to limit your position changes in the barrel, or even catch. If your short board is a 6'3'', then the ideal plan might be to take it along plus a 6'8 and a 7'2". Longboards are usable at many south Lombok breaks.

Hazards

Travelling around can be a challenge with, variable road quality around Bangko Bangko and the south coast. 4WD is a good option, and some roads are only passable by bike. Rip-offs are not uncommon around south coast surf spots. There have been episodes of aggressive behaviour from some locals. Some of these reports are apocryphal, but street-wisdom, diplomacy and caution are a must. The usual reef cut advisory stands, particularly at Desert Point. The odd shark is seen but no recorded attacks. The drier climate reduces the presence of malaria bearing mosquitoes, but check with your doc about prophylaxis before you go.

M	Swell Range		Wind Pattern		Air		Sea	Crowd
	Feet	Dir'	Am	Pm	Low	Hi	°C	
J	1-6	S-SW	NW LO	NW MOD	25	30	27	LO
F	1-6	S-SW	NW LO	NW MOD	25	30	27	LO
M	2-6	S-SW	NW LO	NW MOD	25	30	27	MED
A	2-8	S-SW	SE LO	SE MOD	25	30	27	MED
M	2-8	S-SW	SE LO	SE MOD	25	30	27	HI
J	2-10	S-SW	SE LO	SE HI	25	29	27	HI
J	2-10	S-SW	SE LO	SE HI	24	28	26	HI
A	2-10	S-SW	SE LO	SE MOD	24	28	26	HI
S	2-6	S-SW	SE LO	SE MOD	24	29	26	HI
O	2-6	S-SW	NW LO	NW MOD	25	30	26	MED
N	2-5	S-SW	NW LO	NW MOD	25	29	26	LO
D	1-5	S-SW	NW LO	NW MOD	25	29	26	HI

Gili Air, Gili Trawangan & Gili Meno

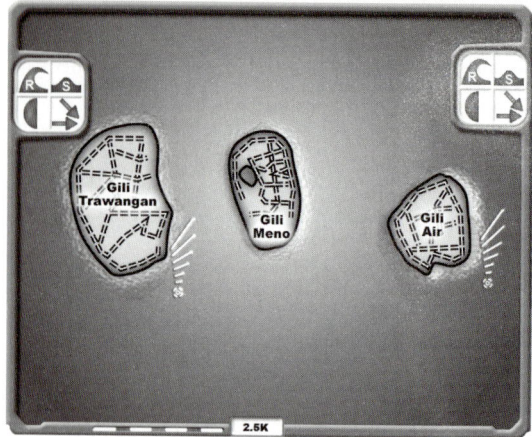

You can get a ferry from Bangsal, which is about 15km north of Senggigi but Bangsal isn't the nicest place, and negotiating the ride can be quite a mission even by Indo standards. The farthest island takes 30min. Ferries also leave from Senggigi; a longer route but ultimately easier. There's also a fast Cat from Benoa on Bali; check the Bounty Bar in Kuta for bookings.

These 3 islands, inaccurately referred to as "The Gili Islands" offer fantastic snorkeling and a laid-back, fairly basic, but idyllic setting for travellers. *Losmen* (cheap accommodation) litter the beaches and you can get very well-priced seafood from the many *warungs* (food stalls). Topless is bathing is an added bonus...or embarrassment.

Gili Air has a fickle right-hand point reef working in massive south-southwest swells and west to northwest winds. It's a long, per-

Gili Air, Gili Trawangan & Gili Meno

fectly combed, fun yet hollow wave if on. It can get critical. Worth a look if you are touring or diving here, but those who make the trip without doing the maths will be disappointed. All levels. 2-6ft. AKA **Perama**.

The next island west is **Gili Meno**, where you can stroll the *losmen* lined eastern beach to it's southern end for some surf discovery on very big southwest swells. Again, extremely inconsistent but pretty.

Gili Trawangan, the westernmost island, isn't known for waves but if Desert Point is in the 10ft plus range there can be a very long, very hollow, challenging right-hander off the southeast reef, and other secret options . It needs major tides, a massive south-southwest swell and preferably norwest winds; a rare combination indeed.

At worst you will have a mellow time on land, some excellent snorkeling and plenty of tripped-out back-packers to talk to. There are reports of girls getting hassled here and it's worth noting.

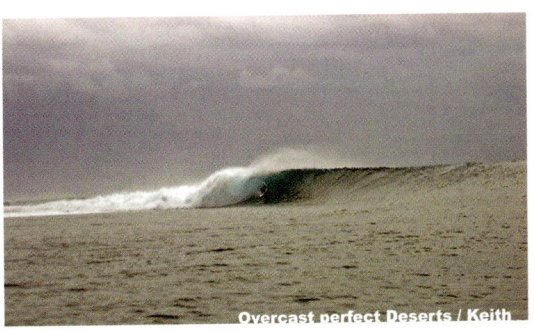
Overcast perfect Deserts / Keith

Senggigi

Bemo from Mataram Airport to this resort area, 6km north of town. Ferries direct to Senggigi from Bali. Head for the Sheraton Hotel.

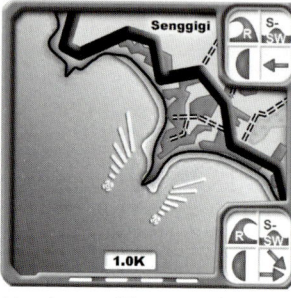

On a major SW swell, a long hollow left-hander can reel in and bend around the reef, with several barrel sections if winds are west. Rarely big, and often flat, but not too crowded. Mid tide best, low very shallow. All levels. Inconsistent. Right-hander round the corner that draws more swell but gets blown out by trade-winds. There are some semi secret left handers of real quality up towards Bangsal.

Desert Point

From Mataram, take the coast road south about 15km to Lembar (or ferry 3.5 hours there from Padangbai in Bali). Then coast road 3 hours via Sekotong and Pelangan, where the road becomes a holey nightmare. West to Bangko Bangko where the road ends, and walk round the point. 4WD essential.

When Desert Point is on, it might be the best left-hander in the world.

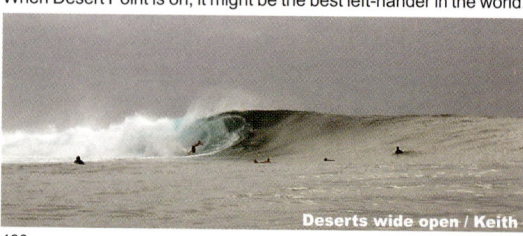

Deserts wide open / Keith

Desert Point

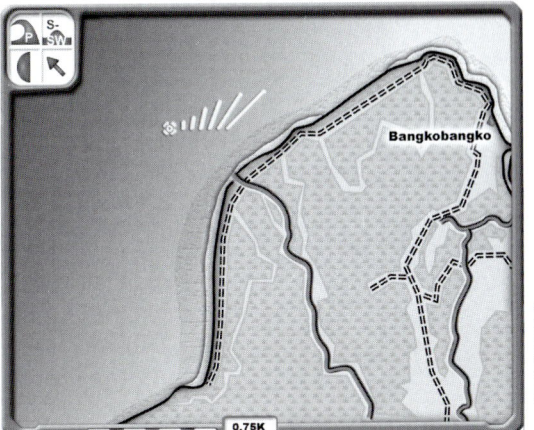

Surfers have camped out here for months waiting for the right conditions, enduring basic conditions and boredom in the hope of catching the day of days. For this to happen, rock-solid south-southwest swell, easterly wind, and low to middle tides (low is super-shallow, high doesn't seem to line up) are needed. The top of the point is a hectic but relatively predictable take-off contested with many others, leading into a hollow, barrelling section that just goes on and on. Convex refraction makes the wave jack up and accelerate as you progress down the line, with the barrel holding all the way to the end, which can dump onto exposed reef, particularly on low tide.

4-6ft is generally acknowledged to be the best size for barrels and length, with 8ft plus being hard-core. Advanced unless very small on a higher tide. Low tide is awesome but for experts only. Around the north side of Bangko Bangko are islands that can yield good waves if swell is massive.

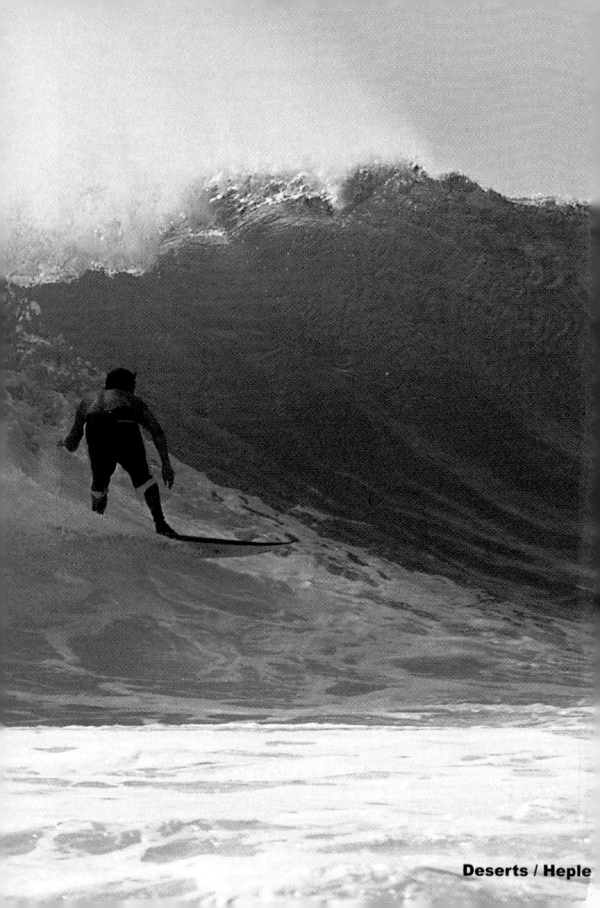

Deserts / Heple

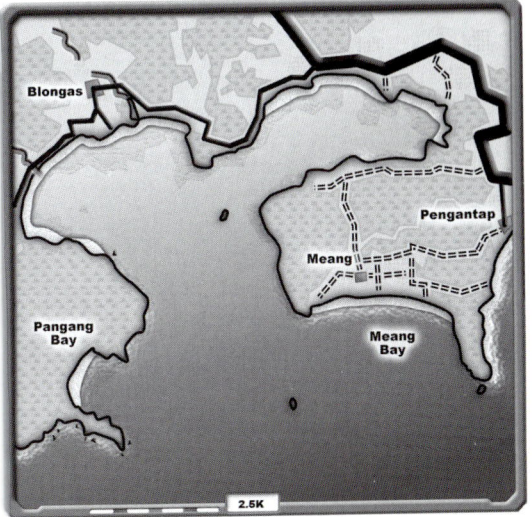

From Lembar, head south to Sekotong, and south again towards Sepi where the road hits the bay and splits. For west side, turn off right down horrid track with awesome views, to Blongas. There's a 4WD track to the right, then walk. For east side, stop before Blongas.

The west side of Blongas Bay inside Cape Pangga, has a wet season, R point break working through the tides on solid SW-S swell. The east side, accessed via Sepi and a major trek, has a classic left-hander working in southeast to east winds and preferably a south-southwest swell. Theres also a bommie peak out in the middle. Remote, beautiful, semi-consistent and adventurous. Sharks known to frequent here, with 1 recorded attack.

193

Mawi

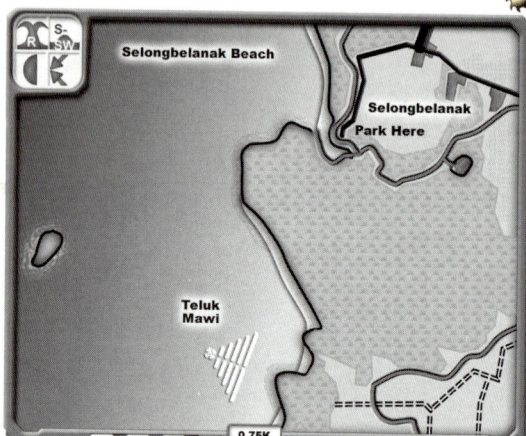

Selongbelanak Beach

Selongbelanak
Park Here

Teluk
Mawi

0.75K

About 7km West from Kuta (3km past the "MTM66" sign), take sealed turnoff L, for 2km (the tarmac stops half way). Pay the dudes at the houses to watch your car, and hike a few 100m to the beach. When you see a little camel-like island off-shore; you know you are there.

Consistent left and right-hand reef breaks in an awesome bay, sucking in more swell than many Lombok breaks. Mawi's reef can throw up dry season barrels to rival anywhere, with lefts on big swells and any tide (shallow on low however, but if big it's fine), and rights on smaller days, starting to work as the tide rises towards mid. High tide isnt a good time to be here. Rips can cause panic, especially on large days, and the end sections (especially on the rights) can dredge or just shut down and swat the unwary. Crowded 1 day, empty the next. Always pay somebody to look after your stuff. All levels, and a good bet in any season as long as winds are light. Different swells and tides open up different waves.

194

Mawun

From Kuta, take a 15-minute drive west to the bay. It's off the road just after the "MTM 66" sign.

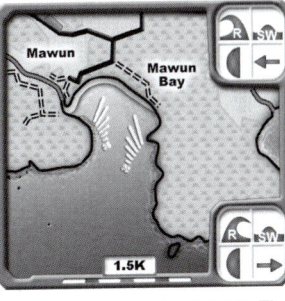

Awesome beach with reef-fringed points at either end. West end has a punchy, lined up right-hander good in the early mornings or in wet season. The east end has a shorter, pretty lame left protected by cliffs, which tries hard in dry season easterlies. Both breaks draw a fair amount of swell and are pretty dependable. The short trip to find them is a low-risk investment given the beauty of the setting. All levels, but advanced if big or low tide.

Air Goleng

West from Kuta. Look out for "MTM64" sign after 2km, then about 1km to a left down a dirt track (bike or walk only). 2km to Air Goleng village (which has many spellings). Boat access recommended from Kuta, 25 min trip.

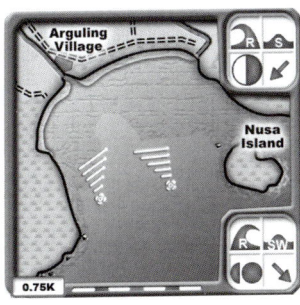

Fun right-hand reef break in an out of the way setting, that can hold some good size. Lower tides generally best and a little more hollow, with an accelerating inside section. Best surfed early mornings if possible because the wind will not be too kind to it. All levels. Uncrowded as not highly regarded. Hollow yet shifty lefts next door can be OK on higher tides.

Kuta

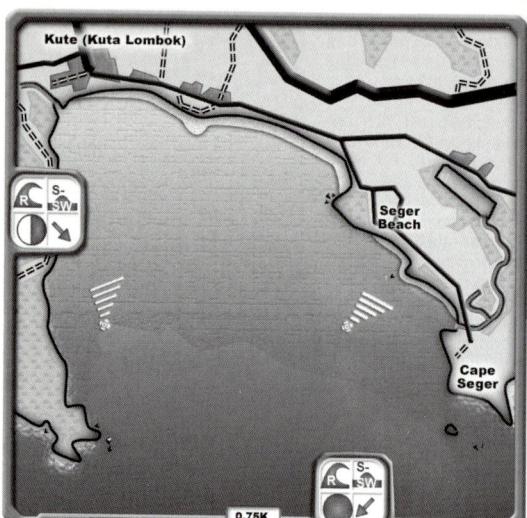

The surf hub / fishing village of Kuta is best reached from Mataram via Praya, or Ferry from Bali to Lembar and again via Praya.

While Kuta is the perfect base camp for South Lombok, It's waves are dreadful in most conditions, with southeast trade-winds making a mess of it. The bay has reef lefts and rights at either end, with straight-handers in the middle. The Rights at the right side of the beach can be good in wet season northwesterly winds. A km or so east lies the exposed, beautiful **Pantai Seger**, where Reef / beach rights of moderate quality and length can hold up to about 6ft on the right day, opposite the Novotel. Despite it's "Vin Ordinaire" status it magnetizes more swell than anywhere else nearby. It can barrel too. All levels, fun spot, mellow. Go early a.m.

A'an

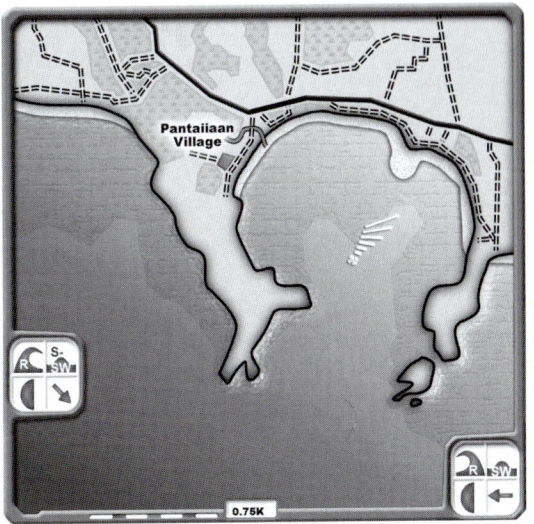

East from Kuta, for just over 4km. Cross the bridge. After another km, just before a tiny creek, take the sealed road to the right for PantaiA'an village & a round protected bay with a rocky outcrop in the middle; it is off this point.

Awesome R that works on most tides, preferring east winds. Barrels always possible, with low tide being very hollow, fast and (too) shallow. Lefts also work on opposing wind, and can sometimes represent equal barrel excellence on the right day. 2-8ft. Advanced, inconsistent spot requiring S swell in generous quantities, and the willingness to get up early. this is one of the few spots around Kuta where a whiff of "localism" can be felt so be cool & careful.

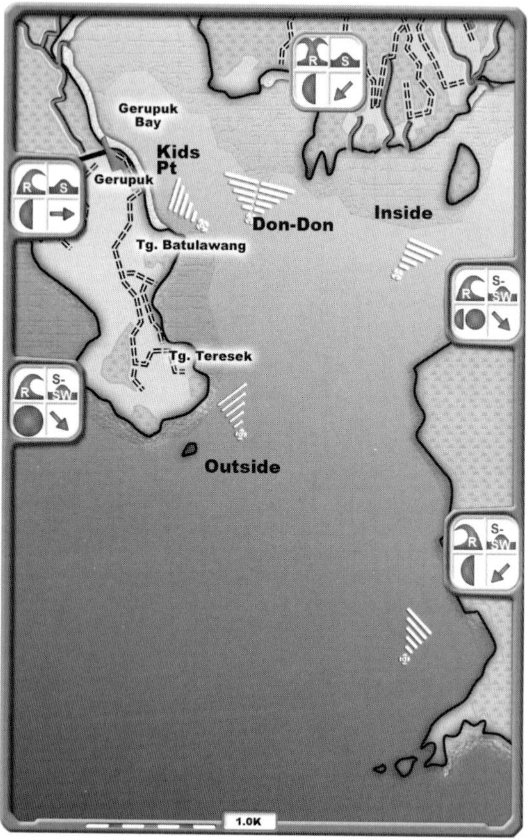

LOMBOK

Gerupuk Bay

Kids Pt

Gerupuk

Tg. Batulawang

Don-Don

Inside

Tg. Teresek

Outside

1.0K

Grupuk Bay

From Kuta, east via PantaiA'an (see previous page) to the village of Grupuk, about 9km in all. Fishing boats can be hired to take you for a look at each of the waves this bay has to offer. This is the recommended option. Known for its fun, fat, sometimes large right, Grupuk hosts a smorgasbord of waves on it's inner and outer reefs.

Outside rights lie off the dramatic headland whose hilly topography inspires the occasional name "Big dipper". Another local name for it is Gili Golong. The set-up here can hold serious size, and does often get very large indeed because it is more exposed than a lot of spots. Barrels are not the speciality here, but the big drops and wide shoulders are an experience, as is the setting. 3-10ft. Needs high tide. Experienced surfers. Consistent. Across the bay at the opposing headland is a major left-hander that isn't often surfed, as it is low quality.

A commonly surfed right-hander, **Insides**, (aka Perigi) peels down the coral reef pass opposite Perigi Island. It needs a very solid south-southwest swell for it to fire, and mid tide. If it's on it'll be the first wave you see when you get to Grupuk. 2-6ft. Intermediates. Inconsistent. Small days can see lefts here too. Again on the inside, soft rights can break on the reef at the village beach at **Kid's Point** as well as another rare inner right point for beginners. These protected waves need a very big swell, preferably from the south.

The main wave however, is the right-hander (with lefts off the peak) out near the middle of the bay. AKA **Don-Don**, It's essentially a fun set-up with a slow-peaking take-off and relatively fat long wall, whatever the size. Any level of surfer can get into this wave, and it works well from mid through to high tide. Semi-consistent spot that can get pretty crowded. The lefts can get good.

All levels. Surf early and avoid crowds. The relatively forgiving waves here encourage some classic bad surfing, so watch the flying boards. You can eat seafood on the beach at Grupuk village, making this a good day-trip destination away from Kuta. If it's not big enough for Tanjung A'an next door, many surfers will make the quick trip across to this more consistent area, thus meaning that small days are busiest here.

LOMBOK

Ekas Village

Awang Village

← Gerupuk & Kuta

Ujungbatu Point

0.75K

Ekas

Head to Awang, about 15km due east from Kuta, on one road all the way to the end. You can hire fishing boats to the breaks from here. It's possible to get a boat straight to the surf from Grupuk too. This is a wise choice if it's small, because you can just continue on around the point towards **Sereweh** and check the whole set-up on that side too while you're at it. It also allows you to side-step the pretty bad roads. You can also drive via Keruak then turn south. This route means passing Ekas village and heading towards Sungkun. The main breaks are off the eastern cliffs, out towards the entrance of the bay.

Inside's is a quality, if sometimes fat, approachable right breaking over deep reef into a channel. It comes into it's own in between tides, when it's faster and gets a little more hollow. On higher tides the long left also works, and can be fun. Needs a reasonable ground-swell to negotiate the angles, and east winds. Crowds vary from none to busy. All levels.

Outsides, located nearer the outside point about a Km south of Insides, is the more challenging pVroposition; an unpredictable left-hander that can yield some very, very long, heavy walls, and the odd barrel. High tide and solid southwest swell generally best. All levels but caution because far from civilisation. Crowds can vary from a totally empty line-up to 4-boats-in-the-bay madness...luck of the draw. Some heavy currents when bigger. Sharks have been seen but no recorded attacks.

If it's huge and winds are light, a cruise around the bay can have results. If both Insides and Outsides are flat, motor east round towards Sereweh. On the way to Seriwe Bay, are a series totally stunning beaches around the **Batudagong** and **Tabuan** areas, with a series of reef passes offering up lefts and rights. The pseudonyms of these breaks vary depending on who you talk to. The whole setup is often too big, presenting a big target to any available swell; If it is flat here, all the indications are that the whole of Lombok will be flat too. This south-facing coast is very exposed to winds so surf early or wet season.

Back inside the bay, up from Inside's you can find some beginners beach-break action on any tide or swell.

Sereweh

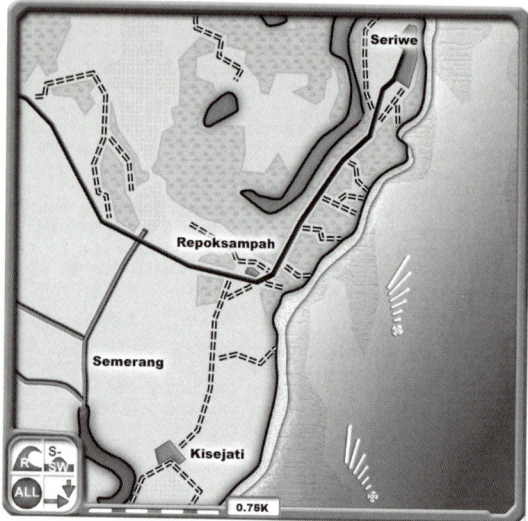

Seriwe

Repoksampah

Semerang

Kisejati

0.75K

A major excursion best taken from Mataram via Praya and turning right just before Keruak. Then take contorted roads south through Tutuk, Pemokong & Kaliantan. Head NE towards Sereweh village from here. Alternatively get a boat from Ekas or Awang.

Series of reef break (mostly) rights that are more exposed and consistent than Ekas. This whole set-up gets destroyed by most winds so best surfed early a.m. or between seasons. This is a hard-core place to get to, which usually means less crowds Remote. Advanced.

Labuhan Haji

At the end of the cross-island road from Mataram, via Narmada, and Masbagik. Labuhan Haji is a small port town, and so it is well sign posted and easy to find.

Several breaks run south along the black sand beaches. A series of right-handers dominate, requiring major swell wrap or a very south swell direction, and west or no winds. Rights also break near the port and there's a good lava reef pass north of the village.

Perhaps only worth an inspection if you are doing the overland route to Sumbawa's west coast breaks, as the ferry leaves from Labuhan Lombok just north of here. Inconsistent, but it can offer severely good quality and plenty of different, quiet peaks. 2-8ft. All levels. Subject to major currents if tides are big.

Beware rip-offs in the area, but it's a fun hangout all in all. The cattle market up the road at Selong is great mayhem on a Monday, and definitely not advised for vegetarians.

Labuaji

Sepolong

Repokbembek

Seliat

0.75K

Sumbawa

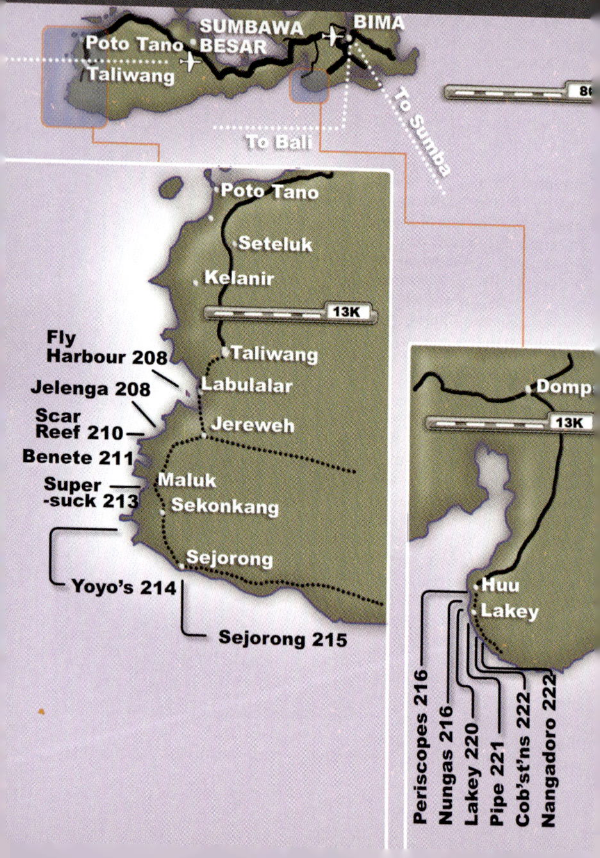

SUMBAWA BESAR

BIMA

Poto Tano

Taliwang

To Bali

To Sumba

8

Poto Tano

Seteluk

Kelanir

13K

Fly Harbour 208

Taliwang

Jelenga 208

Labulalar

Scar Reef 210

Jereweh

Benete 211

Super -suck 213

Maluk

Sekonkang

Yoyo's 214

Sejorong

Sejorong 215

Domp

13K

Huu

Lakey

Periscopes 216

Nungas 216

Lakey 220

Pipe 221

Cob'st'ns 222

Nangadoro 222

Sumbawa Surf Data

Where

Tightly slotted in between Lombok to the west, and Flores to the east, Sumbawa's 300km length twists west to east and lies in the epicenter of the southern trade-wind belt.

Background

If you're nostalgic about olden day Bali then the step back in time encountered on Sumbawa is for you. It's a rugged land, in part sparsely populated, with arid scrub and volcanos as a backdrop.

Transport

Transport is nonexistent outside the centres of Poto Tano (where the Lombok Ferry lands), and the airport towns of Sumbawa Besar and Bima. Horse drawn carts are common. One main road runs from the west (Taliwang) to the East, through the 2 main towns of Sumbawa Besar and Bima. The west coast and it's rich surf zones, is well serviced by road from Poto Tano to Sejorong, where it narrows then stops abruptly, leaving much of the south coast in a time warp.

East of Cempi Bay, there are pretty good roads servicing Hu'u and the Lakey peak area via Dompu. A road from Sumbawa Besar leads directly to Lunyuk, where you can take a gamble on some of the untapped surf resources around.

The Setup

The land mass is heavily influenced by volcanoes, and the coastline is mostly a series of large inlets and bays. Shallow lying coral flats, exposed at low tide, are the predominant sea bottom.

The two established areas are the west coast around Taliwang, and the Hu'u area, which also faces west out of the dry season trade winds. The swell window is just south of due west, to just west of due south, with the most penetrating swell coming from the southwest.

205

Sumbawa Surf Data

The Waves

Sumbawa surfing was put on the map when west coast breaks like Scar Reef and Supersucks were discovered and heavily surfed by boat. The waves here are fast, shallow reef-breaks with several well known lefts and some surprising rights. Lakey beach near Hu'u is the other hot spot, with luminaries like **Periscopes**, **Lakey Peak** and **Lakey Pipe**. These are busy waves during the season, with a host of accommodation options right on the spot. Again, mostly reef breaks of an advanced, though some would say slightly less intimidating nature. In between the two, horrendous road conditions (or no roads at all) have kept surf invasion at bay for now.

Seasons

April to September is the best time to get off-shore conditions on most Sumbawa breaks, although mid season winds are heavy in the afternoon. There is also a trade-off between consistency and population; April and May can be inconsistent. From June onwards the swell is more likely to crank but the place is often overrun. Flat spells are never to be ruled out; it's fair to say that some of the better spots here are less consistent than many Sumatra or Java breaks.

Crowds

As mentioned, mid season can be horribly crowded at Lakey. The west coast is more of a lottery because surfers often arrive by boat, meaning 1 day empty, the next full-on Californian summer.

Hazards

Bumpy roads. Some hassle near the mines at Maluk and around the west coast. It is common for groups of young men to carry machetes in Sumbawa, although not intended as an attack weapon. No major critters although the pythons are enormous, and Komodo Dragons intimidating. Most sharks are reef varieties that are harmless. Some malaria if rains are heavy. Usual reef cut advisory applies.

Boards

See Bali section; the same rules apply. You need something that can handle barrels. Board repair is available at Lakey although not exactly cheap or of good quality....bring spares if you can. Extra leashes are essential, as there are no surf shops although you might luck out with a block of wax etc. at your accommodation.

M	Swell Range		Wind Pattern		Air		Sea	Crowd
	Feet	Dir'	Am	Pm	Low	Hi	°C	
J	1-5	S-SW	NW LO	NW MOD	25	30	27	LO
F	1-5	S-SW	NW LO	NW MOD	25	30	27	LO
M	2-6	S-SW	NW LO	NW MOD	25	30	27	MED
A	2-8	S-SW	SE LO	SE MOD	25	30	27	MED
M	2-8	S-SW	SE LO	SE MOD	25	30	27	HI
J	2-8	S-SW	SE LO	SE HI	25	29	27	HI
J	2-10	S-SW	SE LO	SE HI	24	28	26	HI
A	2-10	S-SW	SE LO	SE MOD	24	28	26	HI
S	2-6	S-SW	SE LO	SE MOD	24	29	26	HI
O	2-6	S-SW	NW LO	NW MOD	25	30	26	MED
N	2-5	S-SW	NW LO	NW MOD	25	29	26	LO
D	1-5	S-SW	NW LO	NW MOD	25	29	26	MED

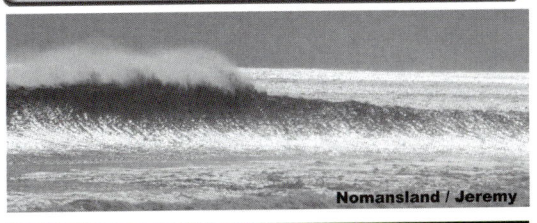

Nomansland / Jeremy

Fly Harbour

From Poto Tano, head to Labuhan Lalar, or Fly Harbour. The fishing village has a rivermouth.

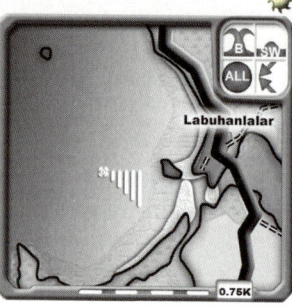

Fun beach-break needing very large swell to work. Mostly rights. Flies is worth checking as part of a trip down the coast, if not necessarily a worthy destination in itself. All levels. Poor water quality. 2-6ft. All levels. On the way down from Poto Tano, if there is a huge south swell, the inconsistent but super hollow **Northern Rights** might merit a check, although you are more likely to stumble across other waves on the way than catch it on the right day.

Jelenga

From Taliwang, head south to Jereweh then Jelenga. Right hand end of beach.

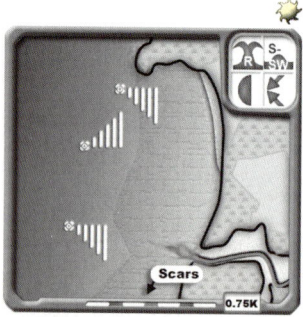

Series of reef peaks working consistently to provide a release when Scar Reef, just opposite, isn't working or is too small. Peaky lefts and rights on any tide. Might not be classic when compared to the name breaks, but all levels of ability are catered for, and it can pull some quality out of the drawer on the right day. 2-8ft. Consistent.

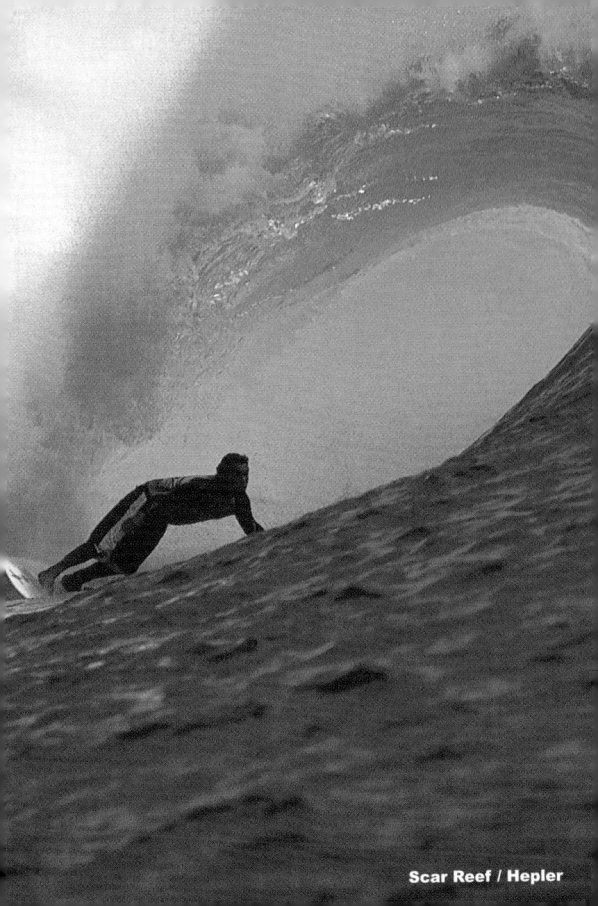

Scar Reef / Hepler

Scar Reef

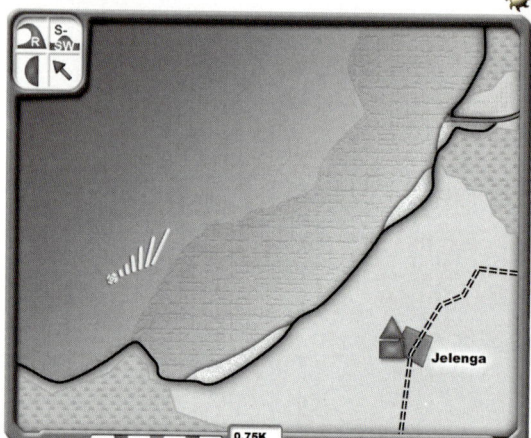

SUMBAWA

From Taliwang, head south to Jereweh and then Jelenga, a total of about 17km. The reef is out the back here opposite the main village area.

An apt name for a grinding left-hander over extremely shallow, sharp reef. The perfection of the barrels entices one to take risks, as the very steep take-off leads straight into the tube. On a good 3-5ft day it is a precision shaped, predictable ride, but the end section has exposed coral. Low to mid tide generally holds the best shape, but water depth at low is minimal and falls will result in a scraping.

You can stay right on the beach at the Jelenga Beach Bungalows. Semi consistent. Advanced.

Benete

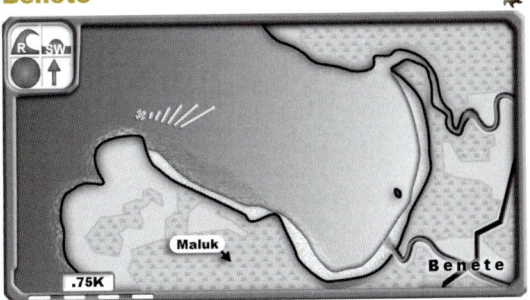

From Taliwang, head to Jereweh. Another 10km or so to the south is the village of Benete, at the head of a deeply recessed bay. Trek to the left headland.

A heavy but rare left-hand reef break for good surfers. the peak is shifty, the take-off concave, and barrels are likely. Consequences are severe if you do not make it. The spot needs a major southwest swell to negotiate the Alas Strait and wrap almost 180 degrees into the bay, but it is a good check if Scar Reef is getting crowded or big and hairy. Advanced.

SUMBAWA

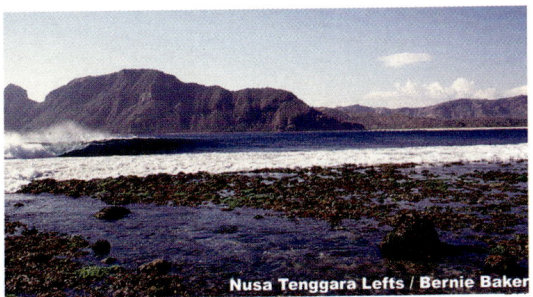

Nusa Tenggara Lefts / Bernie Baker

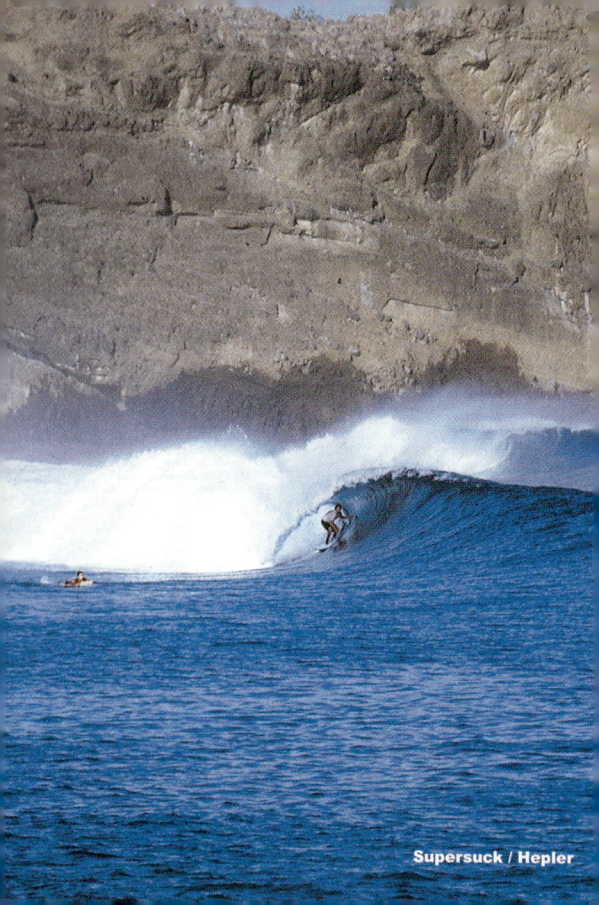

Supersuck / Hepler

Supersuck

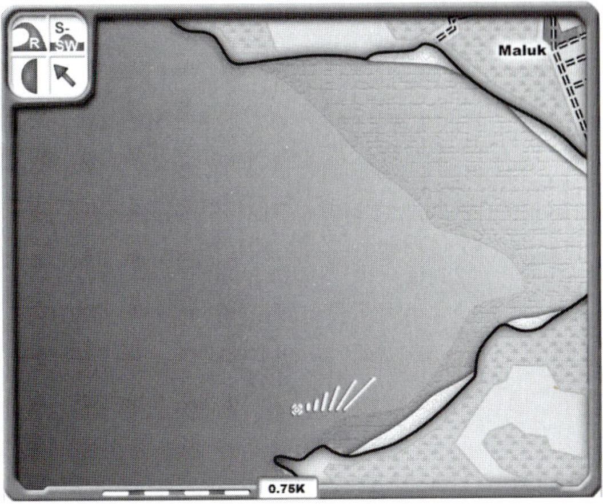

Head through Taliwang south to Jereweh, and about 12km south again to the small town of Maluk. Supersuck, the wave, is located across the bay from the village.

Classic dry season left hand barrel over shallow table reef. Dangerous end section has scraped the skin off many, but the barrels keep the devout coming back. Less consistent than Scars, but a perfect wave when on. Local fishermen have been known to virtually pirate visiting boats, and unemployed youths attracted to the local mine have sometimes robbed unwary land based surfers. Advanced.

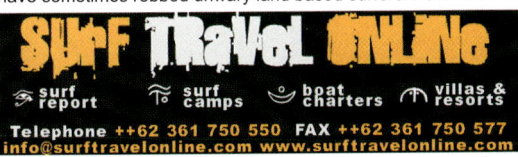

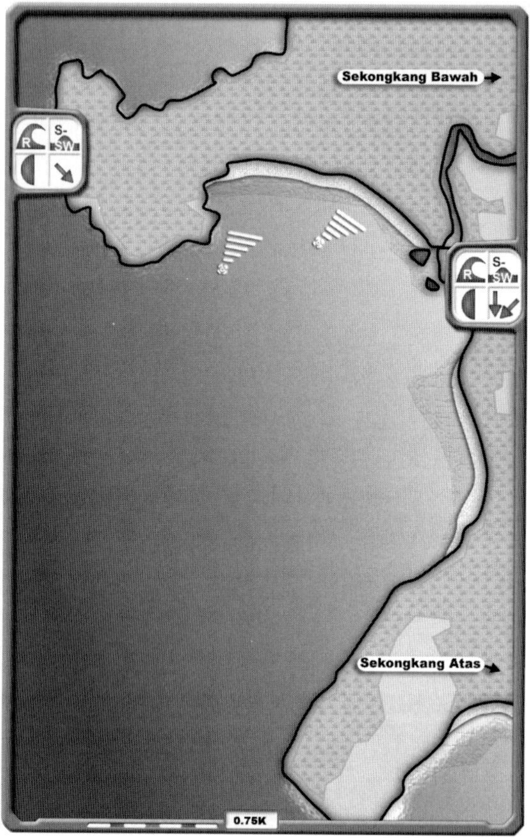

Sekongkang Bawah →

Sekongkang Atas →

SUMBAWA

0.75K

Yoyo's

From Taliwang, head south to Sekongkang Bawah.

Yoyo's has an array of consistent, medium quality surf spots that can be firing when elsewhere is flat. It's often the saviour for those who've sought out supersuck and found it dormant. The main right (aka The Hook) is a nice mid tide peak with possible barrels if there's no wind. Trade winds blow it out so best surfed early or opportunistically between seasons. There's also a good peak off the headland, approachable on take-off but famous for inside reef floggings. It's called The Wedge. Whatever the tide, you will usually find something here on small swells.

Sejorong

From Maluk, head south through Sekongkang Bawah. Go due south to Pantai Pisin where the road bends left. 6km to the village of Sejorong.

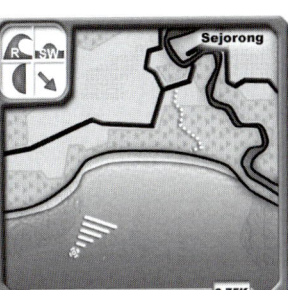

Consistent right-hand reef break that is more likely to be breaking than anywhere. It's draw-back is wind; any wind will destroy it so early morning off-shores or glass are the go. When on it is a very long right-hander. Currents are common, and it is often too big to ride. An intimidating, remote spot to surf and hard to get to overland. Pantai Pisin itself can have a worthy wave on small days with no wind, and Senutuk Bay, about 5km east of Sejorong, has a right-hand reef point that is hard to get to, but can be a rewarding adventure on northwest winds. Beyond here, the roads fizzle out making overland surf exploration very hard.

Periscopes & Nunga's

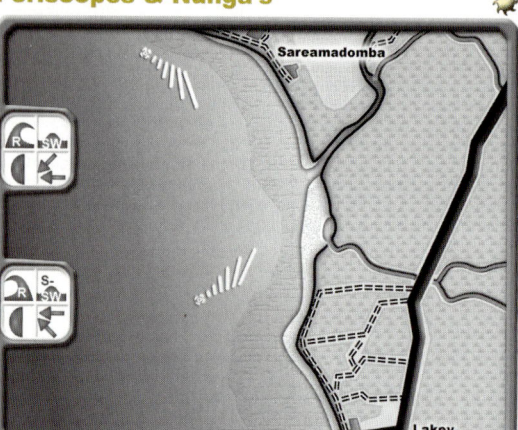

Off to the right of Lakey Peak, is another reef outcrop with a close-out wave called **Nomansland**. It's this reef that photographers perch on to bring you sunlit barrel shots of the peak. Right of this is **Nunga's**. Jump off here at low tide, or walk down the beach on high. L reef set-up with long walls and barrels possible if winds are light in the morning. Solid dry season trade-winds can mess it up. Low tide is shallow, with middle tides often best. Advanced.

Periscopes: A 20 min walk north-west from the Peak at Lakey. Magazine cover reef-break, complete with gaping barrels and a carveable shoulder at the end. Periscopes is the spot to check if Lakey peak is big; it might be 4ft and perfect if Lakey is 6-8ft. It gets slightly ragged in the east trade winds, with light northeast best. Less busy than the Peak due to the stroll required. Good channel to paddle out. This is a wave to respect although the take-off is not particularly bad relative to the hollowness. Not a consistent spot, but brilliant on it's day. 3-8ft. Advanced.

216

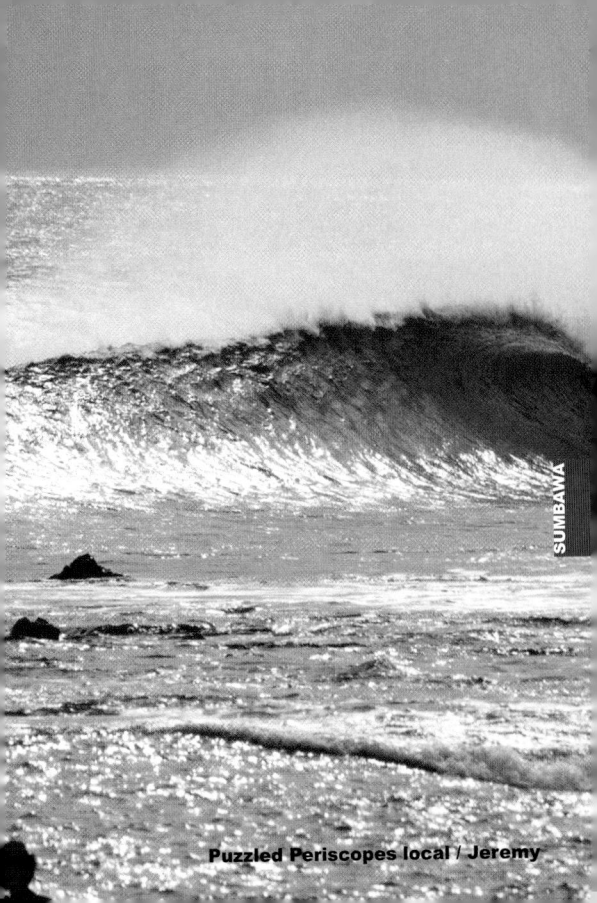

SUMBAWA

Puzzled Periscopes local / Jeremy

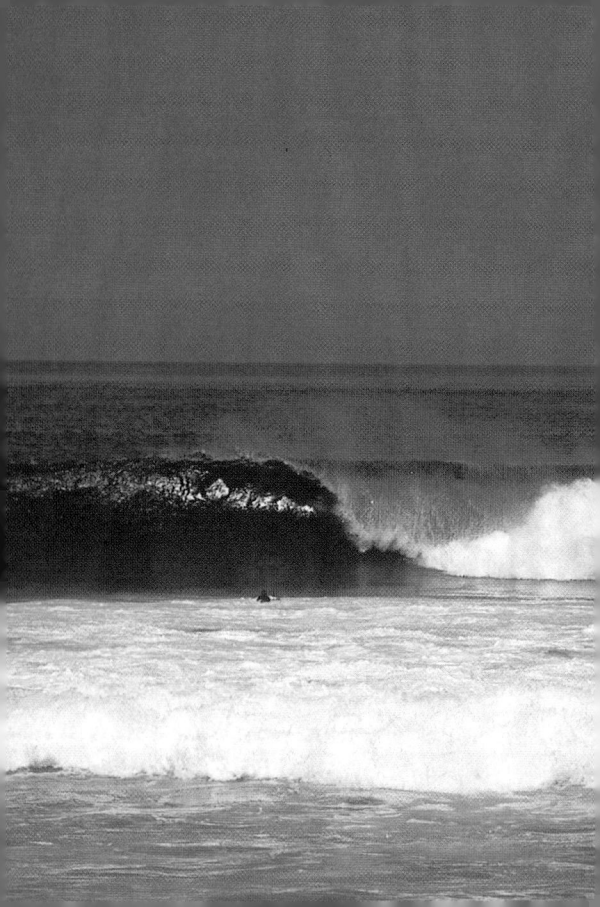

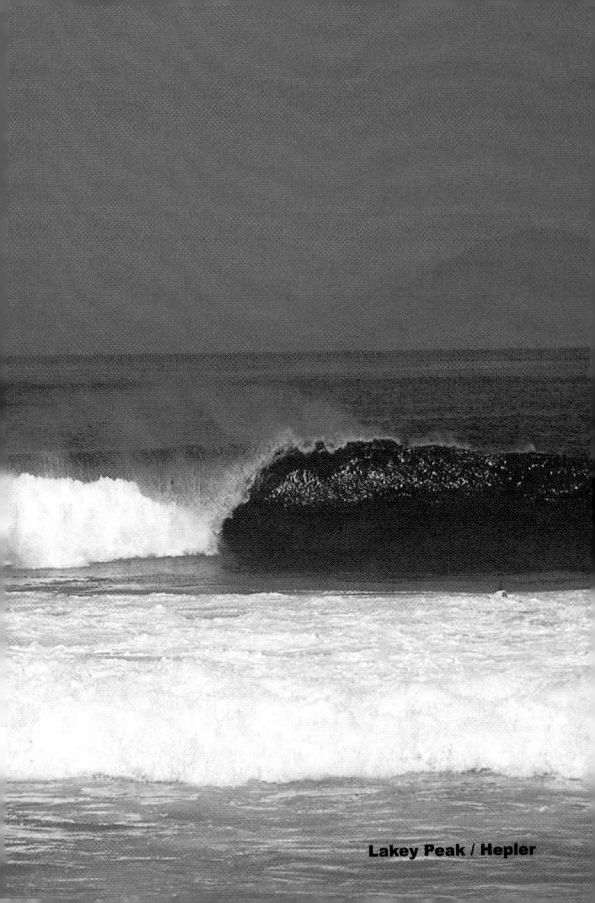

Lakey Peak / Hepler

0.75K

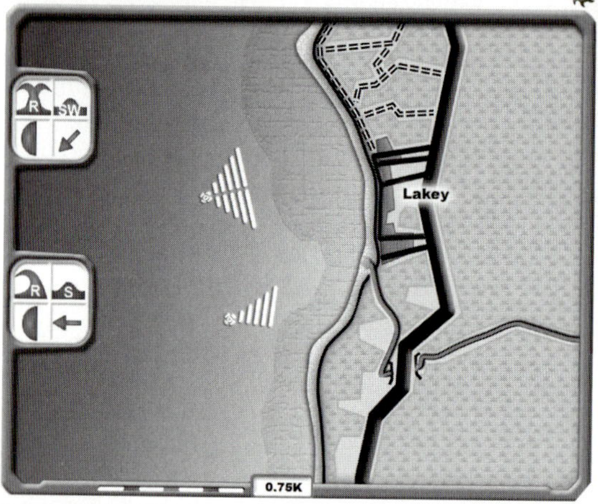

Lakey is the centre for surfing Hu'u area breaks like Periscopes and Nunga's. From Bima airport, you can hire a large *bemo* (taxi) all the way. The road takes you through the fishing village of Hu'u to the front at Lakey, where there are, at last count, 9 camps. The peak is out the front just to the left of Aman Gati (the smart air conditioned hotel), with the rickety judges tower just about still clinging to the reef.

Lakey Peak: "A" frame left and right reef peak. Whackable on a small high tide day with long left walls and a shorter right, the peak comes into it's own on low to mid tide with 4 ft plus swell. Then it becomes a snarling left-hand barrel that jacks up from the deep with genuine power. The wave breaks at perfect speed down the line but it is extremely sucky and hollow. The right off the peak is sometimes hard to finish as it bends in it's final section to make exits difficult. It'll hold up to about 10ft. At low tide you paddle across the lagoon, walk across the reef and time your jump off the edge. High tide in-

Lakey Peak & Pipe

volves some wading and more paddling. Can get horridly crowded, and there's nothing to do when flat. After a small or barren spell the vibe in the water can be aggressive.

Lakey Pipe: On the eastern side of the channel across from Lakey Peak; you can paddle it, or walk around the lagoon and across the reef (ouch!). Left-hand barrel machine at the edge of a steeply shelving reef teeming with sea-life. It may not break all the time, but if there's a wave here it will be barrelling even at 2 ft, with a steep take-off requiring accurate positioning. The wall, although not that long by Indo standards, is perfectly shaped all the way across. Worth sneaking across the channel if the Peak is crowded, and sneaking back again when everybody follows you. Advanced unless very small.

On absolutely huge days, long fun lefts break up the estuary at Hu'u itself, over sand and tidal flats. The Peak needs to be 10ft out of control. Beyond Hu'u are a few secret spots towards Jala, all needing very large swells from the southwest, and trade wind south easterly breezes. There are several fishing villages along the way so exploration up into this bay (Teluk Cempi) is an interesting excursion even if you don't score.

SUMBAWA

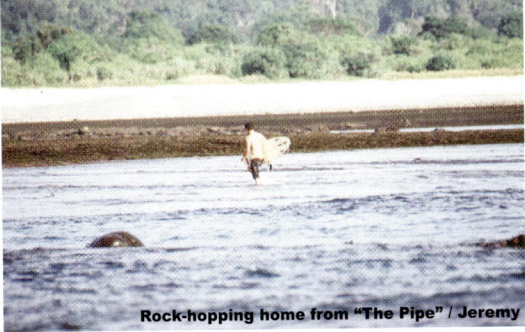

Rock-hopping home from "The Pipe" / Jeremy

Cobblestones

From Lakey, drive S and look for little sign on R, or walk the beach 3km. Wear shoes to get across rocks.

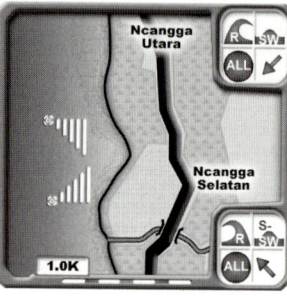

Right-hander that may not be a classic, but can be a lot less crowded than the peak, and often has some action when elsewhere is flat. It gets well lined up, if not as hollow as the peak. Southeast trades mess it up badly. If you look to the other point across the channel you will see some tempting looking left-handers too; they are often cleaner, if they are working. All levels. Don't bring valuables as it is remote and poor here.

Nangadoro

A 4km hike south from Cobblestones. The best method is to chat to your *losmen* guys about getting a ride on a truck; the breaks are half a km south of the village, through rice fields.

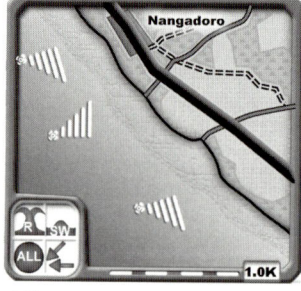

Rarely surfed reef peaks, the two rights and a left need no-wind days and smaller swell than The Peak itself. It's worth having a look here when main spots are very small. Another 3.5km south, after the 2nd bridge, are some more empty reef-break rights that are also good on small no-wind days; again, any trade winds and they are mush.

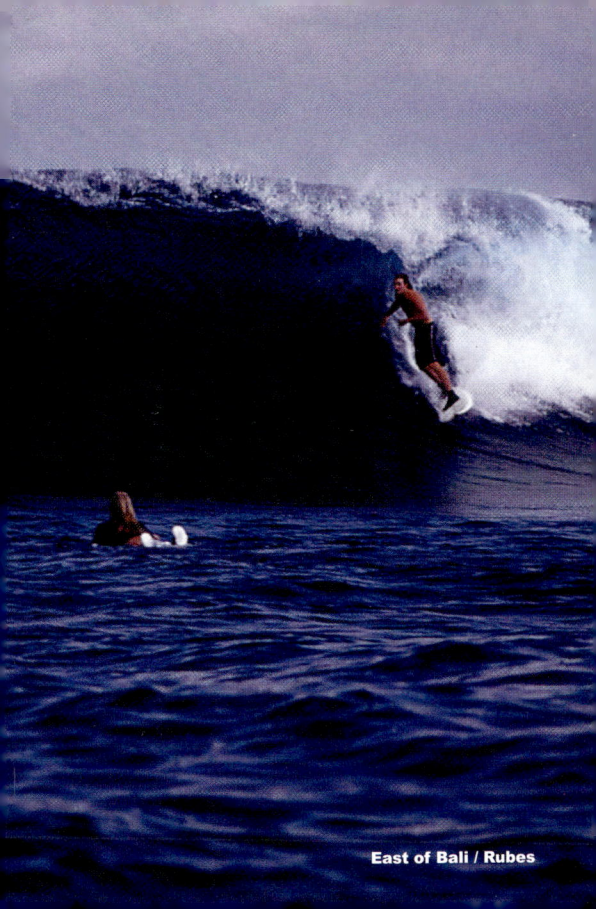

East of Bali / Rubes

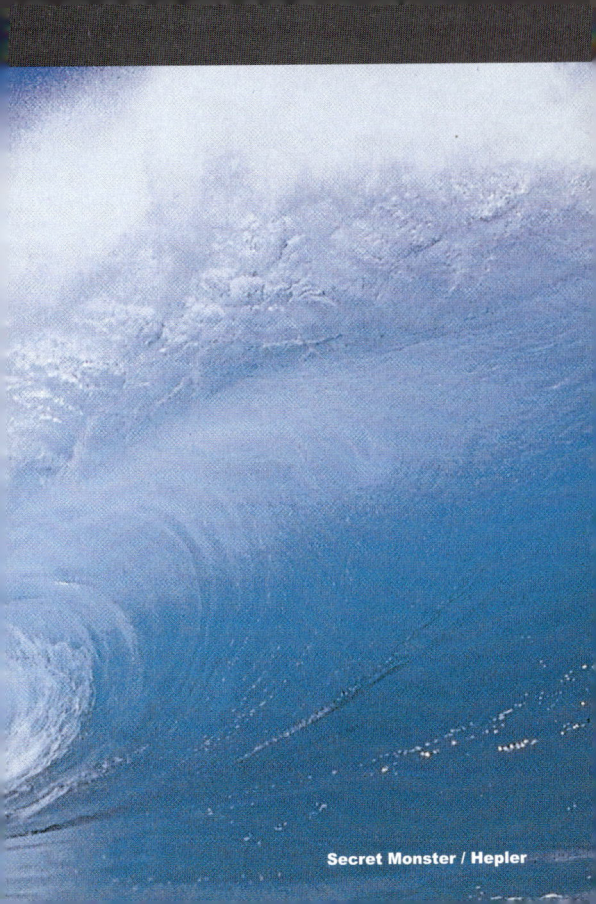

Secret Monster / Hepler

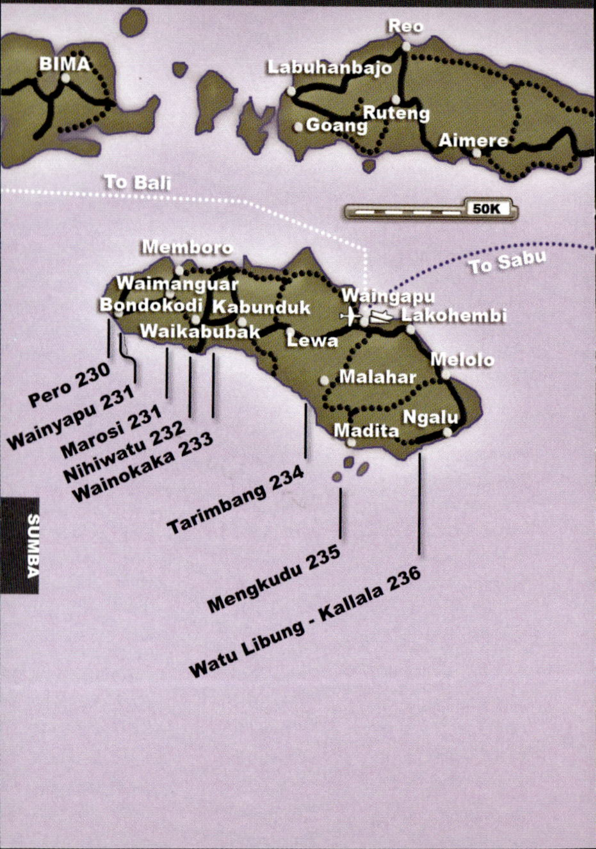

Sumba

BIMA

Reo

Labuhanbajo

Goang

Ruteng

Aimere

To Bali

50K

Memboro

Waimanguar

Bondokodi Kabunduk

Waikabubak

Waingapu

Lakohembi

To Sabu

Lewa

Melolo

Malahar

Ngalu

Madita

Pero 230

Wainyapu 231

Marosi 231

Nihiwatu 232

Wainokaka 233

Tarimbang 234

Mengkudu 235

Watu Libung - Kallala 236

Sumba Surf Data

Background

Some surfers say that the further east of Bali you travel, the more hard-core the set-up. In many ways Sumba bears this theory out. Years of isolation from Indonesia's mainstream religions and culture are one reason why myth and folklore surround the island's people and their ancient culture. Religious systems include Islam and Christianity, but traditional beliefs revolve around *marapu*, the ancestors and gods whose influence pervades everyday life. A good illustration would be the death of the Queen in 2003, when her four hand-servants were voluntarily entombed alongside her in their efforts to reach paradise.

The ancient *pasola* rites, enacted each year before planting season, involve mock fights between machete toting men on horseback with the deliberate slashing of man and horse intended to fertilize the soil with blood. In parts of Sumba, tribal rule holds more sway than any centralized law, and like most of Nusa Tenggara, life throughout the island is centred around the *kepala desa* or village leader.

Transport

For the overland surfer, Sumba is an extremely challenging proposition. Roads and transport are rudimentary. Outside of the few main towns, vehicle hire is impossible, and the word "taxi" irrelevant. Intrepid travellers can use some nouse and diplomacy to advantage however, negotiating rides with locals (keep those mid-size rupiah notes handy). Accommodation near surf spots is extremely limited, with a few exceptions. In certain areas it can be possible to carefully negotiate home-stay accommodation. It is customary to offer betel nut and or cigarettes (a second best in some locales) to the *kepala desa* when arriving in a village. If you follow this protocol, you will improve your chances of finding a place to stay.

In short, overland Sumba trips need to be planned unless you are staying at one of a few established surf-spots. If you aren't a seasoned traveller or prepared for adventure, either stay at one of the spots in the back of this book, on a pre-arranged basis, or go by boat. If you want to travel around Sumba looking for surf, you should at least arrange a guide. This can be done at the Hotel Merlin in Waingapu, or sometimes from the surf camp in Kallala. Negotiate your price clearly in advance to avoid a situation developing at the end of the trip.

The Setup & Waves

Sumba is out on it's own in deep ocean between latitudes 8 and 9 degrees south. The south coast is extremely exposed to most available swell, offering few contortions that could offer shelter from the raw power. The Sumba coast is less craggy than, say Lombok, and there are few islets and inlets, which means that it will often be huge across the whole coast with no hidey hole to find an easy surf.

The Java Trench runs close to shore, so swell arrives with full intensity on the mostly reef break setups. Perhaps the heaviest reef is located on the eastern tip at Pero. A more approachable point-break is the relatively accessible Tarimbang. East Sumba has one of the few genuine big wave spots in Indonesia, and a brace of quality dry season lefts. There are beach breaks too however, such as Pantai Marosi, and some excellent river mouths.

With the Mentawais being the current favourite of magazines, quite a few waves are going unridden out east. Tough but rewarding.

Seasons

Dry season (March to November). Trade winds blow southeasterly at this time, but strong winds can prevail for four or five days and then just die. On an average day, these trades don't kick in until 11 a.m. or later, and the strongest trades occur June through August. These mid-season trades are sometimes a wrecking ball to any spot, so it's generally a good idea to try to surf early morning at these times. Afternoon storms however, are not uncommon in the dry (or any) season, causing winds to veer to a new, potentially off-shore direction for a few hours and turning a break on for the lucky few who are there. With more chance of a solid southwest Indian Ocean ground-swell, this is the best season for waves on West Sumba.

Wet Season (November to March): Sumba's open ocean position means that swell is rarely is short supply for long. There are good wet season waves to be had in the southeast, as well as some out of the way gems off the small island of Mangkudu and it's neighbours. Tarimbang can also get good at this time.

Hazards

Currents and sneaker sets. Heavy, remote big waves far from help. Again it's a poor country so carry yourself well. Most potential situations can be avoided with careful diplomacy and common sense. Parts of West Sumba are pretty wild. Locals will be curious about you. Carry cigarettes and betel nut to help smooth your introductions to them. Whilst almost everybody you meet will be extremely friendly, and quite curious, situations can escalate quickly if you commit a *faux pas*. When travelling in remote areas, carry food and water supplies.

M	Swell Range		Wind Pattern		Air		Sea	Crowd
	Feet	Dir'	Am	Pm	Low	Hi	°C	
J	1-5	S-SW	NW LO	NW MOD	25	30	27	LO
F	1-5	S-SW	NW LO	NW MOD	25	30	27	LO
M	2-6	S-SW	NW LO	NW MOD	25	30	27	MED
A	2-8	S-SW	SE LO	SE MOD	25	30	27	MED
M	2-8	S-SW	SE LO	SE MOD	25	30	27	HI
J	2-8	S-SW	SE LO	SE HI	25	29	27	HI
J	2-10	S-SW	SE LO	SE HI	24	28	26	HI
A	2-10	S-SW	SE LO	SE MOD	24	28	26	HI
S	2-6	S-SW	SE LO	SE MOD	24	29	26	HI
O	2-6	S-SW	NW LO	NW MOD	25	30	26	MED
N	2-5	S-SW	NW LO	NW MOD	25	29	26	LO
D	1-5	S-SW	NW LO	NW MOD	25	29	26	MED

Pero

Head to the village of Bondokodi near the western tip
of Sumba. 2km down the
track to the rivermouth at
Pero. This one of the few
locations where you can
get accom and food near
the break.

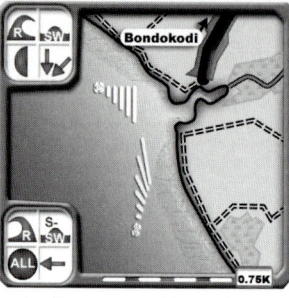

The Left: This long,
prodigiously curved reef
shapes a left that is hard-
breaking, square, and ever
accelerating. After a do-
able take-off, the wave de-
velops an immensely long barrel as it arcs around the reef through
a total of 180 degrees; a bend so pronounced that you often cannot
see round the corner to the exit of the barrel. 4-15ft. Advanced.

The Right: If you are not suitably impressed, There is a big wave
right reef opposite. It gets extremely big, but the real challenge is
in that it ends at the cliff-face. This beast works when at least 8ft
of swell is coming in, and needs to be surfed early morning as the
southeast trade winds destroy it.

Further adventure: The other heavy break in the area, way
east of Wainyapu, involves a major 15km plus bike ride plus a 5km
hike into the Kahala area. It is a challenging, remote left and right
reef-break in the rivermouth, breaking into channels. It holds the
largest swells going, although afternoon winds are on-shore. You'll
most likely surf it alone as there is no accommodation or food here
and any gear left on the beach is likely to be re-appropriated by
curious locals.

On the way in you pass a major *Pasola* site. Hard core only. Definitely not to be surfed alone. Medical kit essential. We'll call it spot
"X" for now.

Wainyapu

3km south of Pero. Best plan is to stay at Pero losmen, and hike in and out across the river and along the beach. Betel nut and negotiation with the *kepala desa* can be used to find lodgings in Ratenggaro.

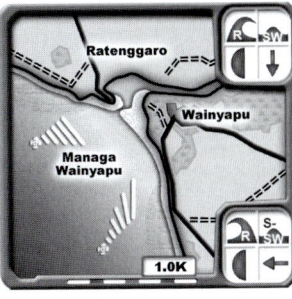

Long left-hander works in dry season trade-winds, and is consistent and makeable. Picks up any available swell. Rights opposite are best surfed early morning before the wind, but can be good. Traditional Sumba scene, with some of the Islands best megaliths right on the beach.

Marosi

Best reached via Waikabu-bak, via Lamdunga.

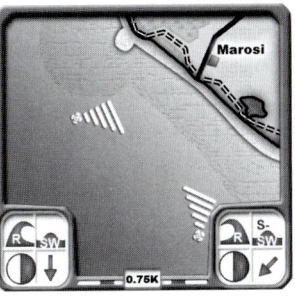

A beautiful pristine beach. Primarily a big shifty deep water right out the back, best on large swells. The wave can peak anywhere so hold-downs are common, but once on it there's a relatively easy charge to the channel. Surf it early as winds do damage. All levels. There are some lefts, and A-frame peaks across the bay too. The misnomer "Sunset" is often applied to the big wave left way out the back at this spot.

Nihiwatu

Access is denied by the resort built right on the break so you may not get to actually surf it. At Waikabubak, turn off south towards Padede Watu. Its a right turn just before Rua. You can see it from above, at the village of Watukarere. If you are prepared to use diplomacy and your very best manners you may be able to organize lodgings here through the village elder or *kepala desa* (see section intro), and hike down the track past the rice paddies and across the beach from there. The likelihood is that you will then be asked to leave by resort staff however. If you have the cash, you can stay there and surf it. Boat access unclear at this time.

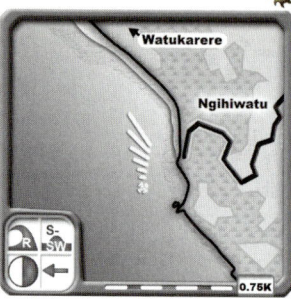

Long left-hander surfable on all tides. It is often fat and lifeless on high, but becomes more and more hollow, and lined up, towards low. At these times, a super steep take-off on the outer point is followed by up to 200m of barrel opportunity. Very low tides can close out except for the final section. The wave holds anything from 2 to 10ft plus but really starts showing it's true character after the 5ft mark... the bigger the better. There's a good channel to the right. Afternoon trades can bring cross-chop. All levels unless decent swell is coming in.

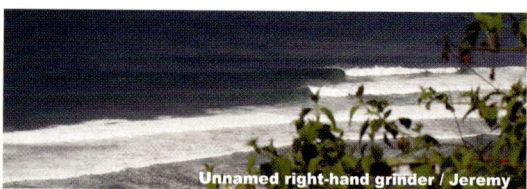

Unnamed right-hand grinder / Jeremy

Wainokaka

Pantai Wainokaka is sign-posted east of Rua, which is reached due south on the road from Waikabubak. The break is just south of the main village.

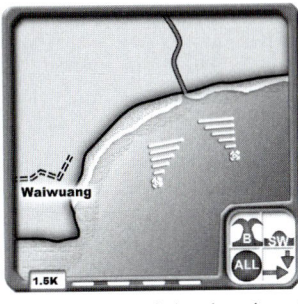

Waiwuang

1.5K

Rivermouth rights and lefts, with the lefts often sensational, lined up and whackable. It works on any tide but sand movement dictates quality and shape. There is an outer reef here that can be surfable although rarely great. Must be surfed early or in wet season. All levels. 2-8ft. May not be the classic Indo reef break, but accessible, and you can stay nearby. Best accommodations are at Rua itself a few km west, with Homestay Ahong a popular hangout for surfers.

SUMBA

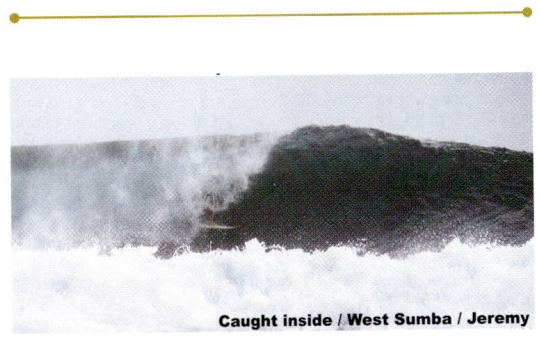

Caught inside / West Sumba / Jeremy

Tarimbang

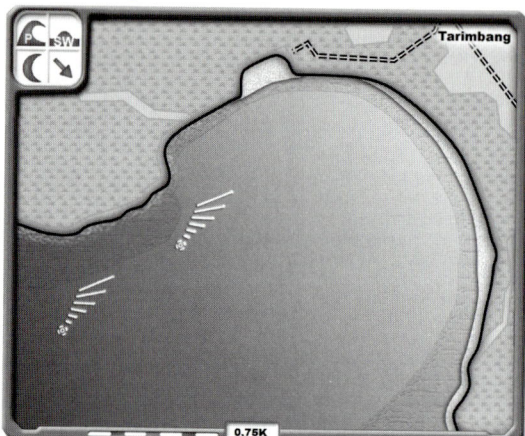

Tarimbang

0.75K

South down the hill from Lahara. 15 min walk from village. The 750m paddle to get to the outer take-off point is a tough proposition when added to the arduous journey, but you can walk along the cliff and hop the reef at low tide+, to a channel behind the take-off.

Extremely long right coral point holding any size, with alternating fat and barrelling sections. NW winds are cross-off-shore, so wet-season is good. Dry season trades are straight onshore but you can steal a quiet early morning session, and afternoon storms can swing off-shore. To maximize your chances, be there on a week when lower tides occur in the mornings, as high tide switches it off unless it is big. All levels can surf it on a shoulder-hopping basis. The most crowded spot on Sumba, but over 20 in the water is still rare. Tempting but hard-breaking rights peel in further around the point, offering very fast square barrels that can close out with severe consequences. There's also a rarely surfed mediocre left on the south end of the bay.

Mengkudu

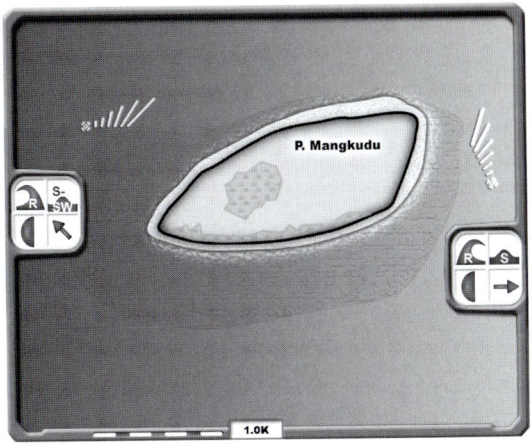

P. Mangkudu

1.0K

Off southeast Sumba. Car or bus from Waingapu to Katundu. Hotel Merlin is good at organizing both . Approx 500,000rp/car (4hr trip) and 20,000rp by bus (8 hours). From Katundu a 30 minute boat ride to Manggudu, approx 300,000rp. 1-2 people can be picked up with the resort's boat for 100,000rp. Call ahead to the Island on 0868 1211 5296.

Lefts: Long left over flat coral reef off the west of the island, holding any size, and offshore in southeast dry season trades. Mid tide best although all tides work. South to southwest swell optimal. It picks up more swell than just about anywhere and is extremely consistent in the dry season. The bigger the better up to 15ft plus. Uncrowded spot as the camp only takes 10 pax. Intermediates can make the easy days, but advanced when big. Manta rays, turtles and tropical fish. At the other end of the island, very long, hollow **rights** get blown off most afternoons, but an early morning session can yield supreme quality. These rights work when wet season north to west winds kick in although the camp is open April to Jan only.

Watu Libung (White rocks) - Kallala

Head for Baing, on the southwest edge of Sumba. Then 2km Down the hill towards Kallala. The breaks are just outside the village. The Hotel Merlin in Waingapu can sort out your transport although roads are sketchy. You can stay in one of 6 bungalows on the beach...just ask for Mr David.

A rarity; east coast waves that are offshore in the dry season, courtesy of a pronounced nose of land fringed by a large protruberant reef that arcs down to the south.

5-0: Hollow, barreling left-hander over shallow coral. It's a demanding wave with real consequences for mistakes. Likes south to southwest swell and straight east wind: southeast trade-winds are side off-shore. Big high tides are best, and safest! 3-10ft. Advanced.

Racetrack: Fast, short shallow barrel. The wave is fundamentally a performance shape, although it speeds up and becomes more critical the further you progress down the line. Likes mid tide, and similar wind and swell conditions to 5-0. 2-6 feet. All levels.

The Point: consistent, very long left-hander over flat coral reef. On small days, this is a fun, makeable wave for all levels and even longboards. Low tide is generally best but you'll always find something up to about 3/4 high tide. 1-6ft. All levels.

On the right swell at the right (big) size, you'll see **Erics** start to show; a big-wave location between the point and racetrack. This not an amateur wave and when on, is a booming outer bombora holding 6-12ft. It links up with a fast inside section called **Bang-Bangs**, which works from 3 to 8ft. There's a good beach-break **right** next to the point too, and other **beach-breaks** on the inside that cater for beginners.

Crowds are generally low here even in season, with limited accommodation and a little bit of a trip to get here. Waves suit all levels of surfer too.

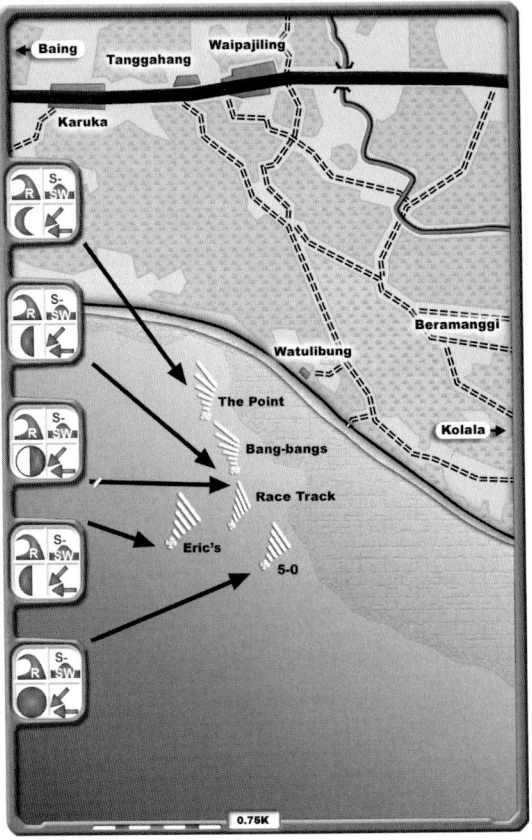

Baing ←

Tanggahang

Waipajiling

Karuka

Watulibung

Beramanggi

Kolala →

The Point

Bang-bangs

Race Track

Eric's

5-0

0.75K

SUMBA

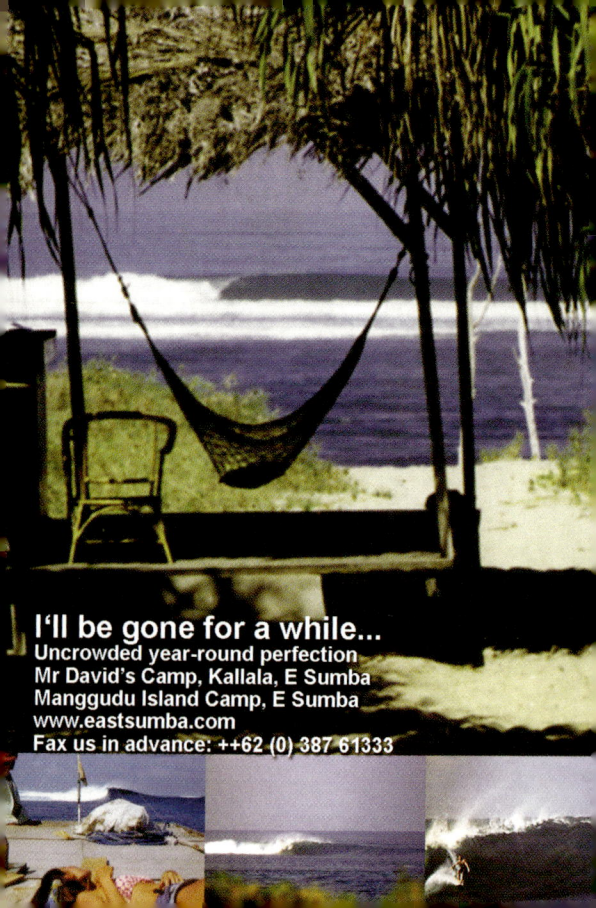

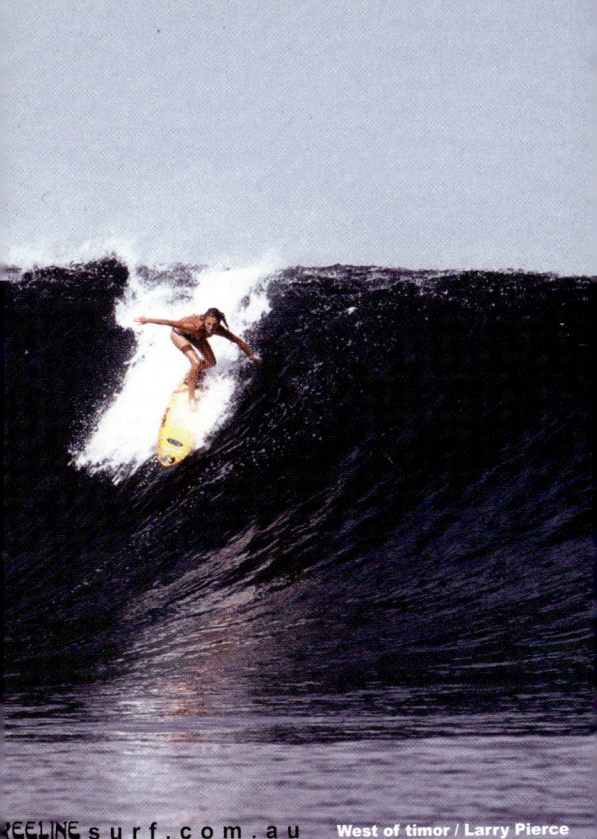

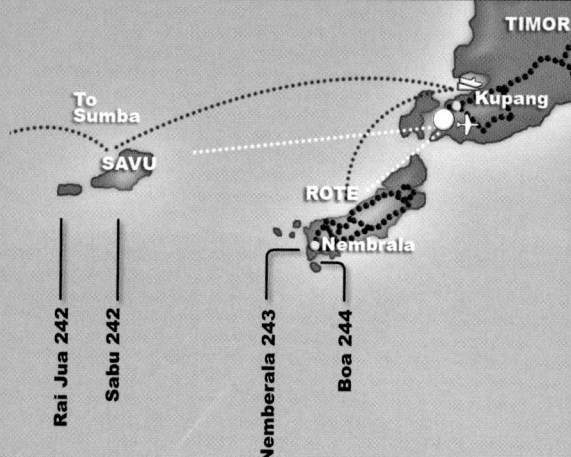

TIMOR

To Sumba

Kupang

SAVU

ROTE

Nembrala

Rai Jua 242

Sabu 242

Nemberala 243

Boa 244

Background

Rote has been on the surfer's map for thirty years, and it's star wave, **Nemberala**, an underground cult wave for most of that. Both Rote and Sabu are part of the Timor district, and are serviced by air from Kupang. There are also yacht charters (see section) out of Kupang, that take in Sabu and Rote and surrounding islands. Nemberala itself has a huddle of surfer accommodation, making it a great base for eastern surf adventures, with waves down at Boa and offshore islands. We will feature some "discovered" waves that are the tip of the iceberg in this region.

Seasons

Dry season (which is very dry in these parts) from April to September, is peak swell season and the name breaks are mostly offshore. Afternoons can get extremely windy mid seasson. The region has a relatively narrow swell window and prolonged flat spells are possible. There are some fantastic right-handers that are offshore in northwest wet season winds although patience is required to catch them firing.

Hazards
- Reef cuts. Lack of medical facilities. Some small-scale theft reported. Remote surf spots beyond medical help. Sabu and surrounds has a lack of food and accommodation.

M	Swell Range		Wind Pattern		Air		Sea	Crowd
	Feet	Dir'	Am	Pm	Low	Hi	°C	
J	1-5	SW	NW LO	NW MOD	22	30	27	LO
F	1-5	SW	NW LO	NW MOD	22	30	27	LO
M	2-6	SW	NW LO	NW MOD	23	31	27	LO
A	2-8	SW	SE LO	SE MOD	21	32	27	LO
M	2-8	SW	SE LO	SE MOD	21	33	27	MED
J	2-8	SW	SE LO	SE HI	21	31	27	MED
J	2-10	SW	SE LO	SE HI	21	31	26	MED
A	2-10	SW	SE LO	SE MOD	22	31	26	MED
S	2-6	SW	SE LO	SE MOD	24	29	26	LO
O	2-6	SW	NW LO	NW MOD	22	31	26	LO
N	2-5	SW	NW LO	NW MOD	22	31	26	LO
D	1-5	SW	NW LO	NW MOD	22	31	26	MED

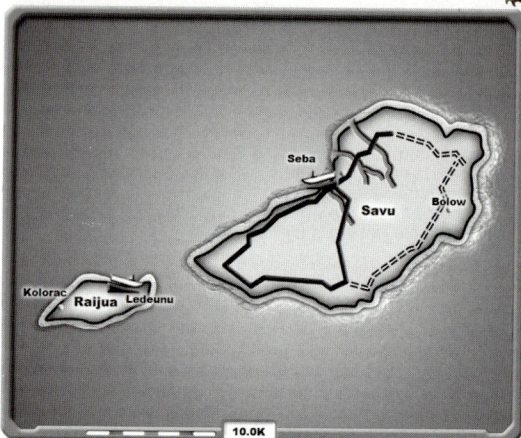

This pair of islands is not an easy prospect. A semi reliable ferry service from Seba connects the 2, and Sabu can be reached by air from Kupang. Once there however, accommodation is scarce on Sabu, and non-existent on Rai Jua. Food, even rice, is a challenge on the latter. Bike and car rental is not yet truly available although initiative can be rewarded when negotiating. Rai Jua is the property of the king of Sabu. Explore by boat for now.

Sabu's northern area has a world class, but *extremely* rare right-hand reef break that requires huge swell from a bizarre direction to create long, perfect barrels. Rai Jua is said to host a long hollow left reef point, again a fickle wave requiring powerful swell to wrap to the max. Other lefts there as well. Reefs fringe the northwest facing western tips of both islands, as it also curves around their eastern extremities. Winds during mid dry season can be too strong even if cross-offshore. The fickle waves and hard conditions mean that this is not a location for the casual surf traveller. The nearby spec of Dana Island is also known to have right and left reef-breaks exposed to winds but showing class on their day.

Nemberala

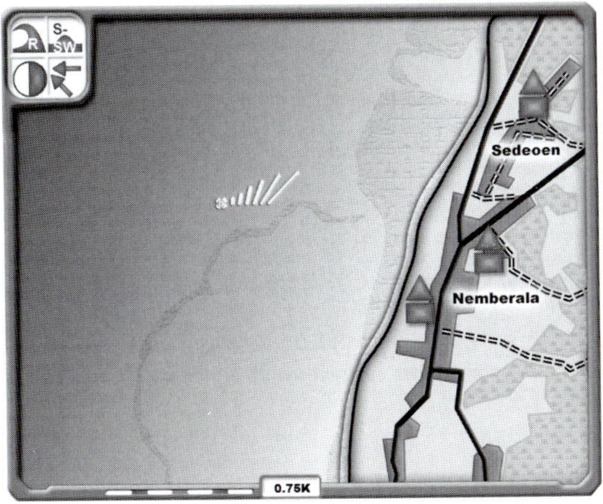

Sedeoen

Nemberala

0.75K

On Rote, head west from Baa. Very well signed and plenty of accommodation on the beach. Nemberala (or Nembrala) is an ideal base for surf discovery in this region. There is a continual presence of surfers who you can share transport with, and get info from. There are also drivers operating around the various *losmen*, who can take you on a guided tour for a small price.

The wave itself is a classic left-hander that put Rote on the map. It works best in dry season southwesterly winds, and holds any size of swell to about 15 ft without losing shape. It can work on any tide, although smaller days need very low tides to get hollow. From 3-5ft it can still be a fun, long wave, but roars back to hollow life over the 6ft mark. All levels. Works often, but not always perfect. Crowds vary from empty to packed with no logic. A.K.A. T-Land. Plenty of good spots nearby.

Boa

8k southeast of Nemberala.

A winding right-hand reef pass requires a fair sized swell. When on, this is a very long, hollow wave arcing around an outer reef. Currents can be a little bit ridiculous. A good wet season wave, and it is a beautiful spot whatever the waves are doing. You can negotiate a guide in Nemberala, to help you 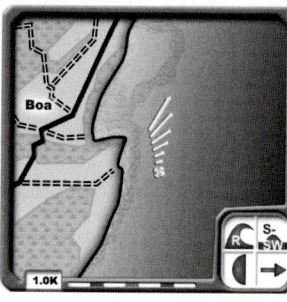 sound out some other spots in the area, and check fickle, wind affected west coast spots on the way.

Rote; the rest

On smaller days with no wind or early mornings, Rote's south coast picks up any available swell. You'll find reef passes in places like Nembedal, and **Landu Island**. Reef-fringed outer islands also have potential, and both **Ndana** (an uninhabited island off south west coast near Boa, teaming with wildlife) and **Ndao** (traditional island west of Nemberala) can be reached by boat organized in town.

Your best bet is to team up, find a local guide, and go explore. Once you think you have it sussed, you can also hire motorbikes in Nemberala. *Bemos* can be arranged at the Nemberala Beach Resort, but not cheaply.

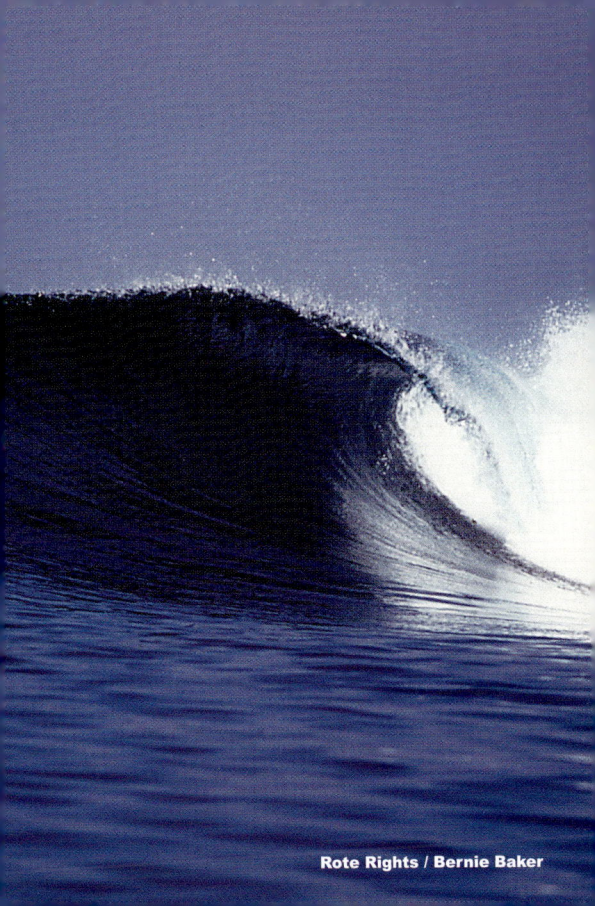

Rote Rights / Bernie Baker

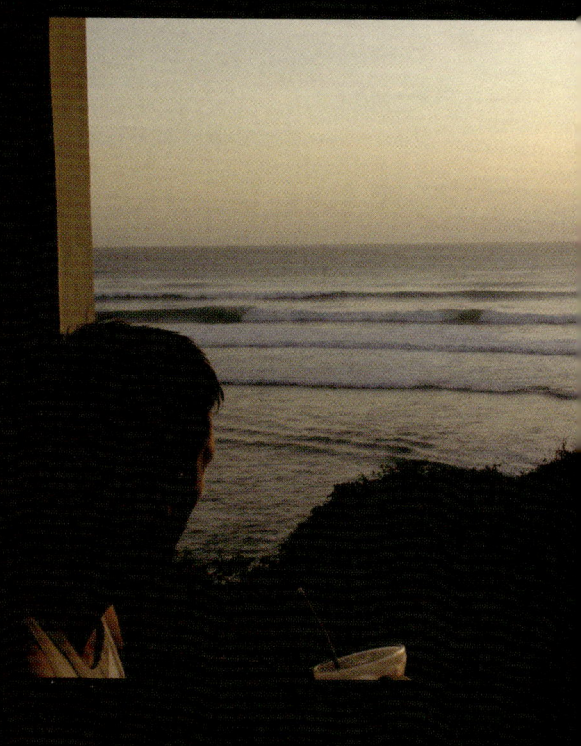

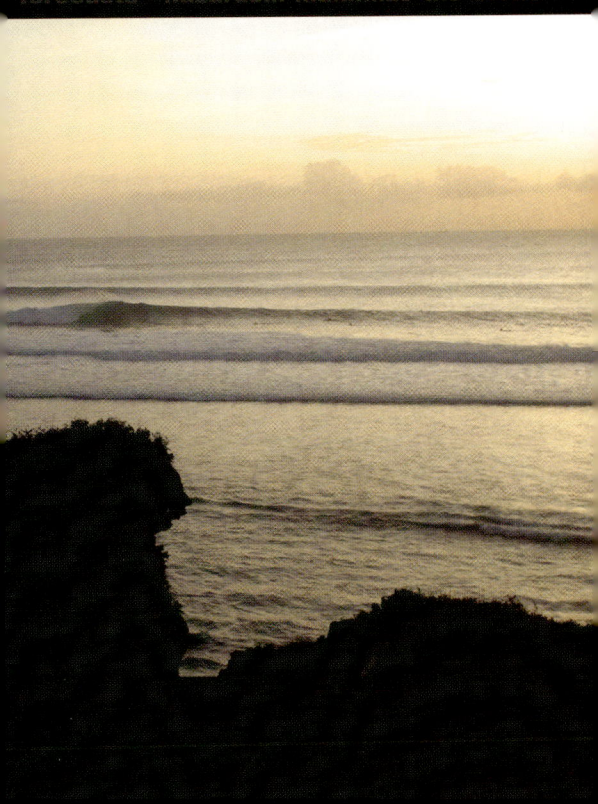

Surf accommodation - transport - surf supplies - repairs - how to get to - boat trips forecasts - hazards... maximize the stoke

Boat Trips

Vessel		Kuda Laut	Indies Explorer
Destinations	Mentawais	X	X
	Nias / Hinako's	X	X
	North Sumatra		X
	West Java/Panaitan		
	Lembongan		
	Lombok		
	Sumbawa		
	Sumba/Rote/Sabu		
Departs From		Padang	Padang
Length (feet)		53	115
Motor (HP)		80	400
Cruise Speed (Knts)		9	9
TV/VCR Etc		TV/VCR/CD	TV/VCR/CD
A/C / Fan		Fans	A/C
Min / Max Pax		4-8	10
Days		6-14	14
Tender; length/power		4.5m, 40hp	5m, 40hp
$ Factor		$$	$$
Luxury Level		***	***
Comments		Good guys, experienced, great value.	Romantic teak yacht
Contact		freeline surf.com.au	indiesexplorer @tiscali.co.za
Photo			

Casuarina	Midas	Wijaya	KM Nauli	Naga Laut
	X	X		X
	X	X	X	
		X	X	
X				
Jakarta	Padang	Padang	Sibolga	Padang
50	74	74	75	70
50	2200,V12	720	760	440
9	20	12	9	10
	TV/VCR/CD	TV/VCR/CD	TV/VCR/CD	TV/VCR/CD
Fan	A/C	Fans	A/C	A/C
4-6	4-8	6-8	6-10	6-10
4-8	6-14	10	10	10
3m, 25hp		3m.25hp	3m. 15hp	4m, 40hp
$	$$$	$	$$	$$
***	*****	***	***	****
Value. Beat the crowds	Super-lux new yacht	Basic Value	Beat crowds in less-surfed destination	Good value, experience.
freeline surf.com.au	insearch travel.com	info@mentawai islands.com	world surfaris.com	surftravel online.com

Boat Trips

Vessel		Moggy	Irish Mist
Destinations	Mentawais		X
	Nias / Hinako's		
	North Sumatra		
	West Java/Panaitan		
	Lembongan	X	
	Lombok	X	
	Sumbawa	X	
	Sumba /Rote/Sabu	X	
Departs From		Bali	Padang
Length (feet)		44	50
Motor (HP)		100/sail	NA/sail
Cruise Speed (Knts)		9	9
TV/VCR Etc		TV/VCR/VD	TV/VCR/VD
A/C / Fan		Fan	A/C
Min / Max Pax		5-8	6+
Days		4-14	10
Tender; length/power			4.5m. 40hp
$ Factor		$	$$
Luxury Level		***	****
Comments		Customised trips, short duration	Friendly skipper, wooden ketch
Contact		world surfaris.com	insearch travel.com
Photo			

Boat Trips

Strictly Business	Santa Lusia	Nomad	Electric Lamb	Purnamah Indah III
X	X		X	
		X		
				X
				X
Padang	Padang	Jakarta	Padang	Bali
58		60	58	90
280/Sail	560		85/Sail	340
8	8	8	9	12
TV/VCR/CD	TV/VCR/CD	TV/VCR	TV/VCR	TV/CD/VCR
A/C		A/C	A/C	Fans
6	5-8	5-8	6-10	12-14
10	10	8-10	10	7
Waverunner	Tin. 25hp	4m	3.5m.15hp.	3.5m. 15hp
$$$	$$	$$	$$	$
****	***	****	***	***
Well appointed vessel		Wild Panaitan is amazing. This is the top boat.	Plying these waters since '82	Uncrowded waves
world surfaris.com	pure vacations.com	insearch travel.com	surftravel online.com	surftravel online.com

Boat Trips

Vessel		Sri Noa Noa	Dream-weaver
Destinations	Mentawais		
	Nias / Hinako's		
	North Sumatra		
	West Java/Panaitan		
	Lembongan	X	X
	Lombok	X	X
	Sumbawa	X	X
	Sumba/Rote/Sabu	X	
Departs From		Bali	Bali
Length (feet)		48	80
Motor (HP)		33/Sail	230
Cruise Speed (Knts)		7	10
TV/VCR Etc		CD	TV/CD
A/C / Fan		Fans	A/C
Min / Max Pax		2-6	12-14
Days		Flexi, 4-14	7
Tender; length/power		3.5m/15hp	
$ Factor		$$	$
Luxury Level		****	****
Comments		V comfortable boat	Recently refitted boat
Contact		freeline surf.com.au	dreamweaver surf.com
Photo			

PLANNER

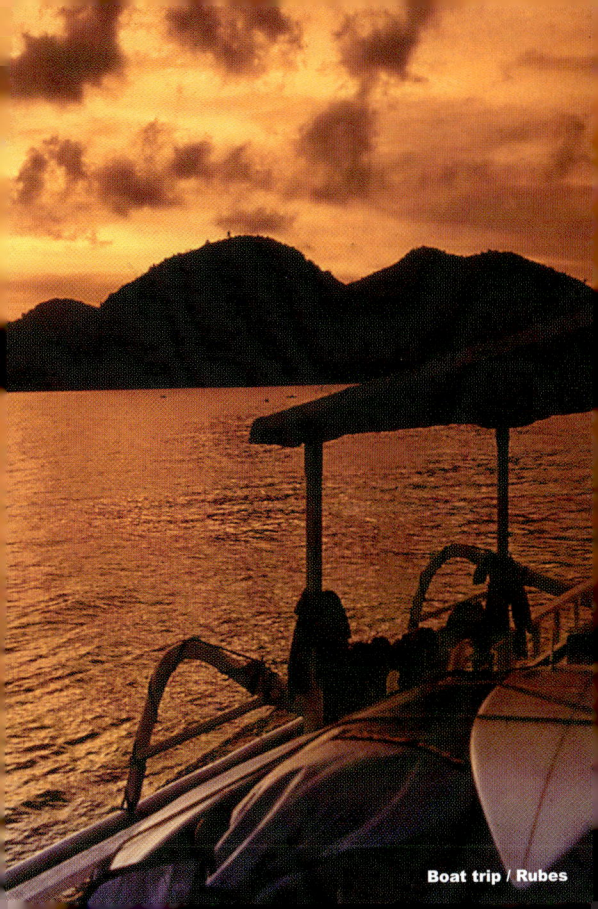

Boat trip / Rubes

Where To Stay Right On The Surf

Places to stay, as reasonably priced as possible, right on or near the surf. Advance bookings sometimes impossible, often essential, always recommended.

Bali - Base Camp

Kuta - You can't beat Kuta as a base for the surfer. It has an outrageous array of accommodation for every budget, and is party central. If you're planning a romantic getaway, this isn't it. It's 25 mins to Canggu, 35 to Nusa Dua, and 45 to Uluwatu.

Nusa Dua - The ultimate place to be during wet season, but it is expensive as hell, being purpose built as a high end destination. It's right on one of the best rights anywhere, and also just 15 minutes ti Uluwatu. 10 min north is **Tanjung Benoa**, which is starting to see a major expansion of all-budget accommodation.

Sanur up north, is a good east coast base too, with plenty of accommodation (albeit mostly fairly expensive), and easy access to Hyatt's, Turtle Island and some quiet east coast black sand spots.

Bali - On The Spot

Medewi - Medewi Beach Cottages, 0361 40 029. $$

Canggu - Pondok Wisata Nyoman. Right on the beach. $

Kuta beach - Palm Gardens, Poppies 2, (0) 361 752 198. $$

Kuta Reef - Mustika Inn, 361 753 298. $$

Nyang-Nyang - Puri Bali Villas. Secluded, (0) 361 701 362. $$

Uluwatu
Villa Istana, Uluwatu, www.balinicerate.com. $$$
Rocky's Bungalows, north side of break. $$

Padang-Padang - Thomas Homestay, up the hill from beach. $

Where To Stay Right On The Surf

Dreamland, Bingin, Balangan
All 3 beaches have rudimentary *losmen* right on the beach; turn up and negotiate. La Joya bungalow at Balangan is pretty cool: intou ch@insearchtravel.com. $

Nusa Dua - Sri Lanka
Nusa Dua Beach Hotel, 361 771 210. $$$

Sanur - Hyatt Reef
Kesumasari Beach Homestay 361 287 824. $

Sanur - Sanur Reef - Ananda Hotel 361 288 327. $$

Lembongan - Shipwrecks & Lacerations
Agung's bungalows 366 24483. $
Jungut Batu Bungalows. insearchtravel.com. $$

Sumatra - Base camp

Nias - As well as being the home of Lagundri Bay, the area around Pantai Sorake on Nias' south coast has a huge array of *losmen* style accommodations, and a few more up market variants. From here you can get to some of the best waves of Sumatra. Charter boats (both of the official, and unofficial fishing type) can get you from here to the Hinako's, and Afulu up north, as well as Telo (Batu Islands).

Krui - There are a half dozen awesome surf spots in and around Krui in the southern province of Lampung. Ujung Bocur nearby, has a good camp.

Sumatra - On The Spot

Simeulue
Baneng Island Resort, in SW Simeulue. www.simeulue.com. Flight charters via Medan to this new, secluded island paradise. $$

Where To Stay Right On The Surf

Nias - Lagundri - Sea Breeze 0630 21224. $$
Sorake Beach Resort. $$

Hinako's - Asu and Bawa
Hinako's Hideaway on Asu, via www.worldsurfaris.com. Unique surf paradise that must be checked out. $$

Ujung Bocur & Krui
Ombak Indah Losmen www.freelinesurf.com.au/sumatra_land.htm. Uncrowded, perfect surf right out the front. Awesome. $

Mentawais - On The Spot

Siberut - Kandui and Bankvaults
Wave-park Losmen www.wavepark.com. Unique and virtually the only place to stay in the islands. Waves out front, and boats to all the "Playgrounds" breaks. $$

West Java - Base Camp

The port / tourist destination of **Pelabuhanratu**, a few hours south of Jakarta, is the hub for surfers in this region. There's heaps of accommodation in town and towards Cimaja. From here you can access Ujung Genteng and Turtles (by boat or overland) to the south, as well as Cimaja and a heap of awesome adventure spots to the west.

West Java - On The Spot

Cimaja & Indicators
Cek Ombak. www.insearchtravel.com. Right in the heart of West Java's surf coast. $$

Turtles
Batu Besar Losmen www.freelinesurf.com.au/westjava_land.htm. Off one of the best surf spots in West Java. $

Where To Stay Right On The Surf

Mama's
Mama's Losmen. Right behind the beach. $

Central Java - Base Camp

Pangandaran is a fun beach-side hangout. Well priced but great food and accommodation abound. The national park has some quiet quality, and waves in and around the nearby **Batukaras** are something different.
Bulak Laut Bungalows 0265 639 377. $

G - Land - On The Spot

Bobby's G-Land surf camp (www.grajagan.com), or G-Land Jungle Surf Camp (www.g-land.com). Book through surf travel specialists, see over. You must book in advance. You can get there via Bali either overnight bus plus quick boat from Grajagan port, or expensive fast boat from Kuta (3 hours each way, but USD 150 just for the ride). $$$

Lombok - Base camp

There are 2 tourist destinations on Lombok that are of interest to surfers. **Kuta**, down on the south coast, has a lot to offer; it's located right between Ekas and Grupuk to the east, and Mawi / Blongas etc to the west. You can (if crazy) take a long and bumpy trip to Desert Point from here too. Kuta has surf shops and all levels of food and accommodation (from *losmen*, through to 5* resorts). There's a fun atmosphere, and a constant stream of surfers hanging about, with whom you can pool transport, trade stories, and get info about swells and secret spots. There are any number of "tour operators" working here, running *bemo* and boat trips to south coast surf spots.

Senggigi, just up the road from Mataram, is West Lombok's answer to Bali's Kuta although it has a quiet feel these days. You can hang here for a few days after landing at the nearby airport, and get waves if a large swell coincides. From Senggigi you can get easy access to the mushroom mecca of Gili Air, Trawangan and Meno, where a

Where To Stay Right On The Surf

laid-back, lotus eating lifestyle awaits. The waves are uncrowded though rare, and the diving fantastic.

Lombok - On the spot

Desert Point

With no surf camp any more, hard core surfers camp here in the dry season, braving rip-offs, flat spells and the most basic conditions. The nearest spot with good *losmen* accomm is Lembar (2-3 hours away depending road condition).

Kuta Lombok

Surfer's Inn, Beach Rd, 0370-65-5582 henryyamada@yahoo.com.br HP: 0818-569027. Excellent. $
Novotel Coralia, Kuta (Pantai Segar). www.worldsurfaris.com. $$$

Ekas

Heaven on the Planet, Ekas, www.heavenontheplanet.co.nz. Secluded "eco" resort right on the main break. $$

Sumbawa - Base Camp

Yoyo's Resort (Sekongkang Bawa) - Hanging about here gives you access to Scar Reef, Supersucks, and Yoyo's itself. On small days, Pantai Pisin next door can have a wave when everywhere else is flat. www.yoyohotel.com. 62 812 3951 899 . $$

Lakey - There are over half a dozen places to stay at Lakey itself, ranging from seedy *losmen* to air conditioned semi luxe. With 5 top drawer spots like **The Peak**, **Periscopes** and **Lakey Pipe** right out the front, this is the place to be in Sumbawa.

Sumbawa - On The Spot

Yoyo's

Yoyo's Resort 0868 1210 4433 www.yoyohotel.com. Beautiful setting, with Scars and Supersuck not too far away. $$

Where To Stay Right On The Surf

Lakey Peak
Fatmah's 0373 623 229. $
Aman Gati Resort, www.amangati.com. Right on the Peak. $$

Sumba - Base Camp

Tarimbang - Roughly half way down the south coast, Tarimbang is one of the few places in Sumba where surf and accommodation combine. You can venture out from here.

Kallala - *Losmen* accommodation on the beach here (see below) makes it the hub for East Sumba. You've got 5 great waves right there, and easy access to Mengkudu Island too.

Sumba - On The Spot

Tarimbang - Bogenvil Homestay. $

Kallala - Mr David's, www.eastsumba.com. $

Mengkudu - Mr David's, www.eastsumba.com. $

Marosi - Homestay Bulu. $

Sabu - Base Camp

Ongka Dai Losmen, or Makarim Homestay are among the better of the few options there are. Sabu is a tough prospect for the overland surfer.

Rote - Base Camp

Nemberala
Losmen Angurah, behind the beach, enables you easy access to T-Land itself, as well as a knot of other surfers who you can pool resources with. There's plenty of this style of accommodation near the beach. From here you can get to **Boa** and other breaks, as well as negotiating boat rides to outer islands.

How To Get To...

Bali

Bali Itself has too many routes and airlines to mention. To find the best for you, we recommend talking to any of the surf travel specialists listed hin this section.

Nusa Lembongan

Boats go daily from Sanur on Bali, and drop you off at Jungutbatu right next to Lacerations. 1.5hr trip. You can also charter one from any Kuta travel shop Sri Noa Noa (see Charters) is a good, flexible bet.

East Java & G-Land

You can get the overnight bus / ferry / speedboat combo from Kuta to the G-Land camps. Companies overleaf can organize it for you, or see the counter at Tubes Bar in Kuta.

Cimaja and West Java mainland

Jakarta is the main international hub for Cimaja area breaks. You can hire vehicles or a *bemo* and take the 3 hour trip south to Bogor, then Cibadak and finally the Pelabuhanratu resort area. Freeline Indonesian Surf Adventures (freelinesurf.com.au) and iNSEARCH Travel (insearchtravel.com) both run guided surf tours in West Java; a good way of getting to good waves with minimum fuss.

Panaitan Island

The island is part of the Ujung Kulon national park, and as such doesn't have any infrastructure to speak of. Overland is not a genuine option, and malaria is a real danger if you make it here. The adventurous can get to the Port of Labuan (2h from Jakarta) and sniff out a ride, or charter a yacht from Carita Beach just by Labuan. By far the most advisable method is to take a boat trip as listed in "Boat charters". Pure Vacations, Surftravelonline, Freeline and iNSEARCH offer hassle free trips via Jakarta.

How To Get To...

Simeulue

One of the most isolated islands, 100 NM west of the Acehnese port of Tapaktuan on Sumatra. **Ferry** from Susoh, or **Fly** from Medan via Meulaboh (about RP750'000). Both routes go to Sinabang in the island's south. Preferred method is by boat; see "boat charters".

Nias

Air: Air SMAC or Garuda from Medan to Binaka (near Gunung Sitoli on the northeast of the island), 3 mornings a week. 0639 21010. About RP 600'000. Boards Extra. Lagundri is 2hrs from Gunung.

Ferry: From Sibolga on the mainland (accessed by road from the airport at Padang), to Gunung Sitoli, Mon - Sat. Also, and more conveniently, from Sibolga to Telukdalam (just 13km from Lagundri), 3 days a week, usually Tue, Thurs & Sat. Call ASDP on 0639 21554 or PT Simeulue on 0639 21295.

Hinako's - Asu and Bawa

Fly SMAC from Medan on Sumatra, to Gunung Sitoli (Binaki) on Nias. 2.5 hour overland from Gunung Sitoli to Sirombu on west coast of Nias, then 1 hour boat ride to Asu Island. Alternatively, charter a **boat** ride from Lagundri. Full boat-based surfaris can be arranged through www.surftravelonline or www.worldsurfaris.com

Mentawais

Boat charters: These days most get there as part of a boat trip, most of which depart Padang. Because of the dangers of malaria and the enormous logistical challenges of the overland route, boat trips are recommended - see "boat charters". This is a tremendous shame however, because it means that thousands of surfers enjoy the awe-inspiring waves of these poverty stricken islands every year without contributing a cent to the local economy. Some guys are try-

PLANNER

ing to address this; see www.surfaidinternational.org.

Overland/Indpendent: Ferry from Padang to Muarasiberut in the south of Siberut island, 4 days a week for about Rp 15'000. Also, The Mentawai Express now goes from Padang to Tuapejat on Sipora twice weekly. Unfortunately, once on the islands you will face a challenge to get around. Although *bemo*s or minibuses can be hired, roads are terrible or non-existent, and rarely lead you to any of the good spots. A new fast launch takes land-based surfers to the Wave-Park Losmen on a small island just south of Siberut in the vicinity of Bank Vaults and Rifles. It's the only official surf accommodation on the islands. www.wavepark.com.

Southern Sumatra

Bandarlampung is easily reached from Jakarta, with 3 flights a day on Merpati. Buses go from there several times per day (6 hour trip to Krui). Freeline Indonesian Surfing Adventures (freelinesurf.com.au) have it pretty wired.

Lombok

For access to south coast breaks: **Ferry** to Lembar from Padang Bai on Bali, every hour or 2. There are also direct ferries from Bali to Senggigi and Kuta (Lombok); see any Perama agent in Kuta - Bali. Cars can be rented at the port.

Air: Merpati flies daily from Bali to Mataram. You can hire bikes & cars here or at Senggigi just north, which is a bustling tourist area. Also Silk Air from Singapore, and Lion Air or Garuda from Jakarta. You can get **boat charters** from Bali for short trips to the top spots; see that section.

Sumbawa

Overland: Ferry from Labuhan Lombok in east Lombok, hourly to Poto Tano on northwest tip of Sumbawa. Poto Tano is the gateway to western breaks like Scars and Yoyo's.

How To Get To...

Air: Air Merpati flies from Bali daily via Mataram to Bima. *Bemo*s easily hired for the 2hr ride south to Hu'u (for Lakey/Periscopes). They also fly to Sumbawa Besar, where you can get to western breaks like Yoyo's; upwards of 3.5 hours driving via Poto Tano to Taliwang and beyond.

Boat charters: See Boat charter section; there is a plethora of short to medium length trips taking in Lombok and Sumbawa, all departing from Bali.

Sumba

Air: Air Merpati fly 1 or 2 times a week from Denpasar to Waingapu and Tambulaka. Pelita Air is another option, 4 times a week. Both are at Denpasar Airport and cost about USD80 1-way.
Boat trips: Departing Bali or Kupang on Timor. iNSEARCH (insearchtravel.com) do guided Sumba tours, worth bearing in mind given the hardships that you might avoid.

Sabu

Air Merpati operate a weekly flight to and from Kupang in West Timor. You can arrange a connection from Bali or Jakarta via here. There's also a ferry from Waingapu on Sumba. Boat charters also depart Kupang.

Rote

Air: Merpati operate a weekly flight to and from Kupang in West Timor. You can arrange a connection from Bali or Jakarta via here.
Boat charters depart Kupang on Timor.

Timor

Air: Merpati have Bali and Jakarta flights going to Kupang on the west coast.

Transport Around

Bemos

In Bali and some other islands, a *bemo* is a large car or minibus. You can hire it for the day (around Rp300'000) and share the cost of it with friends. Similar arrangements can be made in most built up areas or around airports and transport hubs. Other names include **Opelet** (Nias), **angkot**, and **mikrolet**, depending on where you are.

Airlines

Almost every major island has a plane that goes to it. The 3 main domestic airlines are:
Merpati - www.merpati.co.id
Garuda - www.garuda-indonesia.com
Pelita - www.pelita-airventure.com

Car & motorcycle hire

Available from most airports, and all over Kuta and other tourist centres. Don't forget your international drivers licence - fines are heavy and inconvenient. Indonesia drives on the left, most of the time, and it is dangerous out on the roads. Proceed with caution. It is wise to hire a car with driver for your first few days, till you get the feel for the mayhem. You can rent bikes from just about anywhere, for as little as 50'000 RP per day. In Kuta and other surf hubs, some even come with board racks. Bear in mind that it is a dangerous form of transport in Indo.

Taxis

On many islands you are offered the choice of metred travel, or negotiated trip price. Try the latter, if it sounds too much, see if there's a meter in the cab. Don't negotiate too hard. Generally speaking, a cab driver is happy to negotiate a price to wait while you surf, and take you back. Useful if you are going somewhere remote.

Transport Around

Jukungs

Outrigger fishing boats with outboard motors. These are a vital cog in the surf travel wheel, taking surfers further out than most humans can paddle...and back. Softly negotiate a 2-way fare, but ask other surfers what the going rate is if you can.

Ferries

They link just about every inhabited island. Generally slow but cheap. There are many ports and companies, but the biggest is Pelni - www.pelni.co.id

Surf Travel Specialists

Surf travel to Indonesia can be made easy these days. Whether it be a 5 day Bali escape, an overland trek to a remote surf camp, or an island hopping trip of a lifetime, the guys below can hook you up in a single phone call. They are listed by country, but will still be able to help you if you aren't local.

Australia

Freeline Indonesian Surf Adventures
PO Box 479, Surry Hills, NSW 2010
+61 (0)2 9698 2294, info@freelinesurf.com.au
www.freelinesurf.com.au

iNSEARCH Travel, POB 2 North Fremantle WA 6259
+61 (0)8 9336 7700 intouch@insearchtravel.com
www.insearchtravel.com

World Surfaris POB 180, Mooloolaba QLD 4557
+61 (0)7 5444 4011 info@worldsurfaris.com
www.worldsurfaris.com

Surf Travel Specialists

Indonesia

Surftravelonline, Kuta, Bali
++62 361 750 550, peter@surftravelonline.com
www.surftravelonline.com

New Zealand

Surftrip Travel PO Box 27102, Auckland 1030
08 324 4663 - www.surftrip.co.nz

South Africa

True Blue Travel
www.truebluetravel.co.za

USA

Wavehunters
+1 (1) 888 899 8823 john@wavehunters.com,
www.wavehunters.com

WaterWays Surf Adventures, Malibu, CA 90265,
+1 (1) (310) 456-7744 www.waterwaystravel.com

Quiksilver Travel 15202 Graham, Huntington Beach, CA
+1 (1)(877) 217-1091, www.quiksilvertavel.com

United Kingdom

Pure Vacations, 5C Tower Parade, Whitstable, Kent
+44 (0)1227 264 264, info@purevacations.com
www.purevacations.com

Surf Forecast Sites

Bali Daily Reports

www.surftravelonline.com/balisurfreport.asp
Daily forecast with some well positioned wave-cams

www.baliwaves.com/forecast.htm
Good daily reports and forecasts, good links, and some nice pix too

Indian Ocean Swell Heights

www.stormsurf.com
Complete surf forecast site for the serious and the nerdy. Lots of graphs, charts and images.

http://facs.scripps.edu/surf/inda.html
World leader in swell height modelling

www.fnmoc.navy.mil
Best wind modelling on the net

Tide Charts

www.surf-time.com
Detailed printable tide charts; superb. This local surf mag is a must-have anyway, and the site has great pix and local news.

Web-Cams

www.coastalwatch.com
Ever growing site with surf-cams all over the world. Padang and Kuta are worth a look

www.surftravelonline.com
Kuta, Uluwatau and more to come; great

PLANNER

Surfer's Packing List

If you're staying in Bali, you might not need much from this page, but for extended trips beyond the luxury of a well-stocked surf shop, here's a check-list.

- [ ] **Wax - warm water**
- [ ] **Spare leg-ropes, 8ft minimum**
- [ ] **Ding repair kit (with catalyst not UV)**
- [ ] **Rash - vest - SPF 50**
- [ ] **Reef boots. Gath helmet if desired**
- [ ] **Camera & film, spare batteries**
- [ ] **Sun cream - full block, water resistant**
- [ ] **Sunglasses & sun hat**
- [ ] **Mosquito net & coils**
- [ ] **Aloe Vera ointment for belly rash & sunburn**
- [ ] **Make-up bag (er...)**
- [ ] **First Aid Box**
  Betadine & antiseptic cream
  Bandages/dressings/gauze/plasters
  Rid / mosquito repellent
  Headache pills / aspirin
  Swimmers ear drops
  Earplugs / proplugs
  Immoduim / diarhoea stuff
- [ ] **Passport & US $25 for visa on arrival**

Surfboards And Travel

Airlines: As surfers we love them for their disclaimers, their excess baggage charges, and their intransigence. 3 tips:

1. Use removable fins when packing your board. If you don't have them, shove a wet-suit in between your fins and tape it all up to reduce protruberance.

2. Pack boards together, in the same bag, to try to avoid being charged for each board. Separate them using bubble wrap, cardboard, and wetsuits.

3. If you can't fit them all in 1 bag, Tape bags together firmly. This increases stiffness and makes them harder for handlers to snap.

Board repair: Kuta has a gaggle of great surf shops to buy resin and all you need to fix boards. Bear in mind that sun-cure resin products don't work in the wet season if the sun doesn't come out! Try to opt for the traditional resin, catalyst, Q-cells, sandpaper and fibre-glass cloth options.

Surf Supplies & Board Repairs

Where can you go when your leash has snapped, or worse still your board...

Bali
Kuta and **Legian** are littered with surf stores, many offering repairs. The Board Store in Poppies II is one of many good spots in that area near Tubes Bar, but shops are too numerous to mention. We recommend taking a detour here to stock up on ding repair equipment, leashes and any other supplies you might need when venturing anywhere beyond Bali, where supplies are scarce.

Down towards Uluwatu, the street called **Jalan Labuansait** also has a number of board repair stops sign posted, and you can get a fix done at Uluwatu itself.

Surf Supplies & Board Repairs

West Java
The **Cimaja** area has several board repair options around the *losmen.* You can usually score a leg rope or wax, but more advanced equipment is scarce.

G-Land
The camps offer basic repairs and some gear rental or second hand boards might be available. Leggies and wax are available.

Lombok
Kuta village has a couple of board stores and repairs on the main street.

Sumbawa
Lakey Peak has a board repair shed next to Fatma's Warung/ Losmen. The Aman Gati sometimes sells wax and a few bits.

Yoyo's resort has some rudimentary arrangements, at Sekongkang Bawa.

Sumatra / Mentawais
Padang has a surf shop now; Substance on Pondok #1 in town.

Nias
Pantai Sorake has numerous board repair outlets, some with wax and other basic supplies.

Southern Sumatra
Ombak Indah Losmen can help with basic board repairs, at Biha.

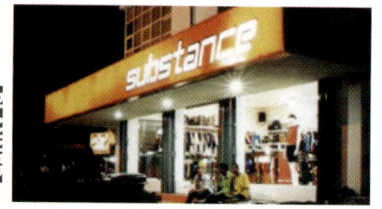

It'll be a while before many more stores like this Padang emporium pop up outside Bali. In the meantime, stock up in Kuta or Padang.

Hazards

In the water

Reef cuts; many spots involve a walk across very sharp coral, especially at low tide. Reef boots (buy them locally in Kuta) save an awful lot of pain, and allow you to put your feet forward during wipe-outs to avoid flaying your back on the bottom. Treat any coral cuts with betadine immediately, and whenever on land keep a disinfectant filled dressing over them at all times.

Urchins: These are present on most table reefs, living in the holes. The spines are agonisingly painful. If you get spiked, try lime juice or vinegar on the wound to dissolve the barb. The above reef boots will protect you, if not, avoid dark spots when walking out!

Sharks: Several types of shark abound although most are harmless, like the white tipped reef shark. If you're surfing the more remote islands and are worried, it is thought that you can reduce your risk by staying in a group, avoiding dusk or dawn, and staying out of the surf after heavy rains (especially river mouths).

Sea Snakes: Mainly in Sumatra and Java. Some are harmless, but avoid them all just in case.

Stone Fish: Rare but deadly. Reef boots help. Seen at G-Land and some Sumatran spots lurking in rock cracks.

Other fish: You may encounter stingrays, fire coral, jelly fish, scorpion fish and any number of stinging sea creatures. The likelihood is fairly slim on a short trip but the general rule of thumb is avoid, wear reef boots, and try to remember what it was that bit you in case you need treatment. None of the above are fatal, but all can be painful!

On land

Police: A scam that has been used on countless surfers over the years is the police drivers licence check. The unlucky are stopped, and given the choice between a hefty fine or a day in Denpasar.

Hazards

Make sure you have an international licence, or hire a *bemo*.

Coral snakes: Many snake varieties across Indonesia. Some harmful, others not. Avoid all.

Scorpions and other creepy crawlies: there are many types of insects that bite although few are fatal. The usual advisories apply; shake shoes and clothes out thoroughly before wearing (when in outlying areas), don't walk around densely vegetated areas without full leg coverage and good shoes, and try to get a look at whatever bites you in case anti-venoms are needed.

Theft: Just bear in mind that your camera, or wallet and its contents may represent a few weeks wages or more to the people whose country you're enjoying. Keep these out of sight, and don't carry valuables on you. Use hotel safes or hide your stuff. Don't strut about drunk late at night. Avoid dark streets...etc etc. Keep your boards in not on the vehicle (or better still hire a *bemo* and the driver will look after your stuff).

Medical Basics

We strongly recommend you get yourself the Lonely Planet books and read their great advice on this subject - see our bibliography for details.

Medical Insurance: Make sure your insurance covers medical evacuation. You do not want to end up in a local hospital if there's something seriously wrong with you, even in Bali. You travel agent can help in this regard.

Malaria: In Bali there's no real problem, but Sumatra, Nias and the Mentawais in particular, as well as other outlying islands from east to west, all have at least some reported cases, with Nias and some Sumatran islands being recognized hot-spots. Adopt a 3-pronged defence - 1 :Check with your travel provider about the latest info for the areas you are visiting. 2: See your doctor about anti malarials well before you go. Bear in mind that these are often useless

Medical Basics

if not started several weeks before departure. 3: Do whatever you can to avoid mosquito bites; use Rid (or other repellent), wear long sleeves and long trousers from dusk onwards, and stay somewhere that has good mosquito nets. Malaria is a very serious, real threat in many parts of Indo, with some strains being resistant to standard prophylactics. Cerebral (brain) malaria is a killer. Wet season, or any period of prolonged rainfall will increase the numbers of mossies, and you chances of being bitten.

Shots you may need: DPT (Tetanus etc.), MMR (Measles etc), Hep A& B, and the Polio vaccine are all potentially indispensable shots you'll need before going; see your doc.

Bali Belly: There's no real strategy for avoiding it, except sticking to boiled or bottled water. The main, quite debilitating symptom is diarrhoea, so take Immodium or Milk of Magnesium type products with you.

Ear infections are quite common; take a bottle of swimmer's ear solution if you're on an extended trip beyond medical help. An untreated ear infection can be agony, keeping you out of the water or worse.

Minor cuts: You are very likely to get some form of cut somewhere. In the tropics, infections are many times more likely and you must disinfect even a small wound. Start with betadine, then keep any cuts covered with a disinfectant dressing. Change twice a day and look out for excessive redness, swelling or pus, denoting infection. If you spot these signs, go see a doctor immediately to get some anti-biotics or treatment. For any larger wounds, see a doctor as a matter of course, even if you would not bother back home.

Kids

Almost all Bali hotels offer baby-sitting, and the Balinese totally adore children. It's super-safe for kids, with plenty of accommodation and food options to suit, as well as kids activities. Outside Bali, the challenge of finding an easy environment for kids under 10 is definitely

Kids

greater, especially when you get near the better surf spots. Malaria and food / water related illnesses are a reality in many of these areas. If your days of hard-core surf travel have been curtailed, Lonely Planet publish a useful book; Travel with Children. It covers medical tips, strategies for keeping kids amused on journeys, and other insights into surviving a trip with them. www.travelwithyourkids.com is a useful resource too. One surf travel co specialising in surf trips with kids are World Surfaris. Shaun knows the deal, and his crew are on +61 (0)75 5444 4011 or www.worldsurfaris.com.

Money

The Rupiah, at the time of press, converts thus:

1 AUD = Rp 6300.00	1 EUR = Rp 10'200.00
1 UKP = Rp 15'000.00	1 USD = Rp 8'600.00

This fluctuates daily! When changing it locally, shop around for rates, and check if published rates include commission or not, to avoid embarrassment.

Trip Bibliography

Wave - finder is a detailed surf guide - not a travel guide. Although we do give some travel tips, there are experts we can recommend. These guys will set you up with all the info you need to get the best out of your trip from both a cultural and comfort perspective.

Books

Indo Surf & Lingo, Peter Neely, ISBN 0957734624
Great photos and surf info, language tips, deals on accommodation and food, & the inside track on places to stay and eat. At surf stores.

Lonely Planet Series
The most comprehensive travel information for Indonesia. Split into territories or the whole lot in 1. At all bookstores or Amazon.com.

Globetrotter Road Atlas Indonesia , C Scarlett, ISBN:

Trip Bibliography

1853684465 72 page map book. Comprehensive. Good for overland trips.

Culture Shock! Indonesia, Cathie Draine, ISBN 1558680578
Insight into varied traditions and culture throughout Indo.

Periplus Pocket Indonesian Dictionary. Bookshops or Amazon.

Periplus Street Atlas - Bali, ISBN 0794600883. Expensive, bulky, but extremely useful.

Periplus fold-out maps; Lombok & Sumbawa, Java, Sumatra etc. Bali bookshops or tuttlepublishing.com. Get into a bemo and point to a location on one of these...you will probably get there!

Websites

www.lonelyplanet.com
Travel advice, maps, books. Check the "travel ticker"

www.surftravelonline.com
Accommodation, boat trips, surf forecasts. The lot.

www.dfat.gov.au
Travel advisories issued by the Australian Government. They're more clued in than some agencies, and less twitchy than others.

Movies

Morning of the Earth, Albie Falzon. The original and best.

Ulu 32. Steve Cooney et al. 32 yrs of Indo surfing... brilliant.

PLANNER

Break Index

Break Index

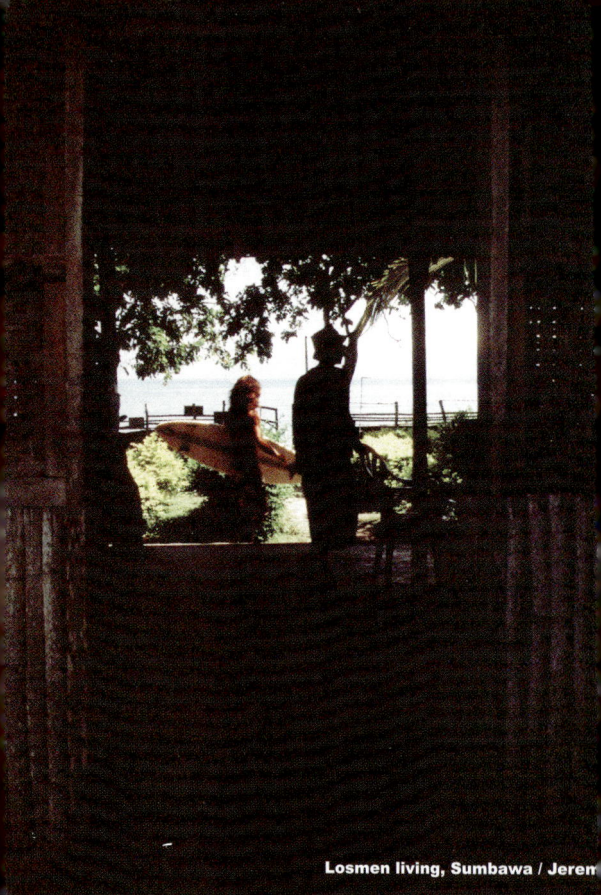

Losmen living, Sumbawa / Jerem

Conversion chart

Temperature

To convert $^{\circ}$C to $^{\circ}$F
Multiply by 1.8 & add 32

To convert $^{\circ}$F to $^{\circ}$C
Subtract 32 & divide by 1.8

Distances	**Multiply by**
inches to cm	2.54
cm to inches	0.39
feet to meters	0.30
meters to feet	3.28
yards to meters	0.9
meters to yards	1.1
miles to kilometres	1.6
kilometres to miles	0.6

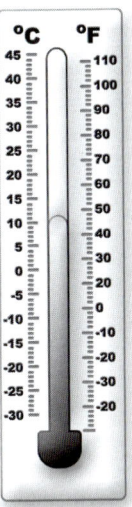

Finding Wave-finder

Wave-finder USA - Hawaii, & Wave-finder Australia are available at all decent surf shops, & surf-friendly bookstores. For details of your nearest stockist, E-mail info@wave-finder.com.

We welcome any comments, corrections or questions, & these can be E mailed to the same address.

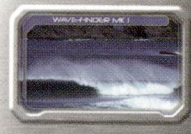

WAVE-FINDER
SURF GUIDE - UK & IRELAND

DATA-MAPS & IN-DEPTH REVIEWS OF EVERY GOOD SURF SPOT IN BRITAIN & EIRE

Wave-finder
Australia

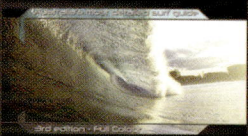

3rd edition - Full Colour

Surfer's eye™ maps
In - depth reviews
Vivid colour photos
Detailed surf data

Larry Blair & Cheyne Horan

WAVE-FINDER
SURF GUIDE - USA - HAWAII

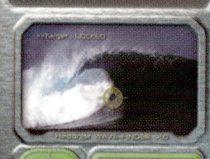

1200 GOOD SPOTS
IN-DEPTH REVIEWS
BREAK DATA-MAPS
SIMPLE DIRECTIONS

LARRY BLAIR
BUZZY KERBOX

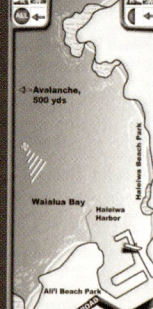

travel.
light on stuff
heavy on knowledge

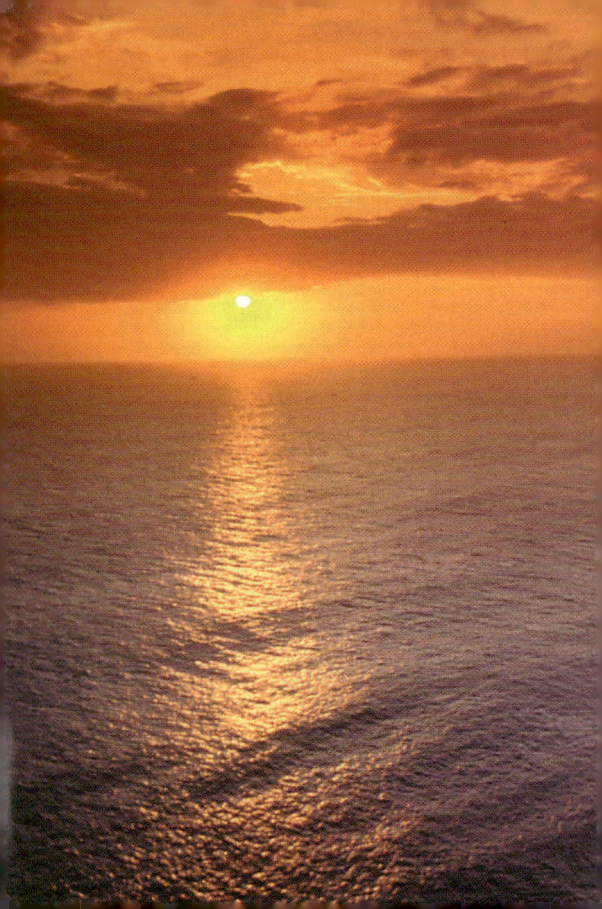

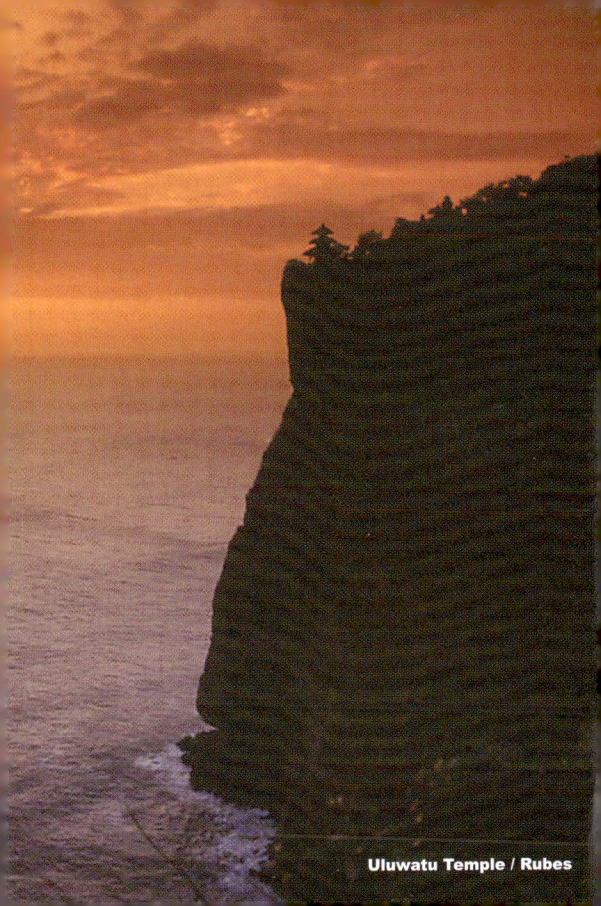
Uluwatu Temple / Rubes

My Secret Spots

Name

Directions

Type   **Direction**   **Swell**
Tide   **Wind**

Description

Name

Directions

Type   **Direction**   **Swell**
Tide   **Wind**

Description

Name

Directions

Type **Direction** **Swell**

Tide **Wind**

Description

Name

Directions

Type **Direction** **Swell**

Tide **Wind**

Description

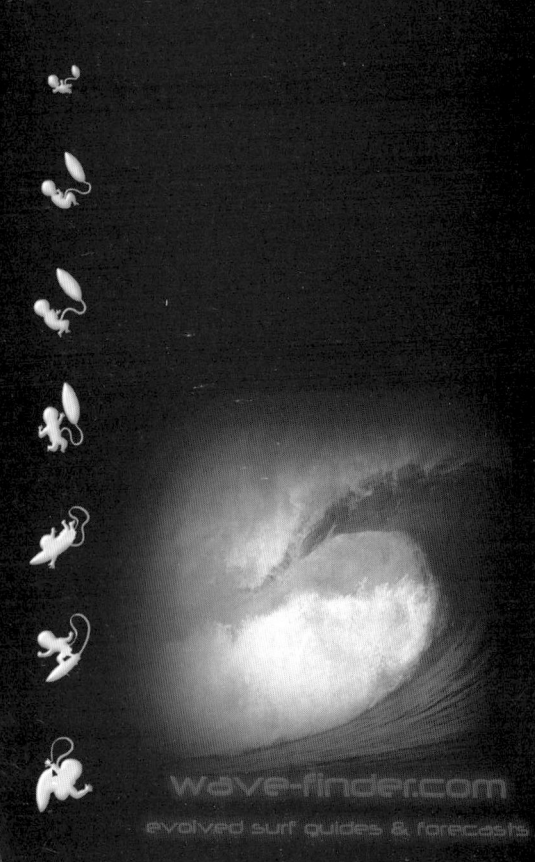

wave-finder.com
evolved surf guides & forecasts